Barach

Hokaia

Crescent Sea

Teek Territory

Lost Moth

Cuecola

MIRRORED HEAVENS

ALSO BY REBECCA ROANHORSE

BETWEEN EARTH AND SKY
Black Sun
Fevered Star
Mirrored Heavens

THE SIXTH WORLD
Trail of Lightning
Storm of Locusts

Star Wars: Resistance Reborn
Race to the Sun
Tread of Angels

MIRRORED HEAVENS

BETWEEN EARTH AND SKY

BOOK THREE

REBECCA ROANHORSE

SAGA PRESS

LONDON SYDNEY **NEW YORK** TORONTO NEW DELHI

SAGA PRESS
AN IMPRINT OF SIMON & SCHUSTER, LLC
1230 AVENUE OF THE AMERICAS, NEW YORK, NEW YORK 10020

First Saga Press hardcover edition June 2024

SAGA PRESS and colophon are trademarks of Simon & Schuster, LLC

Simon & Schuster: Celebrating 100 Years of Publishing in 2024

For information about special discounts for bulk purchases, please contact Simon & Schuster Special Sales at 1-866-506-1949 or business@simonandschuster.com.

The Simon & Schuster Speakers Bureau can bring authors to your live event. For more information or to book an event, contact the Simon & Schuster Speakers Bureau at 1-866-248-3049 or visit our website at www.simonspeakers.com.

Interior design by Erika R. Genova

Manufactured in the United States of America

1   3   5   7   9   10   8   6   4   2

Library of Congress Cataloging-in-Publication Data

ISBN 978-1-5344-3770-8
ISBN 978-1-5344-3772-2 (ebook)

For the outcasts,
the outsiders,
and the unwanted
who forge their own destinies regardless.

THE PEOPLE OF THE MERIDIAN

• THE OBREGI MOUNTAINS •

Serapio – *The Crow God Reborn, Odo Sedoh, Carrion King*
Marcal – *Serapio's father*

• CITY OF CUECOLA •

Balam – *Lord of the House of Seven, Patron of
    the Crescent Sea, White Jaguar*
Powageh/Tiniz – *Serapio's third tutor, a Knife*
Tuun – *Lord of the House of Seven, Jade Serpent*
~~Saaya – *Serapio's mother*~~
~~Paadeh/Paluu – *Serapio's first tutor, a woodcarver*~~
~~Eedi/Ensha – *Serapio's second tutor, a spearmaiden*~~

• CITY OF TOVA •

THE WATCHERS
Naranpa – *Sun Priest, Order of Oracles (hawaa)*
Iktan – *Priest of Knives, Order of Knives (tsiyo)*
~~Abah – *Priest of Succor, Order of the Healing Society (seegi)*~~
~~Haisan – *Priest of Records, Order of Historical Society (ta dissa)*~~
~~Kiutue – *Former Sun Priest (hawaa)*~~
~~Ipep – *Former Priest of Knives (tsiyo)*~~

• THE SKY MADE CLANS •

CARRION CROW
Yatliza – Matron
Ayawa – Yatliza's consort
Okoa – *Yatliza's son, captain of the Shield*
Esa – *Yatliza's daughter, Matron*
Chaiya – Former Captain of the Shield
Maaka – *Leader of the Odohaa, Tuyon*
Feyou – *A healer, Maaka's wife, Tuyon*
Chela – *A crow rider*
Benundah – *A giant crow*
Achiq – *A giant crow*
Yendi – *A giant crow*
Sagoby – *A giant crow*

WATER STRIDER
Ieyoue – *Matron*
Enuka – *Master Engineer*
Suol – *Captain of the Shield*
Aishe – *Barge operator*

GOLDEN EAGLE
Nuuma – *Matron*
Suuakeh – *Nuuma's mother*
Terzha – *Nuuma's daughter*
Ziha – *Nuuma's daughter*
Layat – *Adviser to the matron*

WINGED SERPENT
Peyana – *Matron*
Ahuat – *Captain of the Shield*
Isel – *Peyana's daughter*

• DRY EARTH •

COYOTE
Zataya – *A witch*
Sedaysa – *Matron, boss of the Agave*
~~Denaochi – *Brother to Naranpa, boss of the Lupine*~~
~~Akel – *Brother to Naranpa*~~

CLANLESS
Cazotz – *A laborer*

• CITY OF HOKAIA •

SPEARMAIDENS
Naasut – *Sovran of Hokaia*
~~Seuq – *The leader of the dreamwalkers*~~
~~Gwee – *A dreamwalker*~~
~~Odae – *A dreamwalker*~~
~~Asnod – *A dreamwalker*~~

CITIZENS
Kata – *A shopkeeper*
Japurna – *Kata's friend*

• TEEK •

Xiala – *A sea captain*
Mahina – *Queen of the Teek, Xiala's mother*
Yaala – *Queen Regent, Xiala's aunt*
Alani – *Xiala's friend, a sailor*
Teanni – *Xiala's friend*
Keala – *Teanni's wife*
Oyala – *A wise woman*
Laili – *Oyala's daughter*
Akona

• THE NORTHERN WASTES •

Kupshu – *A wise woman*
Niviq – *A beloved daughter*

And now the Lord of the Region of the Dead takes you . . .
you have gone to the dwelling place of the dead,
the place of the unfleshed,
the place where the journey ends,
. . .
Never again shall you return,
never again shall you make your way back . . .

—*The Florentine Codex*, Book III, 24R

CHAPTER 1

CITY OF TOVA
YEAR 1 OF THE CROW

> On earth, in heaven, and within,
> Three wars to lose, three wars to win.
> Cut the path. Mark the days. Turn the tides.
> Three tasks before the season dies:
> Turn rotten fruit to flower,
> Slay the god-bride still unloved,
> Press the son to fell the sire.
> Victory then to the Carrion King who in winning loses everything.
>
> —Coyote song

Zataya of the Coyote clan was no tower-trained Watcher casting fortunes and charting star maps, no birthright sorcerer from the southern cities dispensing futures gleaned from dark mirrors painted with blood, but she knew enough to read the portents around her, and they told her that something terrible was coming.

First there was the eclipse that lingered over the city since the new year solstice, an impossible thing made real by the crow god's magic. Then there was the tailing comet that had blazed across the twilight sky last month when the Odo Sedoh ascended his throne upon Shadow Rock to break the matrons and rule the city. And now the seasons turned, again, and the constellations of the lesser gods burst to life upon the sky's inky canvas: jaguar and kraken, serpent and spear.

And she understood.

The war on earth may have yet to start as the gods claimed their vessels and set their stakes, but the war in heaven had already begun.

For what was earth but a mirror of heaven?

And what was she but a thing caught in between?

But Zataya would not be idle. She would not wait to be devoured by avatars and armies. She would find a way to survive.

And why not? Her god was a sly god, a god of narrow spaces and narrower paths. He made his own way and did not wait for others to clear it for him.

So she would do the same.

When she had augured the future before, she had used southern sorcery, blood on a dark mirror that revealed the shadow world to those who sought it. But now she wished to walk with Coyote, and his communion manifested in natural things. Rock and flame, leaf and root.

She had been living in a small room in the matron of Coyote clan's house and serving as her Shield captain, a title that allowed her to counsel and observe. But for this, she wanted no witnesses.

The Lupine stood abandoned after Denaochi's death, its gambling tables and drinking cups left to entertain ghosts. That is where she went. Her old room was still there with all of her tools, and she knew no one would disturb her delicate work.

She set the fire in the hearth and stoked it until it burned steadily. Once the logs had diminished to glowing lumps of char, she used a flint spade to rake the largest onto the floor.

Tradition told her that the answer to her question lay within the heated charcoal, so she set her resolve and asked, "How do I survive the war that is in heaven, and the war to come on earth?"

Unhesitating, she struck the lump with the edge of the spade. It cracked into smoldering pieces of black and orange and red. She used a stick to poke around the heated mass, looking for what message the Coyote might send her.

And gasped.

A crow. She saw a crow.

"No," she breathed, shaking her head. That could not be right. Surely the Coyote did not mean to bind her fate to the Crow God Reborn.

Frustrated, she swept the pieces away and lifted another charred lump from the fire. Again, she asked her question, split it open, and again the pieces formed a crow.

With a growl of despair she tried one more time, only to receive the same result.

Perhaps the fire was not the answer.

She went to her cabinets, still intact even after months of abandonment, and searched for the tiny herb that would surely give her a clearer vision. She found it, a crush of dried cactus flower they called Coyote's Paw. It was a powerful medicine known to cause visions, and she swallowed it down.

And then she waited.

It did not take long.

She had expected to see things, but instead she heard a voice. It spoke to her in echoing whispers, a sound that seemed everywhere and nowhere at once. Inside and outside. Above and below.

She knew it was the voice of her god, the Coyote's own song, and she repeated the words with a fervor, letting her lips

3

form to their shape and her tongue learn their weight, knowing that this was the path to survival.

She was not sure how long she sat there muttering the same words over and over again, but when she came back to herself, her entire being resonated with them.

Only they made no sense.

She had memorized a riddle.

She should have known the Coyote's currency would not be so straightforward.

It was the chilling hearth that reminded her that too much time had passed and soon her matron would notice her absence, and that would raise questions, and there were things Zataya did not wish to share with anyone.

She shoveled dirt into the hearth and put away her auguring tools, pausing to tidy her room. And there, cooled to shades of black and gray but still plainly visible, was the crow.

At the thought of the crow, the Coyote song that lay behind her teeth trembled her jaw and burst from her mouth. She found herself repeating the riddle, a whisper under her breath that would not cease. She slapped her hand over her mouth, and the song became a shout. She stumbled to the wall and slammed her head against the stones. Stars danced in her eyes, and she swayed at the pain, but still the words came like a bubbling froth.

Desperate, terrified, she slammed her head into the wall again.

And then again and again until her vision shuttered, and her mind went dark.

She collapsed to the floor, unconscious . . . her lips still moving.

CHAPTER 2

TEEK TERRITORY
YEAR 1 OF THE CROW

May you die at sea.

—Teek farewell

Xiala was drowning.

Seawater, thick and salty, rushed into her mouth. Water weighted her limbs, saturated her lungs, and a growing blackness hovered at the corners of her consciousness. Her instincts screamed at her to resist, to fight. To do something!

But she did not.

Instead, she sank.

Willingly exchanged breath for brine until her feet struck the sandy bottom. She looked up, and her Teek eyes dilated, drawing in what scant light filtered down through the cold water.

Far above her, the hull of her small boat swayed as a figure leaned over the side. She could not see Teanni's expression, but she imagined her childhood friend's face contorted in concern . . . and expectation.

She looked down at her legs—legs, damn it!—and slapped a hand against her neck. The skin under her palm was smooth.

This is not the way, she thought. *I'm forgetting something.*

And she was running out of time, the darkness closing in, her lungs compromised, her mind soon to follow. If she did not act now, she might never be able to.

With her last clear thought, she sliced through the ropes that secured the netting—netting that held the stones that had sunk her to the bottom of the sea—and, with a powerful push, launched herself toward the surface.

She broke through the skin of the water, gasping. She sucked in air, too quickly, and dizziness rocked her, made bursts of light dance in her vision. The sun slapped her face, blinding her too-wide eyes. Teanni's voice came to her, her words a jumble of alarm Xiala couldn't untangle in her breath-deprived state.

She forced herself to slow down, to lie back and float, to trust the sea to hold her until she could get her bearings and convince her body that she was not dying. It took a moment, but finally her head cleared, and she scrambled aboard, Teanni hauling her up.

"Fuck," Xiala swore as she flopped onto the bench, coughing and spitting seawater from between her teeth.

"Nothing?" Teanni's expression mirrored Xiala's own disappointment.

"No. No gills, no tail . . . nothing." She hesitated. "Well, my eyes. I could see well enough, but . . ." She shrugged. "Well enough" wasn't enough, and she knew it, but it was something, at least.

"Did you try Singing?" Teanni asked.

"Of course." But had she? She couldn't recall. Almost drowning had scrambled her brain.

"Perhaps if you let the water into your lungs."

"I've swallowed half the Crescent Sea. That's not the problem."

"Then what?"

Xiala's tone was crisp. "If I knew that, I wouldn't be tying rocks around my waist and trying to drown myself."

Teanni hesitated.

"Say it," Xiala groaned.

"What if, and don't get mad, Xiala, but what if—"

"I imagined it?" Had Xiala not asked herself the same question a thousand times? And come up with the same answer again and again? If she closed her eyes, she could still see the wild storm, the rogue wave, Loob hanging loose-limbed from the rope, Baat leaving her behind to fend for herself after she'd saved him. And then black scales, water sweeter than air in her lungs, the accusing stares of the crew. "It would be easier if I had, but I did not."

"A tail, gills. It is a thing only spoken of in the old stories. It would make you like a goddess."

Teanni's tone held a note of skepticism, but Xiala only laughed. How could her friend understand? Teanni had not seen a man who commanded crows as if he were their master, had not witnessed Carrion Crow clan pilgrims. She could not understand gods alive and working through human beings the way Xiala had learned to.

Teanni dipped her paddle into the water and began to push. "I admit that when you told me your secret, I thought . . . maybe. Maybe it meant the Mother had not abandoned us completely, if she still favored you. It's been hard these past years."

The Teek of Xiala's memory had always been a paradise. Warm sands, secret coves, plentiful food, and freshwater wells. And past the great island chain that marked the edge of their territory, miles and miles of Song-calmed seas where the Teek built their floating islands: platforms a quarter-mile wide and half as long, fashioned from bulrush, a buoyant reed that grew in profusion where the sea touched land.

But that blessed place was no more.

The rains had not come for two seasons, and drought and disease had killed the marshy fields of bulrush. Without it, they could not maintain their floating homes. The Teek were land-bound, as they had been when the enemy had decimated them in the war hundreds of years ago. It was a sign, and it made Xi-ala's stomach knot to think of it. The parallels to the past were too stark, a harbinger that no one among them seemed willing to face. *Whoever said that people learned from the mistakes of history has never met a Teek*, she thought. *Stubborn to a fault.*

"I know it is hard to believe, Teanni, but it happened. Many men saw it." Men who were now dead, although through no fault of her own. "And the Mother has not abandoned us. I still have my Song."

And that had been the greatest shock of all. The Teek had lost their Song, the very thing that marked them as the Mother's favored. Not all at once, Teanni had explained, but relentlessly and without mercy. First the children, and then their mothers, and finally even the elders. Many Teek had left for the mainland as their magic failed; others were so heartbroken they had simply walked into the sea. Song was the soul of the Teek, their very identity, and without it they were broken. It was desperation that had driven them to name Mahina their queen and rejoin the larger world. The elders had read the end of the Treaty as one last opportunity, willfully ignoring any danger.

Xiala understood why Teanni believed her return was a sign of changing fortunes rather than a twist of unpredictable fate. It was an unfamiliar weight to carry, this expectation that she might perform a miracle for a land and a people caught in a net of suffering. But Xiala would do what she could, help where she must. And the first step would be to find a way to awaken her powers again.

"It's getting late." Teanni gestured toward the horizon, where the sun was well past its zenith. "We can try again tomorrow." She flashed Xiala a nervous smile. "Perhaps your aunt Yaala and the wise women's circle will have a better idea of how to wake your magic."

"No, no, no." Xiala felt her jaw tighten at the very idea. "We agreed on that. My aunt will never believe what she cannot see with her own eyes, especially from me. A little more time. I will find a way."

"I know. I'm just . . ."

"Impatient? I understand. But when has the Mother not worked in her own time?"

"The Teek are dying. A little urgency would be appreciated," Teanni said, uncharacteristically tart.

Xiala laughed. "Feel free to tell her. Let's see her reply."

Teanni's eyes widened at the thought, which made Xiala laugh harder. She sobered as they paddled past an abandoned floating island. A dozen thatched reed houses still stood upon the mounded bulrush, but they were steadily sinking. Without more reeds to fortify each new layer of the foundation and the Teek to Sing the waters to kindness, rough tides had rotted the groundwork underneath, and the artificial island sagged, salt-slicked and moldy.

It was a way of life now passing, and it broke Xiala's heart. Had the Mother truly abandoned them? And if so, why? Teanni had said the calamities began after Xiala left, but that could be coincidence. Other factors had to be considered. A generation of elders dying, fewer and fewer babies born each year, drought and disease.

Xiala could see the signs everywhere. If nothing changed, the Teek would be gone within her lifetime.

"Who's that?" Teanni asked.

"Where?" Xiala turned her attention back to the here and now.

A lone figure stood on land, arms raised and waving furiously to get their attention.

"It's Keala." Teanni tensed.

"Your wife? Why is she here?" When they were in Hokaia, Xiala's mother, Queen Mahina, had implied that Teanni might still hold affections for her. Xiala had dreaded their reunion, knowing her heart was firmly set on Serapio and had no room for another. But the concern was made moot when Teanni introduced her wife, Keala. Of course, Mahina had neglected to mention Teanni was married.

"There's something wrong," Teanni said, and they hurried their pace.

As they pulled close, Keala waded out into the shallows to guide the small boat in. Xiala jumped out to help push from behind, and together they maneuvered the boat to shore.

"Ships are coming," Keala said without preamble.

"Sailors?" Teanni asked, hopeful. "It's been a long time since we've had men on the island." She grinned. "It could mean children in nine months."

Keala shared a brief smile with her wife. Xiala had learned that Teanni had birthed a son four years ago. A son given to the waves. Her friend had confessed it in a rush of shameful tears triggered by an innocuous observation about a cloud formation one day. Four years past, and a comment about the shape of a cloud had brought her to weeping. Teek were not supposed to mourn their lost sons, but how could they not? Were they not as much a part of their hearts as their daughters? And with the population dwindling, every child lost seemed a tragedy.

"Yaala did not say what ships are coming," Keala said, "only that Xiala must join her."

"Me?" Xiala asked, surprised. "Yaala hates me. Why does she want me there?" Her aunt had ignored her these past few months, preferring to pretend her long-lost niece did not exist. And when they did cross paths, their conversations were brittle, the past always an unspoken fence between them. Xiala had never forgiven her aunt for the part she played in driving her from Teek all those years ago, and her aunt had not forgotten how close Xiala had come to killing her own mother. So they tolerated each other on Mahina's orders, but at a distance, and often with malice.

"You are the queen's daughter," Teanni said. "It is only right."

Perhaps Yaala should remember more often that I am the queen's daughter, Xiala thought, *and that she is* not *the queen.* But she kept the words to herself and went with Keala and Teanni to the listening house.

Part of her still hoped she might find a way to steal a boat. The one edict Yaala had made upon Xiala's return was that she was not to be given a seaworthy ship. Her paddler, yes, but only for use on the far eastern side of the island. After all, her aunt could not keep her completely from the sea.

The handful of tidechasers had been under guard from the beginning with strict orders not to let Xiala near one. It hadn't stopped her from scheming, and she had considered Singing the guards to attitudes more amenable to a little thievery. But Xiala was not convinced that her Song would not kill, and she had no feud with the guards. She was not quite ready to become a cold-blooded murderer of her own people.

Yaala was waiting for them on the porch of the listening house. She sat straight-backed on a woven grass throne, arrayed in a wealth of shells. She wore abalone in a collar at her neck, moonshell in a crown around her head, and cowries woven through her long, loc'd hair. There was a small cluster

11

of women sitting on mats around her. They were the Teek wise women, their circle of elders, and their hands worked as they stripped yucca leaves or ground corn, and their ears listened so that their tongues might provide counsel.

"Ships have been spotted on the horizon, coming from the north," Yaala said as Xiala approached.

"From Hokaia?" Xiala asked.

"They are too far yet to tell."

"Could it be the queen returned?" Teanni asked.

Yaala sounded relieved when she said, "Let us hope. She has been gone too long."

"You cannot be sure it is my mother," Xiala warned. "Whoever approaches could mean ill. Teek is poorly equipped to fight back."

"Enemies?" Yaala sounded dubious. "Mahina has made us allies in the great Treaty cities. Whoever approaches is surely a friend."

"It would not hurt to be cautious," Alani said, and Xiala shot the woman a grateful look. Alani was the sailor who had escorted Xiala from Hokaia. Over the past few months, they had become friendly despite their rocky start, and she was the only other Teek present who had been to Hokaia. She, at least, understood that sometimes those who called themselves friends wore false faces.

"What would you have us do?" Yaala asked, a touch of irritation in her voice. "Flee to our islands that no longer float? Gather sticks and rocks to fight off the foreigners? We cannot run, we cannot fight, and you and I both know we cannot Si—"

She cut off abruptly. In the silence, the wise women clicked their tongues, a sign of their disapproval. Everyone knew it, but it was still anathema to speak of the loss of their Song, and only a handful of women present were aware that Xiala still possessed hers. Yaala because Mahina had sent a note explaining that Xiala had killed a Cuecolan lord with hers, and that was the reason she was now returned to Teek. Alani because she had escorted Xiala back. And Teanni and her wife because Xiala had told them.

"No," Yaala said, "the arrival of these ships is a gift from the Mother. We shall welcome whoever comes as our honored guests." She mustered her queenly poise and stepped from the porch.

The wise women put down their grinding stones and yucca leaves and gathered to join her. Xiala tried to catch Alani's eye, but the sailor avoided her and fell in with the other women, unwilling to challenge Yaala more than she had. Teanni took Keala's hand and smiled reassuringly at them both, but it did little to settle Xiala's worries.

"Walk with me, niece," Yaala commanded.

Xiala swallowed her foreboding and joined her aunt. Silence stretched between them, until her aunt spoke.

"I know we have our differences," she said as they made their way to the shore, "but I need your support today."

"I have never challenged you."

"Not openly, but I know what you think of me." Her aunt's look was wry.

"And what you think of me."

Yaala acknowledged their animosity with a nod. "There is history between us. Wounds that have not healed. But perhaps tomorrow, once Mahina is home, we might find the time to mend them. All of us."

"Mahina will never forgive me, and I am not sure I can forgive her," Xiala said, thinking of their recent confrontation in Hokaia, and even older memories: her mother's betrayal, their dead lover, Xiala's desperate flight.

"You are her daughter, and she is your mother. This grievance has festered long enough."

Xiala did not think it was that simple, but she realized she wanted forgiveness very much, both to give it and receive it.

"I would like that," she finally said. How could she not? Whether she felt the same tomorrow would have to be seen, but if her aunt was willing to offer her peace, she was willing to try.

By the time they arrived, a small crowd of the curious had already gathered at the edge of the water, all eyes on something farther out to sea, north-northwest.

"Has anything changed?" Yaala asked the nearest woman.

"No, and the setting sun obscures any identifying markings."

Xiala squinted into the distance. The woman was right. The ships were arriving just as the sun cut across the horizon, making it hard to see.

"Perhaps we should send someone out to greet them," Alani suggested. "Surely they would not see that as insult."

"There is another way," Xiala murmured, and waded into the waves. She took a few deep breaths before she sank beneath the water. Here at the shoreline, the sea was calm and welcoming, and she greeted it as a relative. Unlike her earlier attempt at drowning, she only wanted it to speak to her, to ask it what it could see that she could not.

She opened her mouth, exhaled, and let the water hit her tongue. She did not swallow, only tasted. Salt and life, heavy in her mouth. And something else. Something bitter. She spit out the water, kicked up her feet, and dove to the bottom, not so far. She pressed her hands against the sandy floor. It was work to hold herself there, and she wished she had her net full of rocks.

She sought out the Mother's tongue, the language of vibrations and reverberations. And she listened. For the smallest deviation, the barest confirmation in the movement of the waters. And the sea told her what she wished to know.

Satisfied, she rose. Water shed from her skin and hair as she made her way back to shore, her expression grim.

"Ships," she confirmed, "and not Teek."

"I have not seen someone speak to the sea in too long." Tears gathered in Yaala's eyes.

"Have the Teek lost the way of reading the waves along with their Song?" Xiala asked, caught between astonishment and dismay.

The wise women clicked, but Xiala didn't care. She looked at Teanni, who nodded. Mother waters, it was worse than Xiala had imagined, and she had imagined terrible things.

"So it is not the queen, then," Yaala said, disappointment weighting her shoulders.

"That I cannot tell. Only that they do not cut through the waves like a tidechaser, and that they sit heavy in the water."

"Heavy? Merchant ships?" Alani asked, and a buzz of excitement rippled through the crowd.

"Could be a merchant ship laden with goods," Xiala said. "Could be a ship full of people."

"Maybe Queen Mahina has sent men back for us to make children," Teanni said, repeating her previous prediction.

"I don't think so," Xiala said, but the idea had already caught hold, and the women practically vibrated with the possibility.

"We should have prepared a feast," another woman said.

"Light the torches," Yaala commanded. "We will guide them in."

A cheer went up from the crowd.

"Better we wait," Xiala said, but she was not heard over the rising voices, an air of celebration already spreading. She leaned in to shout in Yaala's ear. "Let me Sing the ships back," she suggested. "Hold them at a distance until we know for sure."

Yaala faced her, took Xiala's hands in her own. "No, Xiala. Let them be happy. They need this."

"We have no defenses. We are like minnows in a pond here. You said so yourself. Easy pickings."

"Xiala." Her voice was gentle, but there was an undertone of exasperation. "Please. Not everyone is your enemy."

Xiala looked to Teanni, who was leaning into her wife and smiling. Even Alani was grinning. Yaala was right. The Teek needed something good, and perhaps she was overreacting, seeing danger where there was none. But she still couldn't quite shake a sense of foreboding, and it shivered her shoulders like the first touch of winter.

Soon the shadowy forms of the vessels drew near. Unlike the Teek who stood on the beach under bright torches, the strangers' ships were dark, no lanterns illuminating whoever was on board. Figures paced on the deck, but none called out a greeting to the waiting women.

In the deep twilight, Xiala counted at least four hulking canoes, Cuecolan if her eye for nautical detail served, although it was hard to tell in the dark. Four ships potentially holding fifty bodies each. That meant possibly two hundred sailors. Why would two hundred sailors come to Teek?

A breeze whispered across the beach and sent the torches dancing. Xiala could hear the creak of leather, the shifting of restless feet against wooden decks. Light flared to life on the nearest ship. She caught a glimpse of animal skins, painted faces, and light reflecting against obsidian-tipped spears.

"Not sailors, an army," she murmured, and, as the realization sank in, "Move back!" and then "Run!" and, louder, "Run!"

But no one heard her over the cheering.

Yaala stepped forward in her queenly attire, crown on her head, arms wide. And behind her, the wise women cheered.

And all around, an enthusiastic crowd of those who had come to greet their allies waited, expectant.

Xiala heard it before the others did, or perhaps she was the only one who recognized the sound for what it was.

The huff of an exhale, the whistle of a spear cutting through the air.

It struck Yaala through the stomach.

The regent queen gasped, shock rippling through her body.

Her hands clutched at the weapon protruding from her belly.

Her mouth worked, but no words came out. Only a red-tinged cough, blood spattering the sand.

Yaala toppled over dead just as the sky broke open, obsidian-tipped arrows raining down around her.

The arrows struck the wise women. They fell, shafts protruding from throats and chests. Xiala watched, stunned, as an arrow pierced the eye of the woman next to her.

A wail cut through the shocked silence. Someone at the edge of the circle of dead. Her cry was cut short by the thrust of a blade, as soldiers stormed the beach.

Xiala thought to Sing, but she did not think she could stop two hundred warriors even if she wished to, and she might kill Teek in the attempt.

So she did the only thing she could do.

She ran.

Bodies fell around her; shrieks filled a night that quickly had begun to stink of death and betrayal.

Something hit her from behind.

She staggered, the impact throwing her to her knees.

Get up, Xiala. Get up!

She tried to stand.

But something struck her head, and this time when she fell, there was only darkness.

CHAPTER 3

The tsiyo has but one role: to deal death. It matters not the who or the when, the how or the where. Only that the end is inexorable.

—*The Manual of the Priest of Knives*

It was the last hour before dawn on the first full moon of spring, and Iktan was visiting the war college.

Well, xe thought, *the actual college isn't here anymore. The spearmaidens saw to that, burning what was left after the massacre. Easier to raze the building and the blood-soaked grounds than be bothered to bury so many bodies. So, really, it's more like I am visiting a grave.*

But not simply a grave. More like a graveyard.

Which made sense, as there had been dozens upon dozens murdered that night. In their beds.

Iktan's nephew had been one of them.

A bright boy by all accounts, the son of xir youngest sister. The boy had been born after Iktan had left for the celestial tower, so xe had never truly known him. And the tower forbade familial relationships between those who dedicated their lives to the tower and their birth clans, so xe had not even visited, although xe was certainly aware of his existence. It had been part of Iktan's job to be aware of things.

In light of xir complete inability to predict the Odo Sedoh (or the Crow God Reborn or the Carrion King or whatever the man was calling himself these days), Iktan found the whole notion of knowing things ridiculous. A dark chuckle bubbled out under xir breath. But xe quickly sobered, thinking of xir dead nephew, and all the other scions who had perished.

Another thing xe had failed to see coming.

Iktan looked out over the burned-out field for evidence that this place had once been bustling and lively. Xe could almost hear the clash of staffs as the students sparred, the raucous laughter that must have echoed through the dining hall. Xe had never attended the war college, of course. Xir calling had taken a different direction long ago. But the promise of such a place lingered.

You are getting old and melancholy, Iktan thought. *How indulgent. Next, you will be weeping and leaving marigolds for remembrance. Burning incense like a superstitious Dry Earther or drawing celestial maps to ensure the boy's safe travels back to the stars.*

A yawn cracked Iktan's mouth wide. It was getting late. Or early, depending on how one reckoned time. It was a good hour's travel from the war college to the Mink Palace atop the earth mound pyramid, and no doubt Nuuma Golden Eagle would send one of her lackeys to round up Iktan for breakfast if xe did not show up on time. The woman hated to eat alone, but why Iktan had to be the one to keep her company most mornings was a mystery. Did she not have daughters? Groveling sycophants? Scheming scions who would like nothing better than to spend time at her table?

Ah, and there is your answer, xe thought. *Any one of those would turn an appetite sour. You are by far the most charming and interesting person in her entourage. Is it truly a mystery why she would wish to spend time with you?*

But was it fair? Was it just?

What in life is fair or just? Nothing. You should know that best.

And that is why the gods created revenge. So when events don't go as they should, people like Iktan could do a little correcting.

As xir mind often did when contemplating revenge, Iktan's thoughts turned to Naranpa. Not Naranpa as xe had last seen her: fearful, confused, undone by the treachery of the people she had trusted most (Iktan included). But as xe had first met her.

She had been no more than fifteen and Iktan a few years older. It had been mealtime, and the dedicants were gathered on the celestial tower's terrace in a loud hormonal mess.

Iktan hated mealtime. The forced companionship with people xe was certain were xir lessers, the wagging tongues prone to gossip, and the truly mediocre food the tower served.

What Iktan much preferred to do when xir cohort gathered to stuff lukewarm beans down their nattering mouths was climb the tower walls. Xe used to enjoy climbing the cliffsides of the district of Otsa itself, the sound of the Tovasheh River rushing below. Xe would climb as far down as xe could, always trying to find the best route to the river, daring to hang precariously from some impossibly small outcropping to dip a hand in the deceptively fast flow before working xir way back up the mist-spattered rock, knowing that one poor decision about where to wedge a toe into the wall or what narrow crevice into which to squeeze a finger would send xir tumbling into the deadly waters.

It was exhilarating, relying on one's own abilities to walk the fine line between life and death. And winning. Most important was the winning.

Iktan never fell. Of course not. Despite the thrill, it had not really occurred to xir that xe might.

But someone had fallen. A younger boy who was not as skilled as Iktan. (Who was?) He had made a poor decision and plunged to his death.

Poor decisions could be lethal.

A lesson any assassin knew well.

After that, all the dedicants were forbidden to climb the cliffs, and for a week Iktan paced the halls, restless as a caged cat. Until xe realized that the old priests had not said anything about climbing the tower itself.

So Iktan had spent many a mealtime free-climbing the celestial tower, looking for the perfect holds, building forearm strength so xe could hoist xirself up two and three body spans at a time. From a distance, should someone look up to see a lanky figure scampering up the tower wall, Iktan was sure it would look like xe was flying.

That's how xe had met Naranpa.

She had been sitting on the Sun Priest's balcony, legs dangling between the stone balustrades.

When Iktan popped up just below, hoping to scare her (maybe she would scream, and wouldn't that be funny?), she just stared.

Xe hadn't expected that. Was disappointed that xir surprise appearance had not elicited even a yelp.

"Who are you?" she asked, voice curious.

"What are you doing here?" Iktan channeled all the authority xe could muster. "These are the Sun Priest's private rooms. I could kill you for trespassing, you know. I am a tsiyo." (Xe was not quite an actual tsiyo yet, but xe was certain this strange girl wouldn't know that.)

"I have permission." Her face was placid, not intimidated at all. Xe was going to have to work on xir menace. Some of the older dedicants to the assassins' society had already had their first kills, marking them as tsiyos. The rest of the dedicants gave them plenty of respect. But Iktan had not been chosen for an assignment yet. Not even to accompany a tsiyo as lookout. Xe had not even received an invitation to the inquisition room to practice the methods the Knives used to make traitors spill their secrets. (In truth, they did not use the inquisition room anymore, a by-product of a darker time in the tower's history. But xe had hope, and the Priest of Knives, a bayeki named Ipep, believed in teaching the old ways of blood, even if these days most disputes were settled through diplomacy.)

Iktan noticed the girl was eating something that smelled delicious, a whole class better than normal dedicant slop. It looked to be roasted potato slices that she dipped in oil before popping the bite-sized pieces into her mouth.

A *very pretty mouth*, xir stupid brain supplied, and xe told it to shut up.

"Can I have some of that?"

The girl looked at her lunch. "Not when you just threatened to kill me."

Iktan had been hanging from the ledge for a while, and xir fingers were cramping. Xe scampered up the balustrades, agile as a squirrel, and hoisted xirself up and over the top rail. Xe landed at a crouch by her side.

Up here, next to her, she was even prettier.

"I've heard of you," xe said. "Everyone has."

For the first time, the girl looked uneasy.

"But I don't care about what they say," Iktan assured her. "They're jealous."

The girl drew a hand self-consciously over her hair. It was a dark brown, not a lustrous black like Iktan's own, but there was something nice about it, the way it caught the sun. The same applied to her eyes. Sort of common in color and shape, if xe were being truthful, but they looked kind.

"What is there to be jealous of?" she muttered, running a finger through the oil on the plate beside her.

To Iktan, it seemed obvious. "You're the best, aren't you?"

"At what?" Her eyes narrowed in suspicion.

Iktan shrugged. "Whatever the hawaa society do. Divination. Prophecy."

Xe had a knife strapped to xir thigh, one of four xe always carried (best to be prepared), and unsheathed it now with a showy flourish.

Her eyes widened. Ah, there was the reaction xe had been craving, and a jolt of satisfaction warmed Iktan's chest.

Xe said, "Everyone knows how you bested that dedicant and the Sun Priest picked you over him, and how you came up from the kitchens and aren't even Sky Made."

Xe spun the knife between xir fingers, a simple trick even first years knew, but she looked appropriately impressed. And with a final toss and catch, xe planted the knife in one of the small potatoes. Iktan lifted the tuber to xir mouth and took a bite. It was still hot enough to be soft, and the oil was slightly spiced.

Xe made a little humming noise as the food burst, flavorful, across xir tongue. Heaven.

"But most of the Sky Made are a bunch of snobs," Iktan said as xe chewed.

She lifted a skeptical eyebrow. "Aren't you Sky Made?"

"Not by choice," xe assured her before taking another bite. "Now I know why you hide in the Sun Priest's office. His lunch is better."

She smiled. She had a kind smile, too.

"Would you like to be friends?" she asked.

Xe stopped, mid-chew. "How do you mean?" People did not simply ask to be friends. It took days of time spent together, sometimes weeks. Things in common. "I only just met you."

She huffed, an exasperated sound. "I'm sorry. Do you have too many friends at the moment?" She held a hand to her forehead as if shading her eyes and looked around. "I can't seem to see them."

Ouch. But Iktan was a realist and, in fact, needed a friend. "I see your point." Xe speared another potato. "Tell you what. Bring lunch tomorrow, and we'll see."

"The Knives won't miss you?"

"And if they do? There's no rule I have to sit with them." *And I'd much rather sit with you.*

"A deal." She held out a hand. After a moment, Iktan gripped her forearm. Her skin was sun-warmed beneath xir fingers. Xe held her arm longer than strictly necessary and, even then, was reluctant to let go.

"Here." Iktan handed her the knife xe had used to eat the potato, hilt first. It was one of xir favorites, a delicate thing with carved serpents in the stone hilt and tiny jade chips for eyes. It had been a gift from Iktan's father when xe had left for the tower.

"For protection," xe said, when she looked at xir quizzically.

"What do I need protection from?"

"Everyone needs protection at some time or another. Keep it."

Iktan leaped back over the top rail, catching the bottom beam and hanging suspended in the open air.

"Hey," xe said. "What's your name?"

"Naranpa."

Iktan rolled the name around xir mouth as if it was another tasty morsel of food. "I'm Iktan. Same time tomorrow?"

She nodded.

And that was that.

Such promise, Iktan thought now around the sweetness of the memory. They had both been so young and filled with such promise. But all that had become bitter ash on Iktan's tongue since Naranpa's death.

Better you had never met me that day, Nara. Better we had not become friends.

Become lovers.

And now Iktan had become regret in the shape of a human being.

Revenge, xe thought. *One day, I will become revenge.*

It was a comfort, perhaps Iktan's only one.

A white line across the horizon warned that dawn, and breakfast, was inching ever closer. Xe pushed xirself up from the stump that made for a makeshift seat and dusted off xir Golden Eagle whites. Xe had worn red for so many years, wearing white felt like living in someone else's skin, like xe was a ghost stuck in a sorry, colorless half-life, little left of what xe had once been.

Iktan started back toward Nuuma. And her breakfast. And her war.

In truth, xe cared nothing for war. Had soured on the idea as soon as it started to take shape, if xe had ever been sweet on it at all.

Tova was nothing now without the Watchers, so why Golden Eagle and the Treaty cities were so intent on fighting over who ruled it was lost on Iktan. Mines, the riches of the clans, the jaw-dropping amounts of cacao piled in the stores of the celestial towers, yes, yes. It was not that xe did not understand. But to Iktan, the city was just another graveyard, one soaked in Watcher blood.

More promise squandered, and for what? Money? Power?

What was power?

Once, xe had been ambitious. One did not become the Priest of Knives without ambition.

But now xe cared nothing for it. Power was an illusion, often disabused at the edge of a blade. Xe had known many who thought themselves powerful, untouchable, until Iktan crawled through their window.

Just ask the matron of Carrion Crow.

Oh, you sad sack, Iktan chided xirself. *Enough with the melancholy.*

Distracted, Iktan caught a foot against a root. Xe stumbled for half a step before recovering. Irritated, xe reached down to pluck the offending botanical from the ground, only to find it was not a root at all.

A long white piece of bone protruded from the ground. Iktan pulled at it, thinking it a human bone, but it spooled out twice as long as xir arm. It was a piece of a serpent spine. A winged serpent.

The butchers who had murdered the scions that night had slaughtered their great beasts, too.

To slaughter something so beautiful.

Iktan could not understand the waste of it. The ruin.

What monster would dare?

I will find out and pay them back tenfold.

A satisfying vow. One xe would enjoy keeping.

Iktan broke off the tip of the serpent spine and tucked the bone in xir pocket.

A symbol of the oath made here today.

As the sun came up and the Sovran of Hokaia's pyramid mound rose in the foreground, Iktan hummed a happy tune. Xir mood had improved considerably, and Iktan looked forward to the rising dawn.

Excited for the future and all the bloodshed that it promised.

CHAPTER 4

CITY OF TOVA
YEAR 1 OF THE CROW

> He comes to the feast
> An honored guest.
> To quench the thirst for vengeance
> And fill the righteous tharm.
>
> — Prayer to the Odo Sedoh, recorded at a meeting of the Odohaa

Serapio stalked the halls of the Golden Eagle Great House, shadow billowing like a cloak around him, obsidian knives in each hand. The veins on his neck ran like black rivers under his skin, and ink-colored tears dripped down his hollowed cheeks.

And everywhere he went, death followed.

The trail of dead was testament to his passing, and yet his enemies still came.

A figure barreled in from his right: charging feet, a cry of defiance on doomed lips.

Serapio felt a rush of wind from the swing of a spear that parted the air as it came. He ducked, letting it pass overhead. Now low, he sank his blades into his attacker's legs. The warrior stumbled, audacity turning to screams of agony. Serapio rose, spinning, as graceful as death itself. He wrenched the Shield's spear free, reversed it, and plunged it through the warrior's chest. There was a moment of resistance—bone that did not want to concede.

Serapio persisted.

A startled exhale as flint-tipped spear found flesh and proceeded to beating heart. The Golden Eagle Shield collapsed, dead.

Serapio retrieved his knives and moved on.

He turned a corner. Bowstrings sang out as arrows were loosed from their cradles.

Serapio threw his arms high. Shadow and flesh fused and became black wings. The arrows thudded harmlessly against his feathered armor.

He flung a winged arm out, and barbed quills sped toward his enemies, their tips sharp as any blade. He heard their screams as they fell, pierced through.

He came to the end of a hallway. A cold breeze swept down a staircase.

He lifted his head. Breathed in the frigid air. Above him was the aviary.

He listened, waiting. No sound came to his ears. No Shield with spears or bow and nothing of the great eagles that gave the clan their name. But he had not expected much resistance, was surprised he had encountered any at all. Most of Golden Eagle had fled with their matron months ago, leaving only a limited contingent of Shield behind to protect the scions who had not run when they had the opportunity.

And now it was too late.

Satisfied that he had cleared the halls nearest him, he called to his crows. Within minutes a dozen corvids swept down the stairs and circled around him, a tornado of beak and claw.

"Search the Great House," he instructed the flock. "Every

room, every nook, any place a person might hide. Let no Golden Eagle escape judgment today. If you find them, harry them out, and I will come."

The black storm screamed their reply, and then they were off, swift wings traveling through passageways and breeching chamber doors where only Eagle scions had lived for centuries.

The old ways are dead, Serapio thought. *I bring a new order, and those who do not submit will know only suffering.*

But his new world did not come without personal cost. Exhaustion nipped at him like an unruly hatchling, demanding his attention, but he had no time to rest. His enemies were everywhere. Here, in his own city, even within his own clan. Somewhere out there, across the Crescent Sea, where the Treaty cities gathered their armies. Even in the heavens, where the enemies of the crow god grew restless as he fought to keep Tova in his shadowy grip.

They would come for him eventually, all of them. Serapio knew it like he knew the pace of his own heartbeat, the taste of rage against his tongue.

And he must be ready.

But here in the empty hallway, blood-spattered and battle-weary, Serapio could steal a moment of rest while his crows searched. He pressed his back against a nearby wall, head tilted, eyes closed. Exhaustion became enervation, and he slid to the floor, retreating into himself.

Time passed. The adrenaline that had fueled his rampage faded. The darkness that crawled beneath his skin receded. To anyone who saw him now, he would look like a man stealing a nap when he could . . . save the bodies in his wake.

Familiar footsteps approached. Serapio stirred, ever alert, but did not stand. *One more moment*, he told himself.

Maaka, the leader of his Tuyon, paused a good length away.

Serapio lifted his head. "Speak," he commanded, voice soft with fatigue.

"The scions await, Odo Sedoh."

"How many?"

"Thirty."

"Only scions. No Shield?"

"All were put to the knife."

He held out a hand, and Maaka helped him to his feet. "Take me to them."

As they walked, a crow soared down the corridor. It landed on Serapio's shoulder. He absently stroked a finger across its head. "Have you or the others found anything, little one?" he asked the bird.

The corvid clicked a negative reply.

"Then perhaps you will stay and be my eyes?"

The crow assented, and Serapio reached out with his mind. What had once required star pollen came as naturally as breath, and he knew he was as much crow as he was man. He blinked once, twice, and the world around him came into focus. Stone floors, stone walls, flickering resin lanterns that did little to hold back the darkness.

And dead men. Twisted, eyes staring, blood pooling slick on the floor. Made so by his hand.

He turned his attention to Maaka.

Maaka was much the same as he always was. Stout and barrel-chested, a head shorter than Serapio. His blood armor gleamed in the lantern light that lit the halls, the crowskull helmet casting a sinister shadow along the gore-specked walls. Maaka had once had a warmth and earnestness about him, a trait that had made him a natural leader among the Odohaa. Likewise, his passionate sermons had converted many to the worship of the crow god when such practice was forbidden by the Watchers. But on the night of his ascension, Serapio had demanded Maaka slit his own throat. The pious man had balked at first, seemingly not as devoted to his god as he had thought himself to be. But in the end, he had done as Serapio demanded. Ever since, Maaka had become taciturn and rote, a chastened prophet who made a loyal guard, willing to obey with an unquestioning myopia that Serapio found both refreshing and disquieting. He had no doubt that if he asked Maaka to murder his loved ones and throw himself into the Tovasheh River, the man would be widowed and airborne before Serapio finished speaking.

"Is there anything I should know?" Serapio asked.

"They are defiant."

"They must have known this day would come."

"An eagle cannot change its feathers."

Serapio's smile was grim. "The same could be said of crows."

"They are no Crows, Odo Sedoh." Maaka sounded slightly offended, as if Serapio had suggested something both obvious and impossible. Serapio was tempted to reply, but the commander of his Tuyon often failed to understand Serapio's conflicted opinions about his mother Saaya's clan, so Serapio let his words sit behind his teeth, unspoken.

They arrived at the threshold to the great room, two imposing cedar doors emblazoned with eagles in flight. Maaka threw open the doors, and Serapio entered. The Golden Eagle great room was round and made of lime-washed adobe brick, much like the Carrion Crow great room. It stretched three stories to the ceiling above. Long, narrow windows circled the high edge like a collared necklace. The shadowy rays of the black sun filtered down across the washed walls and floors, casting the room in speckled half-light.

Along the far wall was a dais, and on the dais was a throne, a bench carved from pale stone where the matron had once sat and ruled her clan. The throne was painted gold, but the color had faded and chipped over time, much like the glory of the clan itself. Along the walls were depictions of various matrons, also grown dim with age.

A chronicle of their clan mothers, Serapio thought. *They make fitting witnesses to Golden Eagle's end.*

He took the steps of the dais two at a time and settled on the throne. There, at the doorway and along the curving walls, were thirty soldiers pulled from the ranks of the Odohaa new recruits. They each carried an obsidian-tipped spear and a black blade sheathed at their belts. They were divided into groups of five and commanded by six of his thirteen Tuyon, themselves imposing in their blood armor, crow skulls, and spears. But it was not the eerie armor or the weapons that made the scions in the center of the room tremble; it was the Tuyon themselves. They exuded something unnatural, something of death and what comes after. It permeated the space, smelling of old bones, crow must, and a vow sealed by violence.

He could see the fear in the eyes of what remained of the Golden Eagle scions as they huddled before him, faces as wan and starved as the paintings around him. For the past months, Golden Eagle had been living off scraps, severed from the other clans and the rest of the city as punishment for their matron's treason. Serapio had been content to let them rot, shunned and hated. But Golden Eagle had been unwilling. Instead, they had festered and infected Tova with their treachery.

And now it was up to him to cleanse the wound.

He motioned Maaka close. "Call forward any servants."

"Those of you who serve the Eagle, step forward."

The crowd shuffled nervously, but no one moved.

"Step forward!" Maaka hammered the butt of his spear into the floor, the resulting boom echoing off the rounded walls.

Reluctantly, a few detached themselves from the larger group.

"And the children," Serapio added.

Parents pushed their offspring forward even less willingly, but they did as commanded. Many of the youngest ran to cling to the skirts of the maids. One man dressed in frayed livery scooped up a boy of perhaps five and pressed his cheek protectively against his own. A blanket-wrapped infant handed from mother to nursemaid sniffled in protest.

"Leave us." Serapio gestured toward the servants. "And take the children."

They hesitated, confused, until a woman, silver-haired and wearing a white dress stained to gray, exchanged quiet words with the group. When the soldiers approached to remove them, she patted arms and shoulders in reassurance. Slowly, the servants and children shuffled out, eyes wide, limbs shaking.

Only the adult scions of the clan, those of privilege and power, remained.

Serapio studied them, noting each sweating brow, every rapid inhale.

"Do you know who I am?" he asked.

Defiant silence was his only answer, but he could smell the thick odor of their terror, hear their nervous feet scuffing against the floor.

He sighed. "This will not do." He cast about the room. "You." He pointed to the silver-haired woman who had calmed the servants. "What is your name?"

She lifted her chin and met his black gaze with eyes the color of jade. She had the bearing of a woman who was used to being obeyed, and she, out of them all, was unafraid. "I am Suuakeh Golden Eagle."

Serapio tilted his head slightly toward Maaka, asking a question.

"The matron's mother," Maaka supplied.

Serapio could not quite keep the surprise from his face. He had not expected the matron to leave her own mother behind when she fled. He studied the woman for some sign that she understood the danger she was in and was not disappointed. The too-straight back, as if she had to force herself to outward calm, the slight flexing of her right hand. What he had taken for fearlessness was practiced fortitude . . . and a plan.

He smiled.

"Did you search them all for weapons?" he asked Maaka, his voice too low for anyone else to hear.

"Yes, Odo Sedoh."

"Even the matron's mother?"

"She is an old woman." The excuse was feeble, and Maaka knew it as soon as the words passed his lips. He made to move, but Serapio pressed a restraining hand against his arm. "Wait. Let us see what she does."

He turned back to Suuakeh and repeated his earlier question. "Do you know who I am?"

"The Carrion King." Her voice was mocking.

Carrion King.

He had heard the name whispered through the city, a play on both his affiliation with Carrion Crow and his slaughter of the Watchers.

"Your daughter has betrayed you, Suuakeh. All of you. And your city. Even now she is in Hokaia plotting Tova's fall, and all in this room abet her."

He paused, but there were no murmurs of disbelief. No muttered challenges.

"And none of you denies it." He steepled his hands, tapping his fingers together in thought. "I have been patient with Golden Eagle. Understanding."

"You have ruined us!" Suuakeh's voice quaked with rage.

"Golden Eagle should have come to me at Sun Rock when I called the other clans and they pledged their loyalty. Then your matron's actions might not have stained her kin."

"Never!" Her voice rang through the hall, bounced off the fading portraits of the women who had forged her clan. "We will not bow to a man, and never to a usurper. You are nothing, a passing terror, and once you are gone, Golden Eagle will remain."

In that you are wrong, old woman.

"I admire your loyalty," he said, "but it is misplaced. And so I give you one last chance to renounce your clan and join a united Tova in this war."

"You ask me to fight against my own daughter."

"A daughter who has betrayed her city and left you to die." He raised his voice. "Left all of you to die." They said nothing, not even Suuakeh, although she flexed her hand, again, as if it was empty when it desired to be filled.

Serapio leaned forward. "But you did not stay to die for nothing, did you?"

The woman had lowered her head as he spoke, but she looked up now, her eyes wide. For the first time, Serapio saw something like understanding cross her face.

Ah, now you know why I am here and how you have failed.

He said, "My people have intercepted a spy bound for Hokaia with drawings of Tova's defenses in the Eastern districts. Not only drawings but information disclosing our numbers along the front lines, maps of our supply houses." He paused, letting the implied accusation fill the room.

The stink of fear grew stronger.

He motioned one of the Tuyon forward.

The guard carried a basket tucked under his arm, and at Serapio's direction, he came to a stop at the foot of the dais.

"Show them," the Carrion King commanded.

The guard unceremoniously dumped the basket's contents across the polished floor. A low gasp went up from the families, and someone, a man, groaned, as a tawny-haired head rolled to a stop before Suuakeh's feet. The elderly woman swayed, hands raised as if to ward off the sight.

"He is one of yours." Serapio was not asking.

Suuakeh's gaze stayed fixed on the dead man's severed head. Her voice had been granite before, but now it was as cracked and brittle as early winter frost. "He was my grandson."

Not a child of the matron's, as she had only daughters, but perhaps a nephew. He did not know Nuuma Golden Eagle, but he found her careless with her people. "He confessed immediately and therefore did not suffer."

"Your mercy is a cruelty, Lord Crow, if you name him a coward."

"I have given you chance after chance to repent, and yet you seem determined to die," Serapio mused. His eyes raked the room. Nothing. He shook his head. "So be it. The council of matrons has declared you enemies of the city. They believe the city is safest with all of you dead."

A woman near the back began to cry. No one bothered to comfort her.

Maaka, who had been standing quietly by Serapio's side, spoke. "There is also the war college."

"Golden Eagle is innocent of the slaughter at the war college!" Suuakeh's protest came quickly.

"And yet none of the Golden Eagle scions died," Serapio observed. "Surely you do not expect us to believe this a coincidence. That your children lived while the other children of the Sky Made were murdered in their beds?"

Word of the slaughter had come on the tongues of traders bringing goods and news from Hokaia before the spearmaidens had closed the border. It had been so outrageous, so depraved, that at first the clans had not believed it. Those who studied at the war college were some of the most loved of the scions, children of the matrons' extended families themselves. To slaughter them in their sleep. It did not seem a thing possible.

And yet it had happened. Someone murdered every Sky Made scion as they slept, save Golden Eagle. Others had survived, children of Cuecola and Hokaia, Barach and Huecha. But no one who called Tova home.

The matrons had come to Serapio demanding justice, and he had promised them blood, aware that the war college slaughter had done more to bring the clans to his side than anything he might have done himself. The matrons hated him, but now they hated Hokaia and Golden Eagle a bit more.

Serapio stood.

"Your house is defiled. Rebuke it, or you will be known forever as murderers and betrayers. A debt you will pay with your lives."

"And what of the children you sent away?" Suuakeh asked. "Would you stain them with our perceived sins even though they had no hand in it?"

Serapio spread his hands. "I am not without mercy, although you may consider this kindness a cruelty, too. Your clan must die today, but your children need not. They will be taken into households in the other clans, made to swear fealty to them. Become their children. You will not see them again, but they will live."

"This is heresy!" a man shouted.

"This," Serapio growled, "is war. So choose. Live . . . or die as Golden Eagle."

The woman who had been weeping shoved her way through the crowd. She stumbled to the front, falling to her knees a hairbreadth from the severed head of Suuakeh's grandson.

"I choose to live!" she wailed. "To renounce my clan, my family! Mercy, Odo Sedoh! Mercy!"

Suuakeh flinched as if she had been struck. "You would be a traitor to your clan?" she hissed at the kneeling woman. "Even though Nuuma trusted us to stay and perform our duty? You knew the risks."

"Nuuma is not here. It is not her throat he will cut."

"He will not cut your throat," Suuakeh declared. "I will."

The old woman moved with a speed that belied her age, and before the Tuyon could react, Suuakeh had a blade in her right hand. She plunged it into the woman's neck. The traitorous woman tumbled over, hand clutching at the torn flesh.

Shouts erupted from the crowd, horror sweeping through the room.

Serapio motioned, and two Odohaa soldiers rushed to subdue the old woman. She did not fight them, and soon she was restrained between them.

Serapio felt Maaka shift beside him. Shame radiated from his hunched shoulders. Good. He would not make the mistake of underestimating even the seemingly harmless among their enemies again. Loyalty was good. Competence was better.

"I thought you meant that knife for me, old woman." Serapio's voice was mild.

Suuakeh's gaze was unflinching. "If I could get close enough to carve your black heart out, I would try with my last breath. But I see you now, what you are, and know I cannot. But her?"

She spit at the woman bleeding out on the floor. "Golden Eagle suffers no traitors."

"Then you understand why I cannot ignore what your clan has done."

"You wish to take my life?" Her upper lip curled in contempt. "I will not give you the satisfaction."

She wrenched free of the guards and lunged toward the dying woman. The soldiers scrambled after her, but their footing was precarious on the blood-slick floor, and they could not stop her before she had ripped the knife from the dead woman's neck. Serapio thought for a moment she might try to kill him after all, but instead, she drew the blade across her own throat.

Jade eyes stayed fixed on Serapio as blood poured down across her chest. She moved her mouth to hurl one last curse at him, but it was too late. Her knees buckled, and, choking on blood, Suuakeh fell dead.

Quiet filled the room, the remaining scions shocked to silence.

The shadow's hunger awoke within him, as if it were a living thing separate from himself. Magic rose, uncalled, the veins in his neck blackening, ink-colored tears pooling in his bottomless eyes.

"Travel well, Suuakeh Golden Eagle," he murmured. And then, to Maaka, his voice already shifting to something not wholly him, "Kill them."

Maaka gestured, and the Carrion King's soldiers moved as one.

· · · · ·

Outside of what was once the Golden Eagle Great House, Serapio stood facing the canyon that divided Tova into north and south. He could hear the rush of the Tovasheh below, feel the breeze that gently swayed the bridge that would take them back to Sun Rock, now called Shadow Rock, and the fortress he had built there. The small crow that had lent him its sight had stayed close on his shoulder, as if it sensed his unquiet mind and hoped to soothe him. Serapio absently worried its glossy feathers, his callused fingertips running across the corvid's head.

Maaka came to him, bloody and weary. "It is done. The scions of Golden Eagle are no more."

"And what of the ordinary citizens?" Serapio asked. The streets of Tsay were deserted, the common folk of the district huddled in their homes, no doubt awaiting their fate. "Can they be trusted, Maaka? Or will they turn against us, as their matron did? As their great families did? Will they fight for Tova, or will they betray her?"

Maaka did not answer at first, giving the question the consideration it deserved. When he finally spoke, he was matter-of-fact. "It cannot be known."

No, it could not.

"What do they wish from me?" Serapio murmured, more to himself.

But Maaka heard and said, his voice a question, "Odo Sedoh?"

"Do they wish me to slaughter them all? Pave my path to power with their blood?"

"It has been done before."

Yes, and he had done it himself. What were Sun Rock and his destruction of the Watchers but a path to power paved with blood? He had not seen it that way at the time, caught in his destiny and his god's fervor, but that was naivete. He was naive no longer.

Maaka said, "You could speak to them, tell them of the dangers . . ."

"I am no populist to sway them with speeches," Serapio demurred, a truth they both knew, made even more evident by the encounter with Suuakeh Golden Eagle.

The leader of the Tuyon shifted on unhappy feet. He had once had the gift of oration, but he was no god reborn. He had helped clear Serapio's way, but only the Odo Sedoh could lead.

"Then it is by blood," Maaka said.

"Yes." *My way is death.* Serapio knew it. He had always known it. Even if he wished otherwise.

He dusted his palms against his padded shirt and turned to Maaka.

"Burn the district to the ground. Kill any who try to stop you, but otherwise allow everyone—the women, the children, the commoners—to leave. Those who were once Golden Eagle shall never make their home in this district again. Shall never call themselves Golden Eagle again. Their clan is now anathema. Every door shall be barred to those of that name. Every tongue shall speak against them. Let the people be scattered so they must depend upon the mercy of the other clans. Let the name Golden Eagle mean nothing but ash and mourning from this day forward."

Maaka did not flinch. "It will be done."

Serapio was the Odo Sedoh, and once that had been enough. It was still enough for men like Maaka who would follow him unquestioningly down a road crimson with carnage.

But Serapio knew that he had become something else, too. Something beyond mere destiny. Something grotesque. Something more.

The matron's mother had called him Carrion King.

Called him black-hearted.

She was not wrong.

CHAPTER 5

Dream well, for there is nothing so powerful or so fragile as a dream.

—From *The Manual of the Dreamwalkers*, by Seuq, a spearmaiden

Naranpa walked among the bones of gods looking for god-flesh.

It had rained the night before, soaking the small village of Charna, the place that the former Sun Priest and current avatar of the sun god had called home for the last three months. It was the first moisture that had not simply been an exhalation of cold spittle from gray clouds since she had arrived, and her teacher, Kupshu, had assured her that it was a sure sign that winter was finally over, even in these far northern climes.

And so Naranpa had risen in the hour before dawn when a thick mist still hung over the lakeside on which Charna squatted, and she had gone to the graveyard. It was an hour's walk to the great mounded hoodoos of calcified rocks where legend held that the gods had died. Some in battle, some from ennui. Others from loneliness or remorse or whatever other reason gods died. Legend held that some of the lesser gods haunted the graveyard, reduced to restless spirits and walking night-mares. It was a place one dared not spend a night, but it was reasonably safe during the day, if one kept her wits about her, and had her own god magic.

By the time Naranpa reached the graveyard, the mist had burned away, and the sun was out, sharp and bright. Even so, much of the graveyard remained cast in shadow, the narrow red-dirt path she followed well shaded by the high, round canyons. She stepped lightly, knowing what looked like a solid patch of earth might only be a skin of red mud quick to give way underfoot. Charna was full of stories of unlucky foragers who had stepped on such a false patch and plunged to their deaths.

Her eyes searched for the elusive fungus that only grew here and only after wet, rainy nights and only in the scant months of spring. So far, she had found none. Even with the rain, the small bell-shaped mushroom was rare and hard to find. But Kupshu had assured her that there would be colonies of it hidden in the patchy, needle-sharp grass, so she continued to look.

"You will need it for what comes next," the old woman had said before she sent her out.

"But don't you have some right there?" Naranpa had looked meaningfully at the shelves of dried herbs that lined the walls of Kupshu's round two-room house.

"Better if you find your own."

"I don't see why."

"Of course you don't. That's why I'm the teacher and you're the pupil."

Naranpa, who had been a pupil for most of her life in some way or another, had not argued but had donned her cloak, taken up one of the collection baskets that hung by the door, and gone.

A speck of brown edging white rock caught her eye. She stooped to bend back the weedy grass around it and found a cluster of bell-shaped fungi sprouting off veined white stalks. She took the trowel from her basket and, kneeling, dug carefully around the entire troop, plucking the sacred fruit from the earth.

Naranpa smiled, pleased. There were at least a dozen individual stalks in the cluster. Surely Kupshu could not complain, although the old woman would likely find her at fault somehow. It was the nature of their relationship. Naranpa faltered, and Kupshu corrected. But in truth, Naranpa did not mind it.

It felt familiar.

After her first find, spotting the godflesh became easier, and by the time the sun had crossed half the sky, she had found another four clusters and decided that it was time to return home.

The walk back to Charna was pleasant. The village of no more than a hundred sat along the rocky black banks of the lake. Kupshu had told her it was called the Lake of Flames in the language of the Northern Wastes. It had been formed when the coyote god's heel struck the earth, and later the crater had filled with the tears of his sister. An interesting tale. Naranpa had never heard that the coyote god had a sister. Kupshu had assured her there were many things Naranpa did not know, so what was another?

The lake was also where the golden scales of the sun god had been found, taken back to Hokaia to be mixed with the blood of a sacrifice and forged into the Sun Priest's mask.

Now, with the sun stretching across the vast flat water, Naranpa could see how it had earned its name. Streaks of red and orange spread across the lake, giving the distinct impression that the watery surface burned.

Kupshu was boiling water when Naranpa pushed open

the door. She set the basket on the table and dropped onto a nearby bench.

Her teacher hobbled over. "Let me see."

Naranpa pulled back the cloth she had laid over the god-flesh to keep it moist. "I think you will be pleased."

The woman had a stirring stick, and she gently poked at the fungi, moving them this way and that to examine the gills on the underside and the veiny stems.

"Good," she declared, and Naranpa could not help the small joy she felt at pleasing her teacher. She'd always been a good student.

"Now you're ready to Walk," Kupshu added.

"What, now?" She sat up straighter. "Tonight?"

"Tomorrow. When they dry a bit."

"Tomorrow is so soon."

Kupshu's thinning eyebrows rose. "Did you not come here to learn how to enter the realm of the gods? You have been preparing for a month. It is time."

A thrill of terror shivered down Naranpa's spine. She had been waiting for this day ever since she had arrived and found the old woman. Naranpa had concealed her identity, content to simply be a pilgrim seeking ancient knowledge from a willing teacher. Here, she was not the Sun Priest of Tova and certainly not the avatar of the sun god. It had taken her weeks to even convince Kupshu to speak to her, and then more weeks of backbreaking labor hauling rocks and wash water and anything else the old woman demanded for Naranpa to prove she was a worthy student. Only later, from other villagers, had she learned that Kupshu had not taken on any pupils for a score of years, and those had never stayed, certainly never been deemed worthy of dreamwalking.

Naranpa had outlasted them all, even though part of her

had worried that Kupshu would never declare her ready. But she had, and the moment could not be delayed any longer.

"If you're afraid . . ." Kupshu thrust her chin toward the door pointedly.

"No," Naranpa replied hastily. "I came all this way, learned this much."

"Then hang the godflesh by the fire, and by this time tomorrow, you will be Walking in the realms of the gods." The woman scratched at her bent back. "Until then, go chop some wood. I'll need more, and I'm getting too old for chores."

Naranpa hauled herself back onto already tired feet. "Sometimes I think you took me in only so you'd have someone to chop wood for you."

"Bah," Kupshu grumbled, turning back to her boiling pot. But she did not deny it.

$$\bullet \; \bullet \; \bullet \; \bullet \; \bullet$$

The next day felt like both the longest and the shortest day of Naranpa's life. Sunset found her sitting on a mat on Kupshu's dirt floor, a cup of godflesh tea in her hands.

"Tell me again what I must do." She looked down at the innocuous liquid in the cup. Once she drank it, she knew she would be irrecoverably changed. She had stopped denying that magic existed. How could she believe otherwise when fire burned in her hands, and she could change her shape simply by willing it? But she had not asked for those things. The sun god had chosen her, and she had been the vessel to her divine power. Drinking the tea was a choice, an act of will. Now she would embrace gods and magic and everything that accompanied it. The logic and reason she had once clung to at the tower seemed very far away.

"You must do the same thing that we have practiced every day without the tea."

"So I am not actually asleep."

Kupshu sighed pointedly.

"I just don't understand why they call it dreamwalking if I'm only meditating and not asleep."

"You're stalling. Do it, or don't. It doesn't matter to me. But if you want to know your god—"

"Yes, yes." Her fear was foolish, and she was sick of being afraid. Naranpa drank. The brew tasted like earth and ice, the edge bitter and strange on her tongue.

"All of it!"

She swallowed until the cup was empty and handed it back. Kupshu set it aside.

"Now what?" Naranpa asked.

"Where is your talisman?"

Naranpa wore a small carving of a long-tailed firebird on a strip of hide around her neck. She lifted it up for inspection.

"Take it in hand," her teacher instructed. "When you are unsure if you dream or wake, look at your talisman. It will tell you what is true."

Naranpa clasped the talisman against her palm.

The old woman lit a disk of fragrant peat and let the smoke curl around the room. "Close your eyes and build your house."

The first thing Kupshu had taught her was to build a house inside her head. It could be any kind of house, and it would serve as her retreat and tether once she was in the dreamworld. At first, Naranpa had sought to construct a place like the celestial tower, but as she erected the column in her mind, she realized the tower was not a place of safety anymore. She discarded it and instead fashioned something entirely different.

A round house built into a cliff wall, a painted handmaiden

flower beside the door, its three bladelike leaves peeling back from the starburst center. And on the door itself, a blazing sun. It was the house promised to her by the bosses of the Maw, her once-allies, when she saved her brother from torture and signed her name in their book. But with Denaochi's death and her abdication as matron of Coyote clan, the Handmaiden became a place that would never be, except for a time, while she dreamed. For that brief moment, the Handmaiden could exist both in her mind and in her heart.

She concentrated, bringing the house to life, and soon the structure felt so real that she was sure that if she ran probing fingers along the walls, they would be solid beneath her touch.

She entered it now, its rooms comfortable and familiar to her after days of practice, as if they truly existed on some busy, happy street in the Maw.

Kupshu's distant voice said, "To your workroom."

Naranpa went to her library, a perfect place at the heart of the Handmaiden. Shelves of books and manuscripts lined the walls. There were benches for study, rich tapestries and rugs warmed the room, and a wide wooden table held a teapot and all the tools a scholar and scribe might need, should she wish to write: colored inks, hair-tipped writing pens, lime-bleached bark.

A feeling of joy suffused her. This was the place she loved most. The place where she was safest. The place she was meant to be, even if only in her imagination.

"Stay focused," Kupshu warned. "This is no time to let yourself wander. You must control the dream, not the other way around."

Naranpa understood. Even in her altered state, she corralled her thoughts, glancing down at her talisman to ground herself. The carving shifted on her palm, one minute the familiar firebird, the next the handmaiden flower.

She swallowed hard. That had never happened before.

She was in the dreamworld.

Teacher and pupil had decided that for her first Walk, Naranpa would simply try to peer into the dreams of others. Kupshu had explained that it was easiest to see into the dreams of loved ones, people to whom the dreamwalker had a connection. Her first thought was of Denaochi, but Kupshu had warned that the dreams of the dead were a treacherous place. Best to stay with the living.

So she released the thoughts of her brother and turned to the other person she cared about the most: Iktan.

She did not know if the Priest of Knives lived or not, but she could not contemplate that xe would be dead. Iktan had once assured her that xe was very hard to kill, and she clung to that promise with all the hope her heart could muster.

"Have you chosen?" Kupshu's voice drifted down to her like echoes on the wind.

"Yes," she murmured. She looked around her vast library. Thousands upon thousands of volumes on every wall, as far as the eye could see. More than existed in any library in the Meridian, more books and scrolls, perhaps, than existed in all the world.

And every one of them a person and their dreams.

It was a conceit, a way of organizing the dreamworld that Kupshu had taught her. The method varied from Walker to Walker. Kupshu had explained that when she herself Walked, she organized the myriad of dreams in the world into small clay jars, much the way she organized her precious herbs. For Naranpa, dreams were books.

She moved through the library, her talisman in hand. She glanced down, and now instead of the handmaiden, the talisman had morphed into a black-bladed knife. Her hand closed around it, and the edges of the blade bit into her flesh. She gasped loudly at the pain, and blood welled along the cuts in her palm.

"Control!" Kupshu hissed. "Whatever you see, control it!"

It is not real, she reminded herself. *It is only a dream. Your dream. Control it, Nara. Control it!*

Naranpa concentrated, willing the knife to change, the blood to be gone. When she looked again, her flesh was whole and uninjured, and the knife had shifted back into a hand-maiden flower. She was ready.

She approached the first shelf, envisioning what she needed. Before her was a red-spined book. She pulled the title free.

The book was warm in her hands. Alive. It pulsed like a beating heart, and if she held it to her nose, she knew that she would smell the coppery tinge of fresh blood.

It was Iktan's dreaming world.

Hands shaking, breath held behind tight lips, she opened the volume.

At first, nothing happened. There were pages, but the writing upon them was gibberish, suggestions of glyphs and markings that, if she tried to read them, were not actual words or ideas.

And then she was somewhere else.

A scorched wasteland of blackened earth and charred bones. Lightning flashed overhead, briefly illuminating clouds the purple and green of an aging bruise. A lone figure crouched on the ground in the distance, draped in white.

Naranpa's hand clutched around her talisman, which now fluttered between knife and flower like a locust's wings.

She imagined herself closer, and suddenly, she was there. The white-clad figure was Iktan, as she had known it would be. Xe was searching for something, digging through ash and dirt, throwing bones and branches aside in a desperate flurry of motion. Iktan's hands were bloody, not just from the ripped nails and cut skin that were the wages of this strange excavation but up to the elbows, as if xe had dipped xir arms in a vat of blood.

Naranpa held a hand to her mouth, horrified. The dream was more nightmare than anything else, and a sense of hopelessness pervaded the dark landscape.

Kupshu had warned her not to interfere in dreams. She was only to observe, to see what there was to see. Her whole venture into the dreamworld was meant to expand her consciousness to the god realm and to make room for the sun god's presence. It was not to spy, and certainly not to interfere.

But she could not leave Iktan this way, even in dreams. If she could offer a little comfort, she must.

Her first instinct was to touch, but Kupshu had warned her again and again not to interact directly with a dreamer, lest Naranpa get sucked into the dream and lose her sanity. No, whatever she did had to be something natural to the dream itself.

She remembered a knife Iktan had once given her. Xir first gift to her, in fact, when they were both desperate for a friend. A small thing, the kind of ceremonial knife one might give a child for their birthday or to mark a special occasion. The hilt had been carved into a winged serpent, jade flecks for eyes.

She conjured it now in the dreamworld, imagined it buried deep in the dirt where Iktan's hands scoured the earth. It was something for xir to find, something that might put an end to this miserable digging and remind Iktan that xe was not alone.

Iktan, who had been a whirlwind of motion since she had arrived, froze. Xe felt around in the hole xe had dug, and slowly, tentatively, pulled out the knife.

Xe looked at it in wonder, eyes wide.

"Nara?" xe asked, and Iktan's emotions—ache, regret, fear,

rage, and love, so much love—tore through her as if the feelings were her own.

Iktan crumbled inward, body folding over knees, face buried in hands, and wept.

Wept. Quietly, and then in great gasping heaves, xir whole body shaking.

Oh, skies, this was a mistake! Naranpa backed away. She had not meant this. Had only meant to comfort. Iktan did not weep, did not crumble. In all their years, she had never seen her friend like this.

This is not the real Iktan, she reminded herself. *This is an Iktan born in a nightmare.*

And suddenly, they were not alone but surrounded on all sides. Women with half-painted faces, others with shells woven in their hair, and yet others in cloaks of eagle feathers.

They circled, Iktan still weeping and unaware. Naranpa watched in horror as they attacked. Spears pierced xir back, black knives opened wounds that turned xir white robe to crimson. They struck again and again with blades, fists, even feet.

And Iktan did not fight back but stayed hunched over the small knife, cradling it as if it was something precious and rare.

No! Naranpa screamed. Unthinking, all her caution gone in the moment, she barreled through Iktan's attackers, pushing the dream women aside. But as she touched them, they turned on her, eyes red and menacing. Not women at all but monsters, something dark and violent that wanted very much to hurt her.

She backed away, her hand closing around the talisman at her neck. It cut her hand, a bladed knife, and she remembered her focus.

Take me to the Handmaiden! she thought, and then she was tumbling back, back, out of the desolate dreamscape, into her library, down the hallway, and out the door, watching it slam, a thunderclap reverberating through her bones. And then she was back in her body, lungs heaving, heart racing, struggling to breathe.

Her eyes flew open. She was back in Kupshu's house.

She stared at the talisman in her hand. It was the long-tailed firebird.

She gasped as the world came back into focus, and Kupshu was forcing a cup into her hands.

"Drink, drink!"

Naranpa swallowed it down. It was horrid. A slimy thickness clung to her tongue, and she gagged. She felt her gorge rising. Kupshu held out a bucket, and Naranpa vomited into it. Again and again, until her stomach was empty. Until she fell onto the floor, exhausted, shaking, tears leaking from her eyes.

"Stupid girl," Kupshu chided.

With effort, Naranpa looked up. The old woman stood over her.

"I told you not to interfere."

"I didn't mean to, but . . ." She shuddered at the memory of Iktan being torn apart.

"What did you do? Tell me exactly."

"I . . . planted an object. Something important to the dreamer. As a comfort."

"And what went wrong?"

She gathered herself. "It didn't comfort them at all. It made things worse. And then there were people there with weapons, and they attacked the dreamer, and I tried to stop them, but they turned on me. And then I remembered my talisman and thought of the Handmaiden, and suddenly I was back in my body, and you were feeding me that vile drink." She wiped at her mouth, the bitter taste lingering. "What was that, anyway?"

Her teacher stared at her long and hard, but Naranpa was too exhausted to care.

"Clean up the mess." Kupshu toed the bucket of sick. "And drink all the water in the water jug. That vile drink, as you call it, expelled the godflesh from your body, but it's best to drink water, anyway, to flush it out. And after, bathe with the root I gave you. Godflesh can linger in your sweat, cause you to walk in the dreamworld when you do not wish to and forget the difference between what is real and what is not." She made a sign to ward away evil. "That way lies madness."

The old woman shuffled to the door and paused. Naranpa thought she might chastise her once more for good measure, but instead she asked, "How was it?"

Naranpa considered lying to compensate for her mistake, but honesty won. "Glorious. Terrifying."

Kupshu grunted. "Sounds about right."

"Then I did not fail?"

Her teacher's back was to her, but Naranpa thought she detected satisfaction in the set of her shoulders, the tilt of her head. "Quite the opposite."

"So we will try again?" The experience had been frightening but also exhilarating. "When?"

"We wait. Too soon, and despite all our precautions, you tempt madness. Two days, and this time, you do not interfere with the dreamer."

Naranpa lifted a hand in promise.

Once Kupshu was gone, Naranpa started to laugh. High and hysterical, part elation from the remnants of the drug, part the fear working out of her body.

And no matter how she tried, she could not stop.

CHAPTER 6

It is known that the Jaguar Prince was the Best of Us. A young Man of exceeding Wisdom and great Power. A master Sorcerer and learned Scholar. A Leader and a Friend. But even He succumbed to the Frenzy. Even He fell to the Spear.

—From *A History of the Frenzy*, by Teox, a historian of the Royal Library

Balam watched the girl move across the room and wondered who she was and why he had not seen her before. He knew all the heirs of the Seven Houses, and she was not one.

What she was, was extraordinary.

It was not just her clothes, although her black huipil with the silver starbursts was eye-catching. All the other heirs wore bright yellows and oranges, the epitome of fashion in Cuecola for the season. They lounged on benches, admiring the exotic birds Balam's father had brought in for his cousin Tiniz's welcome home party. They ate his father's rare melons and stone fruits without a second thought for what they had cost to import to the city and how they had been sown, grown, and harvested. They knew only that they deserved them because their families were wealthy and powerful and privilege was the way of their world, and they did not question it.

But this girl in her unfashionable black was different. She didn't giggle and preen and partake of the casual gluttony. She studied the room, much the way Balam studied her. Her big, dark eyes seemed to take them all in and, to Balam's delight, judge them wanting.

Her gaze skimmed over him. Their eyes met.

Balam dipped his head, a small bow of appreciation. Her mouth turned down in disinterest before she glided out the far doors and onto the balcony beyond.

Disbelief like bitterroot on his tongue made him lightheaded. And then a strange warmness that felt like outrage spread through his limbs. He was not used to being dismissed.

But he was not angry. He was intrigued.

And suddenly, this dull party that he had dreaded had become quite interesting.

He had made to follow her out onto the balcony when someone called, "Balam!"

He thought to ignore it, determined to meet his new fascination, but Tiniz came bounding over. Xe may have been a dreaded Knife of the celestial tower only a few months ago, but anyone could see that Tiniz did not have the disposition of a killer.

A scholar, perhaps. Or a midwife.

Nevertheless, seven years ago Tiniz had left Cuecola, bound for Tova and the tower, sworn to become an assassin in service to the Sun Priest. Balam thought it no great surprise that xe had defected from the tower and fled on the night of the Knives' great slaughter of the Carrion Crow clan. What had been a surprise was that his cousin had not returned to Cuecola alone.

She is the Crow girl he saved, he realized, just as his cousin said, "What do you think of her?"

"Hmm?"

"Don't play coy, Cousin. I saw you staring." Tiniz gestured toward the balcony.

"She is . . . interesting."

"Beautiful, you mean." Xe leaned in. "She does not know it yet, but I mean to marry her."

A surge of jealousy darkened Balam's soul. He took a moment to examine the feeling. He didn't even know the girl, and yet he knew instinctively that his cousin would not have her if Balam had any say in the matter. And he would have a say.

"Did you not kill her mother?" he asked casually, knowing exactly the impact his words would have. His cousin paled and took a step back, as if Balam's words had drawn blood. "I mean, that is the rumor. Your one and only kill as a Knife, and it was her mother."

Tiniz's previous energy seeped away, leaving xir hunched and chastened. "It happened so quickly. She had a shovel, and she swung it at my head. It was instinct."

"Hmmm, yes, a woman with a shovel. Terribly threatening to a trained assassin."

Something in Tiniz hardened. "You were not there. You do not know what it was like. The fires, the bodies . . . it was not what I agreed to when I entered the Order, when I pledged myself to the tower."

In fairness, it was not. The life of a Knife was one of training and discipline and the acquisition of a deadly skill set, but most of a Knife's duties were largely ceremonial. The Meridian was at peace and had been for three hundred years. And the very existence of the Knives discouraged most from plotting against the Sun Priest and her Watchers. But the event they were calling the Night of Knives had changed all that, and assassins and bodyguards had become butchers, and Tiniz, kindhearted Tiniz, had failed at being a monster.

Well, Balam should not fault xir for that. Although part of him did. Part of him thought Tiniz lacked commitment. There was something admirable in being a *good* monster.

But would you have done any better? Killed her if commanded? The answer was easy enough, as his eyes wandered back toward the girl. He could only see the edge of her skirt now, billowing in the salty breeze.

"Introduce me."

Tiniz, who had been lost in dark memories, frowned. "Why?"

Balam lifted his shoulders in an elegant shrug. "Why not? She's new to town and needs friends, does she not? Someone besides these vipers."

He spared a glance at the other heirs, laughing loudly and gossiping. He caught the eye of one girl, a girl he had spent a night of passion with, but he could not remember her name. He had enjoyed himself, to say otherwise would be a lie, but not enough to speak to her again. Their parents did not know, of course, or else there would have been talk of marriage, but Balam knew the girl's mother was already scheming to send her daughter off to Huecha to marry into a merchant family there to strengthen a trade contract, so Balam had felt reasonably sure their tryst was nothing of import. Else he would not have indulged.

"Besides." He turned his attention back to Tiniz. "Do you not want me to know your wife-to-be, Cousin?"

At that, Tiniz relaxed. How had anyone in the family ever thought Tiniz had the cunning to be a Knife when xe fell for the shallowest of Balam's lies?

"Come, then," xe said, face breaking into a grin, and together they joined the girl standing alone on the balcony.

This close, Balam thought her even more beautiful. Black eyes ringed with thick lashes, wide cheeks, and a lush mouth. And a sharpness to her eyes, an intelligence she did not try to hide. So many of the heirs played the vapid socialite, but this Crow would have no one mistake her for anything but what she was.

Tiniz took their hands, the girl's in xir left, Balam's in xir right, and said, "This is Saaya, and this is Balam. And now you have met."

They stood for a moment, connected as three. Saaya was the first to let go.

"Are you enjoying the party?" Balam asked, as he let his hand drop, too. It was an empty politeness, but it was a way to begin. And his heart had started to beat very quickly.

She was not particularly tall, not as tall as he, and likely a few years younger, but Balam had the distinct feeling that she was looking down at him.

"I have no use for parties," she said, her voice surprisingly rich, her Cuecolan melodic and quite good, although a hint of some foreign accent shone through. "But Tiniz thought I should come and meet xir uncle. Xe said he could help me."

"Tiniz's uncle? Do you mean my father?" Now that he stood so close, Balam could see that Saaya's beautiful huipil had loose threads, that the ties on her sandals were frayed. "You want money."

Tiniz had the decency to look abashed. If Balam had to guess, Tiniz's reasons for bringing Saaya to the party were twofold: first, to show off his pretty new bird to the gathered heirs, and second, to stoke the rumors of Tiniz's heroism.

But Saaya seemed to believe she was here to implore Balam's father for funds. Anyone who knew the elder Lord Balam would know better than to expect even a single cacao to slip free from his miserly grip. Tiniz had lied.

"Saaya has lost everything," his cousin explained, voice rushed and a shade too high, "and your father controls the purse strings of the entire House. We cannot start a new life on my mother's allowance alone. Surely he will be sympathetic."

"My father will not help you," Balam told her, turning slightly so that Tiniz stood behind him and there was nothing between himself and the girl. "You are a foreigner, and a woman. My father is impressed by neither, nor will he have any sympathy for your plight. It is not personal. It is just his way."

Her expression tightened.

"I do not mean to offend," he continued. "Just to inform. I am afraid my cousin has given you hope where there is none."

"Balam!" Tiniz hissed.

He ignored xir. In fact, if Tiniz would just be quiet, Balam could pretend he and Saaya were alone.

"I, however," he said, "do not share the same prejudices as my father."

She looked at him, truly looked at him for the first time. He took it as an excellent sign, until she said, "What, then, are your prejudices?"

Tiniz had started to speak, perhaps to suggest that Balam's prejudices were terrible and many, when the uncle and father in question laid a heavy hand on xir shoulder.

"Tiniz!" The elder Lord Balam greeted his sister's child. "What are you doing brooding out here on the balcony with my son when there's a whole party in your honor just beyond these doors?"

"Uncle! We were just commenting on what a spectacular party this is. I am honored."

"Only the best for my relatives."

The elder Balam was a robust man on the rough side of handsome, which probably served him better than the off-putting aristocratic polish his only son had inherited from his mother. Men loved the father, wanted to open a barrel of balché with him, do business with him. His son, however, elicited envy from his peers, not a desire for camaraderie. Both were aware of the chasm between their personalities and did not particularly care for each other. The elder Balam found his son cold, and the son thought his father uncouth. It was not open hostility between them as much as it was avoidance, which even now kept the father from making eye contact.

"Have you met Saaya, Uncle?"

The girl straightened, hand rising to tame her long, dark locks before she stopped the nervous motion and smiled. Not coquettishly, as his father would have no doubt preferred from a young girl, but fiercely, as if this orphan and the merchant lord were equals.

Loathing flitted across the elder Lord Balam's face before he took Tiniz in hand. He turned away from Saaya and toward the open doors and the party beyond.

"There are many people you must meet. They want to hear of your time with the Watchers, and of this Night of Knives. Is it true? They slaughtered their own? The barbarity of the Tovans does not surprise me."

Tiniz threw a desperate look over xir shoulder, but there was no escape from family obligation.

With Tiniz gone, Balam and Saaya stood alone. Her black eyes lingered on Tiniz, perhaps on his father, until she abruptly turned away to face the balcony's edge. The city of Cuecola lay spread below her, but Balam did not think she saw it. She wrapped her arms around her middle, her face flushed even in the lamplight, and tears bright as jewels gathered along her lash line, although none fell to her cheeks.

His father had humiliated her. He understood how she felt all too well, as casual humiliation was the discipline his father had doled out since birth. Never a physical beating, his mother would have never allowed it, but the dismissal, the disregard. That was a daily occurrence, even if it no longer made Balam stew in his rage as it once had. Now, at the age of seventeen, he had learned to ignore it.

But he knew Saaya was not so practiced.

He came to stand beside her, leaning his arms against the stone railing.

"If this were all mine . . ." Balam looked out over the city below him. "If this were mine, I would not be a parsimonious merchant lord like my father but someone great like the Jaguar Prince."

He gave her space to answer, and finally she did.

"The Jaguar Prince is dead."

"Killed in the Frenzy of the War of the Spear," he acknowledged. "But that does not mean he was not great." He turned toward her. He was aware of how close they were, how his hand ached to wipe the tears from the corner of her eye. To wipe all her tears away so that she never wept again. "What would you do?"

She did not hesitate. "I would destroy my enemies."

"I can help you do that."

"You? The son of *that man*?" She spit the last with a venom that exposed the depth of her wound and how easily his father had split it open. "What do you know of loss? Your mother sits drinking fruit wine and laughing with her ladies, while my mother's corpse lies rotting along with all my kin."

"And yet you would marry her killer."

If jealousy stirred his tongue, resentment moved hers with equal force. "I am a foreigner and a woman in a city that hates both, as you pointed out. What choice do I have?"

"You do not strike me as someone who settles." He meant to provoke her, but it was also the truth.

"You do not know me well enough to know what I might do. In fact"–she tilted her head–"you do not know me at all."

"I aim to know you very well." He was not sure why he said that or, rather, why he dared to say it, but something about her made him feel bold. "I also know that destroying your enemies will require money and resources. Is that not why you came to my father?"

"He barely even looked at me, and when he did, I wished he had not."

"Do not waste a thought on him. I don't." He leaned close, dropping his voice to a whisper. "I know what the healers say." He glanced back toward the room but could not see his father. "He has an illness, something in his bones. They say he will not live much longer. And when he is gone, all of this will be mine."

She no doubt understood that he meant the money and the great mansion. But he meant it all. The people, the city, even the Crescent Sea beyond. Not because he inherited it from his father, although he would inherit much of it. But because he would take it. Just like the Jaguar Prince.

He smiled, aware that the lift of his mouth lent him a certain attractive arrogance.

"Revenge requires a plan." He moved even closer, his voice even softer. "I have been educated by all the best tutors. I can help you make a plan."

"I already have a plan." She said it, but he could tell she was intrigued. "But it will require someone to help me," she admitted.

A loud laugh boomed out from across the room, and the two turned. Tiniz was surrounded by a gaggle of heirs. Xe was gesticulating, obviously recounting some story to everyone's delight. Something in Saaya's face seemed to crumble, and if Balam could guess what she was thinking, he would say for all the resentment of her fate, she feared Tiniz thought her a passing fancy, something in which xe might easily lose interest.

She does not even understand her power, he thought. *If she did, she would not fear.*

When they turned back toward the night, their hips were touching.

"So your enemies are . . ." He had deduced the obvious, but he needed her to say it.

She lifted her chin. "Does it matter?"

"If you mean to kill the Watchers, then it matters."

"If you are scared . . ." She bumped against him. It was a challenge.

He stayed close, savoring the heat of her body so near his. "Do you know why I admire the Jaguar Prince? Not only because he was a great man who made Cuecola great but because he was a sorcerer."

She threw her head back, the laughter on her lips at once genuine and mocking.

"What's so funny?" That heat again. The emotion that felt like outrage but also like desire.

"Magic is forbidden."

"So is the worship of the gods, and yet it did not stop your people."

Her humor cut off abruptly, and Balam thought perhaps he had learned something from his father, and that was to wield his words like a weapon.

"My people are dead." Her voice was as brittle as grave bones.

"I do not plan to die, if that's what you think. My House is White Jaguar. Sorcery is my birthright. Whether you believe in it or not."

It felt wild to say it. No one in his family spoke of it, although he knew that some of the old families still visited their ancestral temples on high holy days, still hoarded the knowledge of the ways of blood and shadow, stone and sea, and all the other magics of their world.

He said, "My father has a library full of forbidden books. He keeps it locked and does not visit it. But I know a way in."

"So you will study sorcery and become like the Jaguar Prince." She sounded unimpressed.

"No, Saaya. You are not listening." It was the first time he had said her name, and even though he chided her, the shape of it in his mouth was sweet. "Have you not considered that somewhere in those books there is knowledge to defeat the Watchers? Else why would the priests proscribe them?"

Her eyes widened as the revelation took hold. "Magic."

He did not know if the Sun Priest and the Watchers were afraid of Cuecolan sorcery, but if it kept this girl by his side a while longer, he would read every book in his father's library a dozen times, spend every cacao in his father's coffers to make her happy. And when he did finally become the next Jaguar Prince, he would give Saaya the revenge she craved.

"We could discover it together." He held his hand out. Time seemed to slow until she pressed her palm to his. Her skin was warm and soft, her eyes bright with excitement now instead of unshed sorrows.

"You said it was locked."

"I know a way in."

"And if we are caught?"

"We will not be caught." The punishment should his father find out he was learning sorcery would be unfathomable, but he did not care. "Besides, do you never do things that are forbidden?"

Fire blazed in her eyes, and for a moment, he thought he had said the wrong thing, had finally pushed this wild girl too far.

And then she leaned in and kissed him.

Balam had kissed many lips, probably half the mouths of the silly, pink-frilled girls in the adjoining room, but none had made his head spin like this. Saaya's mouth was velvet, but her desire was fierce and consuming.

This was a girl who would change his destiny. He knew it instinctively.

It was not too late. He could walk away with his stolen kiss, go back to the party, leave Saaya to marry Tiniz. Or he could break the rules, follow his savage ambitions, help plot her insane revenge.

It was an easy choice. A choice he would make a thousand times over if only Saaya would continue to kiss him.

She pulled away first, dark eyes wide open. Watchful, wary. But her hand was still wrapped in his. "Where is this library?"

"Two floors below."

"Then what are we waiting for?"

He laughed, pure joy. "Only for you to say yes."

And then they were slipping through the party crowd, fingers laced tightly, and down into the lower levels of the house to discover what secrets the library would reveal. Two teenagers, plotting to bring down the most powerful institution in the Meridian. Two teenagers on the cusp of changing the very heavens with their ambitions.

Balam did not see Tiniz's eyes as xe watched them go.

CHAPTER 7

City of Hokaia
Year 1 of the Crow

The failure to act makes cowards of the brave.

—From the *Oration of the Jaguar Prince on the Eve of the Frenzy*

"I dreamt of her again."

Balam sat overlooking the great plains of Hokaia from the porch of the guest quarters where he had spent the last month. A cup of strong tea warmed his hands, but the rest of him was chilled despite the spring morning. His mood was somewhere between dark and darker, and he did not spare a glance for Powageh when xe took the seat beside him.

Powageh's look was knowing. "Too much godflesh. Your mind has become too porous. Reality, dreaming, life, death. They are becoming one and the same for you."

Balam did not respond, but his silence was admission enough.

"What was it this time?" Xe did not need to ask who the "she" was who haunted Balam's dreams. There was only one woman between them.

"When we first met, at your coming home party." He looked toward his cousin. The party had always been a delicate harm between them.

"You mean the night you stole her away from me?"

Balam sipped from his cup. The liquid burned his mouth, but he kept drinking.

"At the time I thought I was the thief, but now I think Saaya allowed me to think it because it served her ends. I don't think I had much say in it."

"You were never that difficult to read, despite your belief to the contrary."

Balam huffed a breath of mild indignation. "You know how to wound a man's pride."

Powageh waved a hand. "Except we were only children, then. Our pride was a brittle thing. And besides, it is forgotten. Well, perhaps not forgotten, but my romantic ambitions were misplaced at best. You and Saaya. I knew from the moment you met it was inevitable. Together the two of you were . . . a force."

The admission pleased Balam more than he liked to admit, but it also made him unbearably sad.

"We could not have done it without you," he said. "And Paadeh and Eedi." Perhaps it was true, perhaps it was not. But Powageh had always responded well to flattery, and Balam did carry a burden of guilt for the way he had gone about it all. He had been young and selfish, and he had not considered Powageh's, then named Tiniz, feelings in any of it.

"Maybe, maybe not." Powageh echoed Balam's own thoughts. "But we all share in the making of her son, that much is true." Xe smoothed a hand over xir lap, as if hesitant to speak xir next words. "Do you ever wonder . . . ?"

"No." Balam's tone was flat.

Powageh's laugh was forced. "You do not even know what I was going to ask."

"Some speculation about Saaya's son, I imagine. I am not interested."

"Why do you refuse to even consider him, Balam?" Suspicion colored his tone.

A memory flashed through his mind. Saaya, her hand pressed protectively against her belly, a whispered secret in Balam's ear.

He stood abruptly. "Because he should be dead, as dead as his mother. And yet he refuses to die. What should have been a simple claiming of Tova by Golden Eagle in the wake of the Watchers' demise now requires a war."

"Does his tenacity surprise you? He is like his mother in that regard."

Balam was already walking away. "Enough. We are late for council."

"You are late," Powageh called blithely. "I was not invited."

It was all worth it, Balam reminded himself. The dreams, the nightmares, the sacrifices, the ghosts. He had made a promise long ago, not only in word but in deed, and set himself upon this course. And he would not shirk from it now, no matter what memories plagued him.

He slipped on his sandals, affixed his white cloak across his shoulder, and opened the door.

For a moment, he thought he smelled the scent of exotic fruits lingering in the hallway, the echoing laughter of heirs. He touched a finger to his mouth and could almost taste velvet lips against his.

"Damnable godflesh," he muttered, and he shoved the memories away, unwanted.

• • • • •

The dead woman sitting next to Balam leaned over and whispered in his ear. At first, he had mistaken her for an apparition of Saaya, come to haunt him even in his waking hours, but the

69

lingering paint on her half-desiccated face and her straggling braids revealed her as a spearmaiden. Despite the punch of terror her presence had conjured up inside him, he would take this macabre haunting over another visit from his lost Crow girl.

At least a dead spearmaiden could not hurt him.

The woman spoke some ancient version of Hoka of which Balam only understood every other word, if that.

Beware! she murmured. *Beware of . . .*

He couldn't quite make out her last word. His mouth tightened, the only sign of his irritation.

She spoke again, her rotted jaw working, pale bone showing through the gaps in her flesh. But it did no good. No matter how many times she said it, he didn't recognize the unfamiliar word.

"Beware what?" he hissed, exasperated.

"Balam?"

He turned to the living woman on his other side. Tuun's slate eyes stared, curious.

He quickly shaped his mouth into a self-deprecating smile.

"Did I speak aloud?" he inquired, as if he had not just been conversing with a dead woman. A dead woman who still sat beside him, still whispered in his ear, and was obviously visible only to him.

Tuun's eyes narrowed in . . . well, perhaps concern was not the correct word. More like curiosity.

"My apologies if I disturbed you." He made a point of laughing lightly, as if embarrassed. "My thoughts were wandering."

You are walking a very thin line, he chastised himself, *and Tuun is not a fool. She will notice, and then what? Do not be so naive as to think she will not try to eliminate you should she think you a weak link.*

Tuun was his co-conspirator in this war, but theirs was a relationship built on layers of mutual interest and little else. He dared not tell her how his mind straddled the worlds of the living and the dead more and more frequently, how his memories of decades ago seemed as fresh as those of last night.

"I don't blame you for growing bored," Tuun said, seemingly satisfied by the mundaneness of his reply. She waved a languid bejeweled hand around the room. "Naasut is a dullard. How could a woman talk so much of war and yet crave so little conflict?"

Balam glanced around the room. Naasut, the Sovran of Hokaia, stood at the head of the table, droning on, as she had for weeks. A pride of spearmaidens lounged insolently around her, as if daring anyone to interrupt their esteemed leader.

No one did.

The Golden Eagle matron looked as if she desperately wanted to. Nuuma sat stiff and upright, her back straight and chin lifted, her white and gold finery impeccable. She had taken to combing her hair again. When she had first arrived, it had been a tangle of mourning, but now her auburn locks wrapped around her head like a crown. *Not an accident*, Balam thought. *She works to remind us all that she is a queen among her people, equal to anyone in this room.*

Her younger daughter, Ziha was her name, perched beside her mother, attentive. Every so often, her nervous eyes would dart to the older woman, seeking her approval before she so much as plucked a nut from the bowl before her. Balam crudely wondered if Ziha consulted her mother before taking a shit, too. He would not doubt it.

His man within Golden Eagle's inner circle, Layat, had explained the dynamic to him. The older daughter was the favorite, in line for matron after her mother. *And yet*, Balam observed to himself, *she is nowhere to be seen*. Balam envied her that.

The younger daughter, not favored and meant for a politically expedient marriage before war had altered her fate, had been promised control of Golden Eagle's military forces. Balam did not believe that would ever happen. *An empty promise*, *and what does that say about Nuuma and her promises if she can deceive her own daughter to keep her in line? Would she not hesitate to do the same to her allies?*

Nevertheless, he felt confident that between himself and Sayat, Matron Nuuma and her ambitious daughters were well under control. Although he did wonder about the motives of the Watcher who had arrived with her. Ex-Watcher, rather. Balam had immediately identified Iktan as the former Priest of Knives, not simply an adviser, as Nuuma had claimed. Xe was an assassin and a strategist, and perhaps the real threat among the traitors from Tova. Even now, Iktan caught Balam looking and cast a politely wary nod his way.

Balam nodded back, no sign of the sudden hot lick of adrenaline that shot through his veins showing in his demeanor. *A worthy adversary*, he thought. And he did enjoy that.

Balam had quickly deduced that the "favor" the Teek captain Xiala had asked of him before she had been summarily shipped back to Teek was meant for Iktan's ears. "She lives," Xiala had said, but she had not specified who "she" was and why Iktan might otherwise think her dead. Balam had his suspicions.

Since Xiala had not specified when Balam must tell Iktan this news, Balam had decided to keep the information to himself until the proper time to share it revealed itself to his advantage.

With Golden Eagle sorted, Balam had been working to learn everything he could about the Teek queen, Mahina. He had bribed servants to tell him what she ate for breakfast, who braided her hair, which side of the bed she slept on, and with whom she shared that bed. He had also carefully arranged a series of seemingly coincidental meetings with the woman— outside her palace, at the market in the heart of the city—but she had consistently and, he had to admit, wisely avoided him.

"The Teek dislike of men is quite something," he had remarked to Tuun one afternoon as they sipped xtabentún and watched yet another martial parade Naasut had arranged.

Tuun had raised a pale eyebrow. "Is that so? Shall I try?"

He had gestured graciously. "Please."

But Tuun had had no luck, either, and upon her return declared the Teek barbarians who simply hated all foreigners regardless of gender. "I will enjoy ridding the world of their kind," she had exclaimed, outraged.

Balam had blanched at that. Not because he had anything against Tuun's desired slaughter of the Teek; he had reconciled himself to the lives that must be lost for him to win this war. But because he worried that Tuun was blind to the danger the Teek posed, thinking them easy prey.

He remembered his last encounter with Xiala and the very real magic she wielded. She was no easy prey. And while Mahina had shown no signs of possessing a similar power, all Teek Sang, did they not?

His attention was drawn back to the room as Naasut shouted something about future glory and spoils, and her spearmaidens cheered enthusiastically. The woman liked nothing better than to talk of war. The glory of it, the riches won, the land acquired. If only it led to action.

"She has a natural affinity for empire," Balam commented to Lord Tuun.

"So much that she could have been Cuecolan," Tuun remarked.

Balam did not think so. While Naasut had been ruthless enough to dispose of the previous Hokaian leadership, she was in the end a straightforward woman allergic to guile. He suspected the sly politics of his hometown would eat her alive.

Then again, the Sovran was faring better than some of his colleagues had.

Lord Pech, of course, was dead. Killed by the Teek princess.

Poor man, although Balam could not say that anyone missed him. Well, perhaps Lord Sinik had. He had volunteered to accompany Pech's body back to Cuecola. Balam suspected Sinik had been happy for the excuse to leave. He was a decent enough man but did seem a bit skittish around the spearmaidens, never mind the occasional Teek who wandered up to the palace from their ships still docked in the harbor, and he had complained quite pitifully that the foreign food upset his stomach. But he had assured Balam that upon his return to Cuecola, he would inform the Seven Lords of the events that had passed here and ensure that the coffers of the Seven Houses would stay open and available to Balam for the duration of the war. And if Balam needed him, he would return once Pech was properly entombed. Balam suspected he would not see the man again until the war was over.

"Any news from your princess?" Tuun asked.

Balam had confided the basic premise of his agreement with Xiala to Tuun but avoided mentioning Serapio and the promise to spare his life once their allied forces controlled Tova. Tuun thought the girl spied for the most mundane of reasons—a purse of cacao. And, perhaps, to spite her mother.

"She's settled in, it seems, and the navy grows apace. We will have our fleet of tidechasers ready to cross the Crescent Sea when we call upon them."

"Perhaps they could use a push."

Balam tilted his head. "Your hand at their back?"

"My knife at their throat."

He sat back, thinking.

It was not a bad idea. Xiala assured him the Teek were busily building the ships they needed to counter Tovan's water striders and control Tova's riverways. Combined with the Cuecola's larger troop-moving vessels that even now idled at the mouth of the Kuukuh River, they would be formidable. He was sure they could enforce a blockade of the Tovasheh and its tributaries that would bring Tovan trade quickly to its knees.

If only Naasut would give the word and release her spear-maidens to battle.

He could not see outside from within the walls of the palace where they sat, but he knew the weather had turned consist-ently warm and summer inched closer every day. He predicted a quick victory in Tova, a matter of weeks, if that, but he was not so naive as to ignore the fact that this campaign had the potential to drag on for longer if the Tovan clans were able to muster any kind of defense.

He also worried that if the war stretched into autumn and then winter, Naasut's enthusiasm would wane, and Hokaia's commitment along with it.

No, their victory had to be quick and decisive.

He had been subtle, a slow manipulation of people and dreams, but it was becoming clear that escalation was required. Particularly since he was not sure how much longer he could continue to use the godflesh without going insane.

He leaned close to Tuun. "I think you make a fine point, Lord Tuun. It is time for you to go to Teek. Take control of the fleet. Xiala assures me it is almost ready. By the time you return with our navy, I'll have Naasut's spearmaidens on the water."

"And how will you do that?"

He smiled. "Do you doubt me?"

She did not bother to answer. "And what of Queen Ma-hina?" she asked. "Surely she will not simply let me sail to Teek and claim it as my own."

He had already decided that, too. "Mahina is about to grow very ill. Much too ill to spend days at sea. In fact . . ." He shook his head. "Terrible, to die so far from home. But lucky for her, her daughter, who has no desire to rule, is there to help ease the transition to your leadership."

Now it was Tuun's turn to grin.

"Seven hells, Balam. Finally! I've never understood your waiting game, but I've trusted you know what you are doing and allowed you to lead."

Allowed him? Tuun's arrogance grated, but he bit his tongue. Let her have her small moments. He was a practical man, not prone to fits of ego, and he understood that her allegiance was worth the small slights.

"Begin your preparations to leave," he said.

"I'll need soldiers. A squadron of Cuecolan warriors and a pride of spearmaidens, if Naasut will spare them."

"Take two squadrons," Balam encouraged.

"I don't think I need so many."

"Humor me. You'll go under the auspices of taking word back of Mahina's death, bearing her final wishes that the Teek secure victory in her name. The soldiers will be an honor guard. It makes for a fitting memorial, no?"

"You have a dark mind, Balam." She said it half in reprimand and half in admiration.

"Do I?" he asked, bemused. "I thought it a kindness."

She snorted. "Would it be wrong to pick out the location for my new palace while I'm there?" Tuun drummed her fingernails idly on the wooden table. "Perhaps your little spy can help me find the perfect view."

Balam would like very much to see that confrontation, but he was not sure on whom he would place higher odds.

"It seems only practical," he said, "and I'm sure Xiala would be happy to help."

"Then I will excuse myself. Do give Mahina my regards."

She slipped from the room. He watched her go, not without envy, as the war council droned on.

The dead woman behind him whispered in his ear.

Beware! Beware!

CHAPTER 8

TEEK TERRITORY
YEAR 1 OF THE CROW

Speak and shame yourself.
Stay silent and shame your ancestors.

—Teek saying

Xiala woke with a blinding headache and a mouth that felt like she had swallowed sand. Her stomach contracted, forcing her to lean to the side and spit bile. She groaned, and her eyes fluttered open to a room warmed by morning light.

It took a moment for her to recognize where she was—the listening house, on the dirt floor—and another, longer moment to remember why she was there.

The beach, the dark ships. And death. Her aunt, the wise women, and how many others? Surely it had not happened and was only a terrible dream.

"How are you feeling?"

A woman leaned into her line of sight. Light reflected off the sheen of gold powder on her dark skin and rendered her bleached eyebrows almost white. Jewels dangled from her ears, her throat, her wrists. She carried a clay pot to the low round table in the center of the room where someone had laid out a meal.

"I've made tea," she said, and poured steaming liquid into cups. The smell of gingerroot filled the air. "There's wine, too, but I don't know if you're in any condition to drink it just yet." Her lips curled as if they had shared a joke. "But there's food. Some fruit I don't recognize, but also corn cakes and the most delightful smoked fish." She gestured to the table, beckoning.

"Am I dead?" Xiala asked. If she was not, this made no sense.

The woman laughed, the sound as bright and brittle as the sun sloping through the reed roof.

"You are very much alive, Xiala. Although . . ." The woman touched a hand to her own temple. ". . . I apologize for your head. You were not meant to be harmed. I gave strict orders to leave you unmolested. After all, you're on our side." Another intimate smile. "Unfortunately, my soldiers were a bit zealous, but I am pleased to see you are recovering."

Xiala stared. Was this woman serious? Was she calmly pouring tea and inviting Xiala to join her at the table? Did she really expect her to engage in a polite conversation about the slaughter, to accept her grotesque apology?

Apparently, she did.

The woman took a seat. "I'm sorry, I don't think I've introduced myself."

"I know who you are." Xiala remembered her from Hokaia, standing beside Balam when Pech died. "You're Balam's pet."

The woman's gray eyes flashed black, but her expression was carefully neutral. She smoothed a hand over her green dress and breathed deeply before replying.

"I am Lord Tuun of the House of Seven, Jade Serpent by birthright, and I assure you I am no one's pet."

"Whatever lie you need to tell yourself." Xiala closed her eyes and rested her head on the mat, done with this woman. "All you Cuecolan lords are the same."

"Oh?"

"Fragile egos."

Tuun laughed, but it echoed falsely. "Balam warned me that you were difficult."

"Did he warn you about this?" Xiala had been letting her Song build in her throat, and she struck now.

Tuun cried out. Her teacup slipped from her jeweled fingers, clattering to the floor.

Xiala scrambled to her feet and bolted for the door. Her head screamed for her to stop, but she pushed through the pain and dizziness, focused on getting out.

The woman shouted harsh words in a language Xiala did not understand, and the floor moved. Not simply moved but tilted and flowed, as if the ground had suddenly become water. Xiala's arms pinwheeled as she struggled for purchase, but she could not keep her feet.

She crashed to the undulating ground.

A clamor of footsteps and shouting voices rose as half a dozen soldiers rushed into the room. They encircled Xiala, spears out, legs braced, but the ground had already stopped its shaking.

"Get her up," Tuun growled, gesturing to the soldiers.

Xiala was pulled roughly to her knees. As soon as the room stopped spinning, she opened her mouth to Sing, intent on cutting down the men who held her. Pain flared across her face hot enough to steal the Song from her mouth, as Tuun struck her.

"Do that again, and I'll cut your tongue from your mouth," Tuun hissed, her chest rising and falling with heavy breaths, her eyes bright with malice.

But also fear.

Xiala noticed blood dripping from a slash across her palm, just as Balam's had that day in her mother's chambers. A sorcerer. She should have known.

Tuun walked to the table and retrieved a cloth. She dabbed at the trickles of blood in her ears before calmly wrapping the strip of fabric around her injured hand.

"That was my fault," the woman said, mouth in a rueful twist. "A slip of concentration. You see, I thought we were allies." She gestured to a pole in the center of the room. "Tie her there and gag her."

The soldiers dragged Xiala to the pole and bound her there, arms behind her back. Someone forced a cloth into her mouth.

As if it would stop her from Singing. Her Song was magic, the power of the Mother. A piece of fabric could never silence her.

But Xiala understood that she had made a mistake. Underestimated Tuun and her earth sorcery, forgotten there would be soldiers on the other side of the door. So she would bide her time, let Tuun think her tamed.

The woman dismissed the soldiers, pulled a bench up, and sat across from her. Her irises cooled to gray as she studied Xiala. Xiala tilted her chin up, knowing that her own eyes still swirled with power.

"Did you know I have always dreamed of coming to Teek?" Tuun asked, face working to contain her emotions, whatever they were. Dismay, fear, hate?

Xiala stared.

"It is a place of legend. You take it for granted. The peace and tranquility. The ease of this life. Did you miss it when you were gone?"

Xiala glanced down at her gag pointedly.

Tuun heaved a sigh and pulled the cloth free, letting it fall around Xiala's neck. "Speak, but don't be stupid, or I *will* take your tongue. Do not doubt it."

The moment the gag was out, Xiala spit. Saliva struck Tuun's chest. Seven hells. She had meant to hit her face.

The woman's eyelashes fluttered in irritation. "This need not be difficult for you, Xiala," she said. "We need not be enemies."

"You killed my friends, my relatives, the whole fucking village!"

"You exaggerate. The queen regent and her council had to be eliminated. I know their Songs were powerful, and—Yaala, was it?—she was dangerous."

Xiala stared. Tuun didn't know that the Teek, except for her, had lost their Song. She thought of Yaala standing there on the beach, arms wide, the circle of women around her. Had Tuun read that as an attack? It was hard to believe.

"But your friends are likely fine," she continued. "As is the rest of the village." She stepped to the guard standing by the door. "Go to the prisoners and find . . ." She glanced at Xiala, expectant.

Xiala did not want to answer, did not want to give her the satisfaction, but the need to know if Teanni had survived ate at her heart.

"Teanni," she said. "And Alani," she added. If the fierce sailor had avoided death, she would make a much-needed ally.

"Go," Tuun said, and the soldier hurried away.

Tuun turned back to her, gaze lingering, eyes hooded. "I asked about you. From some of the Teek sailors in Hokaia. It seems you are a local legend. A runaway at fifteen, you braved the Crescent Sea, apprenticed to sailors twice your age, and finally commanded your own ships. Not just commanded but sailed for the most powerful merchant lords in the most prosperous trade city in the Meridian. You are a self-made woman, someone to be admired."

"Unlike you." It was only a guess, but Tuun dipped her chin in concession.

"It is true that I inherited my wealth and position, but you would be wrong to believe I have not fought for it. Did you know that I am the only lord from the House of Seven who is not male? The others certainly do not let me forget it." Tuun smiled, a gesture meant to express some shared sentiment. "Teek, with its edict against men, sounds refreshing."

"An edict you broke by bringing your army here." She had glimpsed a handful of spearmaidens on the ship among the attackers, but it did not compromise her point.

"A necessary evil, and a temporary one. Soldiers are expendable by their very nature."

"I wonder if the ones outside know that."

Tuun's mouth tightened. "I see you are blunt with your judgments, so let me not prevaricate. You know what has happened, and what comes next. I am saying that a savvy woman like you can benefit from that, or you can suffer. The choice is yours."

"I want nothing from you."

"I can make you queen."

"A queen under your thumb."

"Power is power. As I said, allies."

"If you asked about me, as you said you did, then you already know that a queen is the last thing I want to be."

"Then what is it you do want, Xiala?"

A noise at the door drew their attention as the soldier who had gone to find her friends returned. He was accompanied by four others, who pushed Teanni and Alani through the entrance. They were both bound and gagged, but they were there. Alive.

Xiala cried out, a soft sob of relief. She made to stand, straining against her bonds.

"Remove them," Tuun said, and as quickly as her friends had appeared, they were hauled away.

"No!"

A slow smile cut across Tuun's mouth, and only then did Xiala realize her mistake.

"Well, Xiala," Tuun purred. "It seems you want something, after all."

"Leave them alone!" Mother waters, she was a fool, her emotions leading her to blunder into the simplest of traps without a second thought.

"Their fate is in your hands. You need only choose. If not for yourself, then for them."

Xiala closed her eyes and swallowed hard. "Why?"

Tuun looked surprised at the question but quickly recovered. "I think you know the answer to that."

"And Mahina?" If Tuun had come from Hokaia, which she clearly had, where was Mahina? Surely she would have never allowed this woman to invade her home.

"You know the answer to that, too."

"How?"

"I was going to tell you she died of the pox, but I don't see a reason to lie to you now. She was in the way, and people who are in my way don't live very long."

The weight of the news bowed her neck. Her feelings for her mother were complicated, but the grief that shuddered through her body could not be denied. She had hated Mahina, and loved her, too. And now there would be no chance at forgiveness, no possible resolution, only this terrible feeling of loss.

"Perhaps you'd like time to think on my proposal," Tuun said. "I can give you that, but I'll expect an answer when I return. Balam informed me that the tidechaser fleet is nearing completion. Our thanks for your efforts. The Treaty cities sail for Tova on the new moon."

Tova. It felt like a lifetime away, and Serapio equally distant. What she wouldn't give to have him here. Perhaps it was a weakness, but she yearned for his unflappable presence, his otherworldly confidence, the protection of his crows and his magic.

But there was no Serapio to help her. There was no one but herself.

And there was no fleet of tidechasers, either. She had lied to Balam.

Tuun gave Xiala one last look and then breezed from the room.

Xiala sagged in her bonds. Grief consumed her, the black clouds of a storm that could easily overwhelm her, drown her with the force of its misery. But she had a choice. She could accept whatever awful designs Tuun had for the Teek and lose herself in the horror of violation. Or she could survive.

She was not sure she believed in fate, but if the Mother had brought her home and gifted her with powers unknown since the time of gods and legends, then surely she did not mean for Xiala to die here at the hands of this cruel foreigner.

But she needed time. Time to think more clearly, to study her enemy and make a plan. So she made herself as comfortable as possible and waited for Tuun to come back.

• • • • •

Tuun returned near sundown.

Long lines of fading sunlight stretched across the dirt floor, and flies buzzed around the food on the table. Xiala's belly had long since ceased to grumble, and even if she had the appetite to eat, she would not touch the food Tuun had left on the table. The very thought turned her stomach sour.

The Cuecolan woman seated herself across from her. "Well?"

"What is it you want from me?"

"Your cooperation. And leadership. I will gather the fleet of tidechasers and return to Hokaia. In my absence, I want you to ensure the peace. Assure your people that I will be a benevolent empress upon my eventual return."

"Empress?"

Tuun smiled. "With my holdings in Cuecola, Teek, and soon Tova, I believe empress is fitting. I will, of course, be leaving a hundred soldiers behind to ensure your loyalty, but I suspect a friendly face, and one who speaks the language and knows the customs, will be more motivation than a foreign man with a sword, no? You will be my cacica in Teek, and I will make sure you are handsomely rewarded."

"You want me to be your puppet and their master."

"I will expect a certain level of productivity from you, of course. Ships, agriculture, taxes that must be paid. But you can manage that, can't you? A small price for continuing to live."

"I want something first."

"I'm sorry, cacica do not make demands. You misunderstand your role."

"You admit you are ignorant of Teek language, ignorant of our ways. Our motivations."

Tuun's eyes went flat, but she nodded.

"We need time to mourn. My mother, my aunt, the elders. It is more than you can understand. There are prayers that need to be said, a meal to cook for the dead to ensure their passage to the Mother. Bodies that must be prepared a certain way and returned to the sea."

Tuun eyed her curiously. "And you want . . . ?"

The words burned her tongue, but Xiala said, "Permission to tend to our dead."

Tuun smiled, indulgent. "Of course. I am not a monster."

Xiala had to bite back a scream. She forced herself to go on. Calm. Reasonable. "As you know, I have been gone many years. I don't remember all the ceremonies, and you've killed the wise women." She could not entirely keep the bitterness from her voice at the mention of the lost elders. "But if you give me Teanni and Alani, they can help."

Tuun barked a laugh. "Is that what this is about? Your friends? Do you think me a fool?"

"It is about the dead," she countered, letting some of her anger leak into her voice. "I have agreed to your bargain to keep them and everyone else alive. Do you think *me* a fool?"

Tuun took her time in contemplation, and Xiala did her best to look harmless. Finally, the woman spoke.

"Very well," she said, as if her concession was a point of graciousness for which Xiala should be thankful. "See to your dead tonight, and we shall survey the tidechaser fleet at first light tomorrow."

"We will need more time for the funerals."

"Tonight is all the time you get. Be grateful for that."

"And my friends?"

Tuun untied the knots of Xiala's bonds. Feeling returned to her shoulders, tingles running down her arms. She rotated her wrists and stretched her fingers.

Tuun rose. "I trust that you will keep our bargain, Xiala. That you understand the stakes for yourself and your people. One mistake, one, and they all die. If you speak a word of rebellion, they all die. If you so much as hum a note, they all die. Do you understand?"

Xiala stood, gently stomping her feet until life returned to her legs. She shook out her muscles and stretched as if preparing for combat. "I understand."

Tuun exhaled, as if she knew the fight had only begun and was realizing that she had not wholly comprehended the difficulty of the battle before her.

"Let's get this over with," Tuun said and walked toward the door.

CHAPTER 9

Upon death, the selfish man asks how he will be remembered.
While the generous man asks how he was loved.

—*Exhortations for a Happy Life*

Okoa read through the glyphs again, working to decipher the
ancient Cuecolan, but the images made little sense. On the page
before him was the drawing of a woman lying on a bed, her bone
spear beside her. The next glyph was a drawing of the woman's
head, opened as if on a hinge. Where a brain might be was instead
a dome and bars with a prominent lock, which was clearly meant
to be a cage. That much he followed. A spearmaiden's sleeping
mind was a cage that could be locked and unlocked, likely a ref-
erence to spearmaiden magic during the War of the Spear.

But then the glyphs became strange and less tractable. Inside the cage was a monster of some kind, its eyes comically big
and tongue protruding from a red face. And in the red-faced
monster's claw was a smaller version of the sleeping woman.

"Something of the dreaming self . . . ," he murmured, finger
tapping the book. "Trapped in the dreaming mind . . . but then
why the monster . . . and what is its significance?"

He groaned and pushed the book away.

"Why can't they just be clear?" he muttered in frustration, running useless hands through his hair. He was sure that the text made sense to a Cuecolan three hundred years ago, but he was a son of Carrion Crow, and the nuances of the language and context were lost to him.

"I should have studied harder at the war college," he chided himself, but he wasn't sure any amount of study would have helped. The book before him was religious esoterica, something one of the librarians had dug up at his request. It was not the kind of text he would have read while studying battle tactics and peacekeeping practices in Hokaia, but he had hoped it would provide clues to how Tova might defeat the spearmaidens when they inevitably came. But no one dreamwalked anymore, so perhaps he was looking in the wrong places.

He sat back, closing his eyes. A dull ache pulsed in his temples from squinting at the text, and his neck seemed stuck at an uncomfortable angle from sitting hunched over for hours. He rubbed at his muscles and gritted his teeth as the cartilage popped. It gave him a modicum of relief, but only sleep would truly solve his aches, and he could not rest until he had answers.

"Any progress?"

He opened his eyes. Esa stood in the doorway, dressed in Carrion Crow black, her long hair loose around her shoulders.

"No," he admitted, motioning his sister in. She paced the room, gaze roaming over the books on the shelves.

"I don't know how you have the patience for such things," she murmured.

"Books?"

She plucked a tome from the shelf at random. She opened it and idly turned the pages, eyes immediately dulling at the wall of glyphs that confronted her. "I've never cared for scholarship."

He grinned, watching her. "I prefer to be on the field, but there is value in ancient knowledge."

Her smile was indulgent. "If you say so." She closed the volume and returned it to its home. Hands free, she reached into her pocket and withdrew a folded note. "I've a missive from Matron Peyana of Winged Serpent."

He motioned for her to hand it to him. He opened it and read it quickly.

"She asks us to meet her and the other matrons tonight," he said. "She has news from Cuecola, and progress on the forging of the weapon she hopes to make from the Sun Priest's mask."

"Then you should go."

He looked up. "You will not come?"

"No, let them think you and I are still at odds. It gives us more space to maneuver should we need it."

"You still believe we need to deceive them?"

"You are a natural at deception, Brother." Her tone was biting, her look arch. "What is a little more?"

He grimaced at that, but it was no more than he deserved. Upon returning from his meeting with the Sky Made matrons and Naranpa, before the Sun Priest had left the city, Okoa had confessed all to Esa. His confrontation with Serapio in the Carrion Crow aerie, the murder of Chaiya and Ituya, and, yes, his own clandestine meeting with the matrons. He had decided he could not keep it from her, and she had a right to know.

Their argument had been long and heated, but in the end, they had agreed that it must be family and Carrion Crow first, Tova and the matrons second.

"They betrayed us on the Night of Knives," she had reminded him. "What makes you believe those women won't do it again? Particularly when it is the Crow God Reborn they must bow to?" She laughed. "It must be like ashes on their tongues to swear him fealty, even if they lie."

"I should have killed him when I had the chance," he admitted. "You were right."

"Perhaps not."

Her answer surprised him, and he said as much.

"I was wrong to cower to the other clans," she said. "You saw his potential. I only saw what we might lose. But now I see what we will gain."

"So you wish to bow to him?"

"I did not say that, but I know we must win this war." Esa cocked her head to the side, a gesture not unlike Serapio's own. "Do you doubt he can defeat our enemies?"

"His power is unquestionable, his sorcery strange and wondrous," Okoa admitted. "The palace he had wrought on Sun Rock is evidence enough. But he cannot single-handedly fight the combined powers of the Treaty cities."

"And that is why he, and we, need the Sky Made."

To all outside appearances, the matrons of the Sky Made clans had promised allegiance to the Odo Sedoh that day he had called them to Shadow Rock. And since then, they had all bowed and called him king and god.

But in truth, they conspired against him. The note in Okoa's hand was evidence of that.

"You'd best make haste," Esa said. "Peyana expects you within the hour."

Okoa waited until his sister was gone to lean across the table and feed the letter to the resin lantern. Once the paper was nothing but ash, he refilled the lantern, took up the plain black cloak he had draped along the bench, and secured it around his shoulders. He pulled up the hood and, lantern in hand, left the library.

By right, Carrion Crow scions traveled by air, but the Odo Sedoh had crow spies that held sway over the skies. So Okoa was grounded. He had no choice but to slither through the earth instead. He did not enjoy it. It made him feel low, reminded him that treachery and deceit had become his norm, and he was not a man on whom deviousness sat well. He wore it like another man's ill-fitting clothes that itched his skin and stank of someone else's sweat.

He took the winding stairs to the lowest level of the Great House and then went farther, down into the baths, and then the kitchens, and finally the storage tunnel. There was a door here behind a shelf. He had rigged the shelf so that it easily moved, and he pushed it aside now and slipped beyond.

He had learned of the tunnel's existence when he was a child. It had been constructed after the Night of Knives, a route to safety should the matron and her family ever find themselves at the mercy of their enemies again.

He followed the path through the darkness, his lantern a bobbing light, his breath the only sound. If he stopped, he could hear the rumble of the river somewhere below, soft like far thunder. He walked, counting his steps, matching them to his breath, until the tunnel began to slope down. The trail quickly steepened, and he had to lean back to stay on his feet. After another hundred breaths, the angle became so acute he slid the rest of the way on his backside.

The tunnel ended at a small embankment, a deep underground tributary of the Tovasheh lapping at the edge. He was inside a cave, a hollow pocket of air hidden well in the belly of the cliffs. He knew that if he dove into the dark water and swam, he would find himself in the Tovasheh proper. But he had no desire to brave the river and its currents. He had another way.

He slipped on the climbing shoes and leather gloves he had left here from previous visits before he doused the lantern. Ropes had been secured in the wall at hand and foot height, and he pulled himself across them now, the freezing waters nipping at his feet. It took him through a long darkness, but he could not hold the lantern and move along the slick rope at the same time, so he endured.

After what seemed like an eternity, the soles of his feet aching, fingers cramping, and body chilled, he came to another cave not unlike the one where he had started. But this one was three times as large, and, at its far entrance, he could glimpse the rushing river.

On the bank were two skimmers. By the small boats sat the matrons of the Sky Made and their Shield captains, warming themselves at a pit fire. Peyana of Winged Serpent was saying something as they passed around a cup. Sedaysa of Coyote clan laughed, a sound like silver bells.

Okoa hopped lightly to land and flexed his aching fingers. A figure materialized from the shadows, and he startled, his hand automatically reaching for the knife at his belt.

"Peace, Okoa Carrion Crow," came a hoarse voice. "It is only Zataya."

"You startled me," he admitted, huffing out a sharp exhale. "You should not sneak around in the shadows."

"And would that ease the burden of your destiny, if I did not sneak?"

He grimaced. The woman spoke nonsense. "It might keep me from putting a knife in your gut."

Her dark eyes glittered in the firelight, amused. "Indeed."

Okoa shook his head and left her there. She was a strange one, a witch he had heard said, and he didn't understand why Sedaysa had chosen her to be her Shield captain. Matrons typically chose men as their Shield captains, and ones trained at the war college. But these were not typical times, and Coyote clan had its own ways. Still, who was she to speak of his destiny as if she knew things he did not? It rankled.

Ahuat, the captain of Winged Serpent's Shield, rose from beside the fire to greet him. They grasped forearms briefly, as the older man welcomed him.

"You are late," Peyana said, once Okoa had settled. "We thought perhaps the courier had failed to deliver the invitation."

"I came as soon as I received your message," he replied, wondering if Esa had delayed sharing the letter for some reason. He couldn't think of what she might gain from it, but his sister's small slights were often incomprehensible to him. "I was in the library and lost track of time." It was a small lie born from an instinct to protect Esa, but it felt sour on his tongue as soon as he'd said it, resentment a knot in his stomach. "I've been doing research, reading through the Cuecolan texts on the War of the Spear."

Ahuat passed him a cup. Steam, redolent with anise and honey, filled his nose. It was xtabentún, warmed at the fire, and he gulped it down in a wash of heat.

"And what have you found?" Ieyoue, matron of Water Strider, asked.

His smile was small and contained. "It is like picking apart the rantings of madmen," he admitted.

"It was a time of high magic," Zataya intoned. She had melted out of the darkness to hover on the edge of the circle. "It may seem like gibberish to you, but it had its purpose, and its purpose was power."

"My same thoughts," he agreed, unbothered by the touch of judgment in her tone. He sipped from the cup again, before passing it to Sedaysa. "I will keep studying."

"And Esa?" Ieyoue asked delicately. "Will she join us?"

"No." Okoa's gaze dropped to his hands. Another small lie for Esa, and the knot in his gut tightened.

"Then we are all here." Peyana smoothed her skirts. "I called this meeting to share what my smiths have wrought from the Sun Priest's golden mask, but first I would discuss Golden Eagle."

Okoa looked up. "What news of Golden Eagle? Something from Hokaia?"

"Did you not see the black smoke?" Sedaysa asked.

"I have been in the library all day."

"He razed the Great House," Ieyoue said, and there could only be one "he" she meant. "Set the district aflame. Forced the people out and then brought down the bridge between Water Strider and Golden Eagle so none could return. Titidi and Coyote's Maw are overrun with refugees."

The shock of it rumbled through him. He had no love for Golden Eagle, but this? It was a savagery he had not foreseen.

"It is the justice we demanded of him," Peyana said, dismissive.

"No," Ieyoue countered, her voice raised. "We asked him to confront the scions with their matron's crimes. We did not ask him to burn down Tsay. There were many in the district who were innocent, and now they are homeless."

"There were many Winged Serpent at the war college who were innocent and will never return home." Peyana's voice was tight with anger. "You were always too soft, Ieyoue. His methods are not the ones I would have chosen, but I will give the Carrion King his credit. It was well done."

"He has gone too far!" the Water Strider matron countered.

A cackle turned their heads. Shadows cast by the fire stretched Zataya angular and otherworldly. Okoa could not stop the shiver that raced across his shoulders, and he found himself tensing, wary of her words.

"Speak plainly, witch," Ieyoue demanded, rare outrage coloring her voice.

"You cannot control the storm," Zataya sang in a lilting singsong that sounded half-mad. "Foolish women to think you could."

"Why should we seek to control him?" Peyana asked. "Let him weed out the traitors from among us, and once he has served his purpose, we eliminate—"

"And are you not a traitor?" Okoa cut in, contempt bubbling within him. He could not condone what Serapio had done, but at least the Odo Sedoh was forthright, never pretending or duplicitous. These matrons were all deception and contradiction, their favor as fickle as spring rain. "Are we not all traitors?"

"We are the rightful rulers of Tova," Peyana said. "We do not betray her. We save her."

"Wordplay." Okoa was unimpressed. "It is sophistry, this dicing of who is a traitor and who is not. But that is not the problem." He cleared his throat. "Zataya is right. Asking him for justice, playing along with this . . . this kingship. We are children teasing a predator who will cry when we are devoured. I did that once before and learned a hard lesson. It seems the rest of you must learn your lesson, too."

"Mind who you speak to, Crow son," the Winged Serpent captain warned.

Okoa raised his hands in innocence. "I mean no disrespect, Ahuat. We are all here for the same purpose, are we not? Then let us speak to it and not bicker among ourselves."

"Wise words, young captain," Sedaysa murmured. She turned to the matron of Winged Serpent. "You were going to tell us how the forging is progressing, Peyana."

"Yes, what of your smiths, Peyana?" Ieyoue asked, sounding relieved to be able to move on. "Have they forged a weapon from the mask?"

Peyana motioned to Ahuat. The captain drew forth a small bundle wrapped in shimmering cloth and handed it to his matron. Okoa held his breath as she carefully unwrapped it. There, in her hands, was a golden dagger.

The handle looked to be shaped from a single piece of dark wood and inlaid with white shell, citrine, and turquoise. The hafting was bound with agave fiber and coated in resin. In the firelit cave, the blade gleamed bright gold, as if it contained a tiny sun inside.

"The essence of the sun god forged into a weapon," she whispered.

Okoa should have been elated, but instead, he was gripped by a grim fatalism. Now that the weapon was before him, his heart felt only heaviness.

"Is this the only way?" Ieyoue murmured, echoing his own thoughts.

"I am open to others," Peyana said.

But no one offered any.

"And who will wield it?" asked Sedaysa once the silence among them had become suffocating.

They all looked at Okoa.

He had known from the moment he brought them the mask that it would be him. For all his protestations, Serapio was Crow clan. It was Okoa's duty to be the one who decided the when and where of his god's death. But it was not only responsibility that moved his hand. It was respect, even something akin to love. He had cared for Serapio once, called him cousin. And in truth he still cared for him, still wished there were another way. But the razing of Golden Eagle proved once again that Serapio was dangerous and answered to only himself and the god within him. He must die, and Okoa had to be the one to do it.

He took the dagger in hand and held it aloft. It was heavy but perfectly weighted. The Winged Serpent smiths had created not only a singular weapon but a work of rare beauty.

"When?" he asked, his voice barely a whisper. He laid the blade back in the cloth, and Peyana rewrapped it. The sunlight it had provided was snuffed out, casting the cave into darker shadows than before.

"The sooner the better," Peyana said, and the others nodded. "Which brings us to the final matter before us. My people in Cuecola have confirmed that the Seven Lords have declared the Treaty officially dead. Accordingly, they refuse to send the tithe owed to the Watchers."

"This is not surprising," Ieyoue said. "They have always begrudged us their cacao."

"There's more." Peyana's eyes turned to Okoa, chin angled at an imperious tilt. "They have also declared Carrion Crow usurpers and oath breakers, and on that pretense, they are mobilizing an army."

Murmurs rippled around the room.

Okoa had expected as much, but hearing it spoken felt like the tolling of his own doom. "So they would lay the blame for this war on the back of Carrion Crow?"

"It was your Crow God Reborn who killed the Watchers," Peyana reminded him.

"Not at our bidding."

"It is bluster," Ieyoue said, sympathetic. "Meant to divide us. We all know they will not stop to sort Water Strider from Crow when their army attacks."

"And I will not be ruled by Cuecola's merchant lords, or

anyone else," Sedaysa added. She pressed a reassuring hand against Okoa's arm. "We will win the war and keep Tova free, so it matters not who they blame."

"It matters in one way," Peyana said.

Okoa frowned at the woman. Sometimes he could not tell whose side she was on, but he guessed the answer was simple: her own. Her jade eyes focused on him. "They will call back their army once the Odo Sedoh is dead . . . or if we surrender the Carrion Crow matron and her captain to trial."

Okoa reeled, his shock echoed in the gasps and protests of the other two matrons.

"Now they play games," Sedaysa said, clearly furious.

The Winged Serpent woman spread her hands. "It is Carrion Crow they blame for the slaughter of the Watchers. They refuse to believe they did not aid the Odo Sedoh, and they know for a fact that Carrion Crow sheltered him afterward. The Crows bear responsibility, and someone must be held to account."

"Enough, Peyana," Ieyoue cried. She turned to Okoa, who had sat stone-faced through it all. "We will not even consider it, Okoa. We are not such cowards as to betray you. We know the truth. You are our ally, and we will fight together."

"It has been done before, your betrayal," he said quietly. His gaze traveled the room, resting on each of them one by one. He might have resented the lies he was forced to tell, but he could not help but think that Esa had been right to not trust these women. "Not a one of your clans spoke for Carrion Crow on the Night of Knives. Is it so strange to think you might not now?"

Ieyoue wrung her hands. "Our clans have lived with the shame of our silence for a generation."

"Have you?" His voice was soft with curiosity.

Sedaysa straightened. "Coyote clan will never agree to surrender you and your sister to foreign forces. Who is to say they would even keep their word?"

Okoa looked at Peyana. "And you?"

She handed him the golden dagger in its wrapping.

"Kill the Odo Sedoh, and the question is moot."

They did not linger long after that, the turmoil between them oppressive. *It is a sorry kind of alliance*, Okoa thought as he made his way back to the Great House. *Half-hearted and cagey. None of us trusts the others, and we are united only by fear of the unknown. There is no higher purpose but to task me with the murderer's work so they can continue to rule their petty queendoms as they see fit and grovel to our enemies for better terms of surrender.*

The more he thought on it, the more it turned his stomach, the knot of resentment growing like a malignancy. He touched a hand to the golden dagger at his belt, heavier on his heart than it had been against his palm.

· · · · ·

He made one stop upon his return to the Great House.

Once the task was completed, he walked the stairs to his rooms, his thoughts troubled and his mood soured. He considered returning to the library, but the meeting with the matrons had sapped him of energy, and if he were to be about the mission assigned to him, he did not see the point of further scholarship.

He pushed open the door to his room to find Esa waiting for him.

"Well?" she asked. She was seated on his bed, looking very much as if it were her room and not his. He bristled to find her there but did not have the will to tell her to go. He had hoped to hold her off until tomorrow, when his thoughts were more ordered and he'd had time to sleep. But he should have known she would not wait.

He hung his cloak by the door and kicked off his boots. He was acutely aware of the sun dagger in the sheath at his side, its heft the weight of his fate, but he did not draw it out immediately. Instead, he walked to the washbasin, where he cleaned his hands and face, taking his time, before turning to his sister.

"Peyana is willing to turn us over to Cuecola to avoid war."

Esa's face darkened, her mouth tightening. "And the others?"

"Their outrage at the idea seemed genuine," he admitted as he pulled his shirt over his head. "And they do not trust the southern lords."

"And why would they? But Winged Serpent are our oldest allies, so why would Peyana lead the way?"

He sat heavily on his bed next to her. She moved to give him room. "Perhaps it is all talk. She did not hide it from me."

Esa's face grew thoughtful. "She wanted us to know she could betray us but chooses not to."

"And she gave me this." He drew the weapon out, unfolded the cloth, and showed her the golden dagger. She leaned forward, mouth slightly open, the light from the blade reflecting in her widened eyes.

"From the mask?" she whispered, a note of eagerness in her voice.

He nodded.

"A weapon to kill a god." Wonder infused her face. "And you, Brother, the godslayer?"

He flinched at the epithet, as if she had cursed him.

"What will you do?"

He carefully rewrapped the blade. "I have already sent a note to the Shadow Palace, asking for an audience with the Odo Sedoh."

CHAPTER 10

A good deed is always punished, but a great deed is punished twice.

—*Exhortations for a Happy Life*

Serapio returned to the Shadow Palace after the razing of Golden Eagle, exhaustion in his bones. The curving hallways of the palace were thick with gloom, an accurate reflection of his own mood. The clock had long moved past what might be considered waking hours, the rhythm of the shadowed city having settled down to sleep, and he longed for nothing more than to join his fellow Tovans in that oblivion.

He shuffled past the Tuyon guarding his door and, once inside and alone, stripped off his bloodstained clothes. Warm water had been left in a nearby basin, and as he washed, he found multiple cuts tracing his hands and arms. There was even a laceration across his forearm that he did not remember receiving.

Before his injury on Sun Rock, the one made by the Sun Priest's mask, he had always been resilient to bodily damage. The crow god had protected him, imbued him with an invulnerability he took for granted. But lately, he seemed more and more susceptible to normal wounds. This new weakness frayed his peace of mind, enough that he contemplated his own mortality more often than he liked. He had been spared once, thanks to the small crows. He was not naive enough to imagine such a miracle would happen again.

His servants had left a meal for him, and the scent of stew made his stomach rumble. But when he thought of walking to the table, of the effort of sitting down and raising bowl to mouth, he found he was too tired, even for food.

He fell into bed, eager for sleep, but the mattress that cushioned his weary body offered him no comfort. Instead, he lay there, body spent but mind unquiet as the events of the day refused to let him rest. He played out the conversation with Suuakeh Golden Eagle repeatedly: her willingness to open her own throat rather than bow to his rule, the treachery of her clan. And of the aftermath: his edict to burn the district to the ground.

Had he done it out of spite because the woman and her damnable clan had defied him? Or was Maaka right and the only way to know the Eagles would not betray Tova again was to eliminate the clan altogether?

He wasn't sure, but he refused to let himself fall prey to regret. Not for the old woman's death, nor the destruction of Tsay. Golden Eagle had forced his hand, had left him little choice even when he had offered them a way out.

And yet Maaka's words troubled his mind. *An eagle does not change his feathers.* If that were true, had it been wrong to punish the woman simply for who she was, when she could be nothing else? And if so, what did it say about his own choices? About Maaka's? About Okoa, who had betrayed him?

And then there were the matrons of the Sky Made. The clan

matrons had demanded their vengeance for what they saw as Golden Eagle's hand in the slaughter at the war college, and he had delivered it. To do otherwise would have only driven a wedge into their precarious allegiance. Even so, it would still not be enough for them to trust him, to bow to him with anything but bitterness in their hearts.

Restless, Serapio threw off his bedding and padded to the small balcony off his private rooms wearing only loose cotton pants. The cold bit at his naked chest and the bottoms of his bare feet. The eclipsed sun pulsed fire-ringed and unnatural on the horizon, still caught in the grip of the crow god's magic. He turned his face toward it, straining to feel some of its heat, finding that he missed the warmth of the sun despite his own role in bringing darkness to the city. Even so, he was wary of what it would mean should he feel the sun against his skin again.

Every day Serapio worried that the crow god's grip on Tova lessened as the seasons naturally shifted from winter to summer. To compound that, he suspected that his god had lost interest in the city now that the Sun Priest, avatar of the sun god, was no longer in residence. The pull to follow Naranpa north to wherever she had fled was ever present. It took effort to stay in Tova and pursue his own ends when his god wanted him to hunt.

Some nights he would dream of Naranpa, their confrontation on Sun Rock, and things would be quite different. In his dreams, she died a hundred times. At the edge of his black blades, under his bare hands, with a blow from his staff. And when she died, the sun died with her, Tova and the continent cast into eternal night.

And his god rejoiced.

But inevitably, Serapio died in those dreams, too.

It was a mutually assured destruction, his and the Sun Priest's, and although it was only a dream, he woke up shivering and drenched in sweat, wondering if he had somehow avoided his true fate, and if so, for how long?

A yawn stretched his jaw, his bed beckoning despite remembered nightmares, and he turned to go inside, ready to try once again for sleep. He had not taken more than a step when he heard it.

Someone called for him.

At first, he was not sure, the sound no more than a whisper on the night wind. But it came again.

"Crow God Reborn!"

Not Odo Sedoh or Serapio. Not even Carrion King.

He tilted his head, intrigued.

And it came again, somewhere below him, past the outer wall that circumnavigated the palace grounds. Something that only his highly trained and attuned ears might hear. Or something that came to him on the wings of magic.

With less than a thought, he shattered into half a hundred crows and took flight. In this form he could see as the flock did, wide-lensed and many-eyed at once. He spotted the source of the summons and swooped down to a figure draped in dark robes, hunched and half hidden in a shadowy corner. Human eyes may have passed them by, but to his crow senses they smelled of earth. The way of roots and rich soil, potions, and herbs. And something else. They smelled of magic.

He landed and re-formed, man once again in form if not quite in spirit. He had come unarmed, unarmored, his body fatigued beyond reason. But he had been trained to fight long past collapse, and with shadow at his fingertips, he was never unprepared.

"Who are you who calls to me?" he demanded.

"They plot against you." The words rushed into the space between them as if forced from the stranger's lips, as if they feared they might not speak at all if not all at once and in a hurry. Serapio heard feet shift nervously, breath come short and anxious. Whoever this was might wield some flavor of magic, but they were clearly afraid.

"They do not see the inevitability of you," the stranger rushed on. "You are the storm they cannot fight, and yet they resist. Those women will always refuse what the gods have ordained, thinking themselves their own deities on earth. But it is earth that mirrors the heavens, not the inverse. What are humans in the face of a god reborn?"

"I know you." Serapio hadn't been sure at first. His crow vision had shown him only a lean form, face hidden well in the folds of a hooded cloak. But the voice was one he had heard before.

"You are Zataya," he said. "The one they call witch."

Zataya barked a strangled half laugh. "Because they fear my power."

"I do not think they fear you," he said, truthful. "I think they mean to insult you."

"And they call you sorcerer," she bit back.

His lips curled, rueful. "They do worse than call me names."

Zataya's breath caught. "So you know."

"I know." He saw no need to dissemble. If Zataya was here, she was here without the matrons' knowledge.

"They think themselves clever," the witch went on. "They believe they can outsmart the Crow God Reborn. But they are small, in thought and ambition."

A strange thing to say, but Serapio was beginning to take her measure. He sensed not only her magic but a seething resentment toward the Sky Made.

"And you? Your ambition is not small?" he asked.

"I only wish to help the Crow God Reborn." She ducked her head as if chastened, but Serapio did not believe her.

"Is captain of the Coyote clan not enough to satisfy you?" he asked.

"I would offer you counsel as I did Denaochi, the brother of the Sun Priest."

"Brother?" He had not known Naranpa had a brother, but it was not that fact that made him ask. It was the way Zataya had said the man's name. Denaochi may have been brother to Naranpa, but he was something to Zataya, too. "You serve him, too?"

"He is dead." Her voice was hoarse with a grief that still seemed fresh.

"The matrons?" It was a guess, but it did much to explain why she was here.

"I do not mourn Golden Eagle deaths as the others do," she said, and Serapio understood that as her answer, that somehow Golden Eagle had been responsible for yet another betrayal, another death, and that she blamed all the matrons. "I have no love for any Sky Made."

"Am I not Sky Made?" he asked, curious.

"You are the Crow God Reborn," she corrected, as if he had said something foolish. "Your place is not here but in the heavens."

"And yet I stand before you." He understood the concept of the heavens as a dwelling place of the gods. Carrion Crow were Sky Made, after all, and spoke of coming to earth from a distant star. But the gods had walked the earth, had lived and loved and bled their magic into soil, into the rivers and seas. Their bodies cratered the land and formed great canyons, their corpses rose as mountains where they fell. The heavens were not above but all around. God or man, his place was here.

"Here only a brief time," she murmured. "Only a little while."

Serapio rubbed his arms, suddenly chilled. "Speak plainly, witch."

She lifted her chin. "My god sent me to you."

He did not like that. He was suddenly reminded that Crow and Sun were not the only deities that claimed Tova. "What does the Coyote want with me?"

"You are a man entangled by the threads of fate who draws all to him, even the eyes of other gods." Her voice took on a note of drama. "I looked into the fire and saw only you. I ate of the god's paw and heard his song, but he sings only of you. Will you hear it for yourself?"

"You have brought me a prophecy." A sense of dismay clogged Serapio's throat. He had always been a creature shaped by portents, spun by destiny, but he thought he had found some freedom when he had been abandoned by his god and saved by the small crows, their gift not only life but the chance to walk a path of his own making. He should have known it would not be so easy.

"Tell me," he said.

Words rang from her throat. "On earth, in heaven, and within, three wars to lose, three wars to win. Cut the path. Mark the days. Turn the tides. Three tasks before the season dies: turn rotten fruit to flower, slay the god-bride still unloved, press the son to fell the sire. Victory then to the Carrion King who in winning loses everything."

The tightness in Serapio's throat became strangling. "A riddle?"

"I only tell you what my god has sung."

Frustration clenched his jaw. "Your god's song makes no sense. Three wars. A path to cut. I will win, but I will lose?"

Zataya lowered her voice. "Just this night, the matrons

gifted Okoa with a blade they call the sun dagger, crafted from the golden mask of the Sun Priest. He means to use it against you."

A phantom pain flared below Serapio's ribs. It was the old wound. He pressed a hand to his side as a sense of betrayal washed over him. Okoa's faithlessness was nothing more than what Naranpa had warned him of, no more than he had earned when he had killed Chaiya and the other Shield man. Serapio should not be surprised, and yet he was. More than surprised. He was heartbroken.

"And is that a part of your prophecy?" he asked, voice cold as he struggled to contain his emotions: the doubts about his own leadership, his fears of war and what came after, the grief of losing Xiala, his mother, his clan, Okoa. And the deep loneliness that never left him.

"That is for you to reason, Crow God Reborn," Zataya answered.

Perhaps it was his exhaustion or the lingering horrors of the day. Perhaps it was that the illusion of free will had come crashing down under the weight of Zataya's prophecy, but unmitigated rage threatened to consume him.

"There is no *reason* in your words, witch!" he shouted, unable to hold back the tide of his ire. His fingers flexed into talons, and he raised them to her face. "Give me a *reason* I should not cut you down where you stand!"

She cowered under his threat. "In earth, in heaven, and within, three wars to lose, three wars to win," she repeated in a rush, her voice high and panicked. "Cut the path. Mark the days. And turn the tides."

"Stop!" he spit through red teeth, exasperation rasping his voice. "Stop!"

But she did not stop. She crumbled to her knees, mumbling

the same words over and over again. "Cut the path . . . turn the tides . . ."

Contempt, and then pity, welled within him. She had spoken her part and could tell him nothing else. He wanted to dismiss her words as the rantings of a madwoman, but his mother had used a scrying mirror, and it had shown true. And had he not heard the voice of his own god before? He would not doubt that Zataya had, too. He could not deny the prophecy simply because he did not understand it or because he didn't like it.

But I will not bow to it, either, he thought. He had not suffered everything he had to be reduced to a pawn once again. He was no longer the boy forced into a mold of his mother's making, nor was he simply the avatar of a vengeful god. Now he was a king with power of his own, with an army to command and resources at his call.

He turned away from Zataya, still huddled and muttering, and took to the sky. His mind churned over the prophecy as he thought about what it could mean . . . and how he could turn it to his will.

CHAPTER 11

> Do not cry, Child. There is already enough salt in the sea.
>
> —Teek wisdom

There were nineteen dead in all, twenty including her mother. It was fewer than Xiala had expected, fewer than it had seemed on that beach under a hail of arrows and the rush of soldiers, but still too many. Each person mattered. Each represented a life lived and a family torn apart.

The loss was not limited to families. The whole of Teek suffered, not only as individuals but as a community that had been robbed of its elders' knowledge, now lost to the next generation. It was hard to fathom the depth of what their deaths meant to the ones left alive, but Xiala did her best to comfort the inconsolable sisters, daughters, and friends and to reassure the grief-stricken that they were not alone. She visited every house, talked with each family. She did not know if her words provided any solace, but she did what she could, spoke from her heart.

All under the watchful eye of soldiers. Everywhere she went, she was accompanied by a spearmaiden and a Cuecolan warrior, resin stuck in his ears as an armor against Teek Song. The foreign soldiers said nothing, but their presence was warning enough, and the mourning Teek stared numbly at their new masters.

By the time Teanni came to tell Xiala that the bodies were ready, it was close to midnight. Xiala rubbed weary hands across her face and gratefully drank from the clay vessel of water her friend offered her.

"Where are they?" she asked.

"Down by the shore."

Xiala gestured for Teanni to lead the way.

Teek custom dictated that the bodies of the dead be washed in saltwater and wrapped in fern leaves. After the proper feasting and songs, they would be carried out to sea to join with the Mother one last time.

Teanni, Alani, and a handful of survivors had prepared the bodies. Nineteen fern-wrapped corpses lay just out of reach of the rising tide. The women had also prepared a traditional funeral feast, one fit for a queen, a queen regent, and her council of wise women. Xiala saw fish, some smoked and some fire-roasted, both seasoned with ginger and lime. A low table heaped with papaya and baked yams, a drink of guava, and small cakes made from cassava and eggs.

"It's wonderful," Xiala said, the closest to tears she had come since the slaughter.

"It is not the feast I had expected to prepare," Teanni admitted. "I feel so foolish." She swiped at her own tears. "I thought they were here to help us."

"It's not your fault." Xiala wrapped a comforting arm around her shoulders.

"Maybe it is," she countered. "Just a little." She sighed. "And now no one is eating."

Teanni wrung her hands, face etched in lines of despair. Xiala patted her back reassuringly and stepped to the nearest table. Likely no one had much of an appetite, but they all had to eat, had to stay strong and honor the dead. It was hard to think of food with so much else taking up space within her, but she knew she had to set an example, so she took up a plate and filled it with something from each dish.

Teanni followed, and slowly, others joined in.

Normally at a funeral, the Teek were a loud, raucous bunch. Fruit wine would flow, and barrels of imported balché would be tapped, and the night would be full of stories. But tonight was subdued. People sat in small groups, their conversations quiet as they picked at their food.

And just beyond the circle of mourners, Tuun and her soldiers, weapons bare, kept a wary eye on the crowd.

Alani dropped down to sit beside them, a plate in her hands and a bottle wedged under her arm. She glared in Tuun's direction.

"Don't let her see you staring," Teanni warned.

"And why not?" Alani complained. "She should know that I know what she is. A butcher."

"No, Alani." Xiala kicked at her leg, forcing the woman to look back at her and away from Tuun. "We play along for now, remember? It will do no good if she sees you as a threat. Remember your promise."

When the friends had reunited, Xiala had explained to them the bargain she had made with the Cuecolan woman and the deadly stakes. She asked for their help, and they swore their loyalty. Xiala accepted, but part of their allegiance meant not provoking Tuun or her soldiers.

"I don't know how you do it," Alani confessed, and took a bite of cake. "Every time I see that smug monster, my blood boils."

"You are not alone," Xiala assured her. Each time she sighted Tuun prowling around the funeral, a drop of rage was added to her already overflowing bucket. But she swallowed it like the bitter bile that it was and reminded herself that first she must survive and ensure that everyone else survived. There would be time for wrath later.

A Teek woman approached. Xiala recognized her as a daughter of one of the murdered wise women. In her hands she carried a small drum.

"Laili," Xiala greeted her.

Laili bowed her head. "Will you sing, Xiala? To honor my mother?"

Xiala shifted, uneasy. She could feel Tuun's eyes on her. The woman had threatened to cut out her tongue if she so much as hummed, but surely she could not have meant to forbid her funeral songs. Still, Xiala did not wish to test it, afraid she might find an arrow through her throat before she could explain.

"I think it best if Teanni sings. She knew your mother well." Xiala smiled to soften the rejection. She knew what it meant for Laili to ask her to sing to honor her loved one and did not want the woman to misunderstand.

Laili's eye flickered to Teanni. She held out the hand drum.

"It would be an honor," Teanni said, accepting the instrument. She handed her plate to Alani and rose to her feet. Voices fell to silence, and eyes turned to her as she took her place in the center of the loose circle, just in front of the dead.

Xiala could feel the soldiers around them tense, could almost hear the bows drawn and spears shifting in nervous hands. Seven hells, whatever notes came from Teanni's throat would be harmless, but they didn't know that.

She quickly stood and thrust out a hand to stop Teanni from singing.

Her friend paused, hand poised above the drum.

"Teanni will sing to honor the dead," Xiala said, projecting her voice across the crowd. She addressed it to the gathered women, but her words were for Tuun. "It is our tradition. And once Teanni is done, any may step forward and sing. It . . . it is not magic. It is simply our way of remembering." It felt like a knife in her gut to admit such a thing, and to say it aloud and clearly for the benefit of their captors, but it was better than more dead. She waited for Tuun to signal her approval, which she did, adding insult to the already smarting injury.

Xiala exhaled, relieved, and motioned for Teanni to continue.

Her friend nodded, eyes big, very aware of the danger she had been in only moments before. But when Teanni struck the skin of the drum and the steady beat filled the night air, her expression cleared, all her fear dissolving into purpose, and she soared.

The first notes of the honor song floated into the sky, bright and beautiful. Xiala felt something inside her shift, some of the burden that had weighed upon her heart lightened, and as the other women's voices joined in, she realized that what she had said was wrong. Teanni might not be able to Sing, but her song was, indeed, a kind of magic. The healing kind.

As the last note faded into the night, Xiala could see that tears marked the cheeks of the women, but she was certain they were not simply tears of sorrow, but of celebration and acceptance. Not of Tuun and her invaders, but of the truth they had known all their lives. The Mother gives, and the Mother takes away. Life began in the sea, and it would end there, and that was a comfort, even now.

Xiala looked around the edge of the gathering for Tuun, but the woman was gone. Perhaps she had felt the magic in the song, after all, and decided she wanted no part in it. The soldiers still stood at their posts. It would be too much to hope they, too, might flee when confronted with the pain they had caused. But then, they had resin in their ears and orders to follow, both a kind of shield.

Another woman rose from the far side of the circle and made her way to the center. She identified herself as the daughter of Oyala, another wise woman who had been slain. As she began her song, Xiala took the opportunity to quietly slip away. Custom dictated that she would be the one who would sing the tribute to her mother, and perhaps her aunt, too. Even if she dared risk singing, she was not sure she had it in her to honor her mother. It wasn't that she begrudged these women their fond memories, but she had none, or at least no good ones that she could share, and she felt like a liar or, worse, a hypocrite.

"I'm not going anywhere," she assured the spearmaiden who stepped into her path, glare suspicious. "I just need to be alone."

After a moment, the woman let her pass.

She did not go far, just to the shoreline, well in sight of any watching guards. She sat in the dark, the sand beneath her cold and damp, and let the sound of the waves soothe her.

Behind her, the woman's song ended, and another took her place. Another daughter whose mother was murdered, another grieving song, and, hopefully, another healing.

Footsteps behind her. She turned, half expected it to be Tuun, and if it was, she wasn't sure this time she would be able to stop herself from saying something she would regret, but it was Alani.

"Thinking of swimming away?" Alani asked, and dropped down beside her. She drank from the bottle of wine in her hand and eyed Xiala. "Teanni told me your secret." She waved fingers around her neck and puckered her lips like a fish.

Xiala cast an irritated glance over her shoulder, but she couldn't see her loose-lipped friend from where she was sitting.

"Don't be mad," Alani said. "She thought I needed to know."

"Shouldn't that be my decision?"

"Normally, yes. But these are not normal times."

Xiala felt her indignation drain away. There was no denying that. And in a way, she was glad Alani knew.

"Drink?" the sailor asked, and offered her the bottle.

Xiala wanted very much to drink, to lose herself and all her problems for just a few hours in a haze of alcohol. It was what she would have done a month ago. Hell, a week ago. But now?

"No," she said, waving the bottle away. "I need my wits about me."

Alani considered her but said nothing. They sat in the darkness, listening to the steady rhythm of the waves and the lilting mourning songs in the distance.

"I'll sing your honor songs for you," Alani said after a while.

Xiala shook her head. "Not if you keep drinking like that."

Alani laughed and drank more.

"Teanni will do it," Xiala said, knowing her friend would do Mahina and Yaala justice. She looked at Alani. "What was she like?"

"Your mother?"

"I mean, after I left. Did she ever say anything? About me?" Seven hells, why was she even asking? Whatever Alani said would only cause the dull ache in her heart to worsen. Did Mahina regret what she had done all those years ago? If so, then Xiala had stayed away for nothing, wasted a decade without her, without a home. And if Mahina had not regretted? Even worse.

"You were her only daughter."

"Oh, skies, is that your answer?" Xiala rolled her eyes toward the heavens.

"She was always kind to me."

"Then perhaps you should have been her daughter."

Alani did not take the bait. "Maybe."

Xiala shook her head, a tired laugh on her lips. "In Hokaia that night? Before I left? She hadn't seen me for years, didn't even know if I was alive or dead before then, and all she had for me was hatred. Said I was a disgrace. A drunk."

"We knew you were alive."

"What?"

"There were stories. An occasional spotting. News would filter back from sailors of a Teek captain with plum hair. She knew it was you."

Xiala's mouth curved in bitterness. "That makes it even worse."

"She would be proud of you now. What you're doing. Helping people."

"The last thing I want to do is make that woman proud." Her words were bitter, but, as much as she hated to admit it, the sentiment had warmed her.

"It's the right thing, playing along."

"I'm not so sure."

"It is," Alani insisted. "You saw what Tuun's army can do. We don't stand a chance if we try to fight them head-on."

Xiala looked out into the blackness of the sea. "I will find a way to drive them from Teek."

"*We* will find a way," Alani assured her, and Xiala smiled, grateful for the support, for the reminder that she was not alone. "And then you will truly be our queen."

Xiala blanched. She hadn't expected that. "I don't think so, Alani."

"What do you mean?"

"I'm not sure queen is something I even want. And besides,

there's a man." She thought of Serapio. "Well, perhaps not exactly a man."

"The Crow God Reborn." She nodded. "I heard of him in Hokaia. The breaker of the Treaty."

"It's not so simple."

"There were rumors that he traveled with a Teek. There are only so many Teek that could be. You're on the wrong side of this war if you mean to be with him."

"I've been trying to get back, believe me. But it seems fate has other plans."

"Doesn't she always." It was more statement than question, and Alani punctuated her profundity with another pull from the bottle.

"Is it a weakness?" Xiala asked suddenly. She wasn't sure what prompted her question, or why she would ask Alani when they were not that close, but she wanted to know.

"Love? No," she declared. "Love is never a weakness."

"People say—"

"People misunderstand. Love is the most powerful force in the world. It can change minds, change hearts, reshape the heavens and the earth. That is why people condemn it, say a woman is stronger without it, but that's their own fear talking. If you are lucky enough to find love, Xiala, you hold on to it with all you have. It is a rare thing."

She grinned. "I didn't take you for a romantic."

"I'm not. I'm a philosopher."

Xiala laughed. "A philosopher who's had too much to drink."

Approaching footsteps made them both look up.

"The tide has come in," Teanni said. "We're ready to return the bodies."

Xiala glanced over toward the fern-wrapped corpses. She

got to her feet, helped Alani to hers, and together the three friends went to say farewell to their dead.

• • • • •

Xiala did not return to the listening house until the early hours of the morning. The sun had not yet risen, but the eastern horizon showed signs of the coming day. She had been staying with Teanni and her wife in a room left vacant by Keala's grown daughter, who had left Teek in hopes of improved fortunes on the mainland. Now that Xiala was cacica of the Teek, whatever that actually meant, she would make the listening house her home.

She crawled into her hammock and pulled the blanket over her tired bones, and within moments, she was asleep. Only to be awoken what felt like minutes later by a very angry Tuun shouting at her.

"Is it necessary to yell?" Xiala grumbled, still more asleep than awake. She squinted into the sunlight. She vaguely remembered Tuun demanding they meet at first light, and it was past that, so maybe that was why the woman felt the need to shout. But it was not going to wake her up any faster.

Perhaps that reality occurred to Tuun, too. She lowered her voice to something more like an outraged hiss. "There are no ships! My men have looked all along the coast, and there are no tidechasers. Where are the ships?"

"Oh." Xiala tried to stifle a yawn and failed. It felt like she had rocks for bones, and her back ached like she had not slept at all. "That."

"Yes, that!"

"I can explain." Xiala's mouth was dry with sleep. She glanced at the water jug on the far side of the room. "Will you bring me the water?"

"There's a whole sea of water!" Tuun said, her voice edging toward too loud again. "What there are not are tidechasers!"

Xiala winced. "The water jug. Over there." Was that not obvious?

Tuun stomped across the room and poured Xiala a cup of water. She returned and thrust it at her, mouth set in disgust. Unmoved by the implied judgment, Xiala gulped gratefully. Once it was drained, she dragged herself to standing.

Tuun leaned close, the jewels in her teeth glimmering in the light. "You have been lying to Balam!"

"Lying is a strong word."

"Do you think this is a joke?"

"I . . ." Another sigh. "No."

"Balam is under the impression that there is a fleet of tidechasers waiting to be deployed to aid the Cuecolan navy in blockading the mouth of the Tovasheh. Ships that are the equal of water striders for an inevitable naval engagement on the river."

"There are ships," Xiala assured her. "I didn't lie. Not entirely. There are just not as many as expected."

"I walked the entire shoreline each way for a mile. I saw none."

"Well, of course not. They're not seaside. No one told you?"

"I didn't see anyone to ask." Tuun's mouth pinched in annoyance. "It seems laziness is yet another Teek trait."

"It was an unusual night." Had the woman already forgotten that the village had spent the night mourning, or did she simply not care? Although, if Xiala was honest, no Teek woke with the sunrise unless it was absolutely necessary.

"Come on. I'll take you," she said. "The ships are in the water."

"I said I saw no ships on the water."

"Not on the water, *in* the water. As in sunk, along the eastern side of the island. We sink the ships once they're done."

"Why?" Tuun sounded truly baffled.

Xiala lifted a shoulder in a tired shrug. "Do you really care?"

"If this is a trick . . ."

"It's no trick. Just . . . give me a moment to dress. And wake up."

Tuun still looked disgusted, but she huffed from the room and out the door. Xiala could see her standing on the porch, arms crossed, waiting.

She took her time through her morning wash, picked something simple to wear, and, after a good half hour, joined Tuun outside.

She didn't speak, just walked across the square toward the cove that served as harbor and shipyard, knowing Tuun would follow.

It was not far, perhaps a twenty-minute walk, and thankfully, Tuun did not try to engage her in conversation. They made their way through a grove of palms, sand giving way to soil and then a raised path that dumped them out on a protected bay. The inlet stretched out before them, a rocky berm making a natural break in the tide a quarter mile out so that the waves lapped gently at the beach before them. Small glassy fish darted through the shallows. And there, under the waves, lay ten black ships.

Tuun let out a small breath of satisfaction. She tied her skirts around her hips, kicked off her sandals, and waded out. As she came up to the first tidechaser, she reached down and ran a hand along its black hull.

"And these are ready to sail?"

"They should be. Yaala didn't allow me near them. But I assume there are sails somewhere."

"Who would know?"

"Alani, maybe?" Xiala shrugged.

"Ten is not enough. How long to make more?"

"A month? Two months?" It was only a guess. Xiala had seen the ships made when she was young but had never shaped one herself.

Tuun shook her head. "It must be faster. We need three times this number."

"Thirty ships total? Even with two women working together, and the fires burning all day, it takes at least nine days."

"Nine days for twenty more ships will suffice."

"Nine days to build one ship."

Tuun trudged back to dry land, the edges of her dress trailing through the water. "Balam expects the fleet to be in Hokaia by the next moon."

Xiala shook her head. "You will have to tell him otherwise. And I am not being difficult," she added quickly, hands raised. "I am only telling you the truth."

Tuun's face darkened. "The problem with this place is that you have no natural predators. No jaguars, no caiman, not even an anaconda. It has made you all soft. No wonder I was able to take this island without the barest hint of resistance."

"We have sharks."

"Sharks." Her voice was flat. "The ones you feed your male children to? Call a meeting. I want the whole village there."

"Why?"

"I don't think you understand your situation, Xiala. None of you does. No matter. It is not the first time."

"What do you plan to do?"

"Call the meeting," she said, already walking back toward the village. "And you will see."

CHAPTER 12

> There is a purity to the ruthless pursuit of power that even
> one's enemies must admire.
>
> —From the *Collected Sayings of the Jaguar Prince*

Balam had hoped to intercept Naasut and her ever-present
entourage of spearmaidens as they departed the great hall.
The morning had been dominated by yet another war council
whose only result was inaction. Naasut had departed in a rush,
leaving Balam loitering uselessly by the wide palace doors, the
last to go.

But he was not alone.

Never alone.

The dead were his constant companions now. They followed him everywhere, sat with him at dinner, slept under his
blankets at night. Sometimes they were strangers, and he found
he could ignore their presence. Other times they were people
from his past—his father, once, who had chastised him for his
ambition; a long-forgotten aunt, who had often sneaked him
sweets when he was still young enough to crawl into her lap,
stared and wept.

And Saaya.

Most often Saaya.

Although she had stayed in his dreams and not seated beside him at council or at mealtime.

At least, not yet.

A spearmaiden sauntered past, and he reached out to draw her attention. He half expected her to be a mirage conjured from his infected mind and was relieved to find her real and solid.

"Where might I find the Sovran?" he asked.

The spearmaiden's sneer was all lazy arrogance. Sometimes he wondered why he labored to convince Hokaia to join his war. The famed spearmaidens who had once driven the Meridian to its knees seemed nothing more than a spoiled warrior class now, content to live off their reputations and do little else beyond bully a few foreign lords.

But even as he thought it, he knew it was not entirely true. He had seen enough sparring matches and martial demonstrations to believe these women were valuable and could, under the right leadership, defeat any force Tova could muster.

And if they could not, they could still be useful as fodder. Bodies enough to clog the Tovasheh and litter the Eastern districts, distract and occupy until he could reach the heart of the city and claim it.

But before he could subdue Tova, he had to subdue Hokaia and Teek, and the battles among allies required a more subtle persuasion.

Subtle, but not gentle.

Teek was well in hand. Tuun was on her way, might even be in Teek claiming the queendom and rallying his fleet at this very moment.

Hokaia. Well, Hokaia he would secure today. It was time.

"The Sovran's in the baths," the spearmaiden said, not even

bothering to insult him before continuing on her way. A rare reprieve that only made him suspicious. Was Naasut plotting behind his back? The idea brought a quiet chuckle to his lips. It would not surprise him. In fact, outwitting her would cheer him up tremendously. Although he did not think much of Naasut's wit.

He nodded his thanks, although the spearmaiden had already crossed the hall, and he headed to the baths.

· · · · ·

There were many public baths throughout the city, but there was one that the Sovran and her maidens preferred. It was not hard to find. Balam had used it several times during his stay. And it was not far from the great mound with its palace and grounds. Down a wide avenue lined with exotic soap and scented oil stands and through a small public garden profuse with goldenrod and purple clover, and he was there.

The bathhouse was a long hut, stone on the outside with a pale sand floor within. An attendant greeted him, a dour man who had shaved his pate clean and wore small earrings dangling from his lobes.

"Ten cacao." He held out a hand for payment, and Balam filled it with the requested amount. In exchange, the attendant offered him a towel and a skin scraper. He saw others had brought fragrant oils and chunks of soap, no doubt procured from the vendors he had passed on his way, but he had no need for perfumery.

Another attendant pointed him to a room where he could store his clothes and sandals. He stripped and hung his cloak and hip skirt on small wooden hooks and tucked his shoes in beside them.

Once nude, he returned to the baths. As he stepped through

the curtain, the heat hit him like a furnace. It took a moment for his eyes to adjust to the hazy interior, and another for his body to welcome the heat, but immediately after, he felt himself relax.

Steam and the low murmur of conversation filled the space. The bathhouse was one room stretching probably two hundred strides before him. Long wooden benches lined both sides in a tiered configuration, allowing those who preferred more heat to climb up a small set of stairs to stay closer to the ceiling where the heat rose, and those who preferred less steam to remain near to the ground. Multiple pits were placed in a line along the center of the room where black volcanic rocks glowed orange. Attendants in white loincloths carried handheld buckets as they strode along the line of pits. They dipped wooden ladles into their pails and poured water onto the rocks, where it hissed before condensing into hot clouds of vapor.

The bathhouses in Cuecola were divided by gender and class, but here it seemed all manner of citizens shared the space, although Balam noticed that women frequented the eastern side of the building and everyone else the opposite. Although the segregation could be attributed to those who lounged idly on the second row of benches in the eastern side, and not to any social mores.

Naasut, naked save the sweat that dripped down her muscled body, lay with her eyes closed, soaking in the swelter. As always, she was accompanied by a pride of spearmaidens. Two clearly were guards. They sat, backs straight and eyes alert, even though they were sweating profusely. His keen eyes picked out another two sprawled on the far end, eyes half-lidded from the heat but clearly watchful. And another two here by the entrance. Watching him, as a matter of fact.

He smiled, if only to let them know that he knew they were

there, and settled the towel over his shoulder. He saw some had tied towels around their waists to blunt their nudity, but he had nothing to hide, and certainly nothing to be ashamed of. He was, quite objectively, a perfect specimen, and he would let that work for him, not against him.

He climbed the short steps and approached Naasut. One of the spearmaidens rose to cut him off. She was unarmed save a wooden skin scraper, but she held it like a knife, and he had no doubt she could turn the innocuous bathing implement into a deadly weapon to defend her Sovran.

"I come in peace." He spread his arms wide to show just how defenseless he was.

At the sound of his voice, Naasut cracked an eye open. Surprise flashed across her face, then alarm, and finally appreciation as her eyes roamed over his naked body. And he knew he had gambled correctly. And while it was a small victory, for what came next, every advantage mattered.

"Lord Balam." Amusement colored her voice.

"Sovran." He took a seat on her bench, close enough to converse but far enough away that he was not crowding her. "I thought we could speak."

She propped herself up on one elbow. "And you followed me to the baths for that?"

"You are a woman in high demand. It is not always so easy to find you alone."

"Hmmm." She sat up, snapped her fingers, and one of the maidens rushed to hand her a towel. "Somehow I don't think you are only here to talk." She draped it modestly over her groin. Interesting. Balam did not for a moment believe Naasut was shy about her body, so the towel meant something else. Perhaps the spearmaiden had passed her a knife which she now hid in her lap?

He considered feigning ignorance but had already decided that the time for downplaying his power had come to an end. Naasut needed to understand who she was stringing along, and that her bluster would no longer serve.

His eyes flickered to her towel pointedly. "Surely you do not think I will attack you in the public baths. A woman as formidable as yourself? A warrior among warriors. What chance would I have?"

He said it all with a hint of disdain. Not enough to offend but perfectly pitched for a gentle reprimand.

She considered him, her expression slightly perturbed. "I think we both know your weapon is your tongue."

A spearmaiden to Naasut's right giggled, although Balam was sure Naasut had not meant the comment to be an innuendo.

Naasut glared at the woman.

"Leave us," she growled, openly annoyed now. The maiden scurried off. "All of you," she said, gesturing, and the rest of her entourage hurried to comply.

With an exasperated breath, she threw the towel off. She placed a small, black-bladed knife on the bench between them, a concession. Or a challenge. Balam wasn't sure, but the provocation sent a thrill through his bones.

"Speak!" she barked, crossing her arms.

He had thought about how to approach her and decided that Naasut would respond best to directness. So he would be direct.

"It is time we leave for Tova."

She bit her lip.

"I have been patient, Naasut," he continued, voice mild but not altogether friendly. "But we have sat here for months while you talk of war but make no move to engage in it. And every day we wait gives Tova time to prepare for our coming. We have lost the element of surprise, clearly, so we must act on what advantage we have left."

She seemed to ponder his words, her brow furrowed and mouth chewing possible replies.

He said, "If we launch our attack on the summer solstice—"

"My scouts have returned from Tova." She glanced at him, and away, and Balam got the distinct impression that Sovran Naasut was afraid. "They say the city still lingers under night. Worse, they say the Crow God Reborn rules the city outright, not the Sky Made matrons. He has built himself a palace where he sits on a throne made of Watcher blood and bones. The clans call him not only god but sorcerer king."

"How colorful."

Her look was arch, and a bit hopeful. "You don't believe it?"

"Oh, no, I believe that is what your scouts told you."

She leaned forward. "When you brought this idea of war against Tova to Hokaia, you promised a city in shambles, no leadership. You said Tova could be quickly taken and all her riches plundered. Her mines, her great beasts, the Watchers' coffers. And most of all, you promised us glory. Revenge against the Sky Made clans for what they did to my ancestors in the War of the Spear."

"And you will have it all, Naasut. No force can stand against your maidens."

"You said nothing about a sorcerer king!"

"King," he repeated, as if tasting the word for the first time and finding it lacked flavor. "What if I told you that he was no king but simply a boy? One who is half your age and has never been battle-tested."

"He slaughtered the Watchers."

"He killed priests and palace guards and now bullies a handful of old women. He is no match for your maidens."

She wanted to believe, he could tell, but there was still trepidation in her voice. "They say he is a god returned."

"A weakened god who every day grows even weaker as the summer solstice approaches. That is why we must arrive—"

"And what of these stories that he practices the forbidden arts?"

Now he met her eyes, let her see something of the power that lived inside him that he had kept so tightly leashed here among the foreigners.

"He may practice, but I am their master."

Her look was long and considering. "So you are a sorcerer."

He acknowledged the truth with a dip of his chin.

She rubbed her hands along her arms, as if suddenly chilled. "I have heard the rumors. I wondered why a merchant lord would want to challenge the Carrion King, why a man of money thought he might win such a contest."

Irritation bubbled at her casual dismissal, but he hid it well.

"The rumors are true," he admitted, "which means whatever small magic this boy possesses is of no concern. We all have our roles, do we not? The Teek will control the sea, Nuuma and her eagle riders the air. You and your spears will conquer the land, and . . ."

He picked up the knife between them, and before Naasut could cry out in alarm, Balam cut deftly across his own forearm. Blood welled immediately, and he murmured a few words. The blood flowed freely, expanding to cover his hand as she watched wide-eyed. He lifted his arm as the blood hardened into a crimson gauntlet covering fingertip to wrist. He brought his gauntleted hand down, smashing it against the bench.

Silence fell around them as all conversation in the bathhouse ceased. Attendants paused in the tending of the fires, and spearmaidens who had idled close, but not close enough to overhear their conversation, snapped to attention.

Balam lifted his hand and spread his fingers to show he meant no harm. The blood gauntlet flexed with him, unbroken.

"And Cuecola brings her sorcerers. So you see, it matters not what he does on his bloody throne. We will crush him, the matrons, their feeble beasts, and Tova herself." He grinned, showing teeth for the first time, letting her see him for the predator that he was. "You need only give the word."

Something in her expression changed.

It was not only in the grin that slowly spread across her face, not only in the sheen in her previously dull eyes, but something deeper shifted. Something Balam had not seen before.

He knew, finally, that she believed.

Naasut stood.

She met the eyes of each of her spearmaidens, one by one, and as their Sovran's gaze rested upon them, they came to their feet.

Balam could feel the energy building, almost magic in itself, something hot and promising. His pulse quickened.

"Lord Balam," Naasut intoned, voice carrying around the bathhouse. "The spearmaidens of Hokaia stand ready to defend the Treaty cities against the threat of Tova and the Carrion King. We join our allies in Cuecola and the Teek isles, and those among the Sky Made who would reject the usurper."

A roar of approval rose from the spearmaidens.

Naasut's eyes shone. She looked at Balam but spoke loudly enough for all to hear.

"We leave for Tova by the new moon, and we will see the great city rid of her tyrant by the summer solstice! We will bring glory to Hokaia, freedom to Tova, and peace once again to the Meridian!"

Wild cheers, not just from the spearmaidens but from the

other patrons in the baths, rose around them in a deafening din. Even the attendants stomped their feet in approval.

Naasut leaned in closely, words only for Balam.

"Bring me victory," she whispered. "Or, sorcerer or not, I will find a way to see you dead."

A silly threat, but he would allow it since he had gotten what he wanted. In truth, triumph sang in his bones. So many years of planning, of sacrifice, of moving people into place, of swallowing his immediate wants and desires to play this very long game. Only a little further, and the world would be his.

No mere merchant lord like his middling father.

Not simply one of seven on the ruling council of Cuecola.

He would be the second coming of the Jaguar Prince, just as he had dreamed when only a boy in his father's house.

And with that thought came memories.

Of her.

Saaya had gotten her revenge. He had promised her that, and he had delivered. Now was his time. And nothing would stand in his way.

Saaya pressed a hand protectively against her belly, whispered a secret in Balam's ear.

He stood abruptly.

Another cheer, this one meant for him, burst forth from the crowd. Naasut turned, a grin cracking her mouth wide, and grabbed his gauntleted hand. She raised their arms together in victory, eliciting another hearty roar from the crowd.

He made himself smile, but his mind filled with the last time he had held a woman's hand and pledged himself to battle, and he trembled.

Ridiculous, he thought. *In the moment of your greatest victory you feel doubt?* Annoyed, he thrust the memory aside.

And then she was there, standing in the cheering crowd that

had gathered in the center of the room. She wore her black huipil, and her dark eyes bored into him. She mouthed words he did not need to hear to understand, as they had been seared into his memory for twenty-two years.

He tried to look away but could not.

No! Tonight he would not dream of her, of his losses, his sacrifices. With victory so close, he would only think of triumph, of Tova conquered and bleeding at his feet.

Somewhere behind him a dead woman whispered in his ear.

Beware!

CHAPTER 13

Woe is me! My Child, My Heart! Your beauty drew the eye
of a jealous god, and now I am alone.

—Inscription on an unmarked grave

Naranpa's days stretched interminably, but she tried to distract
herself with the routine chores of keeping Kupshu's house running. The old woman had a small husbandry of waist-high,
long-haired mammals called tuktuks in the language of the
Northern Wastes, and they required feeding and watering, so
Naranpa did that. In addition, she was tasked with carefully
cutting their overgrown winter coats away to be used for lining
next year's cloaks and providing fiber for blankets. Shearing
the beasts was hard, sweaty work, and Naranpa was a scholar,
not a laborer. But the physical exertion offered the diversion
she needed, and she did not complain.

Once she was done with the tuktuks, Kupshu had explained
that the spring planting had to be done, so Naranpa found herself on her hands and knees breaking up the hard, half-frozen
dirt of Kupshu's small garden plot. And she was still expected
to practice her meditations, building up her mind along with

her body. Kupshu had warned that Walking took its toll, and she would not have Naranpa unable to withstand the mental and physical rigors of the work.

It was no wonder that Naranpa fell onto her tuktuk-hair-stuffed mattress at the end of each day, utterly exhausted. She did not dream, or if she did, she did not remember. Only one minute closing weary eyes, and the next opening them to another day of labor.

But that did not mean that she did not think of the dream-world.

The images from Iktan's nightmare played over and over in her head. The desperate search, the broken figure with the knives and spears piercing xir back, and most of all, that flood of Iktan's emotions that had rolled over her like the tides of a tumultuous sea.

Love, she had felt love. And longing, and regret, and a dark fatalism that felt all too true to Iktan's nature. She did not know what to do with it all, what it meant that Iktan dreamed in such a terrible place and of such terrible things, or that when xe thought of her, xe thought of love. It would be a lie to say it did not move her heart, stir something hopeful to life in a place that she had long given up for fallow. But Kupshu had also warned her that dreams were not real. They were only a mirror of the soul that dreamed, and the mirror could be true, or it could distort. So she awaited her next opportunity to Walk with a grim anticipation, intent on returning and finding Iktan again.

But when she did finally return under Kupshu's careful guidance, she found something had changed. She had been able to visualize the Handmaiden as expected, but she hesitated at the threshold of her workroom, aware of a subtle shift in the air. It was as if someone else had been there.

"Impossible," she murmured, for no one else could enter her imagination, and she had not dreamed all week. That she could remember.

She sat for a moment on one of the padded benches she had provided for herself in this place that she had thought a fortress but now carried the lingering odor of violation, as if someone wearing an unfamiliar perfume had lingered among her shelves or left footprints upon her rugs.

She could almost see the violator, a silhouette moving out of the corner of her eye. And then she remembered. She *had* dreamed. Of the jaguar man.

How had she forgotten? But there was no mistaking his presence in a place she thought of as hers alone.

The first time she had dreamed of him long ago in the depths of the Maw, he had rummaged through her mind, almost at will. Other times, she had seen him in a crowd or passing through her dreams, never again interacting directly with her. She had not thought much of it, considering him something her imagination had conjured in the wake of Zataya's southern sorcery. But now she wondered.

Could the jaguar man be a real person? Could he be a dreamwalker?

Foreboding shivered her shoulders. The very idea that someone had been in her dreams was unsettling.

Well, she thought, *two could play at that game.*

She went to her bookshelves of dreams and imagined the jaguar man in her mind. His face, dark and handsome, cultured and austere. The white jaguar skin around his shoulders. The wealth of jade at his neck. What would his book look like?

At first it did not come, and Naranpa worried that perhaps she had been wrong, or, another very practical complication, he simply was not asleep and therefore was out of her reach.

But then the book was there on the shelf before her. A thick volume bound in white jaguar skin, smelling of heat and jungle and, faintly, of sweet thick copal. She took up the volume and opened it, expecting the same intelligible writing she had seen in Iktan's, but instead, as she turned the first page, something seemed to leap out at her.

She gasped in surprise, a scream reduced to a startled breath, and flung the book away. Whatever had attacked her dissolved into a hazy residue of shadow and dissipated into the air. Had it been a ward? Or simply some strange element of the man's dreaming world? There was still much she didn't understand, and she made a note to ask Kupshu about defenses against other Walkers.

But the book lay there, open and intact, his dreaming mind bare before her.

Naranpa let herself fall.

She stood high upon a mountain.

Not a mountain but a cliffside, overlooking a burning city. Black skies hung low, bereft of stars, and a hot wind seared her skin. The earth rumbled, and in the distance, chunks of buildings broke off and plummeted into a churning river below. Bridges, thin as spidersilk, roared with blue flames and crumbled to ash to be scattered by the scorching gale.

A piercing cry shattered the night. She looked up as a great crow tumbled from the sky and was swallowed by the black river below.

And Naranpa knew where she was, and of what the jaguar man dreamed.

She had tried very hard not to think of Tova since she had come to Charna and the Graveyard of the Gods. It had been an effort, but one she had forced upon herself. For the first month she had been happy to be gone, able to bury the grief of her brother's death and the Watchers' fall somewhere deep inside her. Far away from Tova and with a mission before her, she could almost forget the tragedies of the past. But then her relief had morphed into a kind of homesickness. She missed familiar places, familiar food, and even the damnable clans and their politics. And skies, she missed her brother.

What she did not miss was the Crow God Reborn and the war that he brought with him. But here it was all around her, and she could not keep the tears from her eyes as her beloved city burned.

She became aware of a presence behind her, and she knew before she turned who it would be.

The man stood a distance away, his back toward her. He held something in his hand that glinted with golden light despite the utter gloom of the hellish landscape. And she knew that he held the Sun Priest's mask, and that he must not have it. If he wore it, Tova was doomed.

She willed her feet to move, her arms to stretch toward him. And he turned, as if suddenly aware of her. Before, she had mistaken the man in her vision for the Crow God Reborn, the cloak he wore for corvid black, but now she knew.

The handsome face, the strong jaw, the white fabric billowing around his shoulders.

It was the jaguar man.

His expression was confused at first, and then something else. Shocked. And then enraged.

He shouted her name. Not her name, but "Sun Priest!"

And then she was back in her body, back on Kupshu's floor, the old woman forcing the vomit-inducing afterdrink into her hands.

"No!" Naranpa cried. "I have to go back. I have to stop him!"

"It was a dream! Drink," Kupshu urged, "or you'll go mad."

"I'm not losing my mind." Naranpa shoved the cup away, and its ingredients sloshed over Kupshu's hands.

"Not yet, but look at you. Confusing a dream for reality already. Drink!" And this time, startled at the truth of the old woman's words, Naranpa drank.

After she had vomited into the bucket, guzzled cool water from the water jug, and washed with the root soap, she sat sipping a gentle herbal tea in front of Kupshu's fire.

"Tell me," Kupshu prompted.

Naranpa sighed and ran a hand through her freshly washed hair.

"It was . . . something from my past. Or my future. I'm not sure, but it was . . . awful."

Kupshu took that information in. "What dreamer was this you visited?"

"A stranger."

"A stranger dreamed of your past and future?"

"Not a stranger," Naranpa clarified. "Someone I've seen in my own dreams. I think he is a Walker, too." She looked up. "Is that possible?"

The old woman's eyes widened.

"And there's something else," Naranpa added. "I think he breached the Handmaiden."

Kupshu was quiet for a long time. "An enemy," she finally said.

Naranpa nodded. She had never told Kupshu who she was or where she came from. The old woman knew nothing of the Sun Priest or Tova and the Treaty cities, of the violence that even now brewed far to the south. As far as Kupshu knew, Naranpa was simply a woman who had one day been called by her dreams to find a teacher in the shadow of the Graveyard of the Gods.

"Are there defenses against such things?" Naranpa asked. "Can I keep him out?"

"It is *your* mind."

The tea cooled to tepid in her hands. Her mind. She must strengthen it, but building thicker walls and imagining stronger locks on the Handmaiden would not be enough.

"And can I kill my enemy in my dreams?"

Kupshu's face darkened. "Kill? Not directly. But there are ways to fight back. Dangerous ways."

"You will teach me." It was not a question.

The old woman stood abruptly and hobbled over to her cook pot. Naranpa did not press her but waited. Finally, Kupshu answered.

"Aye. But if it kills *you* in the learning, do not blame me."

Later that night, after she had built up her defenses in all the ways she could conceive of, Naranpa dreamed.

She did not encounter the jaguar man again, but in all her dreams, Tova burned.

• • • • •

Naranpa Walked the next night, and the next, but she could not find the jaguar man's dreambook again, no matter how she tried. She guessed that he had somehow barred his dreams from her, and as long as he did not intrude on hers, she was content to avoid him while she worked on a strategy of her own.

The exercises Kupshu taught her left her unsettled and even more depleted than her earlier excursions, but fear, and a growing foreboding, kept her pushing well into the dawn hours. When, upon finishing her exercises, she would begin her chores.

She did not sleep much, only a few hours in the afternoon

with the sun still well above the horizon. Best not to sleep at night, Kupshu had warned, when her enemy might be looking for her.

And it was enough for a while, but after another two weeks had passed, the urgency Naranpa had felt blossomed into something darker and all-consuming, until one day when Kupshu returned from trading tuktuk hair for lake fowl eggs in the town center, Naranpa was waiting for her.

"I'm leaving," Naranpa announced.

Kupshu shuffled around the room, storing her eggs and rearranging her herb jars. As always, Naranpa waited.

"You're not ready," her teacher pronounced.

"I've Walked in half a dozen dreams, fortified the Handmaiden, and am making progress on the rest."

"You are a child who has learned how to splash in the shallow water and thinks she can swim the length of the lake. You know nothing and are too foolish to know *that*." Kupshu opened a jar, sniffed at its contents, and returned it to the shelf. "You have not even reached into your god consciousness. It may take another year until you're ready. Maybe two." She plucked a bundle of dried roots from a peg and moved it to another peg.

"Kupshu." Naranpa motioned to the bench across from her, voice gentle. "Come. Sit."

The old woman looked ready to refuse, but something in Naranpa's tone must have convinced her otherwise. She sat but with crossed arms, her face set in stubborn lines. Naranpa held out a hand, and, reluctantly, Kupshu allowed Naranpa to take her hand.

"There's a war out there in the world," Naranpa said. "One that I thought I could ignore if I stayed up here and hid away, but there are people I love, and a city I love, that need me. The dreamworld has shown me that. I have to go."

"Stay, or don't stay. Doesn't matter to me."

But Naranpa could see that it very much did.

"I will return," she offered gently.

Kupshu stood abruptly. "I'm going to my sister's. Be gone by the time I come back." She swiped at her eyes but turned away before Naranpa could see her tears.

Naranpa felt her own sorrow. "We need not part like this."

"I had a daughter once."

Kupshu had never mentioned a daughter. In fact, she had never told Naranpa anything about herself. And because Naranpa kept so many secrets of her own, she had not pressed the old woman for hers.

"Her name was Niviq." Kupshu still would not look at her. "She was born on a full moon. People said it was a lucky sign, but all that girl brought me was heartache. Walking too early, getting into trouble, harassing my tuktuks." She croaked a soft tear-filled laugh. "She almost drowned in the lake, and one awful night, she got lost in the Graveyard. No one would go in after dark to help me find her, so I went in alone. I wandered that place all night, determined not to let the restless ghosts get her." Her voice trailed off.

"And did you find her?"

Now the sound from her mouth was a sharp bark of joy. "She found me. Told me she'd made friends with the ghosts, and they'd told her where to find me. That I was the lost one." Kupshu glanced over her shoulder briefly. "She was god-touched like you."

"Like me?" Naranpa had not expected that.

"You think I don't see the god in you? That I'm an ignorant old woman?" She fixed a rheumy eye on her. "You glow, child. Why do you think I took you on?"

"I really thought it was to shear the tuktuks."

Kupshu snorted. "Niviq wasn't touched by the sun god. Perhaps that would have been better. Maybe she would have survived that." She reached onto a high shelf and took down a small figurine. It was a snow fox, carved from white stone. Its small pert ears seemed almost lifelike in detail, and there was an air of mischievousness about it. She handed the fetish to Naranpa, who reverently turned it over in her hands.

"The wind god." Naranpa knew the deity.

"Niviq could call the winds. Conjure up a breeze on a hot day or a gale to match winter's worst. But it did her no good in the end."

"What happened?" Naranpa almost didn't want to know, understanding that Niviq's fate had broken her mother, and, more chillingly, Niviq's end might portend her own.

"She was like you. Gifted at Walking."

Kupshu thought Naranpa gifted? She had never said.

"But unlike you, she found her god there."

Naranpa sat forward. "And then what?"

"The god took her mind. She went into the dreamworld one day, and her mind never returned. Her body was intact, but Niviq was gone. The girl left behind was someone different. Talking about voices that no one else could hear, seeing things no one else could see. She couldn't keep a thought in her head from minute to minute, and the only time she was happy was when she was wandering out in the wilds. Sometimes she'd disappear for days, following those voices, or whatever it was that called her. When she first started wandering, I panicked. I looked everywhere. Even went back to the Graveyard, but she wasn't there. When I did finally find her, I brought her home and tied her up. Don't look at me like that, I had no choice." Her shoulders sagged. "But eventually I accepted that I couldn't keep her home forever, and I let her leave."

"And then?"

"She disappeared. I waited and waited, and then it was a day and another day, and then a week, two weeks. I convinced some of the trackers from the village to look for her, but then the first snows came, and they couldn't look anymore, not until after the thaw." She shook her head. "I knew she was gone by then, and I was right. Hunters from the village eventually discovered her in the Graveyard. They said it looked like she had sat down and just died. Frozen to death. Listening to voices that no one else could hear."

Naranpa shivered. The madness had claimed her. "I'm sorry."

"Animals ate her eyes, her fingers. Foxes, likely." Kupshu sighed under the burden of her grief. "Gods are greedy things."

"I understand, Kupshu. I'll be careful."

"Do you? Understand?" She poked Naranpa with a bony finger. "Because your god is greedy, too, Naranpa, and the sun will eat you up quick as the wind did my girl. And if the sun doesn't get you, the jaguar man in your dreams will. And if he doesn't, then maybe it's this war of which you talk. Or maybe you'll just go mad like all the others. But don't tell me you'll come back when you know good and well you won't."

Kupshu stormed from the house.

Naranpa let her leave, heart heavy, the small stone fox still in her hands.

CHAPTER 14

CITY OF TOVA
YEAR 1 OF THE CROW

> On earth, in heaven, and within,
> Three wars to lose, three wars to win.
> Cut the path. Mark the days. Turn the tides.
> Three tasks before the season dies:
> Turn rotten fruit to flower,
> Slay the god-bride still unloved,
> Press the son to fell the sire.
> Victory then to the Carrion King who in winning loses everything.
>
> —Coyote song

Serapio returned from his confrontation with the witch Zataya, his mind in chaos. *I should never have answered her call*, he thought to himself. *Better to remain ignorant and hopeful than see the path and know it narrow and paved with suffering.*

He came through his balcony door and immediately pulled up short, senses alert. He heard someone's sharp intake of breath, felt the shuffling heat of many bodies.

"Odo Sedoh!"

Serapio recognized the voice and the relieved cries of the Tuyon who had been guarding his door.

"Feyou," he greeted the speaker. It was Maaka's wife who stood in his room with his guards, her voice verging on panic.

"Maaka told me of what was required at Golden Eagle," she said. "I came to make sure you had eaten, that you were not in need of anything. But you were gone."

"I needed to be alone," he lied. He did not wish to tell her about the witch and her god's song. Not yet, anyway.

"You promised you would alert the guards if you left. We thought, I thought . . ." She paused to catch her breath. "Well, I did not know what to think. I worried."

Feyou was a healer by training, but now she was Tuyon, same as her husband. She had taken the vow, opened her throat, and donned the blood armor along with Maaka. But sometimes she mothered him. He did not mind it, exactly. His own mother, Saaya, had never done so. And he could forgive Feyou's henning, as her other skills were invaluable. But tonight, Zataya's words on his mind, it rankled him.

"I am the Odo Sedoh. I need not answer to you or any other."

He could sense she wished to counter him, no doubt to remind him that he was accountable to his faithful, but she held her tongue. "Yes, Odo Sedoh, " she said, chastened.

"Good." He made his way to the chair where he'd left his robe and tied it tight around him. "Now you see that I am well, so you may go."

She hesitated. "There is something else."

"That cannot wait until morning?"

Feyou was not simply Tuyon and healer. She ran much of the administration of the city, handled the mundane things that Serapio had no desire to manage.

"Perhaps we could eat while we talk?" She ordered the guards back to their posts in a soft murmur, and Serapio heard the door close and then a bench being drawn back from the table.

Serapio did not want to eat, did not want to speak to anyone, but he had already insulted her with his sharp words, and short of him ordering her from his room, Feyou seemed determined to stay.

With a sigh, he conceded and joined her at the table.

"Shall I serve, Odo Sedoh?"

"No," he said. "I will do it myself." Serapio found the ladle and dipped it into the pot. Feyou tapped her bowl so Serapio could easily find it. After he filled hers, he turned to his own. The stew had cooled, but the bite of chile nipped at his tongue, and he savored the fire of it. He tasted beans, tomatoes, and small soft chunks of potato, and realized he was famished.

They ate in silence, Serapio working steadily and Feyou giving him time. It was another thing for which he was grateful. Just as she did not try to do things for him to compensate for his blindness without asking, Feyou had an innate sense of when to speak and when he needed silence. Between Maaka and Feyou, the husband was his most trusted adviser, but the wife was the more intuitive of the pair. She was not his mother, *but*, he thought, *if I could choose a mother, I might choose her.*

Once he had eaten his fill, his mood improved. He pushed his bowl away, understanding that an apology was warranted. It was not that he had been wrong to act as he wished but that he had made her worry and then insulted her for it.

"Is there tea?" he asked. "Your tea is always superior, Feyou. You have a gift."

He could not see her blush, but he was sure she did. "The Odo Sedoh is kind."

"No," he said, and let apology color his voice. "I am not."

She did not answer, but he knew she understood, and busied herself with the making of tea. Once they each had a cup of the rich milky brew, he said, "Speak your mind. Tell me why you came."

"I lied," she said, voice unapologetic. "There is nothing that cannot wait until tomorrow. I only wanted to make sure you ate."

He smiled, charmed rather than irritated, since he had in fact been right. "So there is no city business that requires my oversight?"

"Oh, the master engineer is asking for a permit to build a canal through a section of disputed land in the Eastern districts, but I will handle it. Unless . . ." She gave him room to reply, but he waved it away.

"You would be doing me a favor."

"There is one other thing." Her voice was slow, hesitant, as if this she did not wish to share. "A note from Okoa has come."

"Ah." After what Zataya had told him, he had expected it. But so soon? Was Okoa so eager to see him dead? "And what did the captain of Carrion Crow have to say?"

"He saw the smoke from Tsay and inquired as to its cause."

A sorry pretense. "Tell him the clans have their revenge for the slaughter at the war college. That I was true to my word. In fact, send the same note to all the matrons."

"Peyana has already sent a scroll with the names of the scions Winged Serpent lost and the gratitude of their families. But Ieyoue asked if there was another way besides throwing the survivors of the fire into homelessness. She requests funds for their rehousing from the Watchers' coffers that we have claimed. She says Water Strider did not do it, so Water Strider should not pay."

He shook his head, amazed. "Even when I give them what they want, they question my methods."

"They are women of power. It is their way to question everything."

He thought of how Zataya had called them deluded little gods.

"Tell Ieyoue the answer is no. If Water Strider chooses to take the traitors in, they can bear the cost alone."

"It might be wise to placate—"

"No."

Feyou's silence was loud with disapproval, but on this he would not budge. He owed those women nothing, even more so now that he knew they sent Okoa to kill him on their behalf.

"I have kept you too long from your bed," Feyou said finally. "I should let you rest." He heard her push her chair back. "There is one more thing on the Okoa matter, Odo Sedoh."

He motioned for her to speak.

"Okoa has asked for an audience."

"On behalf of his matron?"

"He says only himself."

And there it is. "When?"

"At your convenience. In truth, I recommend against it."

"Are you not at least curious?"

"I . . . no. There is something rotten about it."

"He . . ." Serapio paused. "What did you say?"

"I don't trust it. Why an audience now? What has changed?"

Serapio knew what had changed, but he was more curious about her choice of words. "You said 'rotten.'"

"I, more than most, know of his family difficulties. My mother served his mother until—" She cut off abruptly, and when she continued, she sounded only sad. "If his intentions were pure, he would have come to you sooner. Now he has earned only my distrust."

"You grew up together. I had forgotten."

"No, my mother was a servant, and Okoa and I played together on occasion, but I am older than him by half a dozen years, and I did not see him after his father . . ."

"What of his father?"

"I do not know enough of Okoa's father to speak about him," Feyou demurred. "Maaka is a better source of knowledge. He was his friend."

He remembered now. On the day when he and Maaka had gone to Serapio's mother's home, Maaka had spoken of Okoa's father.

A man put to death as a traitor.

He held back a laugh. Could the witch have meant that Okoa was the first task prescribed by the prophecy? That he was the "fruit" of a "rotten" traitor? Or perhaps rotten himself, as Feyou suggested? Was that why the witch had told him of the matrons' plot? Was she helping him in the only way she knew how?

But if Okoa was rotten, how then to make him flower?

"Send word to Okoa that he is expected before midday tomorrow." He stood, a sure dismissal.

He heard Feyou stand, tracked her footsteps across the room, and listened to the door open and close. He heard the soft inquiries of the guards outside and Feyou's quiet voice telling them he was not to be disturbed.

Serapio was not a man of books. He loved stories, yes, but he could not read or write, could not study books of magic or decipher ancient tomes. But he was smart, well trained in strategic thinking, and was quickly learning the intricacies of human relationships. He need only apply those skills, first to Okoa and after that to the rest of the prophecy.

The desire for sleep had long since fled as his mind churned over the coyote god's riddle, and he knew his best ideas came when his hands were busy. He brought down his carving kit from its place on the shelf, selected a branch of clean pine from a basket nearby, and took up his chisel. He was not sure what his hands would conjure to life, but the first step was always a single cut of a sharp blade.

· · · · ·

He worked at his carving for hours, letting his mind wander, trying to reason out Zataya's prophecy. The first two lines: *On earth, in heaven, and within. Three wars to lose, three wars to win.* It suggested three wars he must fight. The first was on earth against the Treaty cities. That much he understood. And he knew that the crow god battled the sun god, evidenced by the eclipse that still shrouded the city, and that must be the war in heaven. The last war, though. A war within. Did it mean within Tova against the matrons? Or were there plots even closer, a war within his own house? Or was it, he thought wryly, a war within himself?

Cut the path meant he must act. *Mark the days* suggested that things must happen by a prescribed time, likely season's end, although what season? Spring had come already, but summer approached, the solstice the Tovans called the Day of Stillness for the way the sun appeared to hang in the sky. Or did it imply something more figurative? *Season* could mean many things.

Frustration ate at his gut, and he dipped the chisel hard into the wood. It ricocheted, nicking his finger. He hissed at the sudden pain, but it served to bring him back to the matter that needed unknotting most pressingly.

Okoa Carrion Crow.

He is coming to kill me, Serapio thought. *And if the prophecy is to be believed, I cannot simply kill him, even if I wished it. I must convince him to bloom instead.*

And how did one nurture something rotten?

With care, he thought. *Not with violence.*

Care. He almost laughed. What did a man whose way was death know of care?

And yet . . .

There must be a way, something in Okoa's past that would guide him. He considered what he knew of the Crow captain, of his motivations and his character.

Serapio had been surprised when Naranpa had warned him of Okoa. He had not believed Okoa to be the kind of man who would conspire behind his back. The sister, Esa, yes. Even the matrons. But Okoa had seemed honorable.

It was not that he lacked motive. Serapio's hands were stained with the blood of Okoa's kin. He had not known the man he slew that day was Okoa's cousin, Chaiya, but if he had, it would not have slowed him. And yet Okoa had not accused Serapio of murder, had not publicly demanded justice, but had instead lied and blamed the death on a training accident. Why?

And then there was Okoa's attachment to his great crow, Benundah. She was more than his mount. She was Okoa's first and true love. And yet he had shared her with Serapio and never spoken against it. Serapio saw what it had cost the man and that he willingly paid it. Why?

And lastly, when Serapio had held a knife to Okoa's throat and whispered murder in his ear, Chaiya's blood spreading around their feet, even then Okoa had not fought against him. Why not?

It all revealed something about Okoa, something Serapio guessed Okoa did not even realize about himself. He would not call them weaknesses, only soft places where the Crow captain was conflicted and, therefore, ripe for influence.

But there was someone else Serapio needed to understand before he could devise his plan.

Serapio put the carving down and went in search of Maaka.

He found the leader of his Tuyon in the chamber they had set aside as their war room. It was a smaller space off to the side of the throne room, dominated by a table and a tactile map of the Meridian. The map was meant for tracking enemy movements and supply lines, nothing as beautiful or intricate as the wooden one Serapio had carved for himself in Obregi and studied obsessively as part of his training, but serviceable.

Maaka startled as Serapio entered. "Odo Sedoh."

"I expected you to be abed," Serapio greeted him, "but I am glad you are not."

"I could not sleep."

"You are thinking about Golden Eagle. What we did there."

"I do not mean to question," Maaka said, sounding completely opposite of how he had sounded on the streets of Tsay when he had been so certain. But Serapio knew the night hours drew recriminations from the hearts of even the surest of men.

"Regrets will not bring the dead back to the living," he said gently, as much for himself as for Maaka. "They chose their fate. Which brings me to the reason I have sought you out. I wish to know of Okoa's father."

"Ayawa?" Maaka sighed, long and aggrieved, the remnants of some flavor of guilt in his shuddering breath. His feet shuffled as he moved to sit in a nearby chair. Serapio chose to remain standing, his arms crossed as he leaned against the doorway.

"He was a brother to me."

"What happened?"

"What do you know?"

"Only what you shared with me before. That he was condemned as a traitor and executed by the Watchers, a rare punishment."

"Not for a Crow."

"You refer to the Night of Knives."

Maaka grunted, answer enough.

"What did Ayawa do to be named traitor?"

"He plotted insurrection. Murder, to topple the Speakers Council."

"And in truth?" Serapio asked, knowing how the Watchers had often twisted facts to their own ends.

"It was true," he admitted. "We planned to wait until the Watchers and the matrons were in Council on Sun Rock and then cut the bridges and attack."

Serapio blinked. It was nearly the same thing he himself had done, only they had not had the martial training, the gift of sorcery, or the blessing of the crow god. It was not a surprise that they failed.

"Retribution for the Night of Knives," Maaka continued, "and the Crows would be free. We were willing to bleed for it, Ayawa most of all. But we never even made it to the day."

"What happened?"

"We were betrayed." Maaka's fire dimmed. "I cannot be sure, and there was never any proof, but I suspect it was Yatliza who brought our plans to the Council."

Okoa's mother, Ayawa's own wife. "And her motivation?"

"I do not know." His voice was heavy with bitterness. "But she was made matron soon after."

"What of Okoa?"

"Sent him to the war college as soon as he was able, where he stayed until her death. Tova in the aftermath was no place for him. His sister had their mother as a buffer, but the Sky Made held the sins of the father against the son. Had Okoa stayed, he would have carried the mantle of traitor among the scions."

"A difficult burden."

"Okoa carries many burdens. His father's execution, his mother's suicide—"

A suicide that was cover for a murder.

"—the expectations of his clan. And now his sister. He

never had the temperament to be her captain, and yet he is duty-bound to serve her."

"What does suit his temperament?"

"I do not know, but in truth, I do not think Okoa knows, either."

"And am I yet another burden?" Serapio said, thinking of the soft places he had catalogued before.

"You are not a burden, Odo Sedoh." Maaka sounded outraged. "You are the lifter of all burdens. Your coming has given clarity of purpose to the faithful. You, alone, have brought to Carrion Crow what Ayawa and all before him could not." He heard Maaka fall to his knees and press his head against the floor in supplication.

Serapio was quiet, thinking. "Okoa has asked for an audience. Did Feyou tell you?"

"I do not think—"

"I mean to bring him to my side. Make him my general." This was the course of action the prophecy dictated, the flowering of rotten fruit. Serapio was sure of it.

If it could even be done. He was not convinced he could devise a way to persuade Okoa to renounce his sister, his clan, and the matrons by the time he came to commit murder tomorrow, but what else could he do but try?

Maaka was stunned to silence. "It is impossible," he finally sputtered. "You know he conspires against you. You cannot trust him."

Serapio wondered how Maaka might react if he knew Okoa was coming to kill him and bore a weapon forged to the purpose alone, and he decided to keep that detail to himself for now.

"You are right in one thing," Serapio said, a plan forming as he spoke. "Okoa does not know what he wants. But I know what he needs. And tomorrow I will offer it to him. And then we shall see."

CHAPTER 15

> Better to know what lies in a man's heart than to know what he conjures in his mind, for the mind bends toward mendacity even when the heart stays true.
>
> —*Exhortations for a Happy Life*

Okoa tried not to fidget as Esa braided his hair, but her fingers were clumsy with nervousness, and she kept losing her place and having to start over. He grunted in pain as her fingernail snagged along a stray hair and ripped it from his scalp.

"One of the servants can do it," he offered. "There is no need for you to waste your time."

"No. I will do it. I . . ." She pulled against his scalp, jerking his head back.

"Esa!" He reached up to steady her hand.

"Oh!" She exhaled, the puff of her breath tickling his neck. "I'm sorry. I'm just . . ."

"Worried," he said gently. "I know. Slow down. Take your time."

She nodded and started again. This time she moved slowly, more thoughtfully, finishing the first braid and tying it off at his shoulder. She started on the second braid, quiet with concentration, and he breathed a sigh of relief once she had progressed past his scalp and had only to interweave the remaining loose locks and wrap them with the hide tie. The worst was over. She would not cause him any more pain.

Since his return to Tova, he had continued to dress his long hair in the style he had worn since entering the war college: parted down the middle and divided into two symmetrical braids that ended at his shoulders, the loose ends dyed red and trailing down to the middle of his back. He liked it better than the Tovan styles, and it reminded him of happier days. Esa had never really approved, insisting a more traditional fashion would be more appropriate since he represented Carrion Crow, so for her to be here now, helping, was remarkable.

She really is trying, he thought to himself. *And for that I cannot fault her.*

Esa finished and stepped back. Okoa smoothed a hand over her work, checking to make sure the braids lay flat against his head, and was surprised to find that she had, in fact, done well. He was not normally a man worried with appearances, but today, for his audience with the Odo Sedoh, it mattered. And for more than simply presentation. He had learned to favor the braids for their fighting practicality, and he knew that today every advantage, even such a small one, mattered.

"Here." Esa proffered a wooden serving tray. In the center rested twin obsidian earrings, round and flat, the size of his thumbnail. Next to them was a massive turquoise ring and matching cuffs. There was also a jade necklace and headpiece.

"I'm not wearing all this," he complained. "I'll look like I'm going to a feast day, not an audience."

"You must show our wealth. Remind him that we are not at his mercy."

"But we are at his mercy, Sister."

Her look was arch. "If you believe that, he's already won."

Skies, she was dramatic. It used to dig at him like a thorn in his skin, but now he only smiled. He understood her more now, her moods and the pressure she put upon herself as matron, the terrible weight that the loss of their mother had placed on her shoulders.

"Pick one," he said. "A compromise."

"Two." She lifted the earrings.

He fit them into his lobes.

She smiled, something like pride on her face. "You look very handsome. Like a prince of Carrion Crow."

"Too bad the Odo Sedoh is blind and will not appreciate my effort." He made a joke of it, disconcerted by her kindness.

"There are others to see," she said, taking him at his word. "Others who need to be reminded. Maaka, for one."

"I know, I know," he conceded. "It was only a jest. I would not want Maaka to think less of the Crow clan's captain of the Shield."

Am I even Maaka's captain anymore? he wondered. The once leader of the Odohaa had not renounced his clan, but the Odohaa now lived in and around the Odo Sedoh's palace on Shadow Rock, and some of them, including Maaka, called themselves Tuyon and served as the Odo Sedoh's blood guard. Could they be both Tuyon and Crow?

He stood and straightened his uniform. Esa eyed him critically, dusting a hand over his shoulders to correct the unruly lay of the fabric. Satisfied, she nodded.

Two cloaks hung on pegs along the way. Out of habit, he reached toward the one on the right. It was the place where his feathered cloak had always hung, but now the cloak there was half-finished. A pain, sharper than Esa's nails against his scalp, dug at his heart. The cloak was unfinished because Benundah had left him, and he refused to use any other feathers to complete the garment. It would not be the same, would not feel the same, if it did not come from her shed.

He quickly corrected his reach and took up the cloak on the left. It was beautiful in its own right, black jaguar skin polished and oiled to a sheen. But it was not Benundah.

If Esa saw what he did, the hesitation and quick correction, she did not comment. She had not asked about Benundah's abandonment, and for that he was grateful. He did not go a day without thinking of it, without wondering if the corvid knew of his betrayal of the Odo Sedoh and judged him for it. Judged him and found him at fault.

"And for last." Esa had put the jewelry away and returned with another package in her hands. She held out the cloth bundle, the one that contained the sun dagger. He unwrapped it. The blade shone as it had before, beautiful and otherworldly.

An empty sheath of black leather attached to a hide string lay on his bed. He took it up now and carefully slid the blade into it, buckling the dagger securely in place. He dipped his chin and put the string over his head like a backward necklace so that the knife hung down his back. It was not a foolproof way to sneak the dagger past the guards, but it would be impossible to see and hard to feel through the layers of his padded armor. And none among Serapio's Tuyon was a professional soldier. He was counting on that fact with his life.

Esa leaned forward and kissed his cheek. She took his face in her hands, fingers splayed across his cheeks and eyes meeting his. "I will pray for you."

"To whom?" He barked a sharp laugh. "I go to kill our god." There was a note of self-mockery in his voice that he could not suppress.

She pressed her lips together momentarily before saying, "Then I will not pray but wish you luck and wait for your return."

And if he didn't return? If he failed? Then what?

No, he could not fail. For his sake, for Esa's, and for all of Carrion Crow.

They stood there together for a moment in silence, nothing left to say.

• • • • •

The world outside swirled thick with gray mist as Okoa crossed the bridge from Odo to Shadow Rock. A steady drizzle threatened to turn the already treacherous crossing into an ice-slicked hazard. It reminded Okoa of the day of his mother's funeral, when it seemed this had all begun and had been careening toward some sort of tragedy ever since. He pulled the jaguar cloak tighter, but the garment was meant for warmer weather and offered little protection from the chill.

Skies, he missed the sun. Months with nothing but a persistent twilight had frayed his peace of mind as much as the threat of war and the clouds of subterfuge he lived under. The calendar assured him that the year was well into spring and the earth should be offering up her first green shoots and flowering buds by now. But the trees stayed barren, the ground frozen, as Tova stayed tight within the crow god's shadow, locked in a never-ending winter.

He wondered when it would break. Surely the crow god did not mean to deny Tova the sun eternally. Already there were reports of people suffering, elders frozen in their beds, babies sick and unable to be warmed. And the longer the unnatural winter lasted, the harder it would be to grow crops to feed the city. It was as if the crow god meant to punish the city that had slain his chosen in the Night of Knives, but if that were true, why must they all suffer, Crow and not-Crow alike?

Okoa had no idea, and there were no Watchers to consult. Oh, there was speculation on the streets. This was a sign. That was an omen. This thing showed the crow god's favor, but this other thing revealed his disdain. Without the steadying presence of the Sun Priest and her oracles, it was as if the world was determined to slide back into superstition and fear, and his god would lead the way.

He never thought he would admit that he missed the Watchers, if only to explain the heavens and their mysteries with a trustworthy regularity. With the gods risen once again and directly turning the wheel of the sky with their fickle hands, chaos was the new order of the day. If the war college had taught him anything, it was that chaos led to disorder, lawlessness, and, ultimately, war.

By the time he crossed the bridge and was at Shadow Rock, he was shivering. He did not recognize the guards who stopped him and asked about his business. If he had to guess, he would say they were converts to the crow god, not Carrion Crow by birth, despite their freshly carved haahan and red teeth. He could not decide if their appearance was blasphemy or simply a sign of the changing times.

"Your business?" the first one asked.

"I have been invited by the Odo Sedoh."

The guards exchanged a look, clearly dubious.

From a breast pocket, Okoa withdrew the invitation that bore Serapio's seal, a crowskull embossed in black resin on the edge of the paper.

One of the guards picked at it with a fingernail.

Okoa stifled the desire to force his way past these incompetents and said mildly, "I assure you he is expecting me. I am Okoa Carrion Crow, captain of the Shield." He leaned in. "I would not wish to be the man who kept him waiting."

The man who had been digging at the seal looked up, startled.

"Captain of the Shield," the other said, loudly. "Our apologies, Lord."

The more suspicious of the two opened his mouth as if to protest, but the man thrust the invitation back into Okoa's hands and ushered him through. It was a small pleasure to know that his position was still respected, even among these new Crows. But best of all, they hadn't even asked him if he had any weapons, and the sun dagger that rested between his shoulders felt light as air.

He made his way to the edge of what had once been the amphitheater but had now been converted into a tiered camp for the faithful. Once Serapio had built his palace, the Odohaa who had crowded the Great House of Odo had moved here, desperate to be closer to their reborn god. Dozens upon dozens of tents lined the aisles, a forest of dark hide lumps eerie in the mist. Okoa saw few faces, most staying inside and out of the weather, but he did spy a man on his knees, hands raised and cheeks wet, swaying and muttering prayers.

Okoa shivered, and this time it had little to do with the cold.

He finally reached the doors of the palace. The guards here were not as slack as the first pair. These were Tuyon, recognizable by their blood armor, a man and a woman in crow-head helmets. He wondered if they had been there in Maaka's house the first time the Odohaa had stolen him away after his mother's funeral. If they had introduced themselves to him as he sat at Feyou's table with only a towel around his waist. And if so, did they know him now? If they did, they gave no indication.

The woman gestured for him to raise his arms so that he could be searched.

"I would not be so arrogant as to bring weapons into the Odo Sedoh's presence," Okoa said, hoping to strike the right note of piousness.

The man grunted, unimpressed. He slapped rough hands along arms, ribs, and thighs. Okoa could feel the sweat trickling down his back, pooling under the hidden sheath. What had felt light as air moments before now hung from his neck like a stone.

"Take off your cloak."

Okoa unfastened his jaguar skin cloak and handed it over. The man ran hands across it and along the inner lining.

"Boots."

Dutifully, Okoa kicked off his boots, and they were inspected as well.

He felt eyes on him. The woman, gaze narrow.

"I was invited," he said, lifting his lips in what he hoped was a disarming smile. "The invitation is in my pocket."

"You would not have gotten this far if you were not," she assured him, unimpressed.

"He's unarmed," the man said, handing his boots and cloak back. He motioned to a bench just inside the doors. "You can dress there. Someone will come and fetch you."

Okoa stifled a giddy huff of relief and instead gave the man a perfunctory nod. He did the same to the woman and got only lingering suspicion for his efforts. No matter. He had made it through.

He had secured his cloak across his shoulder and was pulling on his boots when the girl arrived.

"This way." She did not wait for his reply but headed off. He hurried to follow, half hopping to tug on his second boot.

She led him deeper into the palace, winding through high-ceilinged corridors and unfamiliar rooms until he was no longer sure of the direction from which they had come. There were no sight lines from corner to corner, and the height made his foot-steps echo deceptively. Okoa looked back over his shoulder more than once, expecting to see someone there, and found nothing.

A place difficult to attack, he thought to himself. *Your enemies would be hopelessly lost, chasing echoes, unable to see what waited for them around the corner.*

They passed an archway, and Okoa caught a quick glimpse of a wing pattern on a tiled floor, a distinctive high-backed chair.

"Is that not the throne room?" he asked, sure that was where they would meet.

"The Odo Sedoh does not wish to see you in the throne room," the girl said, and continued on, not giving him a chance to inquire further.

At last, they entered an open-air courtyard. He was sure the girl had led him in circles, backtracking across reverberating hallways, although he was not sure why. He stepped out into the sandy arena, shielding his eyes from the steady rain and peering into the mist. A cry drew his attention skyward. He caught sight of the edges of black wings as corvids came and went above him.

"Crows," he whispered, knowing that Serapio had built an aerie that had emptied much of the Great House's roost.

He thought of Benundah immediately. Could she have come here and not to the rookery in the mountains as he had guessed? His heart soared at the thought, dangerous hope blos-soming in his chest at the chance that he might see her again. But it plummeted just as quickly with the knowledge of what he was here to do.

"She is not here."

Okoa turned at the sound of Serapio's voice.

The Odo Sedoh materialized out of the gloom. He was dressed only in his black skirts, no armored cuirass, his haahan red slashes along his skin. He was barefoot and unadorned, his curling hair tied back and off his neck, and he held his white staff in his hands.

A wave of emotion rolled across Okoa. What he felt to see Serapio there, looking so human and not the strange god bleeding black blood and lined with inky veins, he did not have the words for. Relief, awe, a touch of terror at what he must do next, and, most unexpectedly, most frustratingly, joy.

Oh, heart, he thought. *How fickle you are. How inconstant. Do you hate this man or love him?* And Okoa could not answer.

"You asked to see me," Serapio said.

Finally, Okoa managed to swallow past the knot of feelings lodged in his throat. "I thought it was time that we spoke."

Serapio ran a bare foot through the sand, as if marking a line. "What is there to say between us?"

For a moment, panic raced up Okoa's spine. Did Serapio know that he had given the Sun Priest's mask to the matrons, that Winged Serpent had forged it into a weapon that could kill a god, and that Okoa at this very moment wore the weapon on his back? He did not think so, but there were eyes everywhere and tongues that wagged, and it was possible that a spying crow had gone unnoticed.

"Come spar with me, Okoa." The edge of a smile turned Serapio's mouth up.

Okoa gaped. "You want me to fight you?"

"Some things are better said through action." Serapio motioned to his left. Along the wall was a rack of weapons. Some were practice weapons, blunted knives and soft wood staffs meant only for teaching.

But others were formed to their purpose—black obsidian blades, a studded war cub, flint-tipped spears. All capable of inflicting a violent death.

Unsure of Serapio's motives but unwilling to forgo the wild opportunity, Okoa made his way to the rack. He ran expert hands across the weapons, all the while acutely aware of the dagger against his back.

"And take off your armor," Serapio called. "Let us make this an even fight. Shoes, too."

Was this a game? Did Serapio know what he had planned? Okoa's mind buzzed as he tried to puzzle out the Odo Sedoh's motivations, but for all his training, he could not read him.

He glanced around. They were alone. Even the girl who had led him here was gone.

Black motion caught his eye. He glanced up. No, they were not alone; the crows bore witness from above.

For the second time in the half hour, he kicked off his boots and removed his cloak. He slid off both cuirass and shirt, careful to lift the strap holding the hidden sheath along with them in one seamless motion.

Once stripped, Okoa stood in only his pants. He could see the turquoise gleam off the hilt of the dagger hidden in the pile of clothes, could almost feel the weight of the thing against his palm. He need only draw it, and the weapon would be in his hand.

He extended his arm, and his hand hovered there for a moment. *There is something I am not seeing*, he thought. *If I draw it, will the crows swoop down to protect him?* Okoa glanced up, but there were no crows paying him any particular attention.

He looked back over his shoulder to where Serapio was patiently waiting. In the unnatural fog, shadows seemed to cling to the man. Okoa had only seen Serapio when he had been injured, the wound in his side a crippling one. But now he was in prime form. He looked strong. Fast. He twirled the bone staff idly in his hands, so quickly that it blurred. A weapon he had mastered, trained by a spearmaiden, Okoa reminded himself. *Could I even defeat him if I wished?* All the Knives in the tower tried, and all paid with their lives.

Doubt prickled his neck. He looked again at the dagger.

"Come, Okoa," Serapio called. "The day is getting long. Pick a weapon."

Pick a weapon.

It is a trap. Okoa could feel it in his bones. He should demur, claim injury or distemper.

But if I do not try now, I may never get another chance.

Somewhere, far off, he thought he heard the baleful cry of a great crow.

Godslayer, Esa whispered in his head.

Is that who I am to be? he thought. *Am I to be remembered as a godslayer?*

He thought of the man on the amphitheater steps with his outstretched arms and whispered prayers. If he succeeded today, no Crow, save his sister, would thank him for it. He had to be at peace with that.

Okoa made his choice.

CHAPTER 16

Beware the woman who is your ally during the day when the world is watching and your enemy at night when none may see.

—Teek saying

For the second time in as many days, the village gathered in the yard outside the listening house. It was not quite noon, and most had to be roused from their beds. More than a few looked as shaky as Xiala felt, the aftereffects of the late night caring for the dead.

Tuun loomed over them from the porch, her cold eyes surveying the gathering. Xiala stood on the edge of the crowd, watching.

Tuun had called her soldiers to the yard, too. The Cuecolans with their obsidian knives and spiked clubs and the spearmaidens with their more elegant weapons formed a loose circle around the Teek. They did not forbid them from leaving, but Xiala was certain that if anyone tried, they would face the bladed edge of a weapon.

Tuun raised a hand to silence the nervous chatter. "Where is everyone?" she asked Xiala.

"This is everyone," Xiala told her.

"I see no children."

"You did not say to bring them."

"Send for them now. We will wait."

Xiala didn't like it, but she motioned Teanni over. "Can you and Keala gather the children?"

Teanni glared at Tuun before turning back to Xiala. "What is this? Why are we bothering the children with village business?"

"I don't know, but do as she says." She eyed their guards meaningfully. "Better you wake them than she sends soldiers to do it."

Teanni pressed her lips together, holding back words. Her normally placid demeanor was stirred to outrage, but she nodded once and then called for Keala to join her.

"Leave none behind," Tuun called after them.

The crowd waited, anxious patter filling the yard. Xiala spotted Alani and made her way over.

"How are you feeling?" Xiala asked, thinking of the wine Alani had consumed the night before.

Alani winced as if Xiala had shouted, and Xiala was reassured that she had made the right decision to abstain, no matter what short-term comfort the wine might have provided.

It did not take long for Teanni and Keala to return, sleepy toddlers and lanky preteens in tow. Xiala had a sudden flash of herself at their age, old enough in Teek to be considered a woman once she had bled, but to look at these girls now? How young they seemed in their awkward growing bodies. How scared they looked, wide eyes searching out their mothers in the crowd, seeking comfort. One girl, grasping her little sister's hand, moved to join the older women, but Tuun stopped her with a word.

"No."

The girl froze.

"All of you, in here." Tuun gestured to the listening house behind her.

Teanni, still among the children, shook her head. "Why bring them at all if you mean to separate them anyway?"

Tuun's look was arch. "I did not ask for your opinion."

"I just think it would better if—" Teanni began.

Tuun gestured, and a soldier stepped forward. He casually struck Teanni across the face with his closed fist. She stumbled. Keala cried out and caught her wife as she fell.

Silence descended, fear so thick Xiala could almost taste it.

She watched as the children marched dutifully into the house. The last girl in line was short and already round-hipped, a beauty with long, lustrous auburn hair and sand-colored eyes. Xiala guessed her to be around sixteen and remembered that she was one of Laili's daughters who had helped her mother make the cakes for the funeral.

Tuun pulled her from the line and forced her to stand beside her. The girl's eyes bulged in alarm, the cost of Teanni's small defiance no doubt fresh in her mind.

"Teek is at war," Tuun declared.

She looked out over the gathering, her expression grim. "I know it must be difficult to understand. Here, on your islands, so far from the world. Cuecola. Tova. Hokaia. These are all just words to you. Not places you know, not people you have sworn an oath to. But you *have* sworn an oath. Your queen promised us ships. Tidechasers. And yet I come and find that there are no ships. How can that be? Was your queen a liar? Are you all liars?"

The crowd shifted, uneasy.

"I do not think so," Tuun conceded with a sympathetic shake of her head. "I think perhaps you only need the proper motivation."

She drew Laili's daughter close. The girl whimpered.

"All girls," Tuun murmured, as if she had been thinking on it. "Behind me in the house, the children are all girls, are they not? It is my understanding that you give your boy children to the sea upon birth to be eaten by sharks." She shook her head, as if disgusted. "Barbaric. My captain finds it particularly distasteful."

She snapped her fingers, and a man Xiala assumed was the captain in question stepped onto the porch. Tuun roughly pushed Laili's daughter toward him. He drew a black blade from a sheath at his waist and held it to her neck.

Gasps rose from the women, a wail emanating from Laili herself.

"Silence," Tuun commanded. "Or I will cut her throat right now."

Laili slapped a hand over her mouth to silence her sob. Her daughter stared back at her from the soldier's grasp, silent tears wetting her cheeks.

"Good," Tuun said. "You can follow directions. Here is your next task. We have twenty days to build twenty ships. That does not seem so difficult." She paused, her gray eyes like granite. "For every day you do not provide me a ship for your fleet, I will feed one of your children to the sharks. Beginning with this one."

Xiala rocked back in shock. Voices cried out around her. Someone was moaning, loud and in pain.

"We will keep the children here, under guard," Tuun said. "As motivation. And so there are no misunderstandings between us, know that if anyone tries to steal a child, not only will you fail, but you will find yourself *and* the child swimming out to meet your Mother with wounds bloody enough to attract every predator for miles."

"Evil," a woman whispered loudly from the crowd, but Xiala could not see who.

Tuun spread her hands, as if protesting her innocence. "I am not evil, my sisters. Can I call you my sisters?" Her smile was the serpent's smile. "What I am is sensible. I strongly suggest you become sensible, too."

"The children are innocent!" someone else cried.

"Your children swore a vow, too. That is what it means to be the subjects of a queen, to be in alliance with an empire." She lifted a jeweled hand. "Now, perhaps no children will die. A ship a day, that is all you must do. If you succeed, I will return your children to you unscathed. If you do not?" Her shoulders rose in a shrug. "The choice is yours."

Alani, arms crossed, her face a thundercloud, said, "But it is not so easy to build a tidechaser. They are made from a special wood that must be harvested and brought to the lagoon. It can take days simply to find the proper tree, a week to carve and burn the trunk. You want us to reduce the work of a week to a single day."

"So you do understand."

"I said it is impossible."

Tuun lifted a pale eyebrow and tilted her head toward Laili's daughter, the captain's knife still at her neck.

"Then you'd best perform a miracle."

Tuun gestured Xiala forward.

She glanced at the terrified women, at the children huddled together around the doorway. They needed her, needed her to be calm, strong, to show them they would survive.

Xiala stepped up onto the porch.

"You know these women?" Tuun asked. "Each of their strengths and skills?"

"Somewhat," she admitted, understanding why Tuun was asking. "But only a handful know ship shaping."

"How is that," Tuun asked, sounding exasperated, "among a people famed for their shipbuilding?"

"There are other tasks," Xiala explained. "Building houses, preparing food, caring for the children. Not everyone shapes tidechasers."

"I will allow a small number of women to continue at such tasks. Everyone else is to build ships. Divide them into groups. Assign them the roles best suited to their talents."

"You want me to be their overseer?" Sourness burned Xiala's mouth. "I cannot ask this of them."

"You are not asking. You are telling. Were you not one of the finest captains on the Crescent Sea? Did you not command crews of men daily? Then surely you can motivate these women to build me my ships. Else you will be responsible for their daughters' deaths."

"Do not blame me for your *sensibility*."

"Do it, Xiala." She clicked her tongue against her teeth. "I look forward to seeing the first ship by morning."

"The day is already half done!"

"Half is not whole." She turned to her captain, who had released Laili's daughter to be herded into the listening house with the other children. "Assign soldiers to oversee the workers." Her gaze dropped to the weapons at the man's belt. "Inspire them, if necessary."

"They will need tools," the captain said warily. "Sharp tools. It seems a risk."

"If anyone so much as swings at anything but a tree, a child dies." She raised her voice so everyone could hear. "If you attack my soldiers, a child dies." She turned back to Xiala. "I look forward to seeing your progress."

• • • • •

Xiala did her best to sort the women into what she thought would be competent work groups. She saved Alani and Teanni until last, allowing for them to be a group of three. With an encouraging word, she sent the other women out, some to harvest trees, others to gather the needed tools and kindling for the continuous fires they would have to tend.

She walked with Alani and Teanni to the cove where the tidechasers waited under the waves.

"Our grandmothers would be ashamed," Alani growled as they walked, her arms still crossed as if she were holding all her rage inside.

Xiala cast a meaningful look toward the two guards who followed them. One was a Cuecolan man, ears blocked with resin, and the other a spearmaiden.

"Walk," Xiala whispered to her friends, a hand pressed against each one's back to urge them forward. "And lower your voice. They are watching us."

"Let them watch," Alani spit, but she lowered her voice nonetheless.

Teanni spoke in a low whisper. "Do you have a plan, Xiala?"

"Not yet," she admitted.

"Can you not just Sing that vile woman to death?" Alani asked.

"I tried, but she is a sorcerer, and there is some magic she knows that blocks my Song."

"And there are the soldiers," Teanni added, "who now wear resin in their ears to block all sound."

"But you can defeat them?" Alani sounded desperate.

"I will think of something," Xiala assured her as they walked past a grove of manchineel trees, their distinctive oval-shaped leaves a bright green in the sunlight. "But we will only get one chance, and we will be putting the children at risk, so before we act, we must have a sound plan."

"And what of your other magic?" Teanni asked. "Can it not help us?"

Xiala's brow knitted. "I don't know. I failed to call my powers last time. I would not rely on it."

Alani shook her head. "All the time you were gone, I thought you rejected by the Mother. And here you are, her true daughter." There was no bitterness in her voice, only surprise. She squeezed Xiala's arm. "It is clear you have been returned to us in our time of need. The Mother provides, and she has provided us you, Xiala. You will find a way."

A startled yelp behind them drew their attention.

Xiala looked over her shoulder. The Cuecolan guard had stopped to harry a small lizard that had obviously surprised him. The poor creature was digging into the sand under the nearby trees, trying to get away. The soldier kicked at it but missed.

"Scared of a lizard." The spearmaiden standing beside the man laughed.

Xiala pressed her lips together, eyes on the grove of manchineel, thinking.

"Teanni, do you remember the brew you made to help me sleep but instead it almost stopped my heart?" she asked.

Teanni flushed. "Sand apple. I made it too strong. I know better now."

"No, you misunderstand."

She motioned for them to keep walking and explained her idea. By the time they had reached the cove, Teanni understood. "I can gather the ingredients under cover of looking for more wood for the fires," she offered, "but it will need a few days to brew."

"As fast as you can, then," Xiala said.

"The sooner, the better," Alani agreed. Her voice had also

risen, the need for subtlety forgotten in her rising passion. "Can you not see it in that woman's eyes? She covets, and what she covets is Teek." She gestured broadly. "We will never see the end of her until she is dead."

A crack, and Alani cried out, falling to her knees. Behind her stood the soldier who had been startled by the lizard. The butt end of his club was still raised from striking Alani in the back.

"Too much talking!" he ground out between clenched teeth in stilted Teek. "Work!"

Xiala stooped to help Alani to her feet. "Are you all right?"

Alani grunted. Clearly, she was in pain, but Xiala saw no broken skin, no blood.

"You'll have an ugly bruise tomorrow, but that's it," she reassured her.

"Work!" the man shouted again. He made a move as if he would hit Xiala next.

"Wait!" Teanni squeezed between her friends and the irate soldier, hands raised. She slipped her arm around Alani's other side, and she and Xiala dragged her away.

This is not good, Xiala thought. She could feel it in her bones. Already the soldiers believed they could hurt them at will. It was only a matter of time until something terrible happened. Teanni said she needed days to prepare, but Xiala was afraid the longer they waited, the more likely someone else would die.

"Sit." Xiala deposited Alani on a log near the water. "Join us when you're ready."

By then, two more work crews had arrived, one bearing tools and the other with firewood. Xiala accepted an adze from one of the new arrivals, and despite Tuun's warning, she envisioned herself planting the thing in the soldier's skull. But she quieted the impulse and got to work stripping bark from one of the logs piled at the water's edge, already designated as the next canoe.

Normally, the Teek would sing to pass the time and make the labor less taxing, but no one seemed to have the heart, so they heaved and chopped and peeled in heavy silence.

Xiala kept her head down, sweat building on her brow and her arms starting to ache. She let her body work while her mind was occupied with other things.

Alani was right, of course. Tuun and her soldiers must die.

Xiala had suspected that it was the only way to save Teek, no matter what empty reassurances Tuun offered about some future freedom in exchange for their willing servitude, but now Xiala understood that she would have to be the one to do it.

And soon.

CHAPTER 17

> There are those who will say I have chosen to walk a lonely
> path, believing the path to power is a solitary one. But I tell
> you they are wrong. It is my friends who have raised me up.
> It is they who have made me great.
>
> —From the *Collected Sayings of the Jaguar Prince*

Balam thrust his hip forward to meet the ball. The crack of impact reverberated down his spine as he sent the ball hurtling forward. His teammate knocked the ball against his shoulder. Balam sprinted to receive the pass, and with a solid thump with his thigh, he launched the small rubber projectile through the stone hoop above his head.

The crowd roared their approval.

Balam lifted his arms in celebration. His teammates, all sons of the lords of Cuecola, swarmed him with shouts of victory. Triumph sang through his veins, and he shouted his joy along with his fellow players. The opposing team, visitors from Huecha, dropped their heads in dejection. Some fell to their knees in defeat, and others began their slow shuffle off the ball court, dishonor bending their necks.

Legend held that the sacred game reenacted the victory of the old gods. Legend also claimed that once, long ago, the opposing team was put to death as a sacrifice to the deities, but centuries of Watcher rule had forbidden any such practices. Balam did not believe the legends, either way. Executing experienced ball players made for sorry competition, and besides, would not the gods demand the best? Losers would not do.

A face among the spectators in the stands caught Balam's eye, and for a moment he thought he saw his father. But that was impossible. The elder Balam had been dead for two summers now, riddled by disease in the end. Balam's mother, the widowed wife, had returned to her family manse as was tradition, leaving Balam the lord of the house in both name and duty.

The duty was not so difficult. His father had surrounded himself with competent men and created a shipping business that ran with little effort on Balam's part. So the younger Balam spent his time on the ball court and filled the house he had inherited with friends and books and all the things of which his father had not approved.

He was free, living the life he wanted, in the way he wished.

And yet he still looked for his father in the stands.

Strong hands slapped Balam's shoulders in camaraderie, and he shook off the specter of his father's absence that seemed determined to mar his joy. Words of congratulation followed him off the playing field and through the streets of Cuecola as he made his way home. He accepted each commendation graciously, but the ghostly sighting had soured his mood.

His disposition lightened when he returned home and found Saaya lying on the library floor, books spread out before her. He loved the way the light from the resin lamps caught in her long black hair, the way she chewed absently at her thumb as she worked to decipher the texts, the look of concentration that curled her perfect lips.

"I return victorious," he announced, hands on hips, and was rewarded with a delighted grin.

She carefully set her book aside before running to him. She leaped into his arms, light as falling leaves, wrapped her legs around his waist, and slipped her tongue into his mouth in a way that made his knees weak. He lost himself in the kiss, letting her affection renew his spirit and remind him that he needed nothing from his dead father or anyone else, as long as Saaya loved him.

"You smell." She dropped to her feet and wrinkled her nose.

He lifted an arched brow. "I return victorious from the battle-field, and all you can do is complain that I stink of the effort?"

"I think it best you take this off." She teasingly pulled at his leather armor, working the buckle at his hip with a sly smile.

He gladly complied, and then she was in his arms again. He pressed her against the wall, hands greedy to touch her skin wherever her clothes allowed, and when they barred his access, he tore them from her. She laughed, the sound pure and beautiful, even more beautiful than the cheers of the crowd, and helped him in his efforts.

He exhaled, contented, as he slid inside her. And Balam was certain that here, in Saaya's arms, with the adulation of the crowd still echoing in his ears, was the only acceptance he needed.

• • • • •

Later, as they lounged among the scattered books and scrolls, she turned to him, a look of doubt on her face.

He had been reading a contemporary manuscript detailing the fortuitous alignment of celestial bodies to the workings of spirit sorcery, but her expression made him ask, "What is it?"

"I've invited friends for dinner."

"Of course." Most nights were filled with friends and food, drink, and late-night conversations. Between Balam's wealth and status and Saaya's charm, they had built a small group of interesting and like-minded friends. Saaya had a way of drawing people together, and Balam had learned some of her talents. How to smile more, how to make others feel important. What came naturally to Saaya was a skill at which he labored, but he did labor and improve. He was no longer the aloof boy of whom his father had disapproved but was growing into someone else entirely. Someone who would be worthy of the Jaguar Prince's legacy.

"I want to invite Ensha and Paluu."

"Mmm."

Balam liked them both. Ensha was a spearmaiden, or so she claimed, who had left the war college and Hokaia because of some disagreement with her instructors that she had yet to reveal. Balam guessed that she liked the mystery of it, that there was romance in Ensha being the outcast warrior. It was a conceit, but she had an outrageous laugh and told the dirtiest stories Balam had ever heard, so he did not mind if she wished to keep her secrets.

Paluu was the opposite. A wood-carver from Tova, he would not stop talking about his past. About how the city was corrupt and had wronged him. Exactly how it had wronged him varied from week to week, but he and Saaya had immediately bonded over their shared hatred of the Watchers. Balam found him pleasant enough, even if he was a bit of an aesthete.

"And one more guest." She hesitated. "I think xe can help us with our plan."

"Xe?" Balam's stomach tightened, certain of whom Saaya had in mind and not liking it. "Well, that explains the look on your face."

"We need your cousin, Balam."

"I don't see why." Balam marked his place in the book with a finger, avoiding Saaya's eyes. He understood he was being unreasonable, but a part of him knew what he had done, taking Saaya from Tiniz, and he did not want to face it.

"Tiniz is a former Knife. Who better to fight the Order of the Knives than one of their own? And xe is House of the White Jaguar, same as you. Can xe not learn sorcery, too?"

"Sorcery is mine."

On the days he was not practicing on the ball court or minding his father's business, Balam was learning sorcery. Just as he had suspected, the library was a treasure trove of magic books that his family had passed down in secret since the War of the Spear, when owning such works became outlawed. His sorcery was more theory than execution right now, but he had gotten adept at spilling his own blood and shaping it. It was not much, but it was a beginning. Still, thoughts of Tiniz practicing sorcery ignited a flame of jealousy inside him.

"Tiniz knows enough about the celestial plane to read the stars," Saaya said. "Xe can help us plot the most auspicious time for our plan."

"I'm reading about that very thing right now." Balam tapped the book before him.

Saaya looked like she might argue, but instead she crawled to him on all fours, pressed him to the floor, and straddled his hips. His breath quickened as he hardened beneath her. His hands trembled as he reached for her hips.

She kissed along his jawline. "Please," she whispered, her mouth wet against his ear. "I want to tell them all our plan."

"Tonight? Is it not too soon?"

"I'm tired of waiting, Balam."

"I know. But we have not worked out the details. The method, the timing."

"They will help us. Five minds are better than two, are they not?"

Balam wanted the secret to be only theirs, for Saaya to be only his, if only for a little longer. If they brought the others into their scheming, things would change. Saaya would change. He knew it in his very bones, and he did not like it. But arguing was futile. He could see that on her face.

"Tonight," he agreed.

• • • • •

The dinner began well after sunset. Balam had asked the kitchen to make Saaya's favorites, an apology for his earlier behavior, and the table was crowded with roasted waterfowl, toasted yucca, pumpkin seeds, and a mix of melons and ripe berries.

His cousin arrived late, just as they were sitting down to eat.

"Tiniz!" Ensha exclaimed, arms wide for an embrace.

Paluu was next, a friendly word exchanged between them, and then it was Balam's turn.

"I thought you might not come."

"I wasn't sure I would until I was standing at the door," Tiniz admitted. Xe wore the thick length of xir hair braided into a crown, a cotton wrap in reds and purples, and an elegant patterned cape over one shoulder.

"You're dressed for a party," Balam observed.

"Is it not a party?"

"Of course it is," Saaya said, coming forward, "now that you've arrived." She kissed xir cheek. "Come in." She took Tiniz by the hand and led xir to the seat next to her, Balam on her other side.

Tiniz seemed surprised to be seated next to Saaya. Balam wondered what his cousin had been expecting from the night. Surely not Saaya acting as if they had never argued, never fought, and she had never left xir for him.

"Let's eat, then," Saaya said. "The cook has made us a feast!"

And for the rest of the dinner, the five friends shared food and jokes and tribulations, until even Tiniz seemed to relax. After the plates had been cleared, Paluu brought out a clay bottle of xtabentún.

"Where did you get that?" Ensha asked. She had bleached and dyed her hair a jarring yellow, quite the fashion in the city, although Ensha wore it with a self-consciousness that struck Balam as striving.

"Yes, where *did* you get this?" Balam took the bottle and studied the markings on the side that indicated the liquor's origin.

"It looks expensive." Saaya smiled at Paluu, and he blushed.

"More than you can afford," Balam agreed, irrational jealousy flavoring the accusation.

"Ho, *Lord* Balam. You're not the only one with wealthy patrons," Paluu protested. His black hair was cut in a terribly unflattering fringe that hung over eyes the color of dead leaves.

Balam sat the bottle on the table. "I don't have wealthy patrons. I *am* a wealthy patron. Now, confess. Did you steal it?"

A round of groans circled the table. Paluu looked offended.

"Don't listen to him," Tiniz said. "He gets envious when someone has something that he does not. But everyone knows Balam's the real thief. You may have a bottle, Paluu, but he has all this." Xe waved a hand around, taking in the room, the decadent feast, the entire palace. "The question is, how did *he* get it?"

The groans were replaced with laughter, but Tiniz did not join in, and Balam knew his cousin had meant it as a barb. Saaya knew, too, and she laid a soothing hand on his arm, asking him for patience.

Well, he would be patient. In fact, he would be magnanimous. He could afford to be, since, despite Tiniz's pique, they both knew Balam had won the girl, had won the family fortune, and would continue to win in whatever matter he chose. He could allow Tiniz a few cutting words, as the wounds they inflicted were shallow indeed.

"It is true," he said, voice dropping into conspiracy. "I am a thief.

But I am not the only thief in the room." He pressed Saaya's hand to his lips. "This thief has stolen my heart."

It was difficult to say who moaned the loudest, but Ensha's eyes watered with sentiment.

"Enough talking," Paluu complained, "when we should be drinking."

"Yes, yes, open it!" Saaya agreed, clapping her hands. Normally, the liquor would be poured into an oversized bowl, and they would dip hollow reeds in to drink, but Saaya placed a small clay cup before each of them. Paluu unsealed the bottle and poured everyone a measure of the anise-and-honey-flavored liquor.

They raised their cups to their lips, but Saaya stopped them with a raised hand.

"Before we drink . . ." She glared at Ensha, who had already sipped from hers. Ensha lowered her cup apologetically. "Before we drink," Saaya repeated, "I would have us make a pledge."

"What kind of pledge?" Paluu asked.

Saaya straightened. She glanced briefly at Balam, and he was surprised to see that she was nervous. Did she not know they hung on her every word? Even now, they all turned toward her, as if they were night-blooming flowers and she the moon.

"I have a secret."

Ensha's eyes widened, and Paluu leaned forward, the better to hear. But Tiniz only looked thoughtful, and perhaps a touch worried.

"Tell us of your secret, Saaya," Ensha urged.

"Yes, tell us." Paluu drank from his cup, but then, remembering he was not supposed to, spit the liquor back in.

"Paluu!" Saaya protested.

Balam frowned, more at the regurgitation than the misstep, and Ensha laughed loudly. Tiniz simply watched them all, as if they were children and xe the only adult in the room.

"Go on, then. Tell us." The seriousness of xir voice seemed to sober them.

"I invited you all here not only because you are my friends but because tonight I ask you to become my co-conspirators. You know my story. What happened to my mother, my people." She glanced at Tiniz. "And my vow of vengeance."

"Hear, hear!" Paluu said. "May the Watchers rot in their cursed tower."

"No," Saaya countered. "It takes too long for them to rot. I plan to kill them well before that."

"Fair," Ensha said, but Balam could tell they thought Saaya spoke as they always did, in hopes and dreams.

"We have a plan," Balam said, voice quiet, drawing their attention.

"What is your plan?" That was Tiniz, who, alone, was beginning to understand the gravity of the situation.

"Balam has been reading about sorcery . . . ," Saaya began.

"Divine transference," he clarified.

"And we think with the proper celestial alignment and the creation of a pure vessel to house the essence, we can perform a magic that has not been seen in an age, if ever."

"Ho! To magic!" Paluu raised his cup. "Now can we drink?"

Tiniz slammed a hand down on the table, the noise making the others startle. "This is not a joke!" Tiniz glared at the wood-carver and then at Saaya. "Is it, Saaya?"

She shook her head, solemn.

"Can you do this, Balam?" xe asked. "Divine transference?"

"Yes." In truth, he was not sure. He and Saaya had worked out some of the necessary elements but not all. "But not without your help. Not without all of you to help."

"I'm no sorcerer," Ensha protested. "How can I help?"

"We need a fighter," Saaya said, "and spearmaidens are the best fighters the Meridian has ever known."

"What of me?" Paluu asked. "Do you by chance need a wood-carver?"

"No," Saaya said, "but we need someone who can teach discipline and be his friend." She graced Paluu with a smile. "You are the best of friends."

"Who are we even talking about?" Ensha asked. "I seem to have missed a vital part of this plan."

"She seeks to make a god." Tiniz's words fell like a stone into the room. "Isn't that right?"

Paluu laughed nervously.

"Gods are forbidden." Ensha turned her cup in uneasy hands.

"As is magic," Balam said.

"This is madness." Paluu's voice was low, thick with disbelief. "What are we even talking about?"

"You do not have to stay," Saaya said, although it was clear that any who left now would never enter her circle again. "But if you choose to join me, you must promise never to speak of our plan to anyone else."

"Easy enough," Paluu muttered. "They would think me insane."

"And you must swear your loyalty to me . . . and my child."

Balam thought he heard the fall of rain a hundred miles away. Ensha was the first to break the silence.

"You're having a child?" She reached her hand across the table.

"Not yet!" Saaya slapped her hand away from her belly. "When the celestial forces align."

The room released a collective breath. Even Balam, who had understood she was speaking theoretically, found himself exhaling in relief.

"And this child will be a god?" Tiniz looked concerned. No, not concerned, angry.

"Not when they are born," Saaya said. "But yes. I will make them one. One who will return to Tova and avenge my people. One who will bring the Watchers to their knees."

Tiniz stood abruptly.

They all stared.

"A moment, if you would, Balam." Xe walked out onto the balcony, clearly expecting Balam to follow.

Balam exchanged a look with Saaya.

"Go," she whispered.

He set down his cup and followed Tiniz through the wide doors. He had barely crossed the threshold when Tiniz turned on him.

"Are you mad?" xe shouted, hands grabbing Balam by the shirt and shoving him against the wall.

"Take your hands off me!"

"I will not!"

"Release me, Cousin. Or you will regret it!"

Tiniz released him with a strangled roar and paced away. Balam took a moment to straighten his wrinkled clothes and calm his hammering heart. Once he felt he was in control of himself, he said, "You knew what she wanted from the beginning."

"Yes, revenge. But it was a dream, wasn't it? A fantasy that gave her a reason to keep living."

"This is no fantasy. This could work."

Tiniz's gaze fixed on him. "That is what I fear."

"This could be the greatest achievement since the War of the Spear, and all you have is fear?"

His cousin shook xir head. "Tell me of the text you found. On divine transference."

"You are not a sorcerer. You would not understand."

"I am older than you, and tower trained. I understand more than you think."

Balam did not want to share, but they had come this far. And

Saaya had already brought them all into her confidence. Still, he balked. "It's complex."

"The basics, then."

Balam conceded. "What Saaya said. A pure vessel dedicated under the proper celestial conditions and with a proper sacrifice should allow the essence of the god to enter the vessel."

"You say 'vessel' like you're talking about that damned clay bottle in there."

"How should I say it?"

"We are talking about a child, are we not? A human being."

"You've never had the stomach for the difficult things."

"And you do?"

Balam thrust his arm forward and shoved his sleeve up above his elbow. His skin was riddled with knife wounds, some older and almost healed, others freshly red. All evidence of his weeks of bloodletting in pursuit of mastering blood sorcery.

Tiniz stared and then, disgusted, said, "What amount of blood do you think it will take to work the sorcery of which you speak?"

Balam lifted his chin, stung by his cousin's dismissal. "We will do what we must."

"*What you must.* Listen to yourself, Balam. Do you even understand—?"

"No, you listen." Anger drove him forward, pushing Tiniz back toward the balcony's edge. Tiniz stumbled, hands grasping the top rail to keep from falling. Beyond stretched only sky.

"You never loved her," Balam hissed. "Not truly. That is why she chose me over you. You wanted to own her, a beautiful thing to preserve. I only want to stand beside her and watch her become a force of nature. She is not mine, I see that. But I am hers, and I will do whatever she wants, even if she asks me to tear out my heart so that she may crush it under her heel. Will it hurt? I do not doubt that it will break me. But I will do it anyway. Once or a thousand times. Because that is what love is."

He was breathing hard, and he worked to catch his breath.

"I will do anything for her," Balam said.

"Even watch her die? Because that is what you will do. How else will she birth this child and bind it to her god?"

Balam looked over his shoulder, back into the room. Saaya glowed under the lamplight, as if the light itself worshipped her. She was telling a story, words that Balam could not hear, but Ensha and Paluu leaned in, laughing, caught on her every word.

He found himself standing at the threshold, not remembering how he had gotten there, as if she drew him closer unawares. Balam loved her more than he loved anything else in his world. His house, his family name, the glory of the ball court.

Even himself.

He tensed as Tiniz came up beside him. Xe watched her, too, and Balam wondered what xe saw. He had never asked Saaya if she and Tiniz had been lovers. He had not wanted to know, and he did not want to know now.

"She is beautiful," his cousin said.

"No, Cousin. She is strong. So strong that I dare not stand in her way lest she leave me behind." And with that, he went back to her, leaving Tiniz standing alone.

"Balam!" xe shouted, but he did not turn back.

Saaya turned to greet him, her smile wide. He bent down and kissed her, tasting sweet melon on her lips. He took up the clay cup. The xtabentún burned a deep gold in its depths.

"We drink now to seal our vow," he said, raising his cup.

The others raised their own cups.

"To Saaya!" he said.

They drank, and Ensha shouted, "To the best fighter in the world!"

They drank, and Paluu growled, "To bringing the Watchers to their knees!"

"To friends!" Saaya said.

Tiniz entered, and Balam thought xe might storm out the front door. They all did, and the room fell into an expectant silence.

Tiniz came to the table and took up a cup, gaze circling the room. Xe rested xir eyes first on Saaya and then on Balam. It was Balam xe stared at when xe said, "To love."

They all cheered and drained their cups. Paluu poured another, and they fell into a discussion of gods and magic and possibility that stretched until dawn.

But Balam could not shake the feeling that somewhere along the way, between the food and drinks and his argument with Tiniz, something had gone terribly wrong.

CHAPTER 18

> A tsiyo is not meant to conquer pain but to embrace it,
> like a lover to their beloved. It is your source of joy and
> inspiration. It is the purest relationship you will ever have.
> Fail to find the beauty in pain, and you will suffer every day.
>
> —*The Manual of the Priest of Knives*

It was proving surprisingly difficult for Iktan to find someone who knew anything about the slaughter at the war college. It seemed that everyone involved was dead.

Xe had asked questions in all the usual places. The docks along the harbor where gossip was as thick as the plentiful catch that weighted the sailors' nets, the less reputable drinking establishments where cutthroats could be hired for the unsavory work one occasionally needed done, the brothels where the morally burdened might seek solace in the arms of bought bodies and confess a bloody misdeed.

Iktan had bribed, cajoled, and persuaded by more direct means (knifepoint), but all xir queries came up empty.

Well, not exactly empty.

Xe learned there had been a nightwatchman on duty at

the war college that fateful night. A dependable man, by all accounts. Born and raised locally, the son of a fisherman, with a family of his own: three daughters and one son with a twisted leg who needed frequent visits to the healer. They seemed to have come into a sum of money recently, enough for the family to travel to Barach and seek out a well-known (and quite expensive) healer there. On the trip back, along what was considered a very safe stretch of road, the father was killed by marauding bandits.

A freak tragedy, all agreed.

Then there was the cook. An older woman who had worked in the Sovran's palace itself in her youth and gone on to feed the scions at the war college in her later years. She was hearty and possessed the energy and drive of a much younger woman, so her neighbors said. She had been the last person seen in the kitchens, laying out the larder for the next morning's breakfast, a feat that required the lifting of heavy bags of grain, to feed the almost one hundred students in residence at the time. And yet, within two days of the fateful event, she had tripped over a previously unforeseen crack in the floor of the house she had lived in her whole life and broken her neck.

Unlucky, to be sure, all agreed.

And last, there was the war college stable girl. She had reported to the city guard that she had been awoken by the restless cries of the beasts she cared for and witnessed men moving through the night, carrying torches and spears. She had hidden, afraid for her life, and run when the stable went up in a conflagration. The day after her report to the authorities, her body was found floating facedown in a muddy inlet near one of the city's busy landfills. With no one to corroborate her story and a distinct reluctance to investigate the murders of foreigners against which Hokaia was about to wage war, the city guard dropped its probe.

A terrible waste, all agreed.

Iktan encountered frustration at every turn, although xe was impressed at the thoroughness with which the villains had executed their plan. And now xe sat alone at Nuuma's breakfast table, a half hour before dawn, mulling over already exhausted options and contemplating what xe might do next, when the answer (unexpectedly) walked through the door.

The answer didn't walk as much as stumble, the unearned swagger Iktan associated with Golden Eagle's scions markedly lacking. This scion's bronzed skin spoke of good health, and the muscles lining his biceps and forearms were a testament to his time on eagleback, but he had a slightly sickly cast at the moment, and he winced at the squeak the bench made when he dropped his weight down upon it. Iktan guessed the young man had come straight from various nighttime indulgences in the city's more questionable quarter to the breakfast table in hopes of being early enough to find the room empty, save the food.

Iktan did love to disappoint.

When the scion spied Iktan sitting at the table, he almost turned back, but Iktan made a show of ignoring him, and it was enough to convince the young man to continue his pursuit of free sustenance. He began furtively filling his plate.

It had been impossible to speak to one of the surviving Golden Eagle scions alone. Iktan had tried. Repeatedly. Despite xir alleged position as a trusted adviser, xe had never been able to discover where the former war college students had been sequestered for the past months. There had been many excuses for why their location was not shared. They were in shock or deep in mourning, or, just this week, they all were struck with an illness peculiar only to them. Iktan had not pushed, content to pursue other methods. But the other methods had run dry, and here was an opportunity xe would not disregard.

"I sympathize," xe said to the scion, face fixed with a commiserating smile.

The scion's brow creased. "What?"

"The alcohol." Iktan waved noncommittally, as if intoxication floated in the air. "I have been there myself, after a night of xtabentún."

"You?" The scion gave Iktan an appraising look. "You are the priest, are you not?"

"Ex-priest."

A low grunt of understanding sounded from across the table as the young man piled the cold roasted hindquarter of some fowl onto an already teetering mound.

Iktan dug into a pocket and withdrew a small folded envelope. Xe pushed it toward the man. "Take some of this."

"What is it?"

It was a common herbal blend found in the market, meant to add some flavor to the Hokaian food that Iktan found terribly bland, but xe said, "A curative that helps with headaches. But if you would prefer not . . ." Xe shrugged and moved to take it back.

The scion nabbed the packet. He poured fruit juice from a nearby pitcher into a cup, dumped the herbs in, and drank the concoction down in a series of long swallows.

"My thanks." He wiped his upper lip.

"So you must have arrived with Ziha and the families from Tova." Iktan knew better, but to catch one's prey, one must first lay a trap.

"That's right," the man said, a bit too quickly.

"A difficult journey on foot." Iktan took the opportunity to move around the table and sit next to the scion. The man's eyes widened, but Iktan made a show of pouring juice into a cup and sipping thoughtfully. "When we came through the high plains, the mud was so thick it made the journey difficult," xe lied. "Was it the same for you?"

"Yes. The mud."

"And the river." Xe shook xir head. "How did you find the river?"

"It was a river." Flat. Confused.

"Yes, yes," Iktan agreed conversationally, "but the early thaw made for difficult rapids. I heard about that poor child who fell overboard and drowned. Such a pity."

"Oh, yes. The child." The scion looked around the room, but no one else had arrived yet to save him from Iktan's attentions.

But they would soon. Iktan had to work fast.

"Do you have children?"

"No." Alarm fluttered across the scion's face.

"You are young, but some in the clans marry early. Especially if they are not destined for the tower or the war college." Iktan tilted xir head, taking in the man's athletic physique. "And a man such as yourself does not strike me as Watcher material." A small, self-effacing grin. "I should know, and count yourself lucky, as the fate of the priests was a terrible thing."

The man's eyes searched the room a bit more desperately.

"Of course, those at the war college did not fare well, either." A laugh. "Well, I suppose Golden Eagle was fine, and the students from elsewhere. But the Tovans . . ." Now a look of deep sorrow, one xe did not have to fake, stained xir features. "A terrible end, and one that no one can explain."

"I have to go." The scion stood.

"Please." Iktan's hand closed viselike around his arm. "Sit. Eat."

Iktan could tell the scion was contemplating whether he

could break free of Iktan's grip, and if he did, what it might cost him.

"Priest of Knives," Iktan said, letting a grin seep across xir face. "I was not simply a priest. I was the Priest of Knives."

The scion deflated, any thoughts of fighting draining away, replaced by resignation.

"I'm not supposed to be here," he muttered.

"Where are any of us meant to be?" Iktan asked good-naturedly, as if their conversation had suddenly taken a philosophical turn.

"I don't know anything." A protest to a question Iktan had not even asked. Xe ran a fingernail down the man's muscled bicep, slow and intimate.

"You're lying," xe whispered, voice filled with terrible promises. "It's a nasty business, lying. First you find yourself lying about mud in the plains when you did not come from Tova recently and know nothing about the state of the roads, and then you are lying about feeling sorry for a child who fell into the river when there was no child, and now you find yourself lying about the war college."

Xe continued down the scion's forearm and across his wrist to tap the back of his hand. The man shivered.

"People lose tongues when they lie." Tap, tap, against his hand. "But first, they lose fingers."

The scion was sweating now, beads gathering at the edges of his tawny hair.

"I am sworn to secrecy! I'll be banished if I say anything. They made that clear enough."

"They?"

The man shook his head, lips pressed tightly together.

"And what do you think I'll do to you, if you don't speak?" xe asked.

"You can't! Nuuma will not allow it!"

A last-ditch effort. Iktan admired the attempt, but it was desperate, and they both knew it. Xe ran the back of xir hand along the scion's cheek.

"Tongue first, then," xe said, "so you won't talk. But I suspect they'll never find your body. However, it is not all despair. I am sure it will be a fine funeral."

And just like that, the scion broke.

"All I know is that we were woken up in the middle of the night and told to go." The words came out in a rush. "We had to leave everything behind, all our belongings. I lost a ring that was precious to me, a family heirloom!"

"A pity." Iktan's mouth turned down, but xir tone was mocking.

"It doesn't matter," the scion said quickly, realizing he would garner no sympathy from present company. "As we were leaving, I saw men entering the dormitories where the other Tovans slept. Men in painted animal skins and blackened faces."

"Men? Not spearmaidens?" That eliminated Naasut, which was unsurprising. If the Sovran had wanted the scions dead, she could have commanded it as soon as she took the throne. Why wait until the night that the party from Cuecola arrived?

And that was an answer. *Slow, Iktan*, xe chided xirself. *How did you miss the obvious?*

"They were men from Cuecola, these soldiers you saw?"

The scion shrugged trembling shoulders. Not a yes or a no, but the answer was plain enough. Still, something didn't quite add up.

"Who told you to keep silent?"

Frightened eyes darted around the room, looking for one last chance at escape, but none came, and the scion whispered, "Nuuma. She said it was for the good of the alliance, that we were at war now and that nothing could be done for it." The scion made a strangled sound. "It wasn't just my ring. I lost friends that night, too! But I swear to you, Priest, I had nothing to do with it."

Iktan leaned back, contemplative. So the slaughter was Cuecola's doing, although Iktan could not quite understand why. To prevent the scions from returning to Tova and joining the forces against them? But if that was the objective, why not simply imprison them and use them as bargaining chips? Similarly, why kill the great beasts? Surely they were more useful alive than dead.

And who among the Cuecolan lords would devise such a plan?

That one lord, Pech, was dead. Xiala had seen to that. But Pech had not seemed the type to order the slaughter of scions. Oh, he probably would have slept fine with thirty Tovans dead in their beds, but he simply wasn't smart enough to organize such a mission and then so thoroughly cover it up.

Then there was the little man who had returned to Cuecola shortly thereafter, the one with the ridiculous forelock. Iktan could hunt him down and ask (not nicely), but that would take some time, and he seemed just as unlikely as Pech.

There was the woman sorcerer, Tuun. She was capable and vicious enough, but she had left to rally the Teek navy in the wake of Mahina's death.

And another puzzle piece clicked into place.

Xe really had become sloppy. Well, perhaps sloppy wasn't the word, but incurious certainly was. Manipulations all around, and Iktan had been sleepwalking through it all.

To be fair, Mahina's death had been unexpected. She was Naasut's favorite and always surrounded by a contingent of spearmaidens in addition to her own bodyguard. It seemed unlikely that anyone could have purposely done her harm, and xe knew from xir time with Xiala that the Teek struggled with illness when away from the sea. Iktan had not suspected foul play, and now xe could only blame such complacent thinking on this damnable melancholy that had taken hold.

Well, the melancholy was cured. Iktan was wide awake, and xe was thinking quite clearly now. If anyone were to ask, say, Naasut at their next war council, Iktan would be sure to mention Tuun's name. And with Tuun due to return with a fleet of tidechasers in only a matter of days, xe was sure Naasut could have quite a welcome planned for the duplicitous sorcerer.

But that still left one Cuecolan lord in Hokaia, who, when Iktan applied a bit more thought, was the obvious villain. They had been avoiding each other, perhaps like recognizing like, while they both played at tame.

That time was at an end.

The most successful predators, Iktan thought, *often hide in plain sight.*

"I think it is time I visited with the jaguar lord," xe mused. Iktan patted the scion on his muscled shoulder and stood. "You've been quite the help. Do enjoy your breakfast."

· · · · ·

The sun had not yet breached the eastern plains when Iktan left the Mink Palace. It would soon enough, but right now darkness still reigned, and the city was only now beginning to rouse itself for the coming day.

Plenty of time to kill a man.

The Otter Palace, where the Cuecolan hosts were housed, hunched low and dark on the far side of the yard. Even in the predawn lowlight, Iktan could be seen crossing the wide, grassy expanse by anyone who cared to look, but xe had ceased to care. Xe was sure that once Naasut learned of the southerners' treachery, particularly in regard to Mahina's death, it would not matter.

The Otter Palace was not empty, of course. There were guards and servants and a household. Despite Iktan's new single-mindedness, it would not be wise to simply march in and slaughter them all, although xe did not doubt that it would bring a measure of satisfaction. Stealth was the way of a Knife, and Iktan was well aware xe was not a soldier but an assassin, and there were better ways to take down one's enemies than through the front door.

There was no time for disguises and subterfuge, but xe did not need it. Xe need only get in, find the right room, and exit before anyone realized Balam was dead. A trick xe had executed dozens of times. And while there were no cliffs to scale, there was a wall left vulnerable by a complacent guard who napped nearby and who never noticed the shadowy figure climbing up to the roof. Once xe was on the roof, it was not difficult to guess which room would be Balam's. All the guest quarters were laid out in a similar fashion, and Otter ran east to west just like Mink, with the largest and most lavish room (the one Nuuma inhabited in the Mink Palace) in the far northern corner. With all the other Cuecolan lords absent from the city, Iktan was certain Lord Balam took the best for himself.

The roof was thatch, bundles of river palm dried and piled together, but there were gaps in the roofing that nesting birds had left behind and soft places where the reeds were weak. Iktan had a number of knives handy (always) and got to work. It was quick business; the thatch was in need of spring repair. As the sun broke over the horizon, the assassin priest eased down through the narrow opening.

Xe hung suspended in open space while xir eyes adjusted to the darkness. Xe had guessed right, and the room below was a copy of Nuuma's. An open space with a low table and cushions and, through a curtained alcove, a sleeping area. And visible, on a low bed, a sleeping figure.

There was a stillness that came with assassin work. It began with breath, long and measured, until a feeling of total calm spread through the body. Senses sharpened, awareness heightened. Iktan's old master had called it a fugue state, one that kept the Knife at a killing edge. It could not be held for long and was often followed by a debilitating crash, but Iktan needed only seconds.

Xe dropped silently to the floor.

The pain was immediate.

Spikes the size of fingers jutted up from the ground where there had been none before. Sharp and pointed, they impaled xir feet, easily breaking through the leather soles of xir shoes and exiting out the top.

Iktan swallowed the scream that knocked against xir teeth, releasing the agony in a huffed exhale. It was barely a sound, no more than a breath that most might mistake for the wind, but the figure on the bed stirred.

"Saaya?"

Lord Balam sat up. His voice was disoriented with sleep, and whoever Saaya was, she was a remnant of that slumber.

Iktan huffed through xir nose, working to control the pain. Blood had already begun filling both shoes. Xe lifted a foot, only a little. The sensation was so intense that xir vision sparked white, but it was enough to see it could be done.

Balam did not approach at first, only watched, as if he expected Iktan might disappear. But after a moment, the man rolled to his feet and padded across the floor, retrieving a robe from the edge of the bed as he went. He wrapped the garment around his body and belted it at the waist. He stopped well out of arm's reach.

A lamp flared in his hand, and light fell across Iktan's face.

Iktan could not help but look down at xir feet, and immediately wished xe had not. Blood seeped from the gruesome wounds without slowing. Xe could not stay like this much longer. Xe lifted a foot another fingernail's span, bracing against the agony.

The knife strapped to xir wrist beckoned, and the one at xir back. But xe would only get one chance. Xe must act with purpose and not out of desperation.

Iktan's breath came harsh and ragged now, control slipping, and still, Balam only stared.

"Well?" Iktan finally broke the silence.

The jaguar lord blinked. "You are real."

A strange thing to say, but Iktan had other immediate concerns.

Balam gathered himself. "I knew you would come eventually. Nuuma might claim that you are simply her adviser, but Layat told me who you are, Priest of Knives."

"Ex-priest." It came out through gritted teeth.

Balam smiled, and it was as unpleasant a thing as Iktan had ever seen. Xir fingers itched for a knife, but xe resisted.

"So why does Golden Eagle choose to send her pet assassin after me now?" Balam pulled up a bench and sat. "Surely the wiser move would be to wait until our victory in Tova is secured. If you ask me, she has played her hand too soon."

"Nuuma didn't send me."

Balam tilted his head. "Then you are here of your own accord?" He leaned in closer. "Why?"

"I know you killed Mahina."

Balam waved his hand. "And what? You suddenly have an affection for the Teek queen? Truly, no one cares about the Teek or their dead queen."

"Naasut will care." Eyes never leaving Balam, Iktan raised xir foot another fraction.

"Iktan, is it? You strike me as a person who has studied their adversaries. Surely you know Naasut better than that. All the Sovran wants is warships, and when Tuun returns with those ships, it will not matter who is sailing them. Now, why did you really come?"

There was no reason to lie. "The war college."

"The war . . . ?" Understanding bloomed on Balam's face. "You lost . . . a child?"

"A nephew."

"Ah." The Cuecolan lord smoothed a hand across his lap, looking thoughtful.

Iktan raised xir foot another agonizing measure. The point of the spike was level with the top of xir foot. Xir thigh muscles burned with the effort, but one more heave, and xir foot would be free.

"It was not personal," Balam said. "But you must know that there will be innocents lost in this war. It is inevitable."

"What is inevitable is . . ." Iktan lowered xir head, and the last part of the sentence came out in a whisper.

Balam leaned in, the better to hear.

And Iktan moved.

With mind-numbing effort, Iktan tore xir foot free and lunged toward Balam, a knife already in xir grip. Balam reared back, and Iktan missed opening his stomach by fractions. The momentum thrust Iktan forward, and xir back foot ripped free of the spikes, too. A scream xe could not control tore from xir throat as xe went careening forward. Xe crashed into the jaguar lord, and they tumbled to the floor, wrestling for the knife. It was an odd angle, tangled limbs and flapping robe and a wooden bench between them, and Iktan was weak from pain and blood loss, while Balam was strong. The jaguar lord slammed Iktan's hand down hard against the ground, and the blade fell from xir shaking fingers.

But Iktan had another hand and another blade, and it was planted in Balam's gut before the first one had hit the floor.

"Wait!" the jaguar lord screamed. He clutched at Iktan's hand, still wrapped around the hilt of the knife buried in his stomach. "Naranpa is alive!"

Iktan froze.

"She's alive," Balam panted, pain etching his face. "And I know where she is, but if you kill me, she will remain lost to you forever."

Iktan's feet were throbbing, xir arms shook, and xir head was spinning. Xe knew it was only training and adrenaline that were keeping xe functioning, and both would fail soon enough. And there were voices somewhere in the palace. Confused shouting, as the house awoke and tried to determine what had disturbed their sleep.

Iktan had seconds, if that.

"Why should I believe you?"

"Xiala. The Teek sailor who arrived with you. She told me. She said you would want to know. That Golden Eagle had deceived you about Naranpa's death."

Iktan remembered the conversation at the inn in the town on the river. Iktan had had suspicions then but had not pursued them. But Nuuma had known from the day she arrived from Tova. Had known for months and kept it a secret, no doubt to keep Iktan at her side and under her thumb. Xe had sat across the table from her day after day thinking Naranpa dead, berating xirself for xir failures, and all this time . . . alive.

"Let me live," Balam coughed, blood spattering his lips, "and I will tell you where to find her."

Iktan lifted a blood-slicked hand and fumbled a necklace free from xir shirt. On the end was a pendant xe had fashioned from the winged serpent bone xe had found on the war college grounds.

"I will find her myself."

Xe buried the bone in Balam's throat.

The last look on the jaguar lord's face was one of complete surprise.

Iktan stood. Pain howled up xir legs, and xe collapsed. Xe tried again, bracing xir weight on the bench, and this time, xir legs held. Xe hobbled to the table and, agonizingly slowly, hauled xirself to the top. With tremendous effort, Iktan leaped to catch the edge of the hole in the ceiling. Xe pulled xirself through, just as knocking on Balam's door echoed across the room. Cries of concern followed, with more insistent knocking, but Iktan was out now and crawling across the roof, thatch nicking cuts across xir palms and knees. Cuts that xe didn't even feel.

Naranpa was alive.

Xe had dreamed it but had not believed it.

A weight lifted from xir heart, and despite the pain, Iktan smiled.

Here was a second chance.

Here was something to live for.

Here was so much promise.

Iktan dropped to the ground outside and slumped for a moment in the shadows under the eaves, breath shallow and pained.

Focus. Embrace the pain. Survive, and find Nara.

You can do this. Will do this.

Xe forced xirself to walk. Bloody footprints left a trail that could not be concealed, but it did not matter.

Xe was done with this place. With these people.

Almost.

First, there was breakfast.

CHAPTER 19

CITY OF TOVA

YEAR I OF THE CROW

> And Grandfather Crow said to First Man, I have cast my children like seed across the earth. May they thrive in my shadow and grow. But if they turn away from me, cut them down like corn in the field.
>
> —From the Crow Cycle, an oral history of the Crow clan

Okoa turned away from the weapons rack with a wooden staff in his hands. He shifted it from palm to palm, working to get the weight of it.

Across from him, Serapio grinned.

Okoa noticed, and his suspicions only grew. "Are you so eager to lose today?"

Serapio spread his arms. "Come."

Despite the invitation, Okoa took his time. It was a sparring match, after all, and he needed time to think. Time to calm the wild pounding of his heart, his too-quick breathing.

He walked to the center of the circle, damp sand under his bare feet. Fog swirled around them, and the rain spattered the ground in sharp, icy shards. His sight was limited, the morning's watery half-light unable to penetrate the gloom. It bathed the arena in otherworldly shades of gray. Resin-heavy torches flickered from their perches along the wall, small bursts of heat and fire, but the world around Okoa was one of shadows.

"I cannot see," he complained.

"There are better senses to use when fighting," Serapio said, sounding amused. "Sound, touch, smell." Serapio pressed a hand against his heart. "Instinct."

"Easy for a blind man to say," Okoa whispered to himself, fully aware that in this environment, Serapio had the advantage, and wondered if the Odo Sedoh had arranged it that way. *Surely he can't control the weather*, he scoffed to himself. But then, his coming had brought down the sun, so nothing was impossible.

Which only made Okoa's stomach twist.

Breath puffed from his lungs as he took a moment to stretch. He raised the staff over his head and then lowered it behind his back, loosening the muscles in his shoulders.

Serapio allowed it, standing patiently, bone staff at his side.

Okoa centered his hands and twirled his weapon with easy expertise. He knew Serapio had been trained by a spearmaiden, but he had trained at the war college and was proficient in this weapon, among others. Serapio would not find him an easy defeat.

The delay had allowed Okoa's pulse to calm, the rhythm of his swings and the pattern of his footfalls familiar enough to provide him the confidence that came with practice. Satisfied, he took up a fighting stance.

Serapio had not moved, his position still relaxed, staff still loose in his hands.

Okoa frowned. Could Serapio not tell he was ready? He stomped his foot and said, "Let us—"

Serapio struck. A two-handed swing that seemed to manifest from nothing, aimed at Okoa's head. Okoa hastily blocked it in an inelegant scramble, a curse on his lips.

Serapio retreated and did not press his advantage.

"Enough talking, Crow son," Serapio admonished. "Let your staff speak for you now."

"Very well," he challenged. "But do not complain when you do not like what my staff has to say."

At first, they were both tentative, two warriors learning about their opponent. But soon they began to trade blows. A thrust to the chest, a swing to the head, a sweep of the feet.

Serapio connected once across Okoa's back as he overrotated on a parry. He stumbled, a hiss escaping his lips. Okoa returned the insult moments later by striking Serapio on the hip, making the other man wince.

They took up their positions again, circling, looking for the moment of advantage.

Serapio found it first.

In one smooth motion, he dropped as he spun, elbows tight to his body. He swung one arm wide as he turned and extended the staff behind his shoulders. He passed the staff to his free hand, gripped the far edge, and swung the weapon like a club, angling for Okoa's knees.

Okoa had to leap to escape the blow, but unlike the earlier strike, this time Serapio did not pause. He used his momentum to continue through the rotation, balanced on the balls of his feet. As he came around, he raised his staff and thrust up toward Okoa's head.

Okoa bent back, letting the blow pass over him. He took two quick steps forward, planted his staff, and, using it as a brace, launched a kick at Serapio's chest as he rose.

Serapio threw himself backward as Okoa's foot grazed his

torso. He rolled, feet over head, and came up in a crouch, left foot forward, staff already raised to counterattack.

He's too fast! Okoa thought as he labored to recover from his charge, even as he realized he was overextended.

Serapio made him pay for it.

He launched a flurry of blows at Okoa's thighs, his midsection, and then his upper body, his staff moving too quickly for Okoa to follow. He tried to block, to find an opening to launch an offensive, but the strikes were relentless and precise, pain blossoming along Okoa's ribs, his kidneys, his lower back.

Finally, Serapio rammed the edge of his staff into Okoa's knee, and Okoa went down. His staff flew from his hands as he collapsed, a cry on his lips.

He rolled, hands searching for his lost weapon, but Serapio's staff hit the ground a breath from his face, and he froze. Serapio loomed over him, staff poised for a blow that would knock Okoa senseless. But he did not take it.

"What are you waiting for?" Okoa shouted, his breath whistling from between his teeth. "Take your win."

Serapio tilted his head, as if considering. And then he tossed his staff to the side, letting it clatter to the ground and be lost in the fog.

Okoa watched, baffled. "What are you doing?"

Serapio walked to the weapons wall, black skirt billowing around him, skin slick from rain and exertion. He went to the bench and rummaged through Okoa's discarded clothing.

"What are you doing?" Okoa repeated, voice rising in alarm. He could see the jeweled handle gleaming through the mist.

Serapio's hand wrapped around the hilt, and Okoa's heart stopped, a surge of panic constricting his chest. Serapio raised the sheath, studied it for a moment, and then tossed it toward Okoa.

Okoa caught it from where he lay on the ground, panic ceding to fear and confusion. He stared as Serapio worked his way along the shelf of bladed weapons. After some consideration, he chose an obsidian dagger, similar in size and style to the golden one Okoa clutched to his chest.

Dagger in hand, Serapio returned to the side of the arena where he had begun. He motioned for Okoa to stand.

Okoa rose slowly to his feet. "You knew," he accused, his emotions a whirlwind.

"I am not a fool, Okoa," Serapio said, voice calm and even. He swung his knife in a wide arching X shape as he tested its balance. "I know the Sky Made plot behind my back."

"Then why am I here?" Okoa asked, his anger prickling. "What game is this?"

"No game. Destiny." Serapio shifted into a fighting position, knees and elbows bent, hands at his center. "I mean for us both to decide our destiny today."

Okoa swallowed. Did he want this? Skies, he did not know. Sometimes he could see no path forward without Serapio's death, and other times Serapio was the only way forward. If he killed him now, did he save Carrion Crow, or did he damn them? And what of himself? Saved? Or damned?

Duty. His cousin Chaiya's words came back to him from the day in the great room when he had first brought Serapio to Carrion Crow. *Duty is all you need to know. The rest will only confuse you. Do what duty requires, and you will always be in the right.*

"Very well, then, Serapio. Destiny." And Okoa took his own fighting stance.

Serapio laughed, a jarring sound from a man about to fight to his death. His laughter was muffled by the mist and echoed eerily around the area.

"You have never said my name before. Always Odo Sedoh. Never Serapio."

Okoa frowned. Was that true? But he had no time to contemplate the charge, as Serapio moved, and the fight began.

Just as before, they circled each other, feet sliding across the sand. The sleeting rain had increased its fury, as if in sympathy, and it bit at Okoa's bare skin like glass. He ignored it, mind focused on Serapio, watching for the barest shift of weight, the smallest twitch of his muscles, the tilt of his torso.

When Serapio moved, arm shooting forward, Okoa was ready. He turned to the side, letting Serapio's blade miss him, and then slashed upward in a backhanded strike. It was the right attack, and against another opponent, he would have drawn blood, but Serapio's speed had him moving before Okoa could connect.

They spread out and circled again, each waiting for an opening.

This time Okoa moved first, a chopping vertical forehand. Serapio avoided it, but instead of countering or making space between them, he crowded Okoa's guard. Surprised, but seeing the opportunity, Okoa's hand shot forward in a quick horizontal jab, aiming for Serapio's heart.

Serapio caught Okoa's arm, stopping the knife a finger's breadth away from puncturing his flesh. Okoa leaned forward, putting his weight into it. It was a risky move. He remembered too late that Serapio liked to make an opponent commit and then take them to the ground, and at the last second Okoa tried to pull back.

But Serapio held him close, denying Okoa's retreat, and dragged them both down.

Okoa fell on top of him, gravity and weight driving the knife even closer until the tip of the blade pressed against

Serapio's bare chest. He winced at the pain but did not try to throw Okoa off, resisting only enough to keep the blade from piercing him further.

"Okoa," he said, voice tight. "I am sorry."

At first Okoa didn't hear, eyes focused on the tip of the golden dagger where it met skin, mind working to puzzle out why Serapio wasn't fighting back and what counteroffensive would come next.

But then the words penetrated, and he met Serapio's gaze.

"I'm sorry," Serapio repeated. "For being yet another burden."

Okoa's mouth worked, suddenly dry, mind scrambling to understand.

"Your father, Ayawa. Your mother. Your sister and the matrons. They have all placed a weight around your neck. You carry too much."

Okoa's breath came in pants, his pulse like a hammer inside his skull.

"Your cousin. I am sorry for that, too."

This is a trick! he thought, wild fear making his heart gallop. He growled and pressed harder against the knife.

"Stop talking!" he barked.

But Serapio would not. "I know what it is to bear the weight of other people's dreams, to be bound to realize their desires over your own. I see your struggle, as it is mine, too. Forgive me for adding to your pain. I never meant to divide you from family and clan, from yourself."

"You overestimate your importance to me," he hissed, but it was a lie, and they both knew it.

"I'm going to remove my hand," Serapio said, voice a strained whisper, "and let the blade find its mark."

"What?" Okoa's head felt light with shock, and his hands began to shake. "What are you saying?"

"I will release you from this burden. It is my choice. You are not my murderer if the Crow God Reborn chooses to die."

Okoa could feel Serapio's grip loosen, and the knife pressed deeper, sinking into Serapio's flesh and drawing bloody ichor to the surface.

"No!" Okoa screamed, an incoherent cry. He flung himself backward, away from Serapio. He let the knife fly from his hand as if it burned him, and it tumbled to the ground.

What was Serapio doing? He was supposed to fight. To call a devouring shadow, to bleed black ink, to become a monster.

But instead . . .

I release you from this burden.

You carry too much.

I am sorry.

Something inside Okoa broke, and the sorrow of years bubbled out in a choking sob, grief he had never allowed himself until now.

He wept for his father and the shame of being a traitor's son. He wept for his mother, betrayed and murdered by her own kin, and for Chaiya, who had tried to do the right thing and done everything wrong instead. He wept for his people, slaughtered by those they had trusted to protect them.

And he wept for himself, foolish lost boy, faithless son, inconstant friend.

His body shook with the weight of it, and he buried his head in his hands, lost in the flood.

He did not know how long he stayed there on his knees, silently sobbing, shoulders quaking uncontrollably in the freezing rain. But he eventually became aware of arms encircling him, of a gentle pressure gathering him close.

"I am here, Okoa," Serapio whispered. "You are not alone. You do not have to bear this life alone."

Relief. That was the emotion he felt. He knew he should be embarrassed by his weakness, should push Serapio away and stand, but he wanted to stay there a little longer in the warmth of his embrace, to know that he was not alone and that his god was with him and did not loathe him for what he had done, did not condemn him for his infidelity. But instead, he asked Okoa to forgive *him*.

"I was ashamed," Okoa whispered. "I wanted them to be proud. To see that I wasn't like my father. But I was. I am. And I . . ." He sucked in a breath and gently pushed Serapio away, just enough so that there was space between them.

"It is I who am sorry," Okoa continued. "After Chaiya, I thought you irredeemable. I could not see that my condemnation was a mirror of what the matrons had done to my own father. I let fear drive me."

Serapio stood and held out a hand. In his open palm was the golden dagger, once again in its black sheath. He must have retrieved it when Okoa was lost to his grief.

"Take it," Serapio said.

"What?"

"Take it and keep it, and should you ever feel I am irredeemable, use it against me. But know that I will not die easily." He smiled. "You will have to earn my blood upon that blade."

"I don't understand."

"You were not wrong to think me lost. I have struggled, too. But when we were in the rookery, you asked me to be the blade and bulwark of Carrion Crow, and I have become that. Not only for our clan but for this whole city. And I vow I will remain that as long as this city needs me. If I break that vow, take up that dagger, and we will meet here again and stay until only one of us leaves. But for now, join me. Be the sword and the shield with me."

Okoa's stomach knotted. He was exhausted, confused, wrung out from heartache. "I . . . I need time."

"Before you answer, there is one more thing." Serapio whistled sharply, and a great crow, somewhere above beyond the fog, replied.

Okoa's eyes widened.

"Is that her?" he breathed, joy rushing into the place where grief had left him empty. He scrambled to his feet, searching the skies, hope blooming.

Benundah swept down into the courtyard, her great black wings spread wide. She landed lightly and clicked her beak in happy greeting, prancing lightly from foot to foot. And Okoa, trembling, reverent, went to his crow.

His fingers brushed across her ruff, and he mumbled nonsense words of regret and reunion. Later, he would not remember exactly what he said, only that he said words of love and Benundah had returned that love in her own way.

Serapio whistled again, and another great crow emerged from the fog, gliding down to join them. She was smaller than Benundah in body, although her wingspan was somewhat greater. And she had a voice unlike any he'd ever heard, a half cry as if her throat had been damaged. But most remarkably, she was white.

"This," Serapio said, affection infusing his voice, "is Achiq."

"She is beautiful."

"More strange than beautiful," Serapio amended, "but there is beauty in strangeness, is there not?" And Okoa thought Serapio meant the observation for himself, too.

"Where did you find her?"

"She came to me. I do not know from where. She appeared one day in the aviary, and she cried until I came." He rubbed his hand across Achiq's head. "I stayed with her for a fortnight. She required hand-feeding, and I dared not leave her alone until she was well enough to eat by herself."

"You cared for her?"

Some emotion passed across Serapio's face that Okoa could not read, and the Odo Sedoh smiled. "I did."

"Sometimes I sleep in the aviary even without a crow to nurse to health," Okoa confessed. "It is the only place I can find peace. And Esa hates it there, so she will not bother me." Oh, Esa! She was probably pacing the halls of the Great House at this very moment, not knowing if he was alive or dead.

"Yes," Serapio agreed. "It is a quiet place to think." He tilted his head toward Okoa. "Shall we ride?"

Okoa had come to the Shadow Palace weighed down by indecision and obligation, fear and shame. But now he felt lighter than the smallest feather. It was as if he had been washed clean of all that had stained him and been given a chance to become someone new. Someone who lived on his own terms and in his own way. He could become the wise man, the faithful son, the loyal friend.

"I would very much like to ride," he said.

Serapio held out his hand. Again, he proffered the golden dagger. And this time, Okoa took it and reverently slipped the cord over his head.

"Allies?" Serapio asked, tentative.

"No." Okoa pulled him into an embrace. "Brothers."

CHAPTER 20

On earth, in heaven, and within,
Three wars to lose, three wars to win.
Cut the path. Mark the days. Turn the tides.
Three tasks before the season dies:
Turn rotten fruit to flower,
Slay the god-bride still unloved,
Press the son to fell the sire.
Victory then to the Carrion King who in winning loses everything.

—Coyote song

Hours later, when Serapio returned alone from his flight with Okoa, Maaka and Feyou were waiting. He could hear them as they climbed the stairs to the aviary to welcome him back, heavy footfalls on stone, their voices echoing up. No doubt they both would have strong words for him.

He had told Maaka that he planned to woo Okoa to his side but not the how of it. He knew his Tuyon would have been appalled by his willingness to put his life in danger to secure Okoa's loyalty, but Serapio had known it was the only way. Had he not, Okoa would have never believed, would have never understood that Serapio was sincere.

And he had been sincere.

He had come to the arena with a plan in mind, but the words he had spoken to the Crow captain had come to him in the moment, inspired by his own thoughts and feelings. He had known what Okoa needed because he had realized that Okoa and he were not so different. They both bore the burden of the generation before them, living under the weight of other people's expectations. Only Okoa had never had a mother to set him on the path of destiny, had never had a god to inspire him.

Until now.

That was what Okoa needed. Someone to take the burden from him, someone who offered him forgiveness from his troubled past, someone who showed him what path he should walk, and then walked it beside him.

Because Serapio had realized something else.

Okoa wanted to believe. He wanted to forgive Serapio for the piles of bodies he left in his wake. He desired an excuse, some reason to look past Serapio's brutalities, to justify the cruelty he could not otherwise accept. Naranpa had told him to show Tova that he was human, but she was wrong. He needed to show Tova that he was a god.

And, just as important, he could be the god that they each desired, a god according to their individual needs, not bound by human weakness or morality. He would understand their hungers, unravel their deepest yearnings, and become many-faced, slipping into whatever mask was required to reach his goals.

After all, was that not what a god did?

The wooden gate to the aviary swung open, and Maaka and Feyou entered.

"Odo Sedoh," Maaka said, and "Odo Sedoh," Feyou echoed.

Serapio acknowledged their arrival with a nod but did not stop filling the crows' trough. He had dipped a hand in earlier and, finding it low, decided to fill it.

He could feel his Tuyon waiting, their impatience at odds with their deference. But he did not hurry. He knew they would wait.

Because he gave Maaka and Feyou the god that they needed, too.

They hung back until he had finished his task, but the moment he turned, they were there, questions bubbling from their mouths.

"Where is he?" Maaka asked, and Feyou, "Are you hurt?"

And then, "He is not to be trusted."

"You are too important to take such risks."

"Why did you not warn us?"

"Why did you not let us help?"

Serapio raised a hand, and they fell to silence.

"Okoa is managed," he explained. "He now serves as my general and is loyal to our cause. I delivered him to the Eastern districts, where he will work with the master engineer to bolster our defenses. She has devised a way to slow any advance should the Treaty armies attack overland from the west."

The master engineer was an ingenious woman, part of the Water Strider clan. She had shown up on the doorstep of the Shadow Palace with a map, a plan, and a note of introduction from her matron. Serapio had listened to her proposal for less than a quarter hour before he knew that her ideas were sound. He had placed her in charge of securing the Eastern districts, the farmlands past Coyote's Maw, against an overland attack, but the insights of someone like Okoa, who had lived in Hokaia and knew the spearmaidens and their ways of war, would be invaluable to her. Later he would need Okoa on the front lines, but right now he was most useful elsewhere.

It also kept Okoa out of Tova proper and away from the clutches of the matrons and his sister. If he could have sent Okoa farther away, he would have. Some kind of diplomatic mission to the Empire of the Boundless Sea to the west or south to the lands beyond the Obregi Mountains. But he needed him close in case his role in Zataya's prophecy was not yet done.

Serapio did not doubt that over the next hours and days, Okoa would question whether he had made the right decision or had been caught up in emotion. He knew that the traitor's son possessed a changeable nature that might be swayed should someone else whisper sweeter words in his ears than the ones Serapio had offered, although Serapio was not sure that was possible. Nevertheless, he would keep him away from the Shadow Palace as long as he could, hidden out in the far farmlands with the engineering corps, where his only purpose was to bloom.

Turn rotten fruit to flower.

"I expect you to keep his whereabouts to yourself," he said to his Tuyon. "It is best to give the matrons time to digest their failure to kill me with Okoa out of their sight."

"They will think he is dead," Feyou said.

"And we will not contradict them."

"It will scare them," Maaka said. "Slow their scheming. They will know that you know of their duplicity."

"Let them tremble," Serapio said. "Let them wait to see what I will do. If I will come to their door demanding blood as I did from Golden Eagle."

"Odo Sedoh," Maaka said, reverent with awe at the audacity of such a thing, but Feyou was silent, and Serapio knew she disagreed. Feyou would not contradict him in words, but she certainly made her opinion known without them.

"I have no desire to raze the clans," he assured her. "Only to make them worry that I might, for them to know that I could. I know we need them. Their soldiers, their armories, their water striders and winged serpents. I am not so impetuous, Feyou."

She made a sound like a hiccup of breath. "Odo Sedoh," she said, her relief evident. "I would never question your judgment."

Would she not? Well, he meant to test that now.

"I have a task for you, Feyou."

The idea had come to him all at once. The talk of the matrons, the need to keep them off-balance and unable to predict what he might do next. It was a good strategy, and the idea had given him an even better one.

One that also served Zataya's prophecy.

Even if it burned his tongue to say it, even if he feared that should he ever find Xiala, she would hate him for it.

"Find me a bride from among the Sky Made scions."

When Zataya had first relayed the prophecy, he had refused to think about the second task, the slaying of the god-bride still unloved. In his heart, his bride could be no one but Xiala, and there was simply no way he would harm her. He would rather die himself, prophecy be damned.

But then he remembered that prophecies were slippery things and could be manipulated. So he would manipulate it. If the sacrifice of a stranger would save Xiala, he would do it, even if the marriage that came before felt like a betrayal.

Maaka inhaled sharply, and Feyou could not stop the small exclamation of excitement that burst from her lips.

"I also do not question your judgment, Odo Sedoh," Maaka said, after the moment of shock had passed, "but why?"

He could see how his request disturbed them. Not because

they objected to him marrying, but because they were concerned that he was acting irrationally. First Okoa, and now this. But could they not see his wild success with Okoa? Could they not trust?

He could tell them about the prophecy, and that might allay their fears, but what then? Confess that he meant to marry simply to have his new bride slaughtered? It was a cruel proposition even for a god, and one that did not make him proud. But if saving Xiala forced him to be a monster, a monster he would be.

He turned to Feyou. "Do you remember when you told me that the city needed something to celebrate? Something to rally the people to my side, not only out of duty and fear but out of joy?"

Their conversation had come on a dreary evening a few weeks ago. Feyou had been giving him the news of the day, a building dispute in the Maw that Sedaysa could not settle, repair requests for a bridge in Kun, when Feyou had suggested he marry.

At the time, he had dismissed the idea, but she had persisted.

"It would secure your position and be a show of commitment not only to the matrons but to any doubters in Carrion Crow. They would see that you are part of this city, that your life is here, and that you have hope for our future."

"I have bled for this city and will bleed for it again. I would die to protect Tova and her clans, and you think I should give them even more of myself?"

"Death, Odo Sedoh. All that you give is noble, but it is the business of death. Is there no space for celebration? For life? There is a saying: A crow cannot feast on famine. You literally starve them of sunlight. Can you not find a way to grant them some small pleasure?"

Pleasure, he had thought. *What is pleasure but the sharp edge of a new blade? The satisfaction of an enemy slain? And—* unbidden—*the taste of honey licked from Xiala's fingers.*

He had flushed at the sudden memory, the feel of her skin against his, the sounds of her sighs as he had brought her to climax.

"Does not the defeat of their enemies give them pleasure?" he had offered weakly.

"All I ask is that you think on it," she had said, and set the matter aside.

Well, now he had thought on it.

"I have decided you are right, Feyou. I owe the city something joyous before the hardships of war set in. It will also unbalance the matrons, which is a boon that cannot be overlooked."

"They will find hope in it," she said, her voice thoughtful, mind no doubt awhirl with possibility.

Hope. Joy. Oh, how he deceived.

"Then it is settled," he said. "How soon can it be arranged?"

"There is much to do to prepare for such an event," Feyou said.

"Can it be done in a month?"

"I do not think—"

"Let me be clearer. You have one month."

Feyou's voice quavered but strengthened as she went along. "It will be done. I already know of two candidates. One of Winged Serpent and one of Water Strider. Both relations of the matrons and of an age. Pleasant young women, and beautiful."

"It matters not what she is like or how pleasant she is, as long as the marriage is secured." The less he knew of her, the better.

"It may be bold of me to say, Odo Sedoh, but perhaps you

will enjoy her company. I know this marriage may be only a duty in your mind, but pleasure can be found in obligation, too."

For all his terrible scheming, he could not hold back. "Are her eyes like rainbows?"

"Pardon?"

"Is her hair the color of plums? Does she smell of ocean magic? Then there is no pleasure for me in this. I will see it done"—*for you, Xiala, to spare you*—"but do not ask me to enjoy it."

"Yes, Odo Sedoh," she murmured, and he dismissed her to go about her new assignment.

Maaka turned to follow, but Serapio called, "Stay one moment, Maaka. I have a task for you as well."

"I serve," he said, voice dropping low.

"There is someone I need to find."

"Tova is large, but it can be done."

"In Obregi."

"I have never traveled so far." Maaka sounded worried.

"You will go with two crow riders. Flying should make quick work of the mission. Two weeks should be sufficient."

"Obregi is wide, is it not? I do not mean to argue, but once we have arrived, it will still take time to search an entire country. I have heard it is mountainous, the terrain steep and difficult."

"I will make you a map. I know exactly where the man is whom I seek."

"Who is he, Odo Sedoh?"

"I need you to bring me my father."

CHAPTER 21

Even the sea cannot stay calm before the storm.

—Teek saying

The great pit fires burned night and day, steaming the seaweed-wrapped black trunks of future tidechasers until the wood became soft enough to carve. To Xiala's surprise, the women had managed to hack out the bulk of a hull on a new canoe by the next morning. They continued apace for the next week, meeting Tuun's impossible deadline. But there was no celebration of their accomplishment. Only a desperate sort of wariness, the threat of violence and consequences thick in the air.

"Another day a child does not pay for your idleness," was all Tuun said when she came to see the progress for herself. She did not stay long, only consulted with the guard on duty before going back to the main camp at the listening house.

"What does she do all day?" Alani asked as she watched Tuun stride away.

"Plot her empire," Xiala said.

"Empire?"

"She fashions herself an empress. She made that clear enough to me. Teek is only the beginning."

Alani pressed her lips together, saying nothing.

The women had taken to sleeping along the edge of the cove. It was easier to keep the fires burning when there was always someone to tend them. And there was other work to do, not only the stripping of bark and carving once the wood was soft but the cooking and keeping of camp. Besides, many of the women had voted to stay at the cove and not go back to their homes. With no children to care for, their thatched-roof huts felt empty.

And so Xiala and the rest labored and lived under constant watch. Two dozen guards encamped at the cove with them, although it was never the same troop for more than one day. And there was always at least one pair of spearmaidens among the men. Xiala noticed that some of the newer guards were lax about sticking resin in their ears, no doubt lulled to complacency by the security of the kidnapped daughters and the total lack of Teek resistance.

Only Teanni, with her seemingly unsinkable optimism, weathered their forced labor with any spirit intact. The rest worked, ate their meals, and longed for the only relief available: an exhausted sleep.

On the first day of the new week, Teanni joined Xiala by one of the pit fires.

"I'm ready," her friend whispered. She leaned the bucket she held in her hands over so Xiala could see that it was filled with small green fruit. "I'll have to brew it, though. They need to boil down."

Xiala tilted her head toward the cooking area. "Can you do it there?"

"They'll see." Her eyes darted toward the soldiers.

"Let them. They don't know what it is."

"What if they ask?"

"Make something up."

Teanni thought about it. "All right." With a sigh, she stood. "Might as well start now."

She took her bucket over to the cooking area. Xiala watched as she dumped the contents into an empty cook pot, poured water over them, and covered the top with a long, thin slice of bark. Laili, the woman whose mother Teanni had honored at the funeral and whose daughter Tuun had threatened, gave Teanni a strange look. No doubt she recognized the poisonous fruit and wondered why she would be boiling it in such quantities.

"Don't ask, don't ask," Xiala whispered to herself, but despite her fervent prayer, Laili made her way over.

"I want to help," she whispered, sitting down next to Xiala.

"It's nothing."

"Xiala." Her hands practically shook with unexpressed rage. "They murdered my mother, assaulted my daughter. I will help."

What could she say to such passion?

"Wait for my signal." She had not planned any kind of signal and did not truly have much of a plan, but it would give Laili something on which to focus, and hopefully keep her out of trouble.

The woman gave Xiala a fierce grin before rising and going back to her work. Moments later, Teanni left the pot over the fire and, trying her best not to draw attention to herself, returned to her duties.

None of the guards seemed to notice, and Xiala breathed a sigh of relief. Now they need only wait.

• • • • •

The next evening, as the sun settled in the west, Xiala, Teanni, and Alani huddled over plates of fish and corn cakes, all of them in good spirits for the first time in days. The pot of poison bubbled innocuously nearby, a merry sound to Xiala's ears. The sound of freedom.

"And there was the year when not a single sailor landed on our shores," Alani was saying as she ate chunks of fish. "Do you remember, Teanni?"

Teanni answered around a full mouth. "Some of the wise women proposed kidnapping raids."

"I remember!" Alani chuckled. "And all I could imagine was old Paamah running down some poor sailor along the mainland and demanding he service her!"

"What finally happened?" Xiala asked, intrigued. She had missed so much when she was gone, and what she had missed most was friendship. She had not had a good friend in a decade, save Serapio, and she had had him for less than a month. Her heart ached thinking of him now, but Tova seemed very far from Teek.

"Well." Alani drank from a cup. "Eventually a ship did come."

"A single man." Teanni held up one finger for emphasis. "He had been fishing off the coast and gotten lost. Looked half-dead when we found him, but as Paamah might say, half-dead is half-alive, too!"

"He must have been a terrible sailor to get so lost," Xiala said.

Alani grinned. "He may have been bad at sailing, but he was a prodigious lover once he'd had a few meals!"

The women laughed, and Xiala could not help but be heartened by their joy. She thought the tale was a story Serapio would appreciate, although she imagined he might blush if she explained Teek sexual practices to him. A smile stretched the edge of her mouth to think of it. She very much enjoyed making him blush.

Alani was the first to catch her breath. "He'd shared a bed with half the village before he collapsed one day and died." She cast a sly look at Xiala. "No sharks for him. We fucked him to death."

"It was the best month of his life, to be sure." Teanni reached for another corn cake.

"A small price to pay," Alani agreed.

The two women's eyes met, and they both burst out into a fresh fit of laughter.

The hard thump of a cudgel against rock startled the three. They looked over their shoulders to find a looming soldier.

"What's so funny?" he demanded to know.

The women lowered their eyes, the ease of the moment gone. Xiala tried very hard not to look at the boiling pot, but Teanni's eyes flicked toward the poison involuntarily.

"And what's that you're cooking?" the soldier asked. He lifted the bark lid with the tip of his weapon. Sweet-smelling steam wafted up. "A compote? Why aren't you sharing?"

Teanni's mouth worked, obviously searching for an answer. The woman was wholly unsuited to subterfuge, but if the soldier tasted from the pot, it would be a disaster. The poison was not subtle, and at its current concentration, it might not kill, but his throat would burn, and he might experience temporary blindness. They could not let him touch it.

"It's medicine," Xiala said quickly. She thought of the Cuecolan sailors with whom she had spent so many years and their superstitions around women. Surely this soldier would not be so different. "We drink it during our moontime."

"Yes," Teanni agreed. "For our monthly cycle. It eases the pain, lessens the cramps and bleeding."

Xiala picked up her cup and motioned as if she would dip it into the pot. "Would you like some? I don't know what it might do to a man, but . . ."

He shuddered. "Do I look like a fucking fishwoman?" he muttered before he turned away.

The women held still until he'd made his way to the other side of the camp and begun to harass another group of women. Once she was sure the danger had passed, Xiala breathed a relieved sigh.

"That was very close." She realized she was sweating despite the cool evening.

"Too close," Alani echoed.

"How long until it's ready?" Xiala asked Teanni.

"Right now, it might cause stomach cramps, vomiting, but it needs two more days to ensure its potency."

"We don't have two more days," Xiala said. "We've already pushed our luck. And when none of us drinks from the pot, he or another will grow suspicious. We have to do it tomorrow."

"What if it doesn't work?" Teanni asked.

"It has to," Xiala said, voice grim, "for all our sakes."

• • • • •

They all worked in nervous anticipation through the next day, but to Xiala's relief, no one asked about the boiling compote, even as Teanni continued to ladle water into the pot throughout the morning and afternoon.

An hour before evening mealtime, Xiala came to hunch down by Teanni as she stirred the mixture.

"Ready?" she asked.

Teanni nodded. "Did you figure out how to get some to the main camp?"

"Laili volunteered to take half back to the listening house as a sweet treat. No doubt the soldiers there will intercept it and claim it as their own."

"What if they don't?"

"We'll have to take our chances. All we need to do is sicken enough of them for the children to escape. Laili will bring them here, and we'll all make a run for the far islands."

Footsteps, and the two women turned. A spearmaiden approached them, a wary look on her face. Xiala waited, mouth tight and heart thumping in her ears.

"I hear you have moontime tea," the woman said. Despite her first hesitation, what should have been a question came out more like an accusation.

"No," Xiala said smoothly. "You're mistaken."

The spearmaiden's brow furrowed. "Don't lie to me, Teek. Give me some of that tea."

"There's not enough," Teanni said, voice too high. "And this batch is not the best."

The spearmaiden thrust her weapon forward. "A cup! Now!"

Xiala's heart sank. What choice did they have? The spearmaiden would take it, even if they did not offer it up. And once she drank, it would only be minutes before their ruse was exposed.

She looked at Teanni, whose eyes were wide with panic.

"Give her a cup of tea, Teanni," she said steadily.

"But . . ."

"I said give her the tea."

Teanni's shoulders fell in defeat. She ladled up a cupful of the sweetly thick mixture, careful not to let it touch her skin, and poured it into a clay cup. Hand shaking slightly, she offered it to the spearmaiden.

The woman blew across the hot liquid before taking a tentative sip. Her eyebrows rose in surprise.

"It's sweet, like apples," she commented, before blowing across it again and drinking it all down. She tossed the cup to the ground and then, with a contemptuous sneer, kicked the pot over.

The poisonous mash spilled across the ground, their chance at freedom draining away with it.

Teanni gasped, and even Xiala could not keep the groan of dismay from her lips.

"Next time, you'll do what I tell you the first time," the spearmaiden spit before she sauntered away.

"How much time do we have?" Xiala asked as soon as the doomed woman was out of earshot.

"I-I don't know." Teanni's voice shook with fright. "I'm not sure of the potency. We could have ten minutes, or we could have a few hours." She wrung her hands. "Mother waters, Xiala, what do we do?"

Xiala looked over at the camp of guards. She counted twenty men with weapons and four spearmaidens. Could she Sing that many people down, and three of them women? She didn't know.

She had Sung enough to offer solace to her crew of twice that many on the Crescent Sea, and she'd Sung to calm the Convergence crowds in Tova. But those instances felt different. Those were gentling Songs, Songs of good memories and kindness. What she needed now were Songs of death, something like she had Sung to Pech. And it had to be strong enough to penetrate through the resin clogging their ears, although perhaps the Mother would decide that a bit of gum in the ear was no barrier to magic.

She looked at Teanni by her side and to the other Teek

around her. There was also the undeniable fact that she did not know what effect her Song would have on them. While she had not killed her mother with her Song, she had wounded her gravely. And that day in Hokaia, her Song had not killed any but Pech. Hurt others, yes, but not killed.

There was no predicting what might happen should she Sing now with the intention of killing. She might fail completely, and the soldiers would rush forward and slit her throat for the attempt and then turn their wrath on the children at the listening house. She might succeed wildly and kill her friends and all the Teek women at the camp, too.

Or . . .

A cough drew her attention. The spearmaiden.

She was leaning on her spear, clutching at her throat. Already there were specks of foam forming in the corners of her mouth. She screamed once, a strangling, awful sound, and collapsed on the ground.

And just like that, Xiala was out of time.

CHAPTER 22

CITY OF HOKAIA
YEAR 1 OF THE CROW

> I have dreamt many times of death, and yet I live. My be-
> loved Gwee says that death is not my destiny but that I am
> meant for something greater. Something more than even can
> be found in the dreams of gods.
>
> —From *The Manual of the Dreamwalkers*, by Seuq, a spearmaiden

When Balam had first awoken, he was sure that it was Saaya standing in his room. But the Priest of Knives had spoken and shattered the illusion.

It was clear xe had tripped the wards Balam had set and impaled xir feet on the floor. How foolish to think one could enter a sorcerer's quarters and not encounter magical defenses. That was the weakness of all the Meridian, spearmaidens and priests alike. They still did not quite believe in magic.

It was magic that saved Balam's life.

Had the assassin strangled him in his bed or poisoned his drink, Balam would surely have perished. But blades? A scrap of bone?

If there was anything Balam had mastered, it was blood.

He had already closed the wound in his stomach, forcing

the blood to congeal and harden, even as he revealed that the Sun Priest Naranpa was still among the living. But he had not expected Iktan to puncture his throat, too, and that had been a dangerous miscalculation.

Three things worked in his favor. First, Iktan was hurt, losing blood quickly and not at full strength, so the blow to Balam's neck with the dull piece of bone did not penetrate deeply. Second, Balam had ducked his chin at the last moment, forcing his airway to the back of his throat, where it was better protected. Still, the cut had burned like fire across his neck. Third, Iktan did not double back or linger to confirm the death blow, likely because the household had already raised the alarm.

Balam played dead, he was not ashamed to admit, until the priest left, climbing out the same way xe had entered. Once xe disappeared through the roof, Balam forced himself to his feet and made his way to the door. Someone was pounding against the wood and shouting his name, but all he felt was irritation. What good did knocking do if he was truly dying?

He worked the latch free, and Powageh practically tumbled through the entrance, blade in hand. Xe took one look at Balam, white robe stained crimson, and paled in horror.

"I'm fine," Balam said, although he did not sound fine. His rich, cultured voice was diluted to a rough, barely audible croak. He drew a finger along the skin at his throat, where the blood had hardened to close the wound. The blow had not severed his vocal cords, but he was not unscathed.

"Seven hells," Powageh breathed as xe took him in. "What happened?"

"I've been stabbed. More than once." He touched a hand to his stomach. It did not feel like the assassin had compromised any of his internal organs, and his magic had stopped any bleeding, inside and out, but, like his throat, that did not mean damage had not been done.

"A healer!" Powageh shouted as xe stepped into the hall. "Find a healer! Now! Get the damned personal healer to the Sovran if you must. But hurry!"

Running footsteps echoed as servants hurried to obey. Balam lowered himself to sit on the low table, exhaustion falling over him like a shroud. "The healer we brought from Cuecola will suffice."

"Two are better than one," his cousin said, "and you need to lie down."

Xe helped Balam to his feet and walked him to the bed. Xe poured a cup of water from the nearby pitcher. Balam drank, but the water seared his injured throat, and he winced in pain.

"Where's that damned healer?" xe muttered, and stalked back to the doorway to shout again at the servants.

"I'm sure they're coming as quickly as they can."

Powageh came back to sit on the edge of the bed. "Did you see who it was?"

"Quite clearly. We even had a conversation."

His cousin stared.

"One of your former compatriots. Iktan was the name, I believe. Priest of Knives?"

"You survived a Knife?" Disbelief colored xir voice.

"Is that so strange?"

"Strange and rare. And lucky. They usually poison their blades."

Balam opened his hand to show Powageh the sliver of bone still clutched against his palm.

"What is this?" xe asked.

"I can only assume it has something to do with the war college."

"The . . . I don't understand."

Neither did Balam, but he was not sure it mattered now.

"Iktan triggered the wards, and they worked as expected. You should find bloody footprints outside that will lead you to the culprit. I am impressed xe could walk at all, but I cannot imagine xe went far in that condition."

There was a commotion, someone running and shouting. A Cuecolan guard barreled through the door, looking panicked.

"Did you find a healer?" Powageh asked.

"It's Golden Eagle."

Powageh looked confused, but Balam pushed himself back to his feet.

"Show me," he said to the guard, already moving past the bedroom door.

"Where are you going?" his cousin shouted, trailing after. Xe caught up quickly, pulling Balam to a halt.

He swayed, hand braced against a nearby wall. He really wasn't well. He should definitely be in bed under a healer's care, preferably lost in a dreamless sleep. But he knew what Iktan had done, and he had to see for himself.

• • • • •

The bloody footprints were exactly where Balam had predicted they would be, and they led across the yard to the Mink Palace. The door was ajar, open to the morning breeze, and all was eerily calm. A handful of people in Golden Eagle livery wandered around, dazed. Others huddled together, hands over mouths, tears wetting cheeks. Somewhere in the distance, a woman wailed, her anguish filling the morning air.

Balam spotted the youngest daughter, Ziha was her name, sitting against the outside wall, knees pulled up tight to her chest and head resting across folded arms. He could not see her face, but it was clear she was in shock. Blood spattered the sleeves of her white shirt and coated her hands. He wanted to ask her what had happened and how she had survived, but she looked in no state to talk.

They crossed the threshold, Balam leaning on Powageh. His cousin had given up on trying to stop him once he had explained what Iktan had likely done, and now simply stayed at his side, making sure he didn't topple over.

The hallway was surprisingly clean, a trail of crimson footprints the only sign that violence had come this way. Of course, the guards had not tried to stop Iktan. Xe was one of them, and they had likely never suspected until it was too late.

But once they reached the central hall where meals were served, the scene changed.

There was a table set for breakfast. It was lavish, pitchers of iced juices and platters of cold meats, fowl eggs, flatbreads, and fruit spreads. There was seating enough for twelve along the low benches, and at the head of the table was the high-backed seat belonging to the matron.

Nuuma sat there now, head thrown back, an obsidian knife through one eye. Her chest gaped open, bone and muscle showing through.

"Skies," Powageh whispered. "Xe took her heart."

Balam could see that it was true. He looked around the table, half expecting the organ to be arranged in some gruesome display, but it was nowhere to be seen.

"And her tongue," Powageh added.

"A liar's tongue," Balam said, thinking of Iktan's face when Balam had revealed that Naranpa was alive.

And there, against the wall, was Layat, his spy. Balam regretted the loss. Layat had done what Balam had hired him to do, subtly influencing Golden Eagle to infiltrate the Watchers. But he had failed to stop Nuuma from replacing Naranpa with an uninvested Sun Priest before Serapio arrived, and that failure had led to the rise of the Carrion King and the necessity of this damned war to begin with. So perhaps his man had gotten the fate he deserved, after all.

Balam bent and examined the body. It, too, was missing a tongue. He scanned the half dozen people dead around the table. Most had died where they sat, but some had tried to run. They had not succeeded. Balam was certain that if he were to look, they would all be missing tongues.

A scream shattered the silence.

A woman burst into the room. She was tall, with a smattering of freckles over light brown skin. Her tawny hair was tangled, and her white uniform hung loose and unbelted, as if she had hastily dressed. She stumbled to the head of the table, eyes wild and searching.

Balam watched her pause, and reach out a hand toward the dead matron.

He knew who this disheveled newcomer was. The elder daughter. Terzha was her name. While the younger daughter clung to her mother's side, Terzha was her opposite. Never once had she attended a war council, and apparently, breakfast was not a priority, either. Rumor was that Terzha preferred to spend her days carousing in the gambling dens and her nights in the brothels. Another time, such behavior might have earned her a reprimand, but today it had saved her life.

She collapsed to her knees with a sob, wrapped her arms around her mother's corpse, and rested her head in her lap as she wept.

"Let's go," Balam said to Powageh. He had no desire to

witness this woman's grief. It felt like an invasion, and he had no comfort to offer.

Naasut was at the outside door, organizing spearmaidens into search parties to track down the murderer. While there was a clear footprint trail into the Mink Palace, there was no departing route. Which meant Naasut's efforts were futile. Balam was certain that Iktan was already out of reach. Someone like that? If xe did not want to be found, xe would not be.

When the Sovran saw him, she stopped. Her eyes widened as she took him in. "By Seuq's name, were you there, Balam? At the table with Nuuma?"

He shook his head, with effort. "Iktan paid me a personal visit before slaughtering half of Golden Eagle." He did not mention that it was he who had told Iktan about Naranpa and set the priest in motion.

"So it was Iktan." Naasut paced, wringing her hands.

He could not blame her. In all their planning, no one had foreseen this.

"But why?" she asked. "Why would Nuuma's own adviser turn against her?"

"Xe was the Priest of Knives," Powageh said. "One of the few surviving Watchers."

Naasut's shock would have been comical had the situation not been so deeply dire.

"In my city? She brought the Priest of Knives to my city?"

"Ex-priest," Balam corrected, and part of him wanted desperately to laugh at the absurdity of it. What *had* Nuuma been thinking, trying to keep someone like that on a leash?

"What do we do now?" Naasut asked, eyes moving between Balam and Powageh, who had slung Balam's arm over xir shoulder to help hold him upright.

"What do you mean?" he asked.

"Do we postpone our attack on Tova?"

"Absolutely not. I have explained to you the importance of the summer solstice."

"But we have lost Golden Eagle!"

"You have not lost Golden Eagle," said a voice from behind them. They turned and made way as Terzha emerged from the scene of the slaughter. Her uniform was bloodstained and her eyes red-rimmed, but her shoulders were set with resolve.

"Terzha—" Naasut began, but the woman cut her off with a look.

"My mother is gone. Foully murdered by someone she trusted. Someone she allowed into our household, someone who ate at our table day in and day out."

Balam did not mention that Nuuma's lies and treachery had likely led to her own demise. It seemed not the time.

"I am the matron of Golden Eagle now, and I will lead our eagle riders." Terzha looked at each of them, as if daring anyone to gainsay her. "We will free Tova from the Carrion King's grip and return Golden Eagle to its rightful place at the head of the Speakers Council."

Again, Balam did not mention that Golden Eagle had wanted that singular throne for itself, and if Nuuma had gotten her way, her puppet Sun Priest would have ensured that she was queen in all but name months ago.

Terzha said, "I will personally hunt down Iktan Winged Serpent and avenge my mother."

A bold promise, and profoundly foolish, but passion often made people reckless. And who knew? Perhaps one day Terzha would be in a position to seek her revenge.

But Balam seriously doubted it.

• • • • •

They held the funeral the following day. It was a small affair, nothing like the state funeral Nuuma Golden Eagle might have received had she died among her own in Tova. But then, a fair number of the Golden Eagle delegation had been murdered, so who was there to arrange the funeral, much less attend it?

Balam attended, of course. Against the advice of his healer. But there were more important things than mending wounds, and assuring Naasut and Terzha that Cuecola stood by their side in this time of crisis was one of them.

While he would not thank Iktan for almost killing him, there were benefits to the assassination attempt. His injuries seemed to have absolved him of any suspicion of conspiring against his allies. He still did conspire, of course, but facing the Priest of Knives and surviving the encounter lent him something akin to celebrity status.

"You're a hero," Powageh informed him some days later. "I was at the market, and a vendor gave me these for free." Xe held up a bag of fruit. "Gratitude from a grateful city that apparently narrowly escaped a murder spree by an out-of-control heretic priest bent on punishing Hokaia for challenging the Carrion King."

Balam caught the persimmon Powageh launched in his direction.

"If I didn't know you were recovering in your bed this past week," Powageh continued, "I'd have sworn you spread that rumor yourself. It's certainly solidified the popularity of the war effort."

"I am innocent, Cousin," Balam assured him as he bit into the fruit. Rich juice burst across his tongue. His throat had mended enough that it no longer hurt to eat and drink, but the healer had not been able to do anything to restore his voice. It still came out in a hoarse rasp. "Everyone imagines themselves a freedom fighter."

Powageh sprawled across the nearby cushions. "How you managed to spin this invasion into the righteous comeuppance of a tyrant is one of your greatest feats."

"Everyone wants to be the underdog. You only need to give them license to claim it." He swallowed his last bit of persimmon and waved off Powageh when xe tried to give him another.

"Any news on the Priest of Knives?" Balam asked.

Powageh raised an eyebrow. "Did you expect any?"

"I imagine we will never see Iktan again."

Powageh considered this as xe ate. "So the priest is no longer a threat."

"Xe will always be a threat, as long as xe is alive. But xe is far from Hokaia by now, and it is doubtful xe will return to Tova." Balam explained that Iktan's parting words had been a promise to find Naranpa.

"Where is the former Sun Priest, anyway?" Powageh asked.

"If I had to guess? Somewhere near the Graveyard of the Gods."

"Why would . . ." Realization dawned. "Dreamwalking? How?"

"I haven't a clue. Perhaps she knew I stalked her dreams and sought a way to banish me."

"Not everything is about you, Cousin."

"Isn't it?"

Powageh ignored that. "Is she a threat?"

"I have taken precautions to keep her out of my dreams."

"Should I?" Xe looked concerned.

"I do not think she knows you exist."

Powageh flinched, as if from a blow. Balam had not meant his words as an insult but could see they had wounded anyway. He gentled his tone and said, "Come look at this. I found something of great interest in one of Seuq's lesser works."

"Just tell me," Powageh said, refusing the peace offering.

"Very well, if you wish to be stubborn." Balam picked up the book at his side and opened to the page he had marked earlier. "I found a passage that speaks of the dreamworld as the domain of the gods. She provides no practical instruction for accessing godhead, but I admit I am intrigued."

"Balam." Powageh's tone was disapproving. "You are about to have all the Meridian at your feet. Do you covet godhead, too?"

"Are you saying it would not be advantageous to have god magic on our side? There are stories from the Frenzy of things outside the ken of sorcery. Deeds the chroniclers cannot explain. Let us not forget that the one we hope to defeat is an avatar of the crow god."

"An avatar made through Saaya's sacrifice and the mutilation of a little boy. It was a steep price to pay."

"A worthwhile price, and you will not change my mind on it. But what if there was another way to create an avatar? *Is* another way?"

"If Seuq could have become a god, she would have. The stories from the Frenzy are just that. Stories."

"But if we could?"

"Stop."

"But—"

"Does your ambition know no bounds?" Powageh asked, incredulous. "Is there no cost too great for you?"

Balam had been leaning forward in excitement, but at Powageh's words, he paused. He stared at his glowering cousin, considering.

"My ambition is why you are here, Cousin." His tone was sharp, slightly condescending. Meant to remind Powageh that without him, xe would be nothing. "You are from one of Cuecola's great merchant families. You should know better than most that nothing is free."

"You think that I do not know that?" Pointedly, Powageh reached into xir sack and pulled out a small dirt-coated bag. Xe tossed the bag at Balam.

Balam peered inside and saw only a few dried caps and stalks of godflesh.

"It is all I could find," his cousin explained, not sounding particularly sorry. Xe had made xir disapproval of Balam's continued use of the godflesh obvious enough. "I tried all the underground markets, even the ones with questionable product. Everyone said it would be late summer before another harvest arrived."

"We don't have until late summer. I expect Tuun to return by the new moon, and then we sail for Tova immediately."

"Then we do it without dreamwalking."

"What about that healer in the Warrens? Did you check there?"

Powageh made a face. "She has a poor reputation."

"Try anyway. Surely you can manage an old woman." He tucked the godflesh into the folds of his robe. "And you? How fares your shadow sorcery? Have you memorized the incantation I found for you?"

Long ago, when Balam had chosen to master blood, Powageh had discovered an affinity for shadow. The sorceries overlapped in many ways, as both the magics were triggered by sacrifice and fed on blood, but it was the manipulation of the element itself that distinguished each discipline from the other.

That was not to say Balam had not dabbled in shadow. The time with the thief upon the jaguar altar, for example. But blood was his domain, and shadow was not a path he pursued very often. Better to task Powageh with the assignment.

But Powageh's gaze had drifted toward the far wall, away from Balam, a particular look on xir face that Balam knew well.

"Do you hesitate to perform the practical requirements of your art, Cousin?" Balam asked, impatient with Powageh's hesitance. "The shadow must feed, and if you do not offer it someone else's blood in sacrifice, it will take yours."

"I'm well aware of what the shadow requires." Xir tone was fractious.

Balam matched Powageh's irritation with his own. "For one who once trained as a tsiyo, you have become quite squeamish."

"Didn't you always accuse me of being a sorry excuse for an assassin?"

"A lackluster Knife, yes, but you were once a formidable shadow sorcerer."

"Careful, Balam. That almost sounds like a compliment."

"Not a compliment. Simply a fact. Magic is your birthright as much as it is mine, although I haven't seen you call shadow since—"

"Since Saaya killed herself? Is it any wonder I soured on sorcery after that? And you're wrong, anyway. I taught our boy, did I not?"

"He's not *your* boy," Balam snapped. "Do stop saying that."

He was not a man quick to anger. In fact, Balam found anger a wasteful emotion, a feeling that clouded one's judgment and led to rash actions that one later regretted, but Powageh's constant claiming of Saaya's son was like an itch beneath his skin. It had always vexed him, but with the recent dreams, the pain that he thought he had long put to rest had blossomed anew.

Powageh bristled. "What, suddenly I cannot claim Serapio as mine, never mind that I was the one who tutored him in Obregi?"

Balam already wished that he had held his tongue. "I did not mean—"

"In fact, we were so close that you once asked me to take his life if need be, because I was the person he trusted most in this world!"

First the accusation about his ambition, then the refusal to practice the shadow sorcery Balam had asked of him, and now this possessiveness of Saaya's son. It occurred to Balam that Powageh was trying to provoke him, but he was not sure why. Balam had done little but lie in his bed since his brush with death. Yes, that meant he had to rely on Powageh a bit more but was not enough to warrant his cousin's belligerence. Balam had been in such good spirits, but now uneasiness tightened his chest with foreboding.

"I concede your point," Balam said in his most gracious tone. "Let us move on."

But Powageh would not hear him. "I have as much right to call Serapio mine as any of our cohort, certainly more than you do, despite you and Saaya fucking every chance you—"

Powageh cut off abruptly, eyes wide, mouth open.

Something clenched in Balam's gut, but he worked to relax it, to keep any stress from his face. "You're right, Cousin," he soothed, reassuring smile firmly in place. "Of course, you are right. *Our* boy. All of ours. You, Paadeh, Eedi, Saaya. Our creation."

Powageh's face was soft with shock, all anger fled.

"And now I need my rest," Balam said lightly. "Still recovering, I'm afraid. The healer insists."

The servants had installed a bell system so that Balam could call them as needed from his sickbed, and he rang it now. The guard who had been standing at his door entered immediately.

"Powageh was just leaving." He gestured toward his cousin, toward the guard. "Xe needs help with xir sack."

Xe did not, of course, but the guard dutifully took it in hand, and now that they were not alone, Powageh had the sense to leave things be.

"We will talk later," his cousin said, annoyingly solemn.

"Whatever you are thinking, you are wrong." Balam's voice was firm, but his heart was racing. "The shadow realm. Think on *that* and not whatever other nonsense fills your mind."

Powageh left without another word, but xir last look had been one of compassion, much too close to pity for Balam's liking. He dismissed his overemotional cousin from his mind and focused on the idea of the dream realm as an ingress into godhood. That was worth his time. Not this sentimentality.

There was work to be done before they left for Tova, and he had been too long in bed recovering. Balam moved to his desk and opened the *Manual of the Dreamwalkers*. He read long into the night, well past supper, turning away all who came to his door, even the healer. He read until his sight was bleary and the words blurred, and he could no longer hold up his head.

He half expected the dead Hokaian woman to appear with her dire warnings, or for Saaya to come and sit with him through the dark hours.

Part of him mourned that she did not.

CHAPTER 23

What is love but a path through the darkness?

—*The Obregi Book of Flowers*

It did not take Naranpa long to pack, as she had brought little with her and had accumulated almost nothing during her time in Charna. By late afternoon, she was on the road.

She decided she would travel on foot until she was well away from the Graveyard. Transforming into the firebird and going by wing would be faster, but Kupshu's story of her daughter's tragic end had reminded Naranpa that this close to the Graveyard, the god's powers were amplified, and what was always unpredictable became chaotic.

There was only one road in and out of the village. It cut through desolate land. Long stretches of barren desert dotted with rough shrubbery and lichen-covered rocks. Occasionally she would spot a splash of color, pink and yellow flowers bunched on fuzzy stems, blossoming under the recent rains, but beyond that, her world was a flat sea of grays and tans. She wondered if godflesh might grow here in the open lands and occupied herself with trying to spot the fungus. She finally gave up. Godflesh, it seemed, truly was confined to the Graveyard.

At night she made camp around a pit fire and slept in the open. Her pack was her pillow, and her cloak served as a blanket. She had brought godflesh and considered making the tea that would allow her to Walk in her dreams, but she did not have water to spare for a bath, and she had completely forgotten to bring any of Kupshu's special soap. She decided the risk without the safety measures was too great.

Even so, on the third night, unprompted, she dreamed of Iktan.

Xe was hiding. Somewhere underground.

Naranpa could smell rich soil and spring grasses and the scent of dried reeds and wet stone. She could feel cold earth at her back and, somewhere above her, voices. And everywhere, blood. Blood on her hands, in her hair, flecking her face like drops of crimson moonlight.

And pain. Pain that had been all-consuming but had now faded to a constant throb. Pain that she strove to embrace lest it reduce her to a feral thing.

And there was something else. Something wet and heavy in a bag that she clutched to her side. Something precious. A gift. A triumph.

Naranpa tried to focus on it, but she was not dreamwalking. She had no power here; she was merely a passenger.

She had been in the ground for two days, and her belly was taut with hunger, her head throbbing from dehydration. She weighed the chance of capture against her other needs and dug herself out.

She had been in the ground, yes, but under a dirt floor covered by a woven rug, and upon that rug, a low table. She pushed it aside now and stood.

Half-forgotten pain roared alive. She stumbled. Looked down. Her feet were ruined, awful things. She swayed, dizzy, but made herself walk. Quietly, carefully, listening for any sound that might expose her, she crept down the hallway of an empty palace where bloodstains blackened the hard-packed earthen floors.

Something had happened here. Something terrible.

Something she had done.

Not her, she reminded herself. Iktan. This was not her dream, but xirs.

And then she was out into the night, atop a great pyramid mound and traveling through a foreign city interlaced by waterways. She made one stop, at a crone's house in the darkened alleys of a night market, and purchased medicine for her infected feet.

And then there was a barge. She paid a captain a small fortune to keep her presence a secret. The captain stowed her in a dank, musty closet that smelled of old, salt-crusted netting and rotted fish, where she starved and slept and tended to her mangled feet with what little medicine she had.

And all the time, through the pain and fear and darkness, one thought kept her moving.

"Naranpa!"

She startled awake, half expecting to find herself tucked into a cramped closet on a boat.

"Who's there?" she called. "Hello?"

Wind across the desert was her only answer, but the sound of her name still echoed. Her fire had faded to embers, and she rose to stoke it. It was cold, still well before dawn, but she had slept enough, dreamed enough, and after a plain breakfast, she set out again.

The dream haunted her, even in the waking world. She

wished Kupshu was with her, and they might discuss it over tea, a tuktuk blanket around her shoulders. But even without Kupshu's insight, Naranpa knew her dream of Iktan had been more than a dream. It was closer to a vision, almost like the one she had seen in Zataya's mirror so long ago that showed her past, present, and future.

"Magic!" she exclaimed. Something in the bush along the road startled and darted away. She caught the flash of a fur-covered tail as the animal ducked behind a pile of rocks.

Of course, it was magic. That magic was still the last possible explanation to come to mind was proof that her years of training in logic died with difficulty. Slowly, she was learning new ways of thinking about the world, but it still did not come naturally.

And yet not all the knowledge that she had acquired at the celestial tower had to be discarded. She had trained as a hawaa, Order of Oracles, and she could still read the heavens. She did not have her tools here, but the memory of how to create a star map to tell one's destiny was embedded in her bones from years of practice.

Naranpa decided she would try to discern Iktan's fate and, from that, determine where xe might be. She told herself that whatever the map revealed would be a comfort. Better than thinking xe was under siege by enemies, as she had first seen in her dreamwalking. Or hurting and hiding, as in her more recent vision.

Once the sun had set and the heavens were a canvas of stars above her, she began her work. Instead of bark paper, she cleared a square of dirt in front of the fire to use as her canvas. Instead of a hair-tipped stylus, she drew on the ground with a dried twig.

She knew Iktan's birthdate and that xe had been born in

Tova in the house of Winged Serpent. She plotted those constants first.

And then she looked to the stars.

Naranpa knew by rote the common aspects of the heavens, the rising and falling of celestial bodies in concert with the seasons. She mapped the current sky above, creating orientations between the sky house of Iktan's clan and the day of xir birth. From there, she drew a curving line stretching across the inky canvas and into the future, the trajectory of Iktan's life.

Too many times, Iktan's life path traveled through the space between stars, signifying death. But xir path did not linger in these empty places. It continued, across the cluster they called the Spider's Web and through the great stretch of the Cosmic River.

She stopped when Iktan's path aligned with the current date. The arc she had drawn rested on the star called Homeland, the star that the Sky Made believed their ancestors had come from and where they would return upon their death.

She sat back, uncomforted.

Her divination meant that Iktan was going home. That much was clear. But what was home? Tova? She did not know for certain that Iktan had even left, although the vision of the mound city suggested that xe had. Home could also mean death, a return to the ancestors, the Sky Made's final home. It was just as likely that Iktan was not dead yet but would be soon.

Frustrated, she swiped a hand across the star map, scattering her careful lines.

It wasn't enough.

Her gaze drifted to her travel bag, to the godflesh within. She could find answers. All she had to do was dare.

She pulled the godflesh from her bag. She broke off half a

cap and stuck it in her mouth, worried that if she took the time to make the tea, reason would set in, and she would change her mind. The taste was overwhelming, so much worse than its liquid form, but she forced herself to chew. Once the godflesh was a mealy paste in her mouth, she swallowed.

Her firebird talisman hung from her neck. Naranpa took it between her hands and settled into her meditative pose, the one Kupshu had taught her so well. Back straight, legs folded beneath her.

Soon she was in her library at the Handmaiden, searching the shelves for Iktan's book. Before, it had been red and alive, a beating heart in her hands. Now it was a wound festering around the edges of the binding.

Dread filled her as she opened the book and fell into Iktan's dreams.

She was back in the scorched wasteland of bones and dead things. Sickly clouds boiled overhead, and lightning punished the sky.

She looked for the figure in white.

"Iktan!?" she called, and her voice was swallowed by the vast nothingness.

She walked, trampling over carcasses bleached by time. Occasionally, she would find a corpse, human and fresh. Once she was sure she saw Nuuma Golden Eagle floating in a river of black blood, eyes staring. She averted her eyes and hurried past.

She wandered for hours, searching, calling out.

The rumble of thunder was the only sound besides her voice.

After what seemed like hours of searching, she dropped to sit on a desiccated tree stump, confused and frustrated. How could Iktan not be in xir own dreams?

Or maybe she was thinking about this all wrong. She already knew that time and space moved differently in dreams. And, unlike the vision, she was dreamwalking, and a dreamwalker could bend the dream to her will. Why chase Iktan when she could make Iktan come to her?

"See me, Iktan," she commanded. "See me!" And her words were not simply speech but the mighty force of her will. She said the command again, pressing the dreamworld to bend to her, to do as she demanded.

The sound was faint at first. Barely more than a sigh above the thunder. But it came again. A voice. Faint, damaged, but one she knew well.

"Iktan?" she cried, hope surging for the first time. "Is that you? Where are you?!"

Find me, Nara!

"I'm trying! Where are you?"

Hurting . . .

"I know, I know. Tell me where you are!"

Nothing, and desperation replaced hope. But this was a dreamworld, a place of perception and sight. Iktan did not have to say where xe was when xe could show her.

"Show me! In your mind. Show me where you are."

Gradually, the landscape changed. The barren waste melted and morphed, and Naranpa found herself standing before a squat plank building that hovered below snowcapped mountains. Rough men wearing animal pelts passed her on a steep stone-paved street.

North. Xe was in the north, on the far slopes of the great mountains. But that was not enough. What she saw could be a hundred different villages, and if Iktan was sick, close to dying, she did not have time to search them all.

"Something else, Iktan. Show me something else!"

The building rushed toward her, or she toward it, and she found herself with her nose almost touching the door. She stepped back. Carved in the wood was an animal head, furred, and with a wide maw and long teeth. Her first thought was of a coyote, but there were no coyotes in the north.

"A wolf?" she asked. "You're in a house marked with a wolf?"

Hurry, Nara!

"I'm coming, Iktan. I promise, I—"

She slammed back into consciousness, eyes wide and stomach heaving. Iktan must have woken up, with her still in xir dream, and the force of it threw her out of the dreamworld.

She stuck her fingers down her throat and made herself vomit up the contents of her stomach until there was nothing left. She could not spare the water but brushed her skin with fine dirt, hoping that it helped cleanse any lingering godflesh from her body.

She had meant to wait until she was at least a week from the Graveyard to call upon the powers of the sun god, but there was no time.

She had risked the godflesh for Iktan. She would risk this, too.

She strapped her travel pack on her back, summoned the firebird within her, and took to the sky.

· · · · ·

The first town she visited was little more than a waystation on the north-south road, and she learned nothing there. The next town was much the same, but by the third day, the snowcapped mountain range she had seen in Iktan's dream had risen in the distance.

Every night, she ate of the godflesh and tried to find Iktan's dreambook, and every night she failed. Either Iktan wasn't dreaming, or . . . she would not let herself think of what other reason Iktan's book might be absent from her library.

Four nights after she had cast her divination, Naranpa sat at a table drinking watered balché and forcing a paste of peppered beans down her throat. Rain had set in, and she had sought shelter and a hot meal at a travelers' inn. There were not many other travelers out on such a terrible night, but a woman and her infant child sat at the far end of her table, and they exchanged a polite hello.

"Traveling alone?" the woman asked. She was young, but her face was already lined by hardship. Her infant was strapped to a cradleboard and propped against the table. She spooned bean paste into the child's eager mouth and looked at Naranpa expectantly.

"I'm meeting a friend."

"Oh? In which direction? Perhaps we could travel together."

"I'm not sure," Naranpa admitted. "All I know is that I'm looking for a plank house marked by a wolf's head."

The woman smiled. "There's a dozen of those."

"I know." Naranpa's shoulders sagged.

"Anything else?"

"No. Well, paved streets and men in furs."

"Oh, paved streets? Then it's a town you want, and there's only one of those, if you're going south."

Naranpa leaned forward. "Where?"

"A day's travel once you reach the river. Follow the river around the bend, and Tleq's right there."

The river. Of course. Iktan had been on a boat.

"I don't know about the wolf's head house," the woman continued, "but chances are—"

"Thank you." Naranpa was already on her feet and gathering her things. "Thank you so much."

"Are you going to finish your food?"

"No, take it." She pushed the bowl toward the woman and hurried out of the inn. The rain had lightened to a cold drizzle, hints of spring in the air. She ran down the road, out of the village and far enough away from the scattered houses that she wouldn't be seen, and then she was flying.

$$\bullet \quad \bullet \quad \bullet \quad \bullet \quad \bullet$$

Tleq was not much of a town, but it did have a wide paved road that ran from the docks to the central square in town. In Iktan's condition, Naranpa guessed xe had stayed close to the docks out of necessity, so she started there.

The first person she found was an older woman standing outside a wooden shack feeding what looked like household trash into a fire.

"I'm looking for a friend," Naranpa explained, hand covering her mouth to keep out the acrid smoke. "Xe might be injured. Or sick. Or both." She dug in her bag and brought out her purse. She offered the woman most of the cacao she had left. "I think xe might be staying in an inn marked with a wolf."

The woman's eyes cut warily to Naranpa. A hand darted out to snatch the cacao, and it quickly disappeared into an apron pocket. "Wolf's Head's down that way." She pointed with her chin down a muddy path on Naranpa's right. "But I heard somebody died there just yesterday."

"Yesterday?" Stars and skies, let her not be a day too late. "Did you hear anything else?"

"Just that it was a foreigner off one of the boats that come in. Could be your friend, could not." She shrugged hunched shoulders and turned away, obviously done.

Naranpa murmured a thank you and left.

The Wolf's Head Inn was a wide cedar-plank house with a small, rounded entrance. Naranpa had to stoop to enter. She straightened once inside and was greeted by a wide welcoming space. A rectangular fire pit dominated the center of the room, and all around the perimeter, people sat on wooden benches talking and eating. She scanned the faces, looking for the one she so desperately missed, but Iktan was not there.

She could see in the distance that the back of the house was partitioned into sleeping rooms by thick hanging drapes. A young boy sat on a bench at the entrance monitoring who came and went down the curtained hallway. She saw a man give the boy a purse of cacao. The boy took the money and carefully counted it before granting him passage.

Naranpa's heart sank. She had given most of her meager funds to the woman at the fire. But Iktan had to be in one of those back rooms, assuming xe was still alive, and Naranpa would not let herself contemplate any other possibility.

Naranpa approached the boy. "I'm looking for a friend."

"Two hundred."

"This is all I have." She emptied her purse. Less than half a hundred fell onto the table.

"Not enough." He looked bored. "You can ask in the kitchen for work."

"I don't have time. My friend is sick."

"Sick?" Curiosity flickered in the boy's eyes. "Heard someone sick died yesterday."

"Are you sure?"

"You can look for yourself for two hundred."

"I don't have two hundred."

He gestured toward her chest. "What's that?"

She touched a hand to her talisman. She had forgotten to tuck it under her shirt. "A firebird."

The boy grinned.

"This," he said, dragging close the money she had already deposited on the table, "and that." He held out a hand for the talisman.

The choice was no choice at all. She lifted the necklace over her head and gave it to the boy. He held it up, eyes wide as he admired the craftsmanship. "Near the back. Red blanket door."

She hurried through without another word, practically running, weaving through the maze of rooms and people until she was there.

The red blanket door.

No sound emanated from within, and even now, she feared she was too late. She pulled the blanket aside, heart hammering in her chest, breath caught in her throat.

"Iktan?"

The figure on the bed stirred and turned toward her. A prominent nose in a face of angles and planes, black hair that brushed the tips of xir ears, and intelligent eyes dulled by illness and pain.

"Do I dream?" Iktan asked in a voice weak with exhaustion but so familiar that Naranpa could not keep the tears from her eyes.

"You do not dream."

"I saw you there, in my dreams."

She nodded and approached the bed. "I know."

She wanted to embrace xir, cover xir much-missed face with kisses, but xe looked so frail. And she remembered how they had parted and was not sure such affection would be welcomed.

Iktan's eyes fluttered shut. "I'm afraid you arrived just in time to watch me die," xe said, voice barely a whisper. "The infection has set in, you see." Xe glanced to feet wrapped in bloody, dirty swathes of yellowed cloth from which wafted the faint odor of disease. "The sickness is in my blood. I'm sorry, Nara."

She laughed, half sob and half wild joy.

Iktan smiled weakly. "I suppose I deserve that, after what I did to you. At least you are here to hear me say that I am sorry. I have done many terrible things, but betraying you was the worst."

She sat on the edge of the bed. "Do you remember when the assassin came for me on Sun Rock, and you told me you were very hard to kill?"

"It seems I was wrong."

"No, Iktan. You were right."

She called upon the sun god. Power flared to life within her. Her eyes glowed golden, and her hands bloomed with light as her healing magic awoke. She reached forward, but Iktan caught her by the wrists, eyes wide and fixed on her shining palms.

"What is this?"

"Do you trust me?" she whispered, tears flowing freely now.

"More than that," xe said, voice filled with soft wonder. "I love you."

"Then let me save you, and then I will tell you everything."

CHAPTER 24

Joy comes not from living a long life but from living a life
with purpose.

—*Exhortations for a Happy Life*

Okoa looked out over the rushing water, his thoughts full
of nothing more than numbers. The length of the tributary
before him, the distance the water must travel, the force and
mass required to divert the water down the newly expanded
irrigation canal.

"More?" he asked the woman next to him.

"I think so."

He signaled to the engineer at the riverbank. "More!"

"More!" the man shouted back, and then turned to relay the
message to the next man who stood within shouting distance
on the stone berm that jutted out into the slow-moving river.

"More!" The cry went down the line until, in the river
proper, two dozen workers hefted more rocks into the current
to build out the makeshift dam.

"Changing the course of a river is not so easy," the woman
next to him observed.

"Nothing worthwhile is," Okoa replied, bending to quantify the impending rise while the woman paced nervously behind him.

"Patience," he murmured, but he felt the nervous anticipation, too. Slowly, slowly, the water demarcation line against the measuring stick rose. Okoa counted the notches and raised three fingers.

"It's working."

The woman beside him could not hide her satisfied smile. "It's time to put it to the test." She glanced at him. "You still going to come? I know the striders are not crows."

"Crow or not, I would not miss it." Okoa was most comfortable on crowback and in the air, but he had sent Benundah back to the aviary for now. The Eastern districts were no place for a crow. She needed food, water, a roost with other crows. It hurt his heart to have her gone, but this time he knew it was temporary.

So it was not a crow Okoa would ride today to monitor the course of their artificial river, but a water strider.

Today was not his first encounter with the giant insects. They were the preferred method of transportation where the ground turned swampy east of Titidi and the Maw. Here the land was marked by the rich silt and the high, slow waters of the Tovasheh's tributaries that fed the farmlands before dumping their riches into the great river. Over the past weeks, as Okoa helped oversee the diversion efforts in defense of the city, travel by water strider had grown commonplace.

If he had been asked a month ago what his life would look like, he would not have guessed this, not even in his wildest imaginings. After he had fought Serapio and been reunited with Benundah, they had gone flying. Okoa would have been content to circle the city, perhaps go as far as the rookery and back, simply for the joy of being with his crow again.

But Serapio had other plans. He had brought Okoa to the Eastern districts outside of Tova proper. It was lush country compared with the rocky cliffs of the city, cut through with irrigation canals and farms. They had flown until Okoa spotted a small makeshift camp of rounded tents, and Serapio had motioned them to land. As soon as they were on the ground, a woman in Water Strider blue had come forward to greet them.

"Ho, Serapio!" she'd called, and Okoa had been surprised at her familiarity, but Serapio had not seemed to mind.

"Ho, Enuka. I've brought a friend."

"Another Crow?" She had a distinct lilting accent. She may have been Water Strider clan, but she had been born in another land.

She looked Okoa over and grinned. "A strong one, and we always have need of that. But I have need of brains, too."

Okoa was taken aback, both by her manner and by the implied insult that he did not look very smart. "I was educated at the war college," he said stiffly.

"Oh, a scion, then." She did not sound impressed.

"But not today," Serapio corrected. "Today he is your apprentice."

Okoa startled. "Apprentice?"

"Maybe not apprentice," she said, eyes on the width of his shoulders. "You're a bit old, no?"

He was only twenty-one, but she was right that he was too old to properly be called an apprentice.

"It doesn't matter, I'll find a use for you." Enuka's look was assessing. "What did you learn there, at the war college?"

"History, philosophy." He glanced at Serapio, who stood unperturbed, gaze focused on the distance. "Weapons."

"Battle tactics?" she asked, brightening. "What the spearmaidens might do? How they might react to disaster in the field?"

"I know how they think," he confirmed. "I've studied their ways of war, read their accounts of the War of the Spear. The Cuecolan accounts as well."

"Spearmaidens, good. Cuecolans, even better!" She clapped him on the shoulder. "Yes, I think I can use you. I am the master engineer, Enuka."

"I am Okoa Carrion Crow."

"Out here we are all the same, Okoa. No scions, no ranks save master engineer, which is me, and you will find that I wear that title lightly." She made a face, as if the title truly meant little. "Does that offend you?"

"Offend me?" What did it matter, unless . . . "Am I to stay?"

"Yes," Serapio supplied, his attention coming back to them.

"But I'm not . . ."

Serapio wrapped an arm around Okoa's shoulders and pulled him into the warmth of his embrace. "She needs you," he said, voice low in his ear. "The city needs you. And you do me a favor."

And what could Okoa say but yes?

That is how it had begun, and since then, Okoa had eaten unseasoned cold beans wrapped in day-old corn cakes, slept in a drafty tent with half a dozen other men, and waded through swamplands and desert both, digging canals until his biceps burned and his back screamed in protest. On the days he did not manually labor, he measured water pressure against sluice gates downriver and advised Enuka on spearmaiden troop formations and attack styles.

And he loved every moment of it.

How Serapio had known precisely what he needed to clear his mind and give him purpose he did not know, but he was grateful for it. Hard work and measurable results for his efforts, every day. People who listened and followed the best idea, not the person with the most power or whose name they feared or wished to please. No subterfuge or casual lies, no betrayal as they all worked toward a common goal, no matter if they be Sky Made, Dry Earth, or clanless.

Best of all, here, among the engineering corps, he was no one of importance. No one knew him as Okoa Carrion Crow, son of the dead matron, captain to the new. No one knew his father or his history or anything at all, except that Okoa was willing to put his back into things, had useful ideas, and could not hold his liquor on the nights they passed a bottle around the fire. That had earned him some mocking from Enuka and the others, but he had taken it good-naturedly, and his geniality had impressed them enough that the mockery quickly turned to affectionate teasing as he was welcomed into the group.

And now here he was, diverting a river.

This particular river was called the Ulaya, and it was calm and placid this far north but raged as it met the boulders and narrow cliffs downriver before joining the Tovasheh.

"So we catch it where it's still calm," Enuka had said, "and bring it across the plains through a canal."

For the months before Okoa arrived, Enuka and her engineers had been widening irrigation canals and building a berm of rocks and logs, diverting the Ulaya so that it gathered against the sluice gate, a mighty tide waiting to be unleashed. Today they would see if their work paid off.

"Ready?" Okoa asked, eyes on the small flood buttressed against the gate.

"Aye," Enuka said, her voice its own ocean of worry. "Now or not at all."

"Shall you do the honors?"

"No." She shook her head. Pressed a hand to her stomach. "Too nervous. You do it."

Okoa grinned and pulled a small bag from their sack of supplies. He hefted it in his hand. Inside were Enuka's special blend of coloring salts: a mixture of dried dye crystals, salt, and bat guano from the caves of Coyote's Maw.

"Well, go on!" Enuka grumbled.

Okoa poured a handful of salts into his palm and flung them into the waiting fire. They cracked and popped until blue smoke rose in a long line, stretching into the sky. He could not see them, but he knew there were signalmen positioned every mile down the line who would see the smoke and throw their own blue dye into their signal fires. The gate operators would see, and one by one, they would open their gates to let the water through.

Once the smoke was steady, Okoa rushed to pull the gate. The lever groaned against the weight of the water, but the pulley finally cranked under Okoa's will, and slowly, slowly, the gate rose.

"Now we see if the flow is enough," he said.

"Or if it's too much and runs the bank," Enuka countered, biting nervously at her lip. It was a tricky balance to keep the flow strong enough to remain high until it reached the end of the course but not so powerful that it overflowed the canal, spreading and losing momentum.

"It comes," he said, voice rising in excitement as the flow started in earnest. The canal they had dug was as deep as a man was tall, and the two watched as the water quickly filled it.

"Perhaps we should step back," he said, mildly alarmed. They were high on the bank and should be safe, but Enuka's warning about the water breaching was well taken.

The woman grunted and took three long steps back. Okoa joined her, and from the safety of land, they watched the rushing wall of water pick up speed, rising all the while.

"Hold, damn you," Enuka muttered, eyes fixed on the canal.

"It will be a near thing," Okoa said, as the flood climbed its way up the earthen walls.

And it was, but as the water hurtled past them and they counted down the minutes, Okoa knew they had succeeded.

"We did it!" He hugged Enuka and whooped with the pure joy of a problem solved to perfection.

She grunted in his embrace but allowed it, and when they separated, he saw she could not keep the grin from her face.

"We follow?" Okoa asked, all boyish excitement.

"Aye," she said, finally believing. "The flow is strong here, but let's see if it makes it to the cliffs."

Twenty miles. The flow had to hold for twenty miles without overflowing its banks before it tumbled off the cliffs and into the Tovasheh.

They jogged to the water strider that waited, harnessed to a sledlike chariot on a shallow irrigation canal that ran parallel to their deep and newly dug one. Okoa and Enuka crowded onto the sled, Enuka trailing her sack of measuring implements and various coloring salts.

"It's working, Enuka," he assured her, taking the salts from her to lighten her load.

"It works when it's ended," she complained, as she tucked her instrument sack between her feet and settled in, but she looked hopeful.

Exhilaration pumped through Okoa's veins as they raced down the canal, their sled gliding along behind the giant insect. He would never have thought being pulled behind a bug the size of a house would be quite so invigorating, but with the spray of water misting his face and the wind blowing his hair back, he could not deny the thrill of it. He had known little about water striders before, but Enuka had proudly informed him of their speed, strength, and stamina, and he had been impressed. His first ride on a sled cutting across the wetlands had dazzled him. It was not the freedom of flying, the world small and far below you, but it had its own joys, and he felt privileged to experience them.

"Keeping apace," Enuka shouted, pointing toward the canal. And they were, the water strider matching the speed of the flowing river.

And so it went as they raced by signalmen and gate after gate, opened to let the flood through. Okoa raised a hand to each as they passed, and they returned the greeting, but there was no time to stop if they wished to see the water as it reached its terminus.

The first rush of adrenaline had fled, and Okoa was resting, eyes closed but not quite napping, when Enuka shouted that they had reached their destination. Once the sled came to a stop, they piled out, smoke and instruments in hand, and hustled to the mouth of the canal. Okoa watched with awe as the icy brown sluice roared over the side of the cliff and plummeted into the racing river below.

"Beautiful," he whispered.

Enuka was already on her knees, pulling her instrumentation free and belly-crawling to the edge where the measuring sticks had already been placed. Okoa waited as she checked the water levels and pressure. Finally, she nodded, satisfied.

"Signal the gates," she commanded. "Shut it down."

Okoa jogged back to where they had left the coloring salts and rifled through the bag until he found the pouch marked with a red dot. He stepped up a small rise where a small firepit waited. He quickly lit the fire, waited as it built to a steady blaze, and then threw a handful of salts in. He watched the smoke turn red, and then watched as the nearest signalman, easily seen from Okoa's superior height on the hill, followed in kind. Soon all the gates would close, and the canal would go dry again, where it would lie in wait until they needed it to form a defensive moat around the city and, if necessary, flood the land to make it impassible for an invading army.

Enuka had envisioned the moat, but the idea of flooding the land to slow the invaders had been his. At first, Enuka had balked, citing the possibility of lingering damage, but Okoa had reminded her that an army would have already decimated the farms and fields. It was then that he realized that for her, much of this was simply a grand experiment, a chance to put her ideas to the test, with little comprehension of the reality of war. Perhaps Serapio had understood that, and that was why he had asked Okoa to join the engineering corps.

But none of that was on his mind now. Now there was only joy.

"Success, Enuka!" he shouted as he rejoined her at the cliff's edge. "You did it!"

"We did it," she said, a grin splitting her wide face.

Yes. He had done his part. Not just the idea of flooding, but he had been in the field every day, taking measurements, hauling rocks. He had been a valued member of the team. It was something he could take pride in.

"Now what?" he asked.

The master engineer clapped his shoulder. "Now we celebrate!"

· · · · ·

Later, when Okoa and Enuka reunited with the rest of the engineering corps at base camp, they were greeted with cheering and foot stomping. After a round of congratulatory back

271

pounding, they breached a keg of balché and drank. Okoa was on his third cup, the alcohol fuzzing the edges of the world around him, when a cry went up for toasts.

Cazotz, the man who had first called for toasts, lumbered to his feet. He was clanless from somewhere south, a hireling brought on for his size and willingness to work. A big man, taller and wider than Okoa, with a voice and demeanor to match. He raised his cup.

"To Enuka!" he shouted, quieting the corps. "Our fearless leader. No idea too obscure, no progress too incremental"—that drew a few chuckles—"and no one else I would rather serve. You have proven yourself worthy of the title of master engineer."

Cries of agreement echoed around the camp, accompanied by enthusiastic clapping. Okoa added his voice to the congratulatory chorus, and they all drank.

Once the cheering had died down, Enuka rose to her feet. "To you all, who have labored with me in swamps and mud"—some shouts of misery there—"dug miles of ditches, eaten cold food, endured rainy weather and midge bites—"

"On my ass!" someone shouted.

"On your ass," Enuka conceded. "But still built the best damn canal Tova has ever seen!"

They laughed and drank. It was only a canal, true, but it was also more, and they all understood that. Their work could be the difference between living and dying, not just for themselves but for thousands of people.

"I'm not done, I'm not done!" she said, waving her hand to quiet them down. "Now, we're all equals here," she said, eyes roving across the corps, "one person no greater or more important to the other."

Murmurs of agreement rounded the circle.

"But I would be remiss if I didn't give a toast to one of the scions among us."

Okoa had not been listening closely, pleasantly inebriated and letting his mind meander over the events of the day, but at the mention of scions, he looked up.

"To Okoa Carrion Crow!" Enuka said, raising her cup. "A son of Tova, not too fancy to be out here in the mud and muck with us."

Some raised their cups, others murmured in surprise. They had not known, and Okoa wished Enuka had said nothing. He knew she meant well, was his friend, but she didn't understand that men like Cazotz would treat him differently now. That they would hesitate to order him around, think twice before they asked him to join them at the fire.

Enuka dropped down by his side, the balché keg in tow, and poured him another cupful. "How do you fare this night, my young apprentice?" she asked, her face warm from the fire of the drink more than the flames that roared in the nearby pit.

"Well enough," he said, but his joy had fled, and he thought he could feel the sideways looks from those around the fire. Evaluating, reconsidering. "Although I wish you would have spoken differently."

Enuka's brows rose in surprise. "Are you ashamed?"

Okoa winced. "Not ashamed." How could he make her understand? He could not, he realized. There was too much to explain, too much that, even if explained, would not make sense.

"You liked the anonymity," she concluded, her gaze weighing him. "Despite your brawn, you're the brooding sort. I can tell."

"It's nice out here in the field," he admitted. "My life back at the Great House among the clans is . . . noisy. This"—he gestured around, taking in her, the corps, the camp, and the vast open land—"is not."

273

"Ah." She was quiet for a moment. "I should have known as much when the Carrion King brought you himself, and on the back of a crow."

Benundah. Okoa would not mind her company now.

Enuka drank deeply. "Well, perhaps I did speak out of turn."

"No matter. It is done." And with that, he realized his time among the corps had reached its natural end. Part of him had known it was inevitable. He could not hide out here forever. Eventually, he had to return and face his sister, face the matrons and the rest of the people he had disappointed, even betrayed.

"You're always welcome here, Okoa," Enuka said, no doubt coming to the same realization he had.

"Aye." He imitated her distinctive accent to make a joke of it, his heart too heavy to do otherwise.

"Your Yamolo is terrible."

He smiled. "Is that where you're from?"

"Aye, along the Boundless Sea. My mother was Water Strider, but my pa—"

"To the Carrion King!" someone shouted.

They both glanced back toward the fire. By now, the toasts had devolved into drunken nonsense, bawdy salutes to the size of one's sexual organs and their presumed proficiency. "May he enjoy his new bride!"

Okoa frowned. Surely he hadn't heard right, the balché warping his senses.

"What was that?" he called.

The woman who had made the toast turned. "The king's getting married. Have you not heard?"

"No."

"You've been out here in the Eastern districts too long," she teased.

"Who's he marrying?" Okoa turned to Enuka, his heart

in his throat. Surely not Esa. He wouldn't. She wouldn't. But, oh, she would if she thought it would help her get what she wanted. Which, he feared, was Serapio dead.

He stood. "I've got to go back." He looked at Enuka, who was watching him curiously. "I've got to get back," he repeated, worried she hadn't heard.

"Aye, but tomorrow, Okoa. We're all too far into our cups now."

"The water striders can take me."

"They're fast and strong, but who's gonna drive?" She shrugged her shoulders in apology and looked toward the clutch of water strider riders drinking on the other side of the circle.

Okoa growled in frustration, but he knew she was right. Tomorrow. It would have to be tomorrow.

He had loved it here, had found peace of mind and the space to heal, but it was time to go home.

CHAPTER 25

We are forced to make a feast of famine.
And invite only ghosts to our table.

—From *Collected Lamentations from the Night of Knives*

Serapio met Maaka in the shadows of the aviary. His most loyal Tuyon had been gone a month, sent south to Obregi to find Serapio's father, Marcal. It was a secret mission, known only to himself, Maaka, and the two crow riders who accompanied him. Although even the riders did not know who they fetched from the far mountains, only that the Odo Sedoh demanded, and they provided. Serapio had Maaka swear to tell no one that it was Marcal he brought to Tova, not even his wife. Only that he was on a mission for the Odo Sedoh and would be gone until the new moon.

"Where is he?" Serapio asked as he reached the landing, not bothering with a greeting.

"Safely tucked away in my old residence in the Odo district."

"Good." Serapio had not wanted his father here at the Shadow Palace, not for what he had to do next. "And he is secure?"

"Locked in an upstairs room, the only way out a sky door that drops down into the Tovasheh."

"I cannot attend to him now. Feyou has planned a dinner where I am to meet my bride."

It had not been his idea. He would have preferred to simply marry and sacrifice whomever Feyou had designated, knowing nothing about the girl. But Feyou had insisted, as had Winged Serpent, the clan from which his bride had been chosen. As it was, Serapio knew only that she was kin to the matron Peyana. But his ignorance was fleeting, as Feyou had arranged for them all to gather in his throne room to feast and celebrate the upcoming nuptials.

"I put a sedative in your father's food," Maaka said. "He will keep for as long as the Odo Sedoh requires."

"You serve me well, Maaka."

"It is my honor."

Serapio turned to go but heard Maaka inhale, as if he wished to say more. He paused, waiting.

"He *is* your father?"

Serapio nodded, his shoulders tensing. His memories of his father brought a muddle of emotions, which he would prefer not to examine, considering the task before him.

"You should know," Maaka continued, "that I did not find him to be worthy of you, Odo Sedoh." Maaka's voice trembled slightly, as if worried his observation caused offense.

Serapio's hand tightened around his bone staff. "What did he say?"

"Words I would not repeat." And now his voice truly shook, not with concern but with rage.

"Ah." He bowed his head, and the memories came anyway. The whispered rejections, the fear of his own son, the drifting away.

"I know you wish him to attend your wedding, but I must advise against it. He does not deserve to celebrate with you."

Serapio almost laughed. Of course, Maaka thought he had fetched Marcal so that he might attend his son's wedding. Serapio wondered how the Tuyon would feel if he knew the truth.

"You need not worry, Maaka. I have no plans for my father to attend the wedding. But I do need you at this feast. Don your blood armor, and meet me in the throne room."

His voice dipped as he bowed. "I shall attend presently."

Serapio left to make to his own preparations, but his mind was on Zataya's prophecy. Okoa managed, his father in hand, his bride impending. He cut the path a bit more day by day, but the knowledge did not bring him comfort. Only a dread of what would happen if he failed, and a heaviness of what he must do to ensure he would not.

· · · · ·

Serapio called a crow to his side to serve as his eyes as he approached the throne room. His engagement feast was to be held there, the receiving area transformed into a banquet hall.

Feyou had assured him that it would be a modest gathering: the matron, his future bride, and a handful of relatives. But when Serapio entered the banquet, dressed in his long skirts, padded armor, and crow feather mantle, he found a hundred people crowded around the table.

He paused at the threshold as the heat of bodies washed over him. His hand sought the crow at his shoulder, his companion for both comfort and sight.

"Odo Sedoh." The whispers traveled around the room as

they noticed his arrival, and one by one, they rose to their feet
and bowed.

He strode to his seat at the head of the table. Maaka had
done as Serapio requested, and he was seated on Serapio's right,
eerie in his blood armor. Feyou was on his left. She had dressed
in more traditional Crow formal wear, a one-shouldered dress
that fell to her ankles, the hem and neckline adorned with
black-on-black beading.

The rest of his Tuyon stood as sentries. If Winged Serpent
took offense at Serapio's military garb, at Maaka's armor, and
at the soldiers, they said nothing.

He sought out Peyana. She was unmistakable, her hair
twisted into two signature horns upon her head like a helm of
office. She wore an iridescent gown, her arms bare despite the
winter outside, her fingers, wrists, and upper arms draped in
sparkling jewels.

"Welcome, Peyana, matron of Winged Serpent," Serapio
said. "And to all of the clan, welcome. You are my guests at the
Shadow Palace."

Once upon a time, his tone would have been stiff, his manner awkward with the formality required. But now the greeting
rolled smoothly from his tongue, his mind already at work,
watching, cataloguing. He had dreaded this dinner, but now
that he was here, he saw the opportunity in it. He would take
this occasion to discern the matron's nature so that he might
predict her behavior and know how best to defeat her when
she inevitably moved against him.

"Odo Sedoh." Peyana bowed at the neck. "I will admit
that it was a surprise to learn that you wished to join our
clans."

"It is only proper that I marry," he said, "for the good of
the city."

"Winged Serpent is honored that you looked to us for your bride."

He had not, of course. Winged Serpent was Feyou's choice, but he had no protest. It mattered not which scion of what clan died.

"This is my daughter, Isel." She gestured to the young woman at her side, who now rose to stand next to her. "She will make a dutiful wife."

If Peyana had not introduced her as her own, Isel Winged Serpent could have been mistaken for a villager dressed for a spring festival, much like the ones Serapio had known in Obregi growing up. Unlike Peyana's, the girl's gown was cut loose around her body and dyed a simple pale green, so light it was almost white. Her only adornments were a single jade bangle on each wrist and a small oblong of jade that pierced her septum. Her dark hair was oiled and divided into a dozen twists that framed a heart-shaped face, unpainted save a sweep of rose pink to color her full lips.

"I look forward to serving you, my king," Isel said, her voice a docile murmur. She smiled but quickly lowered her head, as if unsure.

Serapio considered his bride-to-be. Young, perhaps a few years younger than himself. Thin and willowy, with pretty features, but nothing too remarkable. It was difficult to believe someone so unassuming came from Peyana's household. When Feyou had told him that his bride was Winged Serpent, he had expected someone formidable like the mother, but here was a girl who was more maiden than scion.

Once he might have accepted that Isel was who she appeared to be. But experience had taught him that people lied, and he remembered his mother's warning that the eyes could not be trusted. He had learned to see in other ways. Learned to listen to what was said without words, to take account of deeds, not promises. He had become adept at finding a person's true self, whether they wished to show it to him or not.

What Isel presented was a girl who might appeal to an Obregi country boy, the kind accustomed to dancing in the square on feast days and who valued innocence over experience. The kind whose heart could be won by a shy blush and a submissive nature.

He dipped his head to hide his amusement. So Peyana thought to manipulate him, too. To discern what he wanted and give it to him. But Isel's guise, be it real or for his benefit, said more about what Peyana thought of him than it did anything else.

If the matron knew what he truly loved, *who* he truly loved, she would have been horrified at how terribly she had missed the mark. Isel Winged Serpent could not have been more different from the brash and foul-mouthed sea captain who pleased him because she was wildly and boldly herself and could never be anything else.

And yet, despite his power, his sorcery, his *desire*, Xiala was the one thing he could not have.

Feyou, to his left, touched his hand. "We cannot eat until you command it," she murmured, bringing him out of his reverie.

"Of course. Please." He gestured widely. "Let the feast begin."

Feyou had ensured that her table was worthy of Tova's new royalty, and courses were passed across his plate in indulgent profusion. First came a broth of shellfish and chile peppers, followed by small bowls of apple and papaya. Next were slices of avocado spiced with a mintlike herb, and then chunks of pumpkin and turkey baked into leaf-wrapped corn masa.

Serapio pecked at the rich food. Unsurprisingly, he had no appetite, but he did observe the people seated at his table. Feyou, he noticed, ate heartily, conversing with the person next to her. Maaka, too, had removed his helm and seemed to be enjoying the food, although he kept a watchful eye on their guests.

When only dessert was left, Peyana appeared at his left, Isel in tow.

"Carrion King," she greeted him, and both matron and her daughter bowed low.

"It is Odo Sedoh," Maaka said from across the table, his face set in lines of offense.

Serapio held out a hand. "I would not expect Winged Serpent to call me Crow God Reborn," he assured her, and made another note of the matron's character.

Her smile was tight. "I thought perhaps you and Isel could converse before the wedding. We have heard many stories of your deeds but know little of the man himself."

You know enough to wish me dead, he thought, but said, "A sensible proposal. Perhaps you would like to visit the aviary and meet my crow?" He thought he might get her away from Peyana to interrogate her about Winged Serpent.

Isel took a step back, alarmed, her eyes darting toward her mother.

She is afraid to be alone with me, he thought. *Perhaps a part of her understands the danger she is in.*

"A generous offer," Peyana said smoothly, "but I hear the dessert is a spiced chocolate. It is Isel's favorite. She would not wish to miss it."

Serapio said, "I was hoping for pie."

Peyana's brow furrowed at his pronouncement but only dipped her chin in acknowledgment.

Feyou had been listening, and now she stood. "Please." She gestured to her seat. "Take my place, Isel, so that you two may talk."

"How generous," Peyana murmured, and then Isel was seated next to him, smelling of summer lilies, cheeks flushed, smile shy.

"You go, too." Serapio gestured to Maaka. "I wish to speak to Isel alone."

Isel's eyes widened, as if the suggestion frightened her. Maaka grumbled, but he stood and wandered down the table until he found an empty place and a conversation to join.

Serapio turned to Isel . . . and waited. He knew that he should say words that would put her at ease, but he was much more interested in understanding what game she played, and how she meant to win it.

"It is an honor to meet you, Carrion King," she said, eyelashes lowered. "And it will be an honor to be queen."

Queen? Not my wife, not even my queen, but simply queen. So Peyana wants power and thinks wedding her daughter to me is her most assured path. How quickly she goes from eliminating me to joining me. She must be trembling at Okoa's failure and presumed fate and wondering how much I know of her role in the plot. Perhaps she believes that I would spare her for her daughter's sake.

"You enjoy chocolate?" he asked.

"Pardon?"

"Your mother seemed very interested in chocolate."

"Yes, Lord . . . I mean, Your Majesty. It is my favorite."

"The one with the chile?"

She smiled, nervous, and nodded, looking very much like someone who did not like spice in her chocolate or perhaps didn't like chocolate at all.

"I do enjoy a spiced chocolate," he admitted. "But I have also developed a taste for pie. What about stories? Do you enjoy stories? Of course you like stories," he continued, and noted how the heat rose on her cheeks.

"I like many stories," she offered, "but my favorite is a tale from your homeland. It is about a serpent girl who travels through the seven hells of the underworld to marry the god of death."

"A story of a serpent girl and her lover, the god of death?" A story he had never heard, despite her claim that it was an Obregi tale, and he wondered if it had been created solely for his benefit.

"Her husband, yes."

"And what happens at the end?"

"She saves him with her love."

"And how does she save him?"

"I do not know," she said, "but the story says that they have many children."

"It is only a story." He said it gently, his pity roused. It was not Isel's fault that she was chosen, plumped, and fluffed to be led like a bird to the slaughter. "Why did you agree to this marriage?" He was not sure why he asked, but it seemed important to know.

"It would be an honor."

He waved her glib answer away. "Surely it is more than honor that moves you."

She considered him, lips pursed, and he was acutely aware of his strangeness, the inky blackness of his eyes, the crow that sat on his shoulder.

"You are not what I expected," she admitted, and he thought it was the first honest thing she had said. "You are . . . kinder."

I am not kind.

"Surely your mother has told you terrible stories about me," he said.

Isel glanced down the table at Peyana. "The whole of Tova is filled with terrible stories about you." She looked back at Serapio. "But I will decide for myself."

Ah, Isel. You will decide too late.

The dessert came, chocolate after all, and conversation ceased as they partook. He watched the girl take a small sip and work hard not to make a face of displeasure. He drank his, reveling in the taste, but memories of Xiala and the chocolate they shared on the streets of Titidi turned the confection bittersweet.

He would have preferred pie.

Finally, the table was cleared, and the benches were moved back to make room in the center for the entertainment. Feyou had warned him beforehand that Peyana had insisted on bringing in musicians and dancers, a troupe highly sought after during the current social season.

"They come from the Agave," she had told him.

"And what is the Agave?" he asked.

"A House in Coyote's Maw. A pleasure house, owned by the matron of the clan. Theirs is a sensual dance, no doubt meant to stir your appetites."

He tried to hide his horror.

"You are to be married," Feyou said. "There are certain marital expectations."

"I know that," he snapped, but in truth he had tried to block that part from his mind. The only woman he wanted was Xiala, and while he would marry someone else to save her, sharing his bed with anyone else left him cold and conflicted.

Now Serapio stood to make his excuses. He had endured the dinner, but he would not stay through the dances.

"Leaving us, Carrion King?" Peyana asked.

"I am afraid I must. There is much that needs doing. We prepare for a war, after all. But please, everyone stay and enjoy the performance."

The matron's eyes narrowed, but he did not give her time to protest, instead slipping out the way he had come before anyone else could raise a concern.

Maaka followed, quick on his heels. Serapio walked in silence for a while, his Tuyon by his side. As always, Maaka was wary and watchful, as if he expected an attack around every corner.

"And what do you think?" Serapio asked, once they were well away from the hall.

"I do not trust the Serpent woman or her daughter."

"She knew my favorite dessert and claimed it as her own, and she knew I liked stories and had one ready to share, allegedly from Obregi. One about true love in which I played the role of the god of death."

Maaka grunted. "They dress a viper like a rabbit, send her into the hunter's den as bait, and expect us not to notice."

Precisely. "The Winged Serpents do not worry me," he said, dismissive. Peyana's scheming was but an irritation. He would not tell Maaka that he had no intention of allowing Isel to live long enough to truly trouble him, because at the moment, another death weighed on his mind.

Out of habit, he had led them to the aviary. The night air was cool and welcoming, a contrast to the stifling atmosphere he had left. He paused to savor the chill against his skin, the pleasures of shadow and night, the gentle cry of crows.

"It is time," he said, turning his black eyes to Maaka. "I must go to my father."

They would do as they had done before. Maaka would

walk on foot, and Serapio would follow the flock, moving un-remarked through the district of Carrion Crow. Those who lived there would never know their god moved among them, his mind set to murder.

Perhaps Isel's story names me true, and I am a god of death, he thought.

But, unlike in the story, there was no one who loved him enough to save him from his fate.

CHAPTER 26

> On earth, in heaven, and within,
> Three wars to lose, three wars to win.
> Cut the path. Mark the days. Turn the tides.
> Three tasks before the season dies:
> Turn rotten fruit to flower,
> Slay the god-bride still unloved,
> Press the son to fell the sire.
> Victory then to the Carrion King who in winning loses everything.
>
> —Coyote song

Serapio stood at Maaka's front door, unable to go in. He had been so sure that this was the right thing, the very thing that he must do. Kill his father or lose the war. Do this terrible deed, or the crow god falls, Tova falls, and he himself would be doomed.

His own doom he could endure. Was he not already cursed?

But to let the city fall, to let his god fail?

Over one death?

One death to save thousands.

He pressed a hand to his forehead and rubbed his temples as if that would clear his thoughts, strengthen his resolve.

"Odo Sedoh?" Maaka waited beside him, patient but concerned.

"And you are sure it is him?" he asked, knowing he was stalling.

"I went to the place on your map. An aging white-stone mansion on a cliffside, grand but in disrepair. I asked for the father of Serapio, the husband of Saaya, the man known as Marcal."

Serapio nodded. Of course it was him. But he asked anyway. "And his look?"

"In truth, you must favor your mother, but . . ." Maaka shrugged. "It is hard to say."

"He made my life very difficult," Serapio confessed.

"He did not seem pleased to see me," Maaka acknowledged. "Or to hear of your ascension to king when I told him who I was and why I had come."

"No, he would not. He never forgave my mother for what she did, and he blamed Carrion Crow for her death . . . and my transformation. He was happy to see me go, although he had washed his hands of me well before I left. In truth, I stopped being his son on the day I became the vessel for the crow god. There was not room for both."

"Then you did only as destiny would allow."

Serapio raised his head. "I suppose I did."

So why do I balk at destiny now?

He straightened. "Wait for me here," he commanded, and opened the door before he could change his mind.

Maaka and Feyou's home smelled of the dried herbs important to the healing arts: desert willow, mint, and amaranth. The floor was smooth under his bare feet, intermittent torchlight filtering through windows to cast the whitewashed walls in alternating shades of gray.

A wooden ladder in the center of the room led up to the sleeping chamber, and he knew that was where he would find Marcal.

He left his staff on the ground floor and reluctantly ascended. The upstairs room was dark, no lantern illuminating the room that had no windows, the only egresses the trapdoor Serapio had come through and a closed sky door at the far end. His vision had improved enough that with help from the light below, he could discern a raised sleeping area and, upon it, a shadowy lump.

Marcal.

Serapio groped his way to the bench at the side of the bed. He settled himself there to watch his father sleep. Even in slumber, he could tell his father had aged. Breath labored through his lungs, and his body looked frail and hollowed-out under the blankets. He smelled of medicinal plants, ones he recognized as used to lessen joint pain.

Marcal was not so terribly old. By Serapio's calculations, he was somewhere in his fifty-third year. But the man before him had not lived easy years, and the effects of his hardships showed. His father looked more like a man in his seventies.

They had last spoken on the eve of Serapio's seventeenth birthday, the day before Powageh came as his third and final tutor. Marcal had wanted to mark Serapio's official ascension to adulthood with a celebration. It had been out of character. Usually, Marcal ignored his son, preferring to imagine he had no offspring. But that day, Marcal had awakened him and explained that there would be a feast.

At first, Serapio was thrilled. A party, and for him? He could not recall celebrating his birthday once his mother had died. His previous tutors, Paadeh and Eedi, had made mention of it occasionally, Paadeh only to scoff at how small he was for his age, and Eedi to encourage him to work harder now that he was older. But this was different.

"Who will come?" Serapio asked excitedly.

"I am bringing a soothsayer in from the village."

It was customary to have a wise woman read the calendar and divine one's fate on the first day of adulthood. The "fate" always came out generally the same. Pretty girls would marry and birth many children, strong boys would work the land, clever children would succeed as merchants, creative ones as artists. It all seemed silly to Serapio. No village woman was going to tell him what he already knew. He was a god reborn and had a destiny above all others. Anything the woman said would be rubbish, a poor party trick.

But still, a party.

"Who else?" he asked.

"Well, the servants will be there. Jovi and Taya, your favorites."

"Jovi left last year. Moved to the city to care for her mother."

"Oh. Well, Taya, then. And the others."

"So, no one from the village? No one my age?" Serapio knew he sounded petulant, but what use was a party with only the servants and some false fortune teller?

"I can see if there are others who might come," Marcal said, but he sounded doubtful.

Serapio pulled his knees up against his chest. "Don't bother."

"I have an idea," Marcal said brightly. "Instead of having a party, we can go down to the village."

Serapio had not been to the village since before his mother died. His father had closed himself away for the years following and left the boy to his own devices, cared for by servants, until Paadeh had come when he was fourteen. Paadeh had not ventured out with him, but Eedi had, often taking him on long conditioning hikes through the nearby mountains until his lungs burned and his legs ached. But never to the village.

"Do you mean it?" he asked, sounding more like an eager child promised sweets than an almost-seventeen-year-old on the cusp of adulthood.

"On one condition."

"Name it." His stomach jumped, but whatever it was that Marcal wanted, he would manage it for a chance to be around people again. To perhaps meet a new friend his age, try different foods, hear music.

"You'll have to wear something long-sleeved and high-collared. And a cloak with a cowl. To cover your scars."

"Done." It was late fall anyway, and wearing heavy clothes in the mountains was nothing unusual.

"And you cannot speak, lest people see your teeth."

His red teeth. He had not dyed them since his mother's death, but Eedi had told him that they had never lost their red taint and that it always appeared that his mouth was filled with blood.

"I cannot speak?" he asked. But what would he do if he could not see or speak and had to stay hidden under a cowl and cloak?

"And you'll have to wear this."

Something pressed against Serapio's leg. He touched it. It was soft and smooth.

"What is it?"

"A blindfold. For your eyes."

"I don't understand. I am already blind."

"It is not for you, Serapio," Marcal said, sounding even more cautious than before. "It is for everyone else."

"Everyone else?" And then he understood.

His father was embarrassed. He did not want people to see his blinded son with the stitched eyes, the strange scars, and red teeth. He imagined his trip to the village would be a quick visit to the soothsayer and then right back behind the doors of the mansion where he was safely out of sight.

No new foods, no new friends, no music.

"I don't want it!" He flung the blindfold away.

He heard Marcal grumble and push himself to his feet to walk across the room and retrieve the cloth. "I'm trying to do something nice for you."

"It's not nice! It's not nice if you're ashamed!"

"Why are you so difficult? I thought your tutors taught you more self-discipline than this."

My tutors are dead, he wanted to shout. *The crows helped me kill them. Paadeh hit me one too many times, and the crows harried Eedi off a cliff.*

"Look, Serapio . . . ," Marcal began.

"I can't look," he spit. "I'm blind."

His father huffed in exasperation. "Blind or not, you will be out of this house by tomorrow. Once you are an adult, you must learn to stand on your own two feet."

"Is that what this is?" Serapio's voice rose. "A farewell?" A thought came to him. "Were you going to take me to the village and leave me there?"

"Of course not," Marcal protested, but there was a lift in his voice as if now that Serapio had said it, the idea was worth consideration.

Serapio had never been good at controlling his anger, but now it exploded.

"Get out!" He swung his fist, but he was on the bed, sitting awkwardly, and Marcal was too far away. All his training, his learning to fight, and he was reduced to a wild swing. If he had his bone staff, it would be different, but he had left it propped up against his workbench on the other side of the room.

"Get out!" he shouted again. "Or, or . . . I'll kill you! Like the rest of them! Get out, get out, get out!"

He was breathing hard, panting in shallow swallows, and couldn't catch his breath. He wasn't even sure if his father was still in the room, and he couldn't calm the heartbeat throbbing in his ears long enough to listen.

A heavy thump against the window told him his crows had come, no doubt stirred by his distress. Sniffling and gasping, he hobbled to the window and flung open the shutters. Crows rushed in, squawking and circling, crying out their concern.

"I'm fine, I'm fine," he assured them, holding out his arms. They tucked into his open hands, against his neck, and he sat so they could gather on his lap.

He murmured to them, now more concerned with calming his friends than his own injustices. He told them not to worry, that one day soon they would be gone from this place, that together they had a destiny bigger than a trip to the village, bigger than Obregi, bigger than his father.

Only when his laments had run dry and he lay on his bed nestled among his crows did he hear the door close and realize his father had been there all along.

· · · · ·

Back in Maaka's house, seated across from his father, Serapio shuddered. He stayed bent over, head in his hands, as tears rolled from his eyes. Now there were no crows to comfort him, only himself and this man he had once loved, still loved, but hated in equal measure. If only he could find some of that righteous anger that had fueled him at sixteen, perhaps he could strike now before Marcal even woke and have the heinous deed done. But there was no anger in him, only sorrow.

"You've come to kill me, haven't you?"

Marcal's voice, despite his obvious aging, sounded exactly how Serapio remembered it.

"Yes," he whispered.

The rush of flint and a hiss of air as a flame blossomed to life. Shadows danced, more degrees of darkness than illumination, as Marcal lit a resin lantern on the bedside.

"I thought so," he said, sounding resigned. "Why else send your man to fetch me? Although he looked capable if all you wanted was me in my grave."

"I do not want you dead." It came out barely a breath.

He heard Marcal shift on the bed, sitting up. Serapio straightened, wiping the tears from his face and rubbing his hands dry against his skirts.

His father gasped.

"Your eyes," he breathed. "They are open."

Serapio touched a finger to his eyelid. The last time Marcal had seen him, his eyes were still sewn shut.

"My eyes have been healed," he explained.

"Can you . . ." Marcal swallowed. "Can you see?"

"No, not how you mean it. There is a healer here who has salves that have eased some of the damage, but . . ." He shrugged. "My world is still shadows and light."

And crows, but he did not think his father would understand his crow vision, and it would take too much to explain.

"Oh." There was disappointment in Marcal's exhale.

"Is sight really so important?" Serapio asked, his anger rising. Always with Marcal, the same thing. Even after all these years, his father's disappointment was a palpable presence in the room.

"No. I . . . I meant for your sake."

"I am fine. I was always fine." That was not entirely true, but he would admit nothing to Marcal, lest his father take it as a weakness.

Silence sat between them until Marcal said, "You look well. Healthy. You were such a frail boy."

Serapio laughed, not at the old insult but at the audacity.

"You know that I have come to kill you, and yet you ask if I am well?"

"No, no, I don't mean . . ." Marcal sounded old. "I only wish . . . I worry about you."

"You did not before."

"That isn't true. I always worried. It was just . . ." He sighed and shifted in the half-light. "It was difficult for me after your mother died. You wouldn't understand."

"Difficult for you? What about me? I was twelve, and suddenly"—*blinded, maimed*—"motherless. I needed a father."

"And I was not there," Marcal acknowledged. "Well, in body—"

"Not even in body! You stayed locked in your rooms for the first year and then handed me off to that monster of a tutor at the first opportunity." He could not keep the bitterness from his voice.

"And you hated me for it." Resignation. Acceptance.

"I hate you still!" Serapio shouted, emotion overwhelming him. He squeezed his hands into fists, forced his breath to slow.

"And now you've brought me here to exact your revenge. It is what I deserve."

"No!" Serapio rose and paced toward the sky door. "No, it is not revenge."

"Your mother's god is a vengeful god. How many times did she tell me that? Every day for twelve years, I imagine. I never took her seriously. She had a flair for drama, Saaya did. I wish I would have known."

"Known what?"

"I am not blameless," Marcal continued, as if Serapio had not spoken. "I should have seen her for what she was from the beginning. But for all her passion, I did not think her capable."

"Capable of what? Of this?" Serapio swept a hand down his body, his anger rising again. "Of me?"

"Of hurting you."

It was as if Marcal had reached into his chest, found his heart, and squeezed. For a moment, he was a boy again, flesh opening under a carving knife, eyes closing under needle and thread.

"She loved me," he whispered, emotion thick in his throat. "She gave me a destiny."

"There is a time when love ceases to be love and becomes cruelty," Marcal said. "Somewhere, somehow, your mother lost her way. You were a child. What she did would have broken anyone."

"I am not broken."

"Of course you are."

"I am a god, a king. I rule this city and all in it. I have power you cannot begin to comprehend!" His voice had risen so much he shouted the last.

"A god." Marcal seemed to sit with the idea. "I was there when you were born, you know. You came three months early, but the midwife said you were healthy. You were a little thing, red-faced and puckered, but you didn't cry. Did Saaya ever tell you? The strangest thing. I thought all infants cried. But not you."

Serapio felt hot and his stomach hollow, his head dizzy. He wanted to scream at Marcal to stop, but his mouth was dry and would not form the words.

"Those were good years, Serapio. Me, you, and your mother. Good years. But Saaya's obsession with her revenge got worse and worse, and I could feel her slipping away. I knew I was losing her, but even then, I was too afraid to act."

Serapio frowned. He did not remember that.

"At first, I thought she had someone else, a lover in the village, or perhaps even in Huecha. The city was not so far. I raged like any suspicious husband might, but she would not tell me what had come between us. Would not even admit to

297

our divide. I thought to leave her or throw her out, but how could I when she had given me you? My miracle child, when the doctors had told me that I might not produce enough seed to have children. Against all odds, she had borne me a perfect son, and I would not risk her taking you away."

"I was small. Frail. You said so yourself." It was the only thing he could think to say.

"You were mine." He said it fiercely, but his passion was fleeting. When he spoke again, it was with grief. "If I could go back, do something different . . ."

"You could not," he said, and his sorrow matched Marcal's own. "I understand that now. Destiny decides our fates, not human desires."

"Maybe. Maybe," he repeated, defeat in the sigh that followed. "You know better than me. I am just an old man who wasted his life in bitterness and regrets, driving away the things I loved most. Do you know I live alone? Even most of the servants have left. So now I sit there, day after day, simply waiting."

Serapio wanted to ask him what he was waiting for, but he thought he knew.

"I know you will not believe me," Marcal said, "but I would make amends if I could."

"There is a way," Serapio whispered.

"Anything. Name it."

"A prophecy brought by a witch. A song from her god." He took a breath to steady himself. "*Press the son to fell the sire,*" he quoted. "Or I will lose this war."

"War?"

"The Treaty from the War of the Spear. I broke it with my coming, and now the other cities rise up against me."

"Obregi is not party to such a treaty."

"No, but Tova is."

Marcal was quiet. Thinking. "And they're coming to kill you, these men?"

"Entire armies come to kill me." He said it quietly, the weight of the reality suddenly overwhelming.

"But if I . . . if you 'fell the sire,' you can defeat them?"

"That is what the witch told me."

"And you believe her?"

"My whole life is prophecies. Why would I not?"

He could see Marcal moving in the light, shadows dancing as he nodded his head. He was considering it. Skies, his father was actually considering it.

Serapio abruptly stood. It was too much. Curse the trickster god and the witch. He would find another way.

Marcal's hand snaked around his wrist. His voice was strong now. Stronger than it had been before. "I cannot go back in time and save you from your mother's cruelties or my failures, but if my death is something you need, if it will keep you safe . . ."

"But I do not want it," he whispered.

"No, but you need it, and I failed to give you what you needed so many times."

He pulled Serapio down to sit on the bed beside him.

"I don't understand prophecies," Marcal said. "I am not Saaya or one of your Crow people. But if this will keep you safe, if this will protect you . . ." He took a deep breath. "I know I can't fix the broken things between us, and nothing I do will bring your mother back or mend what she shattered in you and what I made worse. But maybe it will help."

Serapio could not breathe, only tried to memorize the feel of his father's hand on his own, the sound of his breathing, the scent that clung to his clothes and skin.

Marcal reached over and plucked the black dagger from Serapio's belt. He pressed the blade against his son's palm.

Serapio's fingers refused to close around the hilt. Could he do it? He did not know.

Perhaps one life *was* worth losing the war. Perhaps the life of a loved one was important enough to matter over the lives of thousands of strangers.

"Son?" Marcal's hand cupped his cheek. His palms were cold against Serapio's skin, but all Serapio could think about was that it had been so long since his father had touched him with any kind of affection, and he had not realized how the absence gaped and how much he craved it.

"It's all right," Marcal whispered, and rubbed an inky tear away with his thumb.

Serapio closed his eyes and nodded.

"Maybe this will make it easier." Marcal leaned over to snuff out the candle so that they both sat in darkness. A darkness so thick and heavy no light could be seen, but Serapio was aware of the dip of his father's weight, the heat from his body. He had wanted Marcal's love for so long that now that it was offered unconditionally, it terrified him. But he did not have the luxury of fear. The prophecy required this of him, and so, in the end, it would be done. No matter what it cost him, no matter how it chipped away at what humanity he had left. No matter how it broke his black, black heart.

His fingers tightened around the hilt of the knife. "Forgive me."

"There is nothing to forgive."

The quick kiss of a blade, a final breath, and it was done.

CHAPTER 27

TEEK TERRITORY
YEAR I OF THE CROW

The only free thing in life is the sea. Everything else
costs.

—Teek saying

Xiala watched the spearmaiden collapse, blood and saliva
bubbling into a crimson froth on her lips. Her legs kicked,
and convulsions racked her body. A shout of alarm went up
from one of the male guards, and the other spearmaiden beside
her fell to her knees, clutching her dying friend. The woman
shouted for someone to do something, but Xiala knew it was
too late to change the poisoned woman's fate.

Time distended. The dying spearmaiden, the desperate
friend. Soldiers yelling as they sought the source of death that
had come calling on one of their own.

One of the men pointed toward Teanni.

Another was already drawing his weapon.

It was all happening in slow motion, all the sounds coming
to Xiala muffled, as if she was underwater.

Underwater.

And she knew what to do.

"Get everyone into the water," she said, and then louder. "Everyone in the water!"

"What?" Teanni stared in confusion.

She grabbed her friend's shoulders and shook her hard. "Water! Now! Dive as deep as you can for as long as you can. Go!"

Teanni turned and ran. "Water!" she shouted in Teek. "Into the water! Dive! Dive!"

The women who had been watching the commotion of the dying spearmaiden with curiosity broke for the shore, casting aside their tools and bolting headlong into the waves. They moved with an urgency Xiala would not have thought possible, as if they understood their lives depended on it.

"Hey!" a soldier yelled, the one who had drawn his weapon. He pointed it at Xiala. "You!" He strode toward her, long legs making quick work of crossing the camp.

Xiala looked back over her shoulder. More than half the women were already splashing into the water, throwing themselves below the surface. But Teanni had slowed to help an older woman who had fallen behind, and they had barely touched the shoreline.

Xiala whirled back toward the soldier. He had begun to run. Long, loping strides that ate up the distance between them. He was fifteen lengths away, fourteen. Close enough that she could see the spark of rage in his eyes and the gleam of the sharpened obsidian chips on the club he clutched in his hand. Obsidian that would rip her apart.

"Hurry!" she screamed in Teanni's direction, but her friend had barely breached the water.

A shout punctured the night, and Xiala whipped around to see Alani barreling toward the approaching soldier, arm cocked back, an adze raised above her head like a weapon.

"No!" Xiala cried, but it was too late.

The soldier shifted his attention to the charging woman and met Alani's attack head-on.

It was no contest at all.

The man swung his club in an underhanded reel, tearing through Alani's torso in a single motion. The Teek woman split open upon impact, dead before her body hit the ground.

But Alani had accomplished what she wished. She had given Teanni and the other women time. Xiala watched as their heads disappeared below the waves.

And Xiala Sang.

It was a Song of horror. Of blood and loss and pain. Of Alani as she sacrificed herself for another. Of Yaala, trusting and betrayed. Of the wise women, of Queen Mahina, of all the Teek lost to violence.

She Sang a Song of righteous fury, of reckoning, of justice come to call, and it ripped through the soldiers with the same intensity and devastation that the Cuecolan's club had cut through her friend.

Men crumbled, blood erupting from their ears as they vomited. Others flopped and jerked on the ground. The remaining spearmaiden staggered to her feet and cocked back her arm, ready to launch her spear.

Xiala modulated her voice, reaching for a minor note, and hurled it at the maiden. The woman shattered. There was no other way to explain it, as her body burst into pieces.

And still Xiala Sang, and all the terror and pain and rage that she had kept locked inside herself poured forth in a primal hymn of destruction. Until the leaves on the plants began to wither, until the insects that crawled through the soil fell dead, until she felt her own life begin to drain away, and she reluctantly forced her tongue to still and her mouth to close and her heart to slow its frantic beating.

She dropped to the ground, exhausted.

And all was silent.

• • • • •

Sound returned slowly, first in the kiss of the waves along the sandy shoreline, then the soft sigh of wind through the palms. And then in the shape of her name.

"Xiala?"

She lifted her head. The moon was a half crescent above her. The camp was reduced to shadows. She saw the bulk of canoe hulls upturned over untended fires that had reduced to ash, an overturned pot by the embers of a cooking fire from which emanated a sickly sweet smell. *Apples*, she thought. *It smells like apples.*

And then she smelled something else.

Death.

She shuddered.

"Xiala, can you hear me?" Teanni touched her shoulder.

She nodded, the effort costing her. "The others?" she asked, her voice no more than a whisper.

"Safe. They're all safe."

She exhaled, felt the tension release. And then she remembered.

"Alani?"

Teanni's eyes filled with tears. She shook her head.

Xiala's grief sat thick in her belly, like something she could not digest. She thought she had expunged the grief from her body through her killing Song, but here was more. Always more. What had her life become but an ongoing parade of death and loss?

All the more reason to fight, to protect those I have left.

She thought of what Alani might say. She could see the woman's brash smile, the challenge that had simmered in her ocean-blue eyes. And she knew, not just for Alani but for all the Teek, and for Serapio, and especially for herself, fight was exactly what she would do.

Even if it killed her.

She reached out a hand and let Teanni pull her to her feet.

"What did you do, Xiala?" a woman in the crowd asked, her voice choked with awe.

Xiala looked over her shoulder at the field of dead. "I . . ."

"You obliterated them," Teanni provided. "Your gift from the Mother is a killing Song. You have been sent to protect us in our time of need, a warrior for your people."

Xiala appreciated the thought, but said, "I can't even wield a knife."

"Who needs a knife when you can do that?" Keala, Teanni's wife, asked, sand-colored eyes wide with wonder.

Teanni squeezed Xiala's arm. "I am sorry I ever doubted you."

"You doubted me?"

"What do we do now?" another woman asked. "More soldiers will come soon, and the children are still captive. Are you sure you have not put us in more danger?"

"Hush," Teanni scolded.

"She's right." Xiala met the woman's gaze. "We've got work to do. The replacement shift of soldiers could be here any moment, and I don't think I can Sing again, at least for a while."

"We can run," Keala offered. "Like we planned before."

"Alani sacrificed herself to save me, to save us all." Xiala's gaze swept across the Teek gathered behind her. They were still damp from their dive into the sea, but whole. "I will not let that be simply so that I can hide."

"Then what?" Teanni wrung her hands, eyes begging Xiala for an answer.

And Xiala had one: "I'm going to the listening house to free the children."

A murmur rumbled through the crowd.

"You don't have to come," she continued. "In fact, most of you should not. You should do as Keala says. Take these tide-chasers and hide in the outer islands until the invaders are gone and this war is over."

"I won't let you go alone," Teanni protested. "You can't take on Tuun's sorcery, the remaining soldiers, and free the children, too."

The grief Xiala was trying desperately to ignore bubbled in her gut. "I can't lose you, too, Teanni. Please."

Her friend straightened. "Better to die as Alani did than live under their yoke and shame my ancestors. If we do not end the invaders now, they will never leave us in peace. You said so yourself. Tuun covets."

"And the children need a friendly face," Keala added. She grasped her wife's hand. "We are going." And then softer. "It is our choice, Xiala. Let us help."

Your choice to die? Xiala thought, but she knew her friends were right. And she did need the help. "If you mean it, then I have a task for you. Both of you. And for the rest of you, too. We must hurry and strike while we still have the advantage."

Teanni nodded, solemn with purpose. "Tell us what we need to do."

The women worked for the better part of the hour, dragging bodies into the water, gifts to the predators of the sea and payment to their Mother. They kicked sand over the blood and tidied the camp so that a casual inspection from a distance would find nothing amiss save their absence. Another cluster of women hastily carved paddles from tree limbs since the tide-chasers were without sails. Once done, they armed themselves with sharpened adzes and set out for the chain islands, well out of Tuun's reach. At last, only Teanni, Keala, and Xiala remained on the shore.

"You and Keala will take a ship around the island and come to the listening house from the far side, through the jungle," Xiala explained. "But don't approach the house until I draw Tuun and the guards away."

"How will you do that?"

Distant thunder rumbled somewhere far off over the sea, a storm heading their way. "I'm not sure, but I will think of something once I'm there."

Teanni looked grim. She embraced Xiala tightly. "We will see you on the other side of this." And then they were dragging a tidechaser into the water. They soon disappeared along the twisting coastline.

Once they were gone, Xiala went back to the pit where the women had nursed the cookfires. She found what she was looking for and slipped flint and dried seagrass into a small waterproof sack, making sure to seal it tightly. Satisfied, she lugged the last remaining tidechaser into the waves and paddled in the opposite direction, back toward the listening house and Lord Tuun, flashes of distant lightning illuminating her way.

· · · · ·

Xiala left the tidechaser a short distance down the coast from the camp and swam the rest of the way, invisible from the shore to even the sharpest lookout. She moved soundlessly through the water to approach the nearest Cuecolan canoe. A hundred fifty paces long and twenty paces across, with a cavernous reed-covered awning in the center and paddles for twice a dozen men, it floated fat and smug under the waning moon, anchored along a floating makeshift dock the invaders had built for the purpose.

The approaching rain hadn't yet reached the island, but Xiala could feel the air thickening with moisture. She hoped the rain gods Iktan had once told her about were as kind to her as her Mother was and would hold their bounty back just a little longer.

A single guard stood watch on the dock, club swinging idly in his hand. His expression in the fading light looked distinctly bored. He faced the beach, no doubt convinced that any threat would come from land.

Xiala watched long enough to make sure he was alone before she slowly worked her way up the side of the ship, using the anchor rope and what footholds she could. It was taxing work that threatened to blister her palms, but the canoe did not sway, and the lapping waves covered what little sound she made.

Once on board, she slipped into the captain's quarters, identical to the ones she and Serapio had been confined to on another Cuecolan ship at another time. The space was arrayed just like that one, with a bench, a table affixed to the wall, and a dresser. For a moment the memory of the first time she had seen him there, eyes sewn shut, lips parted, his mind soaring with his crows, rushed back. A wave of longing washed over her, but instead of crippling her, it suffused her with strength. She remembered what Alani had said, that love made one strong, could move mountains, and Xiala felt the truth of it.

Invigorated, she got to work, looking for the items she needed. They were easy enough to find. A sheaf of bark paper filled with numbers and glyphs, likely ration and pay logs, and, most important, on a bottom shelf, a tub of resin used to plug leaks.

That was the thing about the viscous putty. Once cured by the saltwater, it made a paste that kept the water out. But in its natural form, especially if you added a little bird shit scraped from the side of the canoe to it, the resin was highly flammable.

She drew the waterproof bag from her neck and opened it. The flint and seagrass she had collected from the shipyard camp were still dry. She pinched off a block of resin and rolled it together with the bird droppings and the grass. Then did it three more times, tucking all but one palm-sized ball into her waterproof bag. That one she placed into a nest of paper.

She lit the paper and watched the flames spread. She slipped out and down the side of the ship just as smoke started to fill the cabin.

By the time she got to the second ship and had hauled herself aboard, she could smell the smoke in the air, but no one on shore had noticed, and the bored guard on the floating dock was peering toward land, as if the smell must be coming from there.

She worked fast to set the other fire and was off the ship and climbing onto the third canoe when an alarmed shout went up from the first, the guard finally discovering what had now turned into a steady blaze.

Xiala squinted against the firelight back toward the shore. Soldiers stood on the beach, eyes on the burning ship. They stared slack-jawed, not quite comprehending the fiery vision before them.

A figure rushed out of the cabin in front of her. Xiala threw herself back against the wall at the last moment, crouching in the shadows.

"What is it?" A voice rose from inside the cabin.

Xiala's pulse soared. She had been about to enter, and if

she had opened that door, she would have found people inside waiting for her.

"Fire," answered the shadowy figure before her.

She had not recognized the first voice, except that it was masculine, but this one she knew well.

Tuun stared across the water at the burning vessel. Xiala had been sure Tuun would be on shore in the listening house. What was she doing here, on the canoe?

As if in answer, the captain who had threatened Laili's daughter trailed Tuun out of the cabin, a blanket wrapped loosely around his hips. He draped a hand over Tuun's shoulder, but she shook him off, clearly irritated.

"Cursed Teek," she spit.

"It could have been an accident," her captain offered.

As if in rebuttal, a bellowing huff sounded from the second canoe as it went up in flames.

Both Cuecolans hissed and stepped back as the new conflagration built in earnest.

"Is that an accident, too?" Tuun's face, lit by the fires, tightened in disgust.

Xiala could not see the captain's face clearly, but his shoulders tensed.

"Get dressed," Tuun commanded, "and meet me at the listening house. Clearly, I need to make an example."

The listening house was a dark block on the far shore, but Xiala hoped Teanni and Keala had used the distraction of the fires to rescue the children and were even now reuniting with the other women somewhere safe.

The men at the beach camp had finally lurched into action and were hurrying toward the burning canoes, buckets in hand. Lightning flashed from above, quickly followed by thunder, and Xiala cursed the first drop of rain against her face.

As the captain disappeared back into the cabin, a shout rose from the dock. A soldier, firelight gleaming off his weapon, ran toward Tuun's ship, shouting. His footsteps clattered against the planks.

Tuun went to the edge to meet him. "What is it now?"

"The shipyard camp," he huffed, flustered and short of breath from his run.

"What of it?"

Xiala could almost feel the edge of Tuun's words, sharp with violence.

"Everyone is gone."

"What do you mean, gone?"

"No soldiers, no women, nothing."

"Impossible."

"Nothing, Lord Tuun. I swear it!"

"Look again!"

The soldier looked confused in the firelight, but he turned to obey.

"No, wait." She called him back. "What of the ships? The tidechasers?"

"Gone, too."

Tuun emitted an incoherent growl and slammed her hand against the railing.

The captain reappeared, this time fully dressed.

"I'll go," he said, already striding toward the gangplank.

Tuun grabbed his arm, and he slowed. "The listening house. Check the listening house first!"

The captain dipped his chin and clambered down the plank, motioning for the messenger to lead the way. The two men headed for the listening house at a steady pace.

Tuun paused, face framed by the flames, chin lifted as if scenting the air. Xiala made herself small in the shadows and held her breath. After a moment, Tuun swept the hem of her robe up over her arm and marched down the gangplank. Xiala counted to ten, and then ten again, before slipping around the corner and into the cabin.

She drew the third resin ball from her bag and was about to strike the flint when the door banged open behind her.

She whirled, expecting to find Tuun, hand dripping blood as she prepared to unleash some strange sorcery.

But instead she found the captain had returned. The man grinned lazily and twirled his battle club.

"You set those fires, little fish?" he asked.

Xiala scampered back, putting as much space as she could between herself and the warrior, but in the small, confined space, there was nowhere to go. She desperately scanned the room for a weapon, but there was nothing. Only her voice. She would have to try to Sing her way out and pray the Mother would not fail her.

As if sensing her plan, the man's grin spread. "You can try, but I can't hear a sound from that pretty throat," he said. With his free hand, he tapped a gob of thick black resin stuffed in his ear.

Xiala swallowed past a lump of fear. The resin had not protected the soldiers on the beach, but they had been careless, too secure in their invulnerability. She was certain this one had not made the same mistake.

Think, Xiala! But what did she have to fight this warrior but her Song and the ball of resin in her hand. *Of course!*

Ball balanced in her palm, she awkwardly struck the flint. Sparks danced in the air.

The captain paused, eyes on the threat of fire.

She struck the flint again.

The grass in the ball caught.

The captain launched himself forward, club raised.

She threw the ball at the charging guard just as the black putty began to glow. It glanced across his cheek and clung to his hair in flaming bits. Xiala watched in horror as his long locks ignited. The fire hopped to the resin in his ears. An inhuman scream shrieked from his mouth as he dropped his club and batted uselessly at his head.

Xiala ran, pushing past the burning man.

She had not taken more than three steps before she heard a thunderous crack and felt a whoosh of conflagration push her forward.

Suddenly, she was flying, hurtling through the air and into the dark water as the canoe she had been standing on exploded. She felt heat and pain and then the cool kiss of water as she plummeted into the sea.

She sank, momentarily dazed, her mind trying to reconcile the change of circumstances. But quickly enough, her senses returned, and she surfaced amid fire and blasted bits of wood.

The canoe had been reduced to wreckage. There must have been some kind of explosive hidden on the ship. Surely her little fire couldn't cause that much damage.

And the captain was nowhere to be seen. Dead, she hoped.

Shouts of commotion at the shore drew her attention. Some soldiers stood and gawked as yet another ship was destroyed, others shouted desperately for more buckets and more water, and pleaded with others to search for survivors.

But above it all, the most beautiful sound of all.

"Where are the fucking children?" Tuun shouted, voice cracking in rage.

Xiala laughed. Teanni and her wife had done it.

But her joy was short-lived, as she caught sight of a soldier dragging a struggling woman out of the jungle. He threw the woman at Tuun's feet. Torchlight caught in her frightened eyes, and blood dripped from a cut across her forehead. She had been gagged and her hands bound.

It was Teanni.

Xiala shuddered, horror bubbling in her gut. What had happened? She could only guess Keala had gotten the children away while Teanni stayed behind to distract the guards. And now—*oh, Mother waters, not Teanni!*

Xiala watched from the water as Tuun dragged her friend down the pier, all the while shouting orders at the remaining soldiers. She stopped in front of the ship that had unexpectedly exploded and stared. Xiala could see the horror and rage etched on her face.

Tuun grabbed the nearest soldier by the arm.

"Where is your captain?"

The man shook his head, his meaning clear enough.

Tuun visibly shuddered, grief flashing across her face before a mask of implacability fell across her patrician features.

"You are my new captain," she said to the man. "Ready the remaining ship to sail. We're leaving."

The soldier looked momentarily stunned but quickly came to his senses. He bowed and then ran, shouting orders, everyone bustling to follow Tuun's command.

For a moment, it was only Tuun and Teanni on the dock, and Xiala realized that it was now or not at all.

Xiala swam to the dock and dragged herself up.

Tuun turned at the sound of her exiting the water. As soon as she spotted Xiala, her eyes flared with hate.

"This is your doing."

"Mine alone," Xiala acknowledged. "Let Teanni go."

"I'll let her go if you give me my ships. Where are my tide-chasers, Xiala?"

"They were never yours."

Tuun's fingers dug into Teanni's arm, and the woman cried out.

"Ships," Tuun spit from between jeweled teeth.

"They're gone."

"And my soldiers? My captain?" Her voice cracked.

"I think you know the answer to that," Xiala said, echoing what Tuun had told her when she had asked about Mahina's fate.

"Dead, then." Tuun nodded, as if accepting the inevitable. "You understand this means that our truce is at an end."

"To be honest, my heart wasn't in it." Xiala flexed her hands, eyes flicking between Tuun and Teanni.

Tuun saw her look, and her smile sent a shiver of dread down Xiala's back.

"Your friend is no use to me," the woman admitted. "Only another body on an already overcrowded ship." Her eyes turned toward her burning canoes. "This was foolish," she whispered, almost to herself. "You were so close, Xiala. Only a few more days, and I would have had my ships and left you in peace. You could have been a queen."

"You would have never left us in peace. You said so yourself, *Empress*. And besides, I already told you I wasn't interested."

"You think you've won something here? Is that it? You're free now?" She clicked her tongue in disapproval. "When this war is over, I will return to this cursed island with ten times the warriors I have now, and there will be no bargains, no kindness from me. I will crush you and your kind simply because I can. So enjoy your victory now, Xiala, but spend every day and every sleepless night wondering when I will return. Today will give you no comfort."

Rows of soldiers stomped down the pier, packs on their backs. They had retrieved only what they needed to make the journey back to Hokaia. They tramped past Xiala with little more than a glance, more concerned with getting off the island before their last ship burned than disposing of a single Teek whom Tuun seemed to have well in hand.

If they had known that Xiala had set the fires or that she had butchered their friends, perhaps they would have hesitated. Taken the time to exact their revenge. But as it was, their only concern was escape.

When the last soldier was aboard, Tuun dragged Teanni up the plank while Xiala watched.

"Let her go!" she shouted, as Tuun kicked the plank away.

Tuun stared at her for a moment, and—*foolish Teek!*—Xiala almost believed she would. Instead, she forced Teanni up onto the rail, hands still bound, gag in her mouth, her eyes pleading for Xiala to save her.

But they both knew it was too late.

Tuun shook Teanni by the collar, leaning her precipitously over the open water. "You didn't really think I'd give her back, did you? Especially after you killed my captain. What is the saying? Blood for blood?"

Her expression flattened, and she drew a knife across Teanni's throat.

Xiala screamed.

Tuun pushed, and Teanni tumbled into the sea.

Xiala was swimming before she knew it, arms and legs churning through the water. A volley of arrows pierced the waves around her, and she dove deeper, Teek eyes widening in the darkness until the depths of the sea were as bright to her as the land above. She caught a glimpse of Teanni in the distance, her body slowly sinking.

Please, Mother. Not this. Not Teanni!

Teanni, who had been her first kiss.

Teanni, who had never judged her for running away, who had never spoken against her even after Xiala's own mother had condemned her.

Teanni, who had welcomed her into her home with Keala and called her friend and sister.

Xiala felt when it happened. The surge forward, the waters parting before her with no effort, the sea flowing through her lungs sweet as air.

She did not need to look to know she had finally transformed.

But it was too little, too late.

She gathered Teanni into her arms, her friend's throat leaking a watery trail of blood, her eyes wide and staring, neck limp and almost severed by Tuun's obsidian knife. Xiala desperately pressed a webbed hand to the wound, but it was a useless gesture.

No!

She kicked to the surface with her powerful tail, bringing Teanni with her. They broke through the surface, and she scrambled to lift Teanni's head above the water, hands cupped under her chin.

"Breathe! Damn you, breathe! Please . . . oh, Mother waters, please!"

A sob broke from Xiala's throat.

"Breathe!"

But Teanni would never breathe again.

She held Teanni's body close, the salt of her tears mixing with the sea, her powerful tail keeping her afloat.

"I did it," she whispered. "I've changed. You were right. The power was there all along. I just needed your help."

Oh, skies, but not like this. Why like this?

She was not sure how long they floated there together,

Teanni draped across Xiala's chest as Xiala drifted on the tide. An hour? Two?

This is too much, she thought. *They have finally taken too much from me. Family, friends, home. And now I have nothing left to give but hate.*

Hate for hate.

So be it.

She relaxed her hold, letting Teanni go. She watched the body bob for a moment until the waves rose and she was lost in the darkness among the swells.

Xiala looked back toward Teek, now small in the distance. Keala must be wondering what happened to her wife, but Xiala didn't have the heart to return and tell her. She had cried all the tears she meant to cry, grieved all she could grieve.

Now there was only a reckoning.

She turned north, in the direction Tuun had gone.

And she followed.

CHAPTER 28

> Do not dwell on the past when the future has yet to be
> written.
>
> —*Exhortations for a Happy Life*

The healing took all night and most of the next day. Twice
Naranpa had to rest as the life she forced into Iktan's failing
body drained from her own. But by nightfall on the second day,
the infection was gone, the wounds were healed, and xe, freshly
bathed, was sitting up in clean sheets and drinking some of the
tea the local healer had left behind.

"It strengthens the blood," Iktan explained, "but it tastes
like reconstituted animal shit."

"It might be. Have you heard of tuktuks? My teacher said
they cure a number of ills."

Iktan smiled. "You must have many stories to tell."

"And I will share them all. But tell me first, how did this
happen?"

Iktan moved xir toes, looking relieved they moved at all.
"I was rash. I acted on impulse and did not plan well, and the
jaguar lord outsmarted me."

"The jaguar lord?" Surely it was not a coincidence.

"I killed him for it, of course. But he almost reciprocated the honor."

Naranpa hesitated. "Are you sure he's dead?"

"He looked very dead when I left, but why do you ask?"

"I think he has been in my dreams."

"Recently?"

"No, and death would his explain his absence. But I think he may still live. I had a vision of him holding the Sun Priest's mask."

"A vision?" xe asked. "Like an oracle vision?"

She hadn't thought of that. There were stories of oracles of old who did not just read the stars but were able to see time— past, present, and future. Had the sun god stirred yet another ancient power within her?

"I don't know," she admitted. "But I saw you in a vision. You were hiding, and then you were on a boat."

"That is accurate. And if you saw true then, it is likely you saw true for Balam." She could tell xe did not like the news that the jaguar lord might have survived.

"So you were in Cuecola?" she prompted.

Xe came back from wherever xir mind had wandered. "Hokaia."

Iktan told her of xir journey there with Golden Eagle and of how the southern merchant lords plotted with the spear-maidens and the Teek to invade Tova and kill the Odo Sedoh. Things she had suspected and Iktan now confirmed.

She smoothed a hand across her skirts. "I fought him, you know. The Odo Sedoh."

Iktan inhaled sharply. "And yet here you are. It seems we are both hard to kill."

"He was injured, and I healed him. I know it sounds

implausible, but you weren't there. You didn't see. He was just a man, and barely that. Young, and just as confused by his god's demands as I was."

"He slaughtered all our friends."

She sighed, conceding the point. "It gets worse. I told him he should rule the city."

"You—?" It started as a chuckle and built, until Iktan was doubled over with laughter.

The humor was infectious, and Naranpa found herself laughing, too. It felt surprisingly good, a much-needed cleansing.

"It really isn't funny," she said, after their laughter had died down.

"It is absurd, Naranpa." Iktan wiped tears away. "In the best way. You are responsible for the Carrion King."

"Carrion King? What an awful name. He was not so terrible."

"A legion of dead would say otherwise."

"You are not one to judge, my Priest of Knives." It came out more tartly than she had intended, but Iktan only grinned.

"*Your* Priest of Knives. I like the sound of that."

"Do you?" Naranpa bit her lip. "Iktan, before, when you were delirious with fever, before I healed you, you said something."

"I remember."

"Not the apology, although it is appreciated. I mean the other thing."

Iktan reached out a hand.

"Come here, Nara."

Naranpa had been sitting at the foot of the bed, her back against the wall and Iktan's legs resting across hers. Xe held xir arms open, and she crawled across the mattress to wedge herself against xir chest. She rested her head in the crook of xir neck. She could feel the steady thrum of xir pulse against her cheek, heartbeat strong and steady.

Iktan's arms encircled her, and the weight of loneliness, of regrets and mistakes, lifted from her heart.

"I missed this," xe said, chin resting on her head. "I missed you."

"I thought you hated me." She almost didn't want to bring it up, worried it would poison this perfect moment. But unkind words had passed between them, cruel deeds had been done. She could not pretend it was otherwise.

"I took you for granted." The admission was heavy with grief, and she remembered the intensity of emotions she had felt in xir dream. "I thought you would always be there, as you had been since that first day we met."

"On Kiutue's balcony." She smiled. "I remember."

"And you had those wonderful potatoes."

Her stomach rumbled at the mention of food, and they both laughed.

Iktan shifted, sliding down to meet her, hands cradling her face. They were eye to eye, so close they breathed the same air, lips near enough to touch if Naranpa tilted her head even the slightest measure.

"I cannot change what I did," Iktan whispered. "And I know words are not enough to heal your wounds, Naranpa. But I will perform whatever penance you ask of me, do what I must to prove that I will never, ever leave you again. Will never let your enemies touch you again. Only tell me what is required, and I will do it."

She brushed her lips across xirs. "Show me."

"What?"

"You are right. Words are not enough, but I ask no penance of you, Iktan. Only that you show me that you love me."

The softest of sighs escaped Iktan's lips.

"Gladly."

Naranpa wound her hands in xir hair and pulled xir mouth to hers. Iktan tasted of home, of comfort and all the things she thought she had lost. Xir arms tightened around her, and the ache of years melted away. For the first time in months, years, Naranpa felt safe.

"Why are you crying?" Iktan asked. Xe pressed lips to wet cheeks and kissed away her tears.

"Because I love you, too," she said.

Iktan rolled onto xir back, pulling Naranpa up to straddle xir hips. Xir black eyes gleamed with mischief.

"Then show me," xe said.

And she did.

• • • • •

The next morning, Naranpa sat with Iktan at a table near the fire in the plank house hall and ate like she had never eaten food before. Everything was a revelation. The dried elk meat was wonderfully chewy and perfectly salted, the honeyberry jam that she spread over the hard, dry, crackerlike bread common to the north was richer and juicier than she had ever had. Even the water, no doubt hauled from the river nearby, tasted crisper than she remembered water could be.

Iktan sat next to her, their thighs and hips touching, and every so often she would smile for no reason, and xe would smile back, and Naranpa felt like they were teenagers in the tower, newly discovering the joy of first love. Only it was better now. Fought for and earned, deepened by time and hardship in a way that their first relationship had never been.

A clamor at the entrance drew their attention, and Naranpa

stuffed the last bite of her breakfast into her mouth as they both turned to look. A man dressed in a green mantle and short hide kilt was drawing a crowd.

"Who is he?" Naranpa wondered.

"Hokaian," Iktan said. "By the looks of his clothing, at least. He must have arrived off the boat this morning."

"With news?"

"Shall I go see?" Iktan asked, already standing. Naranpa watched as xe edged into the crowd, talking to a woman standing in front of the Hokaian stranger and then another man to her right. After a moment, Iktan was back, face grim.

"What is it?" Naranpa asked, dread already pooling in her belly.

"Hokaia sets sail for war. The Sovran has declared the day."

Naranpa pressed a hand to her mouth. She had known it would come, they had both known, but to hear it was in motion, that in only a matter of days Tova would be under attack . . . Her stomach roiled at the reality.

"Some good news." Iktan's voice lifted. "It seems that most of the Golden Eagle clan is dead."

Naranpa remembered Iktan's dream and Nuuma's body floating in black water.

"Did you have something to do with that?"

Iktan's gaze drifted. "And if I did?" Xe did not meet her eyes.

She touched xir cheek to turn xir gaze to her. "Nuuma was horrible. She may not have killed my brother directly, but his blood is on her hands. Do you think I mourn her death?"

Iktan relaxed. "Then we are in agreement. But"—and the tension seem to come back, shoulders lifting—"there is some bad news. It seems you were correct, and Lord Balam lives."

"Balam. That's the Cuecolan jaguar lord."

"And sorcerer."

She knew all too well. "Then he will come for me. There is a reason he Walks in my dreams."

"And what exactly does that mean, Nara, that he Walks in your dreams?"

She explained it all. Kupshu and the dreamwalking and, before that, waking up in her tomb under the Maw and the awakening of the sun god within her. She was hesitant at first. It all seemed so unbelievable, so out of character for who she had been at the tower.

"You are a wonder," Iktan said when she had finished. Out of habit, Naranpa looked for the mockery in xir tone, but xe was entirely sincere. Xe grasped her hand and pressed lips to her palm. "And to think I doubted you once upon a time. Thought that you were not capable of leading us."

"You may have been right," she admitted, "but I am not the same woman I was then." The past months had been a kiln that had fired and reshaped her into something, and someone, new.

"Yes and no," xe said, and did not elaborate.

Xe did not need to. She understood. The core of who she was had always been there, but it took betrayal and devastation to sharpen her into something more. She would not repeat it, especially not the loss of Denaochi, and she would give all her newfound power back if it would bring her brother back. But here she was, and for the first time she realized she was more than just a victim of circumstance.

She was a weapon.

And with that realization came a choice. A choice that felt inevitable now that it manifested before her. Iktan was watching her, keen eyes reading something in her face. She had never been able to hide her feelings from xir.

She pressed a hand to Iktan's cheek. Xe had always been

beautiful, a face of planes and angles, a geometry of perfection that she had always loved, would always love. Was she truly going to say goodbye, again?

"We cannot let this assault against Tova go forward." Her voice was quiet, determined.

Iktan frowned. "We are days, maybe weeks, behind the Treaty armies, even if we left now."

"I do not mean for us to go to Tova."

"Then what?"

"I said Balam would come for me, and I believe that is true. To him, I am still the Sun Priest, and I must be defeated."

"Then I will kill him and be certain of it this time." Iktan's voice was hot with passion.

"No, Iktan. Where Balam is you cannot follow." She smiled as a plan began to form in her mind. "But he cannot come for me if I come for him first."

• • • • •

They left the next morning, traveling north, retracing the road Naranpa had taken only days before. The journey was slow. Iktan was healed, feet shod in new hard-soled boots that xe had "found," but xe still moved tentatively as xir body worked to restore what had been lost after the torturous time in hiding and the subsequent period bedridden.

The weather cooperated, and the roads stayed passable and the skies clear. At night, they would make a small fire and marvel at the northern sky overhead. And when the wonder of the stars waned, they would delight in the splendor of breath and touch and sensation, limbs tangled, mouths hungry, and souls aligned. They were the best days of Naranpa's life.

But as they drew closer to their destination, she knew they must end.

They reached Charna on a sunny midmorning two days before the summer solstice. The days this far north stretched forever, the sun dominating the sky and denying the night its due. Naranpa felt the shift of seasons in her bones. She knew that the sun god was quickly approaching the height of her power, and so was she. If she was going to face Balam, it must be soon.

But first . . .

"I want you to meet someone," she told Iktan as they made their way through the village.

Iktan looked around, amused. "This is where you lived?"

"Yes." Along the single dirt road through town were some mud and stone huts and animal pens, mostly empty, their tenants out for grazing. Near the middle of town was a common well and market stalls. A handful of people carried woven baskets full of fish, and a man mended the hull of an overturned ship, no doubt meant for trawling the nearby lake. "Is it so strange that I called this home?"

"A Maw girl moved to the countryside," xe said, grinning. "Did you milk the tartars?"

"They're called tuktuks," she said primly, "and I sheared them."

Iktan laughed.

"If Kupshu has her way, you'll be out in the pens working, too."

"No, I won't," xe assured her, but xe smiled when xe said it.

They passed through the village and along the path near the lake until they came to Kupshu's home. It was smaller and dingier than Naranpa remembered it, but it warmed her heart to be able to keep her promise to return. She quickened her step and pushed the door open without knocking.

"I'm back!" she cried. "Kupshu?"

And now she understood why the little house looked so sad. It was empty. No fire in the hearth, no tea brewing over the fire.

"Kupshu?" she called again, but the shack only had two rooms, and the old woman was in neither.

Iktan idled by the door.

"I don't understand," Naranpa said, disappointed.

"It looks like no one has been here for a while."

Naranpa ran a hand across bone-dry water buckets, peered into a cold and empty ash pail. "She said she was going to her sister's, but that was weeks ago."

"Perhaps she decided to stay."

Naranpa's shoulders sagged. "But I wanted to show her that I came back."

"She will be just as happy to see you in a month as she would have been today. Maybe happier, since by then Balam will be dead."

Naranpa swallowed her secret and nodded. She could not tell Iktan that she did not expect to be alive in a month, or even next week.

"Let's stay here tonight," she said. "Kupshu would not mind, and I'd like a roof over my head and a mattress for a night."

"A mattress?" Iktan's arms slid around her waist. Xe kissed her neck as xir hands wandered. "A mattress has possibilities."

She closed her eyes and let herself fall into the feeling. *At least I have this for another night*, she told herself.

And that would have to be enough.

CHAPTER 29

Mother waters, first and last.
Mother waters, spot the mast.
Lightning flashing, winds lashing,
Waves crashing, ship smashing.
Mother waters, first and last.
Mother waters, no more mast.

—Teek children's game

Xiala swam through the night, moving through the water as if she was born to it. And the sea? It had always been her mother, her sustainer, her friend and first love.

But now it was a revelation.

She had known the sea was life. After all, she ate from her bounty, sailed merchant ships full of riches across her waves, and the Teek called her Mother. But in her newly transformed and revelatory state, so much more complete than the change she had experienced before, Xiala was as much sea creature as human woman, and she realized she had only scratched the surface.

The sea was more than a life giver. It was life itself.

Life, in the smallest sandworm. Life, in the boneless, glutinous jellyfish. Life, in the undulating manta rays. And everything that lived within the sea, including the gestational waters themselves, sang. From the creatures that were barely a speck against her fingernail to the mightiest leviathans, the whole of the underwater world communicated in chorus. Her world was filled with the uncanny beauty of whale song, the bubbling chatter of sand divers, the sonorous keening of sea turtles. It all exclaimed in riotous choir.

Xiala had always believed herself in harmony with the Mother, but this was something more. She *was* the Mother, or at least a form of her. And as her instrument, Xiala held the very font of life within her: both the creatures that lived and died and the unfathomable might of the tides.

It was power. Power like she had never imagined, and for the first few hours after her transformation, she simply struggled to contain the deluge of energy that surged within her. After a time, she managed to reduce the terrifying flood to the gentler drag of a dangerous but survivable riptide, and by daybreak, she had reduced it further still, to something more like the rise and fall of a normal tide.

In and out. High and low. It was a constant balancing. After all, such immense and varied power could not be controlled. It existed in reciprocity. Taking and receiving, a tidal ebb and flow. She had only to find a way to float in it, to hold the power in her open hand and let it flow through her fingers at the same time.

Teanni had been right about one thing.

Before, when Xiala had tried to drown herself, she had been trying too hard. The sea did not want her surrender. It wanted her cooperation. It was a state of mutuality, not submission.

The thought of Teanni dampened some of her wonder. If only her friend could see her now, breathing water through delicate gills at her neck, cutting through the waves with a flick of her powerful, black-scaled tail, her hair trailing behind her like a bed of rich kelp.

But the transformation did not free her completely from the limitations of her humanity. Xiala still tired. She still grew hungry. Only now she was far from land, and without knives and nets, she wasn't sure how she was supposed to eat. Simply catch a fish, apologize profusely for her cannibalism, and take a bite?

The thought was surprisingly disconcerting, even though she knew fish ate each other all the time. She even had the teeth for it; a tail, gills, and webbed hands were not the only changes to her form. Her teeth had become sharp and elongated, a predator's teeth.

If the tail had been enough to scare the Cuecolan sailors on her voyage to Tova, she could only imagine the terror her teeth would provoke from Tuun and her murdering crew. They would think her a monster.

And they would be right.

Xiala's stomach rumbled, a very un-monstrous thing, and she decided, fish kin or not, she had to eat. She began by finding a mass of free-floating seaweed, the thick algae bloom offering her nutrient-rich food. Small silver fish dipped and dived within the flora, and she partook of the bounty, reminding herself that with teeth like hers, it was meant to be.

Balance, she reminded herself. The sea, while brimming with life, was certainly no stranger to death.

Her hunger sated, she swam on. Always north, northwest. Always listening for the passage of ships in the reverberations of the waves, the canticles of passing sea life.

She found that she could hold her mermaid form effortlessly and swim for miles, and while she did fatigue, it was no more taxing than walking on land. At some point, she would have to sleep, but she told herself there would be time for sleep once Tuun was dead.

On the third day, she felt it. The heavy dip of paddles rhythmically punching the surface of the water and the surge of something big slicing across the waves.

She rose to take stock of her enemies.

An overcrowded Cuecolan canoe sat heavy in the water before her, rows of soldiers bent over paddles as they pressed their vessel through the water. In the glint of the sun off the open sea, the sheen of sweat glistened on hunched backs and exhausted muscles. They must have been paddling with almost no rest from the time they fled, no doubt fueled by the threat of Tuun's wrath and a desire to get as far from Teek as quickly as possible. Tuun herself was nowhere to be seen, likely hidden away in the captain's quarters away from the heat.

Xiala swam closer, careful to stay unseen while at the same time thinking of how she might draw Tuun out. She could think of only one way, and it meant exposing herself on the open sea with nowhere to hide but under the waves. A risk, but she could see no other way. The longer she waited, the closer they drew to Hokaia, and the more likely they were to encounter other vessels coming and going. Other vessels meant a greater chance of losing Tuun in the confusion. The Cuecolan lord would never be more isolated and vulnerable than she was right now.

Xiala plunged back below the waves to surface a few lengths away, this time in full view of the ship's lookout. She slammed her tail against the waves, sending a huge plume of spray high in the air. And then did it again. Once, twice, a third time.

The sighting took no time at all.

"Man overboard!" the lookout shouted, waving wildly.

But of course, they saw a humanlike figure in the water and assumed. In a way, she was touched. But "man overboard" would not do.

She leaned back, flicking her black-scaled tail, her plum-colored hair spreading out around her.

She could not see the lookout's face from where she was, but she heard the panic in his voice. No, more than panic. Fear.

"Sea monster! Sea monster! Starboard quarter!"

That was better.

More cries from the deck followed, now accompanied by the thump of running feet. Heads popped up along the rail to point and shout.

Show yourself, Tuun, Xiala thought. *Come and face your fate.*

The first arrow that arched across the sky toward her took Xiala by surprise. Awash in her newfound power, she had forgotten about the Cuecolan archers.

Suddenly, she was on the beach again, facing down an invading army. Instead of the arias of the ocean, her ears filled with the twang of bowstrings, the thud of obsidian spears as they pierced flesh, the screams of the dying wise women. She threw her hands over her ears and squeezed her eyes closed, her vision overwhelmed by memories of her aunt toppling to the sand, a bolt protruding from her belly.

An arrow nicked Xiala's arm, drawing a fiery streak of pain and a cry from her lips. Shaken, she dove. Arrows sliced through the water around her, but she swam faster and farther than a human could go. Soon the deadly rain ceased, unable to follow so deep.

She stayed below, dazed by the shock of her failure. She had let herself forget how dangerous humans were and that even she, beloved by the Mother and a creature of the sea, was not invincible.

And worst of all, it had all happened so fast that she had seen nothing of Tuun.

Her arm ached, and she peered at her shoulder. Blood billowed in wispy trails from the place where the arrow had hit her. It had taken a piece of skin and flesh with it and now bled freely. It hurt enough that when she moved her arm, her vision sparked with stars.

You are a fool, Xiala, she chided herself. *And with nothing to show for it.*

With both her pride and her body injured, she decided to rest before trying again. She let herself drift, trusting the Mother to hold her in the cradling sea. She must have lost consciousness, because sometime later, she awoke to a bump on her side.

She opened her eyes in time to see a silver and white body, twice as long as her own, glide past. It took a moment for her mind to comprehend what she was seeing, some part of her brain still not able to reconcile a lifetime on land with the fact that she was underwater, but when she did stutter to understanding, she knew she was in trouble.

She was weakened, she smelled of fish and blood, and she had come to the attention of a very large shark.

But she didn't panic. After all, sharks could be fought. They were sensitive creatures, their eyes and gills vulnerable. But their sense of smell and their relentless stamina meant that she could not run and hide. She would have to fight.

But with what weapon?

She looked around and saw only miles of water, and in the distance, the shark was already turning back toward her to make another pass. And now she started to worry, if only a little.

She tried to think of the stories she had learned growing up, but her mind was a jumble. There were tales of Teek who had faced down the predators of the sea. Greater ones than sharks. Stories of leviathans and krakens that lived in the darkest depths and ate ships whole.

If only her Mother had given her the power to command a kraken.

And Xiala realized with a laugh that was exactly what her Mother had done. The creatures of the sea were not her enemies, and she was not theirs. She didn't need to fight the shark, she only needed to Sing to it.

But not all beasts of the sea sang the same song.

What would sharks sing of? she thought. *Besides, well, eating me?*

She knew the answer as soon as she asked the question. Sharks sang of the hunt, as Xiala had expected. The thrill of chase and capture, the pleasure of feeding. But even more, they sang of a life of forever moving, of days gliding through miles of open waters. They also sang of swimming through time, of ancestors and long solitary decades of individual existence. There were brief fluttering notes of mating, offspring, and a deep undertone of kinship with others like themselves. Xiala took it all and shaped it into a melody that poured from her throat in a song of the hunt, the aching loneliness, the fleeting kinship. She added her own notes, a warning that she was a predator, too, and would not be easy prey.

And it worked. Mother waters, it worked.

The shark swam away, disappearing into deeper water, looking for an easier meal.

She waited a while, shark song still on her lips, but it did not return.

Finally, she let herself relax. Her arm still ached, but the bleeding had slowed. She would have liked to rest, but she had already wasted an untold amount of time, and she was scared Tuun was only getting farther away.

Determined, she continued her pursuit, a new idea already forming in her mind.

It took a full day to catch up to the Cuecolan canoe, but this time she did not approach. Instead, she stayed a healthy distance away, only rising out of the water enough to confirm that it was the right ship. Unfortunately, she also saw a stretch of thin, wispy clouds in the far distance. That meant land. They were closer to Hokaia than she had expected.

· She could wait no longer.

Xiala descended. Down, down, to the darkest depths of the Crescent Sea. Soon the canoe above shrank to a distant sliver, and then a dot. And still she descended.

The world began to change around her, light lessening and then disappearing altogether. She moved through darkness, a world of crabs and krill, and then even those passed from sight. The weight of water pressed against her, and it felt like the entirety of the world's ocean was trying to crush her.

And still she dove, until she was in total darkness, and the life that had teemed around her seemed very far away. She finally stopped, unable to go any deeper, her own life already at risk. She only hoped she had gone deep enough.

With her remaining breath, she Sang.

It was an ancient song, one that vibrated through the waters like the rich and heavy hum of the world itself. If the sharks sang of centuries passing, the song she Sang now spoke of eons, of the shifting of continents and the falling of stars, of the turn of the heavens and birth and death of great seas.

It was a song rarely heard, a song that, as it reverberated through the sea, sent the smaller creatures that knew only light and life scattering in terror. It was a song that shivered even Xiala's heart. But it was the song of a creature that knew something of dangerous men on ships and the necessity of revenge and the fire of righteous hate. And so it rose at Xiala's call, its great body shifting tides, the long reach of its tentacles unfolding like the flowering of a deadly bloom.

It moved past Xiala, and opened a single curious eye to see

the thing that had dared to awaken it from its slumber. Xiala watched it ascend, ten times larger than any ship, its girth more akin to an island than anything made by human hands. A sinuous limb slid past her, and she grasped the slick appendage to let the kraken pull her along toward the surface.

It was not a fair fight, but Xiala had never wanted fair. She had wished for total destruction, and that was what she received.

The kraken breached the surface with a deafening roar. Its monstrous battle cry was echoed by the screams and shouts of soldiers as the great beast fell upon them.

Xiala had positioned herself a reasonable distance away to watch the slaughter. Some part of her felt a kinship with those doomed souls on the ship. After all, she was a sailor, too, and knew the terror of living and dying at the mercy of the sea. But any sympathy she might have had, any hesitation at calling down death upon the men and women aboard, was quickly stifled by the memories of what these soldiers had done to the Teek, to her aunt and the wise women, to Alani and Teanni. The memories transformed the monster's roar and the dying's screams into a sweet song of justice, a melody of reckoning, and not simply a violent dirge.

To their credit, most of the soldiers did not panic but instead reached for their weapons. A burst of arrows flew toward the kraken as it rose higher and higher from the sea. For a moment, its massive body dwarfed the ship as the arrows bounced uselessly off its thick, purpled skin.

Its size alone disrupted the waters, sending wave after wave rushing toward the canoe. But Cuecolan ships were built to withstand the unpredictable storms of the Crescent Sea, and while the vessel tilted, sending a handful of soldiers into the water, the ship righted itself quickly, and those who were left continued their assault.

A massive tentacle rose from the depths, so high that Xiala

craned her neck to see. The arm rippled with muscle and ended in a fearsome hooked club that was peppered with serrated suckers. The creature brought the arm down with a horrible screech. The wooden hull shattered under the impossible weight, and bodies were tossed skyward before plummeting below. Xiala saw a man impaled on a splintered paddle and another flattened by falling debris. More bodies struck the water, some still alive, limbs flailing in the punishing waves. Most dead, their blood already darkening the waters.

Xiala watched as a spearmaiden flung herself from the bow of the ship, now angled vertically out of the wreckage, hoping to plant her spear in the kraken's eye. Xiala screamed, a single note meant to kill the maiden, but the beast had already wrapped a razored tentacle around the woman, snatching her from the air before she could find her mark. The beast squeezed, and the woman burst.

Xiala did not turn away, even though her stomach turned. This was her doing, and she would not hide from the horror of it. She did not revel, but she did bear witness.

The carnage did not last much longer. Most upon the ship had died when the vessel was torn asunder, and those who did not survived only long enough to drown in the furious tumult that rolled relentlessly from the kraken's colossal body.

Xiala knew it was over by the silence. No more screams, no more desperate cries to indifferent gods, no more cracking wood or bestial roars. Just the soft lull of waves where once a hundred lives had been.

She Sang her thanks to the kraken, and the great beast bellowed its reply before it sank below the waters. The sea was littered with broken bits of boat: smashed barrels, splintered paddles, scraps of cloth and food and weapons bobbing on the surface.

And everywhere the dead.

Xiala worked her way through the wreckage, stopping to inspect the bodies, looking for one in particular. It was nightmarish work, but she did not cower from it. In fact, she was eager. But despite her diligent hunt through corpse-filled waters, she saw no sign of Tuun.

She dove below the surface, where more of the dead littered the depths. Again, she was thorough in her search but came up empty-handed. Somewhere she had lost Tuun. Either the woman had somehow evaded the kraken's attack, or she had made her escape before Xiala had brought the ship down.

In truth, Xiala had never actually seen Tuun once the canoe had departed from Teek. It was possible the ship had crossed paths with another vessel long before Xiala even caught up to them, and she had been chasing a phantom across the Crescent Sea.

Frustration at her failure bubbled up inside her, and she screamed her fury to the sea, fists beating against the tide and tail thrashing uselessly. Tuun had taken so much from her and deserved any retribution Xiala might rain down upon her. And yet it seemed that even the Mother could not bring the Cuecolan lord to justice.

No matter.

Xiala gazed toward the coastline in the distance, no more than a day's swim. She would chase Teanni's murderer across the whole continent if she must.

A song reverberated through the water. Far away but coming closer. A song Xiala recognized, which sang of hunt and hunger.

Sharks, and this time more than one. Of course, they would be called to the carrion, and this time, Xiala did not think they would be dissuaded.

"Hokaia, then," she whispered, and swam on.

CHAPTER 30

I would not ask for your sacrifice if I did not believe that it
is through blood that the gifts of the gods are bestowed
upon us.

—From the *Oration of the Jaguar Prince on the Eve of the Frenzy*

Someone was shouting his name, and for a moment, Balam
was certain he had fallen asleep and was dreaming.

It was well into the night. He was seated at his desk, once
again reading through Seuq's manual. A wad of dried yaupon
was lodged between his lip and gum. The stimulant was meant
to keep him awake, and yet.

The shouting continued, growing more aggressive. The voice
was angry and exhausted and edged in panic. Even worse, the
owner of the voice seemed to be blaming him for their current
state. They were calling him some very colorful names, most of
them pertaining to his parents' sexual mores and their impact
on his lineage. The others were outright insults.

"If this is a dream, it is a poor one," he muttered. He pressed
fingertips to temples and worked to rub the nightmare away.

Balam had done his best to forswear sleep. Not simply on

this night but on all nights. He would have abandoned the practice entirely, if possible. Unfortunately, and to his great disappointment, he was still human and therefore required rest.

It was not that he was opposed to slumber in general, but his head had become an uncomfortable place, full of dead women, difficult memories, and self-reproach. On the nights when his mind granted him a reprieve from his past sins, it was eager to have him dwell upon his encounter with the Priest of Knives. He did not care to live through his attempted murder again, even if only in his imagination.

The voice became a hammering on his door, and then, "By all the gods, open this door! Or I will bring this roof down on your head, you cat-fucking son of a whor—"

Tuun. It was Tuun banging on his door and disparaging him so creatively.

Not a dream at all.

Curious. He had not expected her back until the new moon. She was early.

He padded to the door and opened it just as she launched into a string of curses so vile even he felt the need to blush.

She stopped abruptly.

"Finally," she huffed, and stormed past him. He looked down the hall, where half the household stood in their doorways, eyes wide in shock.

"It's fine," he assured them. "Back to your beds."

Slowly, they obeyed, but not before giving him lingering looks of pity. He understood the implied condolences; Tuun was his problem now.

He closed his door firmly.

"What happened to your voice?" she threw over her shoulder.

He touched a hand self-consciously to the scar on his throat. "A story for another time. Why are you here?"

Tuun had already made her way to his personal collection of xtabentún. She broke the lip of the clay vessel against the edge of his travel trunk and tipped the bottle over her mouth, letting the liquor run down her throat.

"Would you like a cup?" he asked. She was drinking a particularly fine botanical blend he had meant to save for a special celebratory occasion.

She swallowed and shot him a sour look.

"No," she said, voice curt. She took the bottle and dropped onto his bed.

He grimaced but decided it was not worth telling her he didn't like other people lying on his blankets. Something about the lingering smell of another body bothered him. He didn't think Tuun would appreciate his eccentricities in her current state of mind, and he wasn't planning to use the bed anyway.

"You've arrived early," he said, trying again. "I expected you tomorrow, or the next day. At a decent hour. Say, after breakfast."

"Don't start with me, Balam. I'm not in the mood." She drank more.

"Well, you're using my name instead of calling me a cat fucker," he observed, voice dry, "so that's progress."

She flushed. "I'm sorry. I thought perhaps you wouldn't let me in. That there was nowhere safe for me . . ." Her voice drifted off, and Tuun looked distinctly haunted. In fact, Balam had never seen her so unnerved.

He was not unmoved, having recently been through his own unexpected trauma. "Perhaps if you begin at the beginning." He retrieved two cups, handed her one, and kept the other for himself.

"I'd rather not." She poured them each a measure of xtabentún. "You know most of it already, and the rest is quite prosaic." She grimaced. "Until it's not."

"When last we spoke through the mirror, you said all was in hand. What happened?"

"The Teek princess happened."

"Xiala?"

"You told me she was docile, a drunk. That she would be happy to help. I believe those were your exact words."

"I thought she *was* helping. You said she had organized the workers, that the fleet of tidechasers was coming along apace." He frowned. "You did bring me my ships, didn't you?"

"Fuck you, Balam," she muttered, and drained her cup.

"Am I to understand that to mean no, Tuun?" He had been patient through the insults and the drinking, but this was untenable. "You assured me you would be a knife at their throats. I believe those were *your* exact words."

She did not meet his glare and instead made to pour herself more drink, but the bottle was empty. With an irritated growl, she stood, obviously meaning to pilfer more from his private collection.

He rose to meet her, arm extended to block her path. "You owe me an explanation before you drink yourself into oblivion."

Her shoulders drooped, deflated, and she sank back onto the bed. She studied her hands, as if what she wished to say was written there, and did not look up at Balam when she said, "She is magic."

"The Teek Song. Yes, if you recall she killed Pech with—"

"I didn't say she had magic, I said she *is* magic."

"The Teek are such skilled sailors that their talent at sea is often confused with magic."

"You're not listening to me, Balam. She didn't calm the fucking waters or speed the tide, she set a kraken upon my ship. Has a Teek sailor ever done that? I should have drowned, almost did but for stupid luck. But that is not the worst of it. I left her on that beach without a single ship with which to follow me, and somehow she caught up, and not just caught up . . ." Tuun shivered. Her eyes wandered toward the liquor on the other side of the room, but she only looked.

"You won't believe me." Her sigh was heavy with his assumed doubt. "But she transformed into a creature I've only heard of in a story. Half fish, half woman. And she hunted me across the Crescent Sea."

Balam cleared his throat, turning his cup in his hands. "Just to be clear, you are saying the woman that I found in a Kuharan jail turned into a sea monster out of a child's story and stalked you from Teek to Hokaia?"

"I know how it sounds. I hear myself."

"And where is she now?"

"I don't know. But I do know I'm never going near the water again."

"Well, that might be a problem. I need you back on a boat heading for Tova."

She shook her head, adamant.

His irritation flared. "What happened to the Teek isle as your birthright? Of claiming the throne?"

"I want nothing to do with them."

"Lord Tuun." He set aside his cup and tried his best to stay calm. "This will not do. We have a plan. A very specific plan, I might add."

"I can't, Balam."

She sounded genuinely terrified. It fascinated him, as human weakness often did. What had Xiala done to her? But it was only idle curiosity that made him wonder, and there was no time for that now.

"Of all the things I expected from you," he said, letting some of the disdain he felt leak into his voice, "it was never to be craven."

"Call me names, if you wish, but it is not cowardice to know what you can survive and what will surely kill you."

His smile was thin. "You need to be upriver on the To-vasheh commanding the blockade. You are the only one I trust to do it."

"I won't!"

"I'm afraid you must."

"You cannot make me."

"Can I not?"

She opened her mouth, and Balam opened his hand. Blood from a cut already pooled in his palm.

"You wouldn't," she breathed.

"Wouldn't I?"

"Then give me something with which I can fight her!"

"Are you not a sorcerer?"

"Of land! My magic is the magic of the earth. I am power-less on the sea."

"Is not the sea simply on top of land?"

"Yes, but the weight of the water. I cannot . . ."

"Enough." He contemplated her there in her diminished state, his mind caught on the precipice of possible failure. No, he would not let this one person bring his plans to ruin. He was resourceful, was he not?

And there was always another way.

A dangerous, audacious way.

Balam stood up abruptly and walked across the room. There was a bottle there on a high shelf, a very special bottle, and he took it down now. He was careful not to touch the clay seal when he pried it open with a small blade, and he turned his head so he did not inhale the fumes of the drink directly. It smelled sweet, of honey flowers.

He took down a fresh cup and poured Tuun a measure of the drink and then carefully pressed the molded clay to the lip of the bottle to reseal it.

"Perhaps I have been too harsh." He approached Tuun with the cup, expression conciliatory. "Perhaps there is another way you can serve."

She took the cup and greedily drank its contents down. Balam watched, face neutral, until the cup was empty. And then he allowed himself a smile.

Tuun scraped a hand over her face. "Name it. As long as I don't have to set foot on a fucking ship until that Teek woman is dead."

Idle curiosity or not, he could not resist asking, "What happened to you?"

She shook her head, as if trying to clear her thoughts. "Just . . . scared . . ." She frowned, as if the words had not been her own.

He supposed they had not. Poison did make people say strange things before they succumbed.

She shook her head again, more violently this time, and then her eyes widened in shock. Her gaze fixed on him, and hatred flared in her eyes, hot enough to sear him had he not been immune to her feelings on the matter.

"You bastard . . . !" She managed to spit the epithet before her neck bent and her limbs went limp, and she collapsed sideways onto his bed.

He gingerly held a finger to her throat. Not dead. But she wasn't going to wake up anytime soon.

Nevertheless, because he respected her magic, Balam restrained her hands, bound her eyes, and tied a gag between her lips. It would be best to move her through the city before dawn. Probably in a sack, carried over a porter's capable shoulders.

"Such an indignity," he whispered to his former ally as he straightened her hair, fingers smoothing back the long strands. They had gone gray at the root during her time in Teek bereft of her dyes. Her skin, too, lacked the golden sheen he associated with her, another vanity sacrificed to primitive island living.

Why she had ever wanted those damned islands he would never understand. But it had been her undoing. If there was a lesson to learn about ambition within her fate, he was determined to ignore it. After all, now she would achieve a kind of glory she had not even thought to dream of.

In a way, she should be grateful.

Yes, he liked that. Grateful.

He went to call the porter.

• • • • •

The morning that the combined armies of the Treaty cities were to leave for Tova dawned gray and rainy. Balam contemplated the turn of the weather as he drank his customary tea and reviewed his plans for the day. He had not spoken to Powageh since their disagreement days before, and he wondered if he had pushed his loyal cousin too far. There was no denying that Powageh had been treating him differently since Iktan's attack, but Balam could not quite decipher the why of it. Was it that Balam's brush with death had prompted Powageh to consider xir own morality? Or did xir absence have more to do with the shadow work with which Balam had tasked his cousin?

Or maybe it was that the recent talk of Saaya had stirred old jealousies? Whatever the cause, today he would either reap the rewards of involving Powageh in his scheming or suffer the punishment.

He dressed in his formal whites, jaguar skin cloak fastened at his shoulder. Despite the weather, he wished to look his best. He was, in a completely unexpected turn, a hero of the city now. It was amusing at first, but as he thought more about it, he realized he could use his burgeoning popularity to his advantage. When he had initially begun this war endeavor, he had only thought of ruling Cuecola and its sister cities along the coast. With Serapio's survival, his scope had expanded to include Tova. And now the idea that his reign might extend across the Crescent Sea to Hokaia intrigued. The entirety of the Meridian lay ripe and ready before him.

But first he had to get through the day.

His morning appointment was with Naasut. The rain had turned much of the lower city to mud, and by the time he reached his destination, his sandals were ruined, and black bits of sludge dotted his legs and the hem of his hip skirt. But the dirt on his garments was nothing compared with the stench that assailed him as he entered the city jail.

Perhaps the smell was tolerable on a dry winter day, but now, in the wet and heat, the overwhelming odor of bodies and human waste in a confined space made Balam sway in the doorway.

There was a wooden stairway to his right, and Naasut appeared on the high step, eyes searching. Her gaze found him, and relief crossed her face before her features settled back into irritation.

"You're late, Lord Balam," she groused, and motioned him up the stairs.

The Hokaia jail was more animal pen than proper facility. He, Naasut, and a man who introduced himself as the warden stood on an elevated walkway that circled the wooden walls. As always, Naasut was not without a handful of spearmaidens, but they stood unobtrusively to the side. Somewhere along the way, Balam had passed from suspect foreigner to trusted ally, and the warden was elderly and stooped, someone Naasut could surely best with little effort if he was foolish enough to attack his Sovran.

Muscular men with long spears were stationed along the walkway at regular intervals. Below them, dozens upon dozens of humans were gathered in an enclosed open-air pen. Some slept, curled up on a loose scattering of reeds that did little to prevent the floor degrading to overtrodden slop. Others clustered around an impromptu game of patol. And yet others verbally assailed their jailers, heads tilted back and rotten-toothed mouths shouting that they had been unjustly imprisoned and demanding release.

"And which ones are the ones I requested?" Balam shouted over the din.

Naasut shrugged. "You said round up all the criminals, so we rounded them up."

"I said find me all the thieves."

"Thieves, vandals, arsonists, rapists. What does it matter?"

"It matters."

The warden said, "If I may, aren't they all thieves in some way?"

Balam tilted his head. "What do you mean?"

"They took something from someone, didn't they? Something without permission, whether money, property, or dignity. It's all stealing."

A smile crept across Balam's face. "A philosophical man. I

like it." He turned to Naasut. "They'll all do." He shifted back to the warden. "How many prisoners do you have here?"

"Around two hundred, Lord."

"My, Naasut," Balam said, delighted. "I believe you have a crime problem in your city. Rest assured, you will not after tonight."

"You still haven't explained why you need them."

"Hold them here until nightfall. Then bring them to the war college with the other items I asked for."

"The war college?" Naasut asked. "Why there? They say it's haunted."

"Of course it's haunted," he said, thinking of his own ghosts and what might await him there, but it could not be helped. It was one of the most desolate places within a short walk of the city, and they would need their privacy.

"But you will be at the parade, won't you, Balam? To see off the fleet."

He smiled. "I'm quite looking forward to it."

· · · · ·

As expected, the parade to the docks was spectacular. Even the rain could not dampen the spirits of the crowd that turned out in number, enthusiastic and loud. Balam walked with Powageh through the streets, nodding and waving to the citizens of the city he was now considering conquering once Tova was sub-jugated. Despite his moment of misgiving, his cousin showed up at the appointed time and in the appointed place, loyal as always.

"I know that look," Powageh said, eyes narrowed. "You're scheming."

Powageh was dressed in Cuecolan formal wear: a knee-length white garment edged in a pale blue pattern, thick jade in xir ears and at the collar. But over the finery, Powageh wore a common Cuecolan green cloak, likely in deference to the elements.

"Can a man not simply enjoy the weather?" Balam asked.

Powageh snorted and lifted a hand to catch the rain.

"Naasut has certainly outdone herself," Balam observed, changing the subject.

"Appearances are where she excels," Powageh agreed, obviously content to allow Balam at least this secret. "But let us hope she and her maidens are more than spectacle. Say what you will, but to see them like this? I think I understand why the Meridian trembled before Seuq and her dreamwalkers."

Balam had to admit the spearmaidens made for an intimidating presence in their battle regalia. Divided into squadrons they called prides, they marched in precision, making their city and Sovran proud.

Not to be outdone, Cuecolan soldiers stepped smartly in formation behind them. Some had stayed on the ships docked at the mouth of the river downstream, but Balam had ordered a hundred of their most elite to join him in the city for the parade. They also wore their battle best, animal skins and painted faces, and they carried fearsome obsidian-studded clubs and flint-tipped war spears.

The only thing the parade was missing was Terzha's golden eagles. The new matron had explained that while her eagle riders could fly in the rain, they preferred not to. It was less about getting wet than the difficulties posed by changes in the air caused by humidity and atmospheric pressure. It had been a disappointment to have the birds grounded. They would certainly have added to the grandeur of the moment. Instead, Terzha and her younger sister, Ziha, walked beside Naasut near the head of the procession, dressed in their riding clothes. From the volume of the crowd, they appeared to be favorites, the wronged daughters of a slain mother and an occupied city.

Powageh exhaled heavily beside him, and Balam braced himself. "There's something I wished to speak to you about," his cousin said.

Balam cocked his head. "I am right here."

"About last time we spoke."

"Ah . . . it is forgotten," he said hurriedly. "We both spoke in anger."

"No, not that."

Truly, would xe not allow this to lie? Well, xe could not ask questions if Balam gave xir no room to think. "You've been reading up on the shadow world, as I asked?"

This time, Powageh frowned at his change of subject.

"For tonight," Balam clarified. He had hoped to keep his plans secret, but Powageh's unwanted sincerity meant he had to at least offer his cousin a bone.

"You still haven't explained exactly what we are doing."

"The details will become apparent soon enough."

Powageh's expression darkened. "Does your plan tonight involve the shadow world?"

"Did I tell you that Tuun has failed to bring me my tide-chasers?" he asked, hoping to keep Powageh off-balance. It seemed to be working, because his cousin grimaced.

"I wondered," xe said. "I thought perhaps they waited downstream. What happened?"

"The Teek bested her."

Powageh's look was incredulous. "She had a pride of spear-maidens and two full squadrons of Cuecolan warriors against an island of unarmed women."

"I am well aware."

"Seven hells. What is her excuse?"

"Sea monsters."

Powageh laughed, but it was more shock than amusement. "She lost almost two hundred souls to sea monsters?"

"Not only did she lose two hundred fighters, but she also failed to bring me my fleet of tidechasers," he reminded xir.

"What will you do?"

"Fortunately, I have devised a contingency plan. Tuun's failure, while disappointing, is not wholly unexpected. I knew she underestimated Xiala."

"Care to explain?" Xe snorted at Balam's look. "Of course not."

"Tonight," he assured his cousin.

"And Tuun? I cannot imagine you will allow such failure to go unpunished."

Balam spread his hands. "Who am I to punish a lord of the House of Seven?"

Powageh did not bother to reply.

"Tuun will still serve our efforts," Balam said. "She is still a powerful sorcerer, if an entirely mediocre conqueror."

"And what does she say about that?"

"I'm afraid she has forfeited her ability to say anything."

Powageh gave him a look, as if xe meant to ask more, but they had crested the final hill that led down to the waiting ships, and they had an unobstructed view of the docks and bay from their vantage point and, beyond that, the river. Dozens of ships filled the harbor. Sturdy Hokaian vessels that would carry the infantry along the shoreline until their land forces reached Tovasheh, sleek Cuecolan canoes with crews of paddlers that would maintain a blockade of the great river where it met the sea. But not a single Teek tidechaser.

"And there is the fleet," he observed, voice dry with disappointment. He turned to Powageh. "Give me your cloak."

Powageh pulled the garment closer. "Why?"

Balam motioned, impatient. "I must go. There are still things I must attend to before tonight."

Powageh reluctantly took the green cloak from xir shoulders and handed it to Balam. "You're leaving the parade?"

"It cannot be helped," he explained as he slid the cloak across his own shoulders and raised the cowl. He had only planned to stay long enough to make an appearance, but Powageh's prodding meant he certainly had no reason to linger now. "Please convey my apologies to Naasut."

"But . . ." Powageh shivered. Xir beautiful finery was already getting soaked.

"Until tonight." Balam extended his hand.

Powageh gripped him by the forearm, more reflex than intention, and then the jaguar lord was slipping anonymously into the crowd, well aware that he had successfully avoided his cousin's prying but knowing that he could not keep Powageh at bay forever.

CHAPTER 31

Some women are born to always stay in sight of the shore.
Others are meant to cross the oceans.

—Teek wisdom

Xiala stood in the rain and watched the combined armies of Hokaia and Cuecola parade through the city. It made her queasy to see the hundreds upon hundreds of warriors in their colorful armor, queasier still when she caught a glimpse of the ships waiting in the harbor, knowing that they were bound for Tova. Her only consolation was that there was not one Teek ship among them. She had done that much. Been willing to bring down Tuun and everyone with her to ensure her people did not contribute a single tidechaser to their effort.

A shadow fell over the crowd, and Xiala looked up, expecting to see a golden eagle soaring overhead, but it was only a flock of very normal birds, rushing to get out of the rain. Nevertheless, she pulled the hood of her cloak a bit closer to hide her face and checked again to make sure her hair was completely covered.

The leaders of the Treaty cities were gathered on a platform in the distance. She was close enough to recognize the woman with the antler crown, the one they called Sovran, and the spearmaidens who surrounded her. Beside her were Terzha and Ziha Golden Eagle, not on eagleback but resplendent in the white and gold Xiala had grown to hate. They, too, were accompanied by a contingent of riders. She wondered if Iktan was among them. She had hoped to catch a glimpse of her once-friend, but if xe was mingling with those people, whom xe certainly loathed, she could not spot the ex-priest. Alongside the sisters stood a Cuecolan dressed in white and blue whom she did not recognize. Another lord, no doubt.

But no Tuun.

She flexed her fingers into a fist, imagining the woman's neck in her grasp. She had been so close it still rankled.

But if Tuun was not here, then where? The creatures of the sea had assured Xiala that her corpse did not float among them. Which meant she had to have made it to shore. And if she made it to shore, the first place she would run, no doubt, was here.

Xiala pushed forward a bit, eyes scanning across the dozens of minor governors, bureaucrats, and otherwise self-important minions who crowded the platform. They were a blur of rich fabrics, colorful feathers, and priceless jewels, all looking bedraggled by the rain.

But no Tuun.

A figure moved through the masses a short distance from her. She could not say what drew her eye, except that everyone else was focused on the platform where the Sovran had begun to give a speech, and this person was headed in the opposite direction. She watched them for a moment. There was something familiar about the set of their shoulders, their almost arrogant stride, even as they worked against the tide, as if they expected the rabble to part and make room.

Ah. She knew that swagger! She almost hadn't recognized him without his white jaguar skin, but Lord Balam was hard to miss, even in a crowd.

She did not know where Tuun was, but Balam would know. She had no doubt that he had had a hand in Tuun's invasion of Teek, and she would make him confess his role, and then, if he was suitably contrite, she would only throw him into the sea to drown and not actively feed him to the sharks.

She pulled her cloak closer and followed, keeping her distance, wary of being spotted. But Balam was focused ahead, not behind, and the rain was her ally, bowing heads and obscuring vision. Nevertheless, her Song rested ready in her throat; she had learned her lesson about allowing a sorcerer to see her coming. She did notice that Balam gestured sometimes, as if talking to someone, but there was no one there that she could see.

Balam led her down into a part of the city she did not know. It was a warren of tarp-covered stalls, most of them abandoned to the poor weather. Balam entered a small shop, one of the few with stone walls and a wooden door. Xiala thought to wait outside, but on an impulse she had grown to trust, she slipped through the door behind him.

The air inside the shop was humid and damp and smelled strongly of copal, a scent she had not smelled since Cuecola. Shelves stretched along all the walls well up to the ceiling and created aisles handy for hiding. Xiala quickly dipped behind a shelf lined with clay pots all labeled with small drawings that identified their contents. She spotted yarrow separated into seed, root, and ground to a paste. Fever bark in the next pot and, beside it, a plant she did not recognize.

Balam was at the counter, arguing with an elderly woman who bore the traditional tattoo on her cheek that Xiala knew signified a healer among the Hokaians.

"But my servant arranged to have me pick up the package today," Balam was saying.

"I have no order for a man named Balam," the woman insisted, thumbing through a large book of glyphs and hashmarks.

Balam's voice was calm, even charming, but Xiala recognized small signs of exasperation in the annoyed flutter of his eyes and the way his hands lay purposefully still upon the counter, as if he was working to control his temper.

"You must. Xe was here only yesterday."

"Xe . . ." The woman's mouth worked. "But this is for you?"

"Yes." Balam smiled. "And I will pay handsomely for it, of course."

She could see the woman considering it and then deciding.

"No." Her voice was flat, and she slammed the book closed. "Sorry. Try the merchant down the street. His shop is marked with a red bird."

Balam's voice dropped low and lethal with threat. "So you have it but will not sell it to me?"

The door banged open loudly enough to make Xiala jump, and a woman bustled in, shaking the rain from her cloak.

"It was glorious, Kata, despite the heavens pissing upon us. Did you get out of the shop to see at all? Oh, you've got a customer!"

"Hello, Japurna. He was just leaving." The shop owner's gaze was cool, and at some point during Japurna's arrival, a rather intimidating woman who looked very much like she had recently been a spearmaiden had materialized from somewhere to stand just behind Kata's shoulder. A clear threat.

And one Balam seemed to take to heart. He acknowledged the former spearmaiden with a dip of his chin and, voice a font of regret, said, "I am disappointed we could not do business, Lady Kata. I hope you do not grow to grieve your decision."

The shopkeeper crossed her arms over her chest. "I will not."

Balam offered her a nod, and Japurna, too, who was now watching wide-eyed. And then he left, closing the door firmly behind him.

"A strange man." Japurna's eyes lingered on the door. "Perhaps you shouldn't have offended him."

"Bah! I don't fear any man. He should have known better than to deal in my shop, but he sent a bayeki thinking to trick me." Her face was set in stubborn lines. "I have never sold godflesh to a man, and a foreign one at that. It is sacred and does not belong to his kind."

"Nevertheless." Japurna looked thoughtful.

"Can I help you?"

Xiala had been doing her best to not be noticed, but she'd finally come to Kata's attention.

"Godflesh." Xiala drew close to the two women. "I thought it was legend."

The shopkeeper snorted. "It is real enough."

"What would a man want with such a thing?" Japurna murmured.

"Blasphemy, that's what!" Kata said, voice prim. She motioned Xiala closer. "Where are you from, Child? I hear the sea in your voice."

"Teek."

"Ah. I am sorry to hear about your queen. She was well liked."

Japurna added a sympathetic glance to Kata's condolences.

"I . . ." Xiala hesitated, unsure what to say, her grief still too fresh. She settled on "Thank you."

Japurna cleared her throat loudly. "As I was saying, Naasut and her pride looked splendid, as always. But I am sad we did not see the eagles. After everything those girls have been through. Losing their mother like that." She pressed a hand to her heart, as if deeply moved. "And the daughter, the eldest who is matron now? Oh, she was beautiful. All in white and gold like that."

"Terzha is matron?" It came from Xiala's mouth before she could stop herself, but the women took it in stride, as if everyone knew the woman's name.

"Did you not hear about the 'Butcher at Breakfast'?" Japurna asked, no doubt delighted that Xiala was a willing audience and warming to her subject.

"I've only just arrived in the city after being away."

Japurna's voice dropped to a conspiratorial whisper. "The Butcher killed the mother and her advisers, but the elder daughter fought the killer off and saved her little sister. A hero!" She relayed the story with relish, the most delicious of gossip.

"One of her own!" exclaimed Kata, also enjoying the gossip. "Can you believe it?"

"Not one of her own," Japurna protested. "A spy and assassin priest working for the Carrion King."

Iktan. They must mean Iktan. But Xiala found it impossible to believe that Terzha could best Iktan at Guess the Shell, much less in a fight. The women must be mistaken. And who was the Carrion King whom Iktan was allegedly in league with against Golden Eagle?

They mean Serapio, she realized. And on the heels of that thought, *King? He's a king now? Seven hells. What is going on?*

The women had moved on, talking now about someone else's daughter who was part of the contingent of spearmaidens sailing to Tova.

"Thank you again," Xiala murmured, and received a distracted nod from both women. With no reason to linger, Xiala slipped back into the rain-slicked streets.

So much had happened in her absence. She had been so focused on Teek that the larger world had faded from her immediate attention, but as she spied the shop with the red bird farther down the road and headed toward it, she tried to sort out what she had learned.

Iktan had killed Nuuma and a contingent of the Eagles elite. That seemed clear enough, and she guessed that xe had spared Ziha of xir own accord. It was likely that Terzha had had nothing to do with saving her sister's life, contrary to the women's gossip. She suspected Iktan had a fondness for Ziha, did not blame her for her mother's transgressions, and therefore allowed her to live. Why xe would spare Terzha, too, Xiala couldn't guess, and part of her wished Iktan had done otherwise. Terzha was dangerous in a way her younger sister was not. She remembered well the woman's threat to crush Xiala under her foot like a pretty seashell, as opposed to her sister's willingness to pluck out the eye of the scion who had threatened Xiala with violence.

But what could have prompted the slaughter? Xiala had a guess. Balam must have kept his vow and told Iktan that Naranpa was still alive and that Nuuma had known all along but held the secret so that Iktan would not stray. Iktan's rage must have been a dark thing.

She shuddered. That had not been her goal. In fact, she had hoped that Iktan might learn that Naranpa was still alive and leave the company of the treacherous Eagles, which, she supposed, was exactly what xe did. She could not dictate the method of departure, and, perhaps, part of her knew Iktan would never depart without drawing blood. Only where was the ex-priest now? Surely not dead, or the women would have shared those salacious details, too.

But then where?

Tuun and, by association, Balam were her primary concern, but following the jaguar lord would have to wait. If Iktan was imprisoned and facing some gruesome execution, she could not allow it, especially if it was in part her fault.

She took a moment to orient herself, trying to determine in which direction lay the city jail. She had been spared a sojourn behind its bars, but she remembered spotting it after she killed Lord Pech and wondering what it would be like to be counted among its murderers.

She turned north.

As she walked, she thought of the other information she had gleaned from the women. Serapio was a king. Her instinct had been to deny that it was possible. After all, she had insisted to Iktan that Serapio wanted nothing to do with earthly power. Something must have changed. Was it the war alone? Or had the man she had found so maddeningly contradictory, both gentle and caring and a cold-blooded killer, finally succumbed to the darkness that she knew lurked within him?

Skies, Serapio, she thought. *Do you need me to save you, too?* It was a dark kind of humor, even if she meant it.

But first, Iktan.

The street she walked deteriorated to slop as she grew closer to the city jail. The air turned fetid with the smell of unwashed bodies and bad sewage. Even the rain could not dampen it. In fact, it made it worse. She drew the edge of her cloak over her nose in a futile effort to keep some of the stench out.

The streets here were deserted, most of the lower city no doubt at the docks to watch the parade and partake in the city-wide celebration or wisely tucked inside out of the weather. So it was a surprise when Xiala turned the final corner and found the grounds outside the jail filled with people.

She slipped back around the corner to draw her cloak and

hood tighter before stepping back into sight. She had not thought of what she might say, how she might free Iktan if she found xir here, but she had her Song and the will to wield it as necessary.

But not against a crowd. A persuasive tune for the guard or the warden, yes, but before her were at least a hundred bodies, most shackled and looking morose. They were surrounded by a circle of cruel-looking men with long spears, eyes wary and suspicious.

She paused near an older woman who was sobbing as she hugged a young man, face etched with lines of guilt.

"How?" the woman asked around deep hiccuping sobs. "How did they catch you? Did I raise a son to be so careless?"

A mother and son, then, and the mother only mad that her boy was foolish enough to get caught, not that he was a criminal. Xiala moved on. Next, she passed a handsome young man talking quietly to a woman who held a baby close.

"It's work," he was saying. "If I do it, they say I will be freed early. They have work for you, too."

"With the baby?" The woman sounded doubtful.

"Can you not leave her with your mother?" They both looked back toward a dour-looking woman standing beside a far wall. "The war college is no place for the little one. They say it's haunted, but I'm not scared." His words were brave, but his voice quivered.

Xiala spotted a man holding a writing tablet and made her way over.

He looked up, eyes baleful, but she was undeterred.

"I'm looking for someone."

"Not my problem."

"You've got a list of prisoners, don't you?"

It was a guess, but an easy one to make. He was clearly a clerk of some kind.

"My sibling," she improvised. "I think xe was arrested. Probably a mistake. Xe has a fondness for drink." She worked to look embarrassed.

The clerk was unimpressed.

Xiala took a handful of cacao from the purse she had pilfered earlier and held it out.

The clerk took it, confirming what she already guessed. Bribes were not only common but expected.

"Name?" he asked.

What should she say? She was committed to the sibling lie, and the 'Breakfast Butcher' would not do.

"Iktan." She hoped it was a common name.

The warden frowned. "An unlucky name to have these days."

"The Butcher. I know." She mimed a shiver. "Wouldn't want to share a cell with that one."

"I'm not afraid of no priest, assassin or no. Give me an hour with the Butcher, and xe wouldn't be so tough no more."

Which suggested Iktan wasn't here.

The warden scanned his list. "Have you checked the brothels along the docks? Maybe they're sleeping off the drink."

"Maybe," she conceded.

"You can look in the pen. Everyone in there is waiting for work. Volunteers on the left, prisoners on the right."

"Volunteers?"

He shook his head, eyes wide with unspoken meaning. "I wouldn't."

"I hear the work they offer pays generously."

"I don't care what that White Lord is paying, it ain't worth it. Trust me."

"Who is the White Lord?" she asked, but someone else was there, drawing the clerk's attention and offering the man a purse of cacao for information. She stepped aside, thinking. Could the White Lord be Balam? Surely not. But what other "White Lord" could there be?

"Head out!" someone shouted from the pen. "Volunteers on the left, prisoners on the right."

To follow or not follow. She had seconds to decide.

She quickly fell in with the volunteers, blending in with a group of mostly women. She spied the mother of the incompetent son among them and the young wife, who must have handed her child over to her mother before joining the work crew.

"Do you know where we're going?" Xiala asked, as she walked beside the wife.

She looked up, as if surprised someone was speaking to her.

"War college," she said. "They said there's work. Kitchen, I think."

She supposed it made sense. If they were going to march all these prisoners out there and work them all night, they would have to feed them eventually.

The procession continued through empty streets. It seemed the whole of the city had either been drawn to the docks to watch the launch of the fleet or was locked away before a warm hearth. Whatever this sorry walk of criminals and desperate women was, it was second to the spectacle of impending war and absolutely no match for the weather.

By the time they left the city proper, the spotty sunlight was lost in earnest behind a fresh bank of weeping clouds. The intensity of the rain seemed to double, and Xiala huddled, miserable and wet, in her cloak. As they left the city walls, she could not help but feel that no one had witnessed their leaving, and no one would miss these poor souls.

They crossed a bridge over a loudly rushing river swollen by the storm. The bridge led them along a path that cut through wide fields and farmland. The ground was saturated, and the path had become a shoe-sucking mess. More than one person lost a sandal to a greedy mudhole and was forced to limp along barefoot.

They walked for another quarter hour until they came to a cluster of burned-out ruins.

The war college.

Xiala knew little of the place. It was not something that interested her, an elite institution for the privileged children of the Meridian, where the descendants of the continent's powerful met and created alliances. She supposed that in another world, if the Teek were not what they were and if her life had been different, she might have attended the war college as the daughter of the Teek queen. She tried to imagine herself there and laughed. There could not be a worse fit.

The procession drew to a halt. A woman with a tablet similar to the clerk's back at the jail walked among them, a spear-maiden at her side. She tramped her way down the line, sorting people into work details. From what Xiala could gather, it was as the young mother had said. Volunteers were sorted into kitchen duty or portering, and the prisoners . . . Xiala looked around. Where were the prisoners? They had all walked together, but at some point, the others had been taken somewhere else.

Well, she wouldn't find Iktan among the volunteers.

She started to shuffle her way back toward the end of the line, hoping to slip away unnoticed in the dark. And if she was stopped, she would claim she had changed her mind about work. And if that didn't convince, there was always her Song.

"You!" a familiar voice shouted.

Xiala froze, every muscle tense. She knew that voice. Had seen its owner on the raised platform by the piers only hours ago.

"I am speaking to you," the voice said.

Xiala braced herself and turned, but Terzha Golden Eagle had not been talking to her. The now-matron was calling a man in a Cuecolan uniform over. It had nothing to do with her.

But why was Terzha here at the abandoned college standing in a muddy field?

"Kitchens, then?"

Xiala turned. The woman with the tablet was there, looking bored and waiting for Xiala to answer. She reached out and pinched Xiala's arm. "Although you look strong enough to fetch and carry."

"Kitchens." Xiala had been ready to leave, but now all her internal alarms were ringing. Terzha would not be at a simple work detail, especially not in the dark of night and in the rain.

Something was happening. Something to do with the war effort.

"Over there." The woman gestured with a thrust of her lips. "Tie the rope around your waist, and hold on to these until we give you further instruction." She handed Xiala a strip of black cloth and a sack on a cord.

"What are these?" she asked.

"You don't like it, you're out. No arguing."

Xiala didn't like it, but she took the items and joined the women tying the rope around their waists. The rope was one long length that, once secured, would bind them together. It was the same method Cuecolans used at sea to keep a man from going overboard.

"Do you know what this is for?" she asked the nearest woman as she stepped into a circle of rope and pulled it to her waist.

The woman was short, her dark hair braided.

"Magic," she whispered.

"No talking!" A spearmaiden sauntered down the line. "Rope around the waist. Shoes off and in the bag. It goes around your neck. Blindfolds on, hand on the shoulder of the person in front of you . . . and follow me."

Seven hells, what is going on?

Xiala slipped her stolen shoes into the bag, her feet cold on the wet earth. She looped the bag around her neck and tied the blindfold loosely around her head, leaving a gap at the edge that allowed her to see the ground and, if she tilted her head up, more. She placed her hand on the braided woman's shoulder and walked.

They had not gone far when the spearmaiden barked, "Stop!" And then, "Step forward slowly to wash your feet. Keep the blindfold on!"

Xiala shuffled dutifully forward until her toes touched the edge of a pan. She lifted her feet and stepped over the lip. Something hot and thick touched her soles.

She shuddered.

Blood, her mind supplied. The liquid lapping between her naked toes felt like blood, not soap and water.

A breeze kicked up in a fetid gust, and the stench of something awful came with it, worse than even the odor at the jail.

The woman in front of her gagged noisily.

Xiala tilted her head back, peeking around the blindfold.

Immediately, she wished she had not, as her mind struggled to make sense of what she was seeing.

Bodies.

Torsos and limbs, heads loose on lifeless necks.

A face she recognized. The son, the one whose mother had chastised him for getting caught. He was dead, his arms still bound and his throat cut as a Cuecolan with a blue-painted face drained his blood into a pan.

A pan just like the one she was standing in.

Mother waters! Her mind reeled in shock. Fear gripped her, and she had the overwhelming urge to run. She closed her eyes and forced herself to breathe deep calming breaths, but each inhale tasted like the dead against her tongue.

Calm, Xiala! You are not helpless. If they wanted you dead, they would have bound your hands. You are meant for something else, so watch and listen, and find out what evil this is.

With great effort, her heart rate slowed, and her breathing evened out. She forced herself to look ahead to where the line of kitchen staff was being led, and all her hard-won calm fled, horror shivering through her bones.

At first, it looked simply like a massive black door in the middle of the field, freestanding and unattached to any building. But the longer she stared, the more it became clear that the *thing* before her was no door at all but something slithering and alive that bubbled and frothed with shadow.

She watched as the blue-faced Cuecolan carried his pan of blood to the not-door and poured it across the threshold. The shadow door groaned, *groaned!* And grew another handspan in height.

They were feeding whatever that was with blood, and it was eating it.

Fuck! This! She took a step back and collided with the woman behind her.

"Hey!" The spearmaiden was there, hand gripping her shoulder, and Xiala brought her Song to her lips. She would Sing this madness down before she got any closer to that thing.

But her Song died on her lips as she saw what she had missed before.

At the threshold was a body she recognized.

Tuun was propped sitting against a makeshift altar of stone.

She had been opened from sternum to pubis, her insides removed, her body now a gaping cavity. Her hands rested in her lap, and in her palms lay her heart.

Oh, skies! Not even in Xiala's darkest revenge would she have wished this fate upon the woman. Eaten by a sea creature, yes. But this violation? This abomination?

Why? Who?

As if in answer, Lord Balam walked out of the terrible shadow door.

He was wrapped in a heavy cloak but barefoot, his face painted. He threw back his cowl, and Xiala saw frost clinging to his hair, ice twinkling on the jade plugs he wore in his ears.

The Cuecolan in blue and white, the one she had seen on the platform at the parade, approached him, and they consulted before Balam motioned a group of people forward.

Among them were the Sovran, now wrapped in a winter cloak, and dozens of spearmaidens. All were barefoot, and Xiala could see blood glistening on their feet. They stepped around Tuun's horrible corpse, as if it wasn't there.

And they followed as Balam led them into darkness.

Once they had passed, another Cuecolan returned with a pan of fresh blood. He poured it across the threshold, and the shadow expanded. Another, and another, and now the door was large enough to pass a giant through.

Or a giant eagle, for next came Terzha, leading her eagle riders and their mounts. The birds wore hoods covering eyes and earholes, and their talons and wings were smeared with blood.

And Xiala began to understand.

It was a door, after all. Or, rather, a gate. Some kind of passage into the shadow world just like the mirror Balam had given her to communicate. She had heard of it in the stories the sailors told, of the great wizards of the Cuecola who could walk across hundreds, even thousands of miles in an instant through a shadowgate.

That must be what gaped before her like an open mouth of darkness, and the blood must purchase their passage. And there was only one place such a gateway could lead with an army of spearmaidens and eagle riders.

Tova.

The spectacle at the harbor was for show, so Serapio and his allies would think the Treaty cities approached from the sea. A passage that would take weeks. He would never see this army coming.

Her group was nearing now. She could still run, maybe sneak away and not be seen in the darkness, but if she did, Serapio would never know of the danger massing behind his back.

She remembered what Iktan had said about seeing things through, and she meant to see this through, no matter the cost.

She straightened her blindfold, gripped the woman's shoulder in front of her, and walked toward the shadow.

CHAPTER 32

Take care that you do not become the very thing you seek to defeat.

—*On the Philosophy of War*, taught at the Hokaia War College

Despite his best efforts, it was more than a week before Okoa made it back to the Shadow Palace. One of the water strider insects had come up lame, so the handlers were reluctant to take their beasts out unnecessarily, and then Enuka had insisted he consult on a new weapon idea that had come to her in a dream, an attempt to turn light and sound into a wave weapon. He had begun to think he might never leave, when Benundah arrived to retrieve him, a note tied to her ruff explaining that he was needed back at the palace. Enuka could not argue with their king, so she loaded him up with a keg of balché and bid him farewell, drawing promises from him that he would return. The rest seemed willing to let him go. The camp had never quite been the same since it was revealed that he was a scion.

Serapio was waiting for him when he landed in the aviary.

"How was it?" he asked, but Okoa could tell he was distracted. And he looked hollowed out, as if the past weeks had carved away at his spirit. He wanted to ask Serapio if he had been eating well and getting enough sleep, but it wasn't his place, and he thought he knew what weighed on the Odo Sedoh's mind.

"Enuka is a genius," he said instead as he stripped Benundah's tack. "You were right. Any army approaching from the east by land will find it difficult, if not impossible, to enter the city."

"Good. And you. How are you?"

"Better. It is a simple life, to be an engineer." He could not keep the longing from his voice. "But I cannot avoid my sister and the matrons forever. What has happened since I left?"

"Nothing."

He paused, hands halfway to the saddle hook. "Nothing?"

"No inquiries into your whereabouts, no accusations. It is as if you disappeared, and everyone is too afraid to acknowledge it."

He finished hanging the saddle. "They think I am dead and don't want to admit they sent me to kill you."

"I imagine that is precisely it."

He laughed. "What will happen when they discover the truth?"

"That is why I have asked you to return. Political alliances are shifting, and I need your help."

"Of course. I meant it when I said we are brothers."

Serapio's face tightened momentarily, as if he was in pain.

"Are you well?" Okoa asked, alarmed.

He exhaled. "I am to wed."

"The news reached us, even in the field. But they did not say who. It is not Esa, is it?"

"Your sister?" Serapio's chuckle was low and amused. "No.

Skies, no. I am sure your sister would sooner claw out my heart with her bare hands."

Okoa relaxed, but his feet kicked against the flagstones. "I would not be so sure. If she thought it would benefit her, she would certainly consider it, the way a sick man drinks the oil of the castor bean." The plant was known to cause vomiting and severe diarrhea, but if the patient survived, they were often cured.

Serapio blanched. "I think I would rather not be a poison to be endured. No, it is Isel Winged Serpent."

"Peyana's youngest?" He was surprised.

"Do you know her?" Serapio gestured for Okoa to walk with him, and they strolled along the parapets. From here, Okoa could look out over the southern half of the city, stretching from the abandoned celestial tower in the west, across Otsa and the Carrion Crow Great House, all the way to the far edges of Winged Serpent's territory.

"I used to." Okoa scratched his cheek, drawing old memories forward. "She is a few years younger than me. Her mother and mine were close. But I haven't seen her since I left for the war college."

Serapio's face clouded. "I was hoping you might give me some insight into her character. Tell me if she is trustworthy."

Okoa frowned. "Forgive me for asking, but wasn't there already a woman you loved? The Teek who came looking for you at the Great House. A sea captain?"

Serapio leaned against the wall that kept him from a long fall into the Tovasheh. "What I do with Isel is not a marriage of love. Feyou has been pressuring me to make peace with the matrons, even more so since your assassination attempt."

Okoa winced to hear his actions described in such a way.

"She says this is a way to reassure the Sky Made that I am

one of them," Serapio continued. "That if I show my dedication through marriage, they will cease their plotting."

"I am not sure anything could make them cease their plotting," Okoa said, "but it is not a terrible idea. Give Peyana a peaceful path to power, and maybe she'll stop trying to kill you, at least until after the first grandchild is born."

Serapio paused and turned to face Okoa, his black eyes uncannily unerring. "I don't know that she will wait. I worry that this wedding is the excuse she needs to breach the security of the palace."

Okoa tipped his head back. "Possible," he admitted after a moment of thought. "I would certainly increase the guards, have all the guests thoroughly searched, and not by the same ones who searched me."

Serapio's look was quizzical.

"They did not find the sun dagger," he reminded him, and Serapio made a sharp sound, as if amused.

"Can you do this for me?" he asked.

Okoa's brows knit together. "I serve, Serapio. But what is it you need?"

"I would like you to oversee my safety during the wedding. The Tuyon are at your disposal, and the rest of the soldiers. However many you need."

"I will be recognized." He had not planned to make his return to Tovan society in such a dramatic manner, but he would not say no if the Odo Sedoh insisted.

"I will make you blood armor." He lifted a hand as if in anticipation of Okoa's protest. "No need for you to cut your throat. I can do it with only a bit of your blood. Beneath the helmet, you will be indistinguishable from any other of the Tuyon. Do you agree?"

Of course he agreed. "When is the ceremony?"

For a moment, Serapio looked hesitant, as if he had changed his mind and didn't want Okoa's help after all. But then he steadied, and Okoa was certain he had imagined it.

"The wedding is tomorrow."

• • • • •

The wedding guests were scheduled to begin arriving by midday, so after a brief breakfast, Okoa visited the baths and then dressed in his new blood armor. The making of the armor had not been as unsettling as he had feared. Serapio had made him open a vein and bleed into a bowl. Just as Okoa had begun to feel lightheaded, Serapio had signaled that he had enough, and then, as Okoa watched in awe, Serapio had added his own blood and then spun the mixture into a dark red crowskull helmet, cuirass, and forearm guards.

"So the . . . ?" Okoa had mimicked slitting his own throat, making the accompanying gagging sound.

Serapio had smiled at his playacting. "A test of loyalty. But you have already been tested, Okoa. I have no doubts where your allegiances lie."

Okoa had been pleased by the praise, more than he cared to admit, and it had fueled him through the night. His first point of order had been to map the layout of the Shadow Palace. He walked the halls, muttering to himself and employing the drawing techniques he had learned from Enuka to quickly surmise that the damn place was a maze. A good structure to defend if an enemy breached the walls but a disaster if one was trying to keep out a solitary assassin.

After much arguing with Feyou, his maps as evidence, he convinced the woman to move the main ceremony to the steps just outside the palace doors, where the center of the amphitheater had once been. It was a much more easily defensible point, and it kept the wedding guests out of the palace itself. They would designate the first few amphitheater rows for the clan matrons and other important guests, and, against his wishes but in compromise, they would allow the denizens of the city to fill in the remaining seats.

"If we let the citizenry onto the palace grounds, I want crow riders monitoring from the air," he had insisted, "and Tuyon and the rest of the armed guards spread out among the crowd."

Feyou had agreed, seeing at least the reason in that, and Maaka had left to make sure it was done.

And now it was time.

Okoa had personally instructed the Tuyon in proper body-searching techniques and what could and could not come into the Odo Sedoh's inner circle, and now he stood at his vantage point, watching the Tuyon do their work from behind the anonymity of the crowskull helmet.

The problem began with a raised voice, too loud and obviously inebriated. The man was a Winged Serpent, young, dressed in an elaborate shirt made of iridescent scales. He was waving his arms and protesting loudly that his arrowhead necklace was no weapon, and he should be allowed to keep it.

The Tuyon was doing her best to placate the scion, but he was only getting louder. Annoyed, Okoa stepped in and confronted the scion.

"No weapons," he said, voice flat behind his helm.

He blinked, taking in Okoa's broad and muscular form, and swallowed. In a much quieter voice, he tried to make his case. "It is only a necklace, and I have no intention of killing my new in-law. We're all happy he's marrying into the family."

Okoa snapped his fingers, and the Tuyon lifted a basket.

"In the basket," Okoa commanded, "or you leave. There

are no exceptions." And then, with a thought toward a diplomacy he did not feel, he gave a small bow from the neck and added, "Even for family."

Understanding he was defeated, the scion dropped his necklace into the basket. "I want it back when this is done," he said meekly before he went to join the rest of his party in the second row.

"Fool," Okoa muttered as he turned to resume his position . . .

. . . and walked directly into Esa.

Their eyes met, and Esa let out a small gasp, her dark eyes widening in shock.

"Okoa?" she whispered. "Is that you?"

Skies, what had he done? Careless. How could he be so abominably careless? Of course, Carrion Crow would be here. Serapio was still a Crow, and by all outside appearances, the clans of Tova were allied with the Carrion King. He should have stayed at his post, and he certainly should have never spoken. But now it was too late, and Esa had recognized him.

"Not here," he hissed. He looked around for a private place where they could speak. "Through the side door," he said, thrusting his chin in the direction of a small door in the palace wall. And then he stepped away, praying that no one took note of the Crow matron conversing with a Shadow Palace guard as if she knew him.

He wove his way through the growing crowd, taking the longer route, giving himself time to think. Part of him had known that at some point, he would have to face Esa and explain what happened and why he had not written to let her know he was alive. He had meant to a dozen times while out in the Eastern districts digging ditches and puzzling out water flow. But he had not.

And he knew why.

He was scared, some of the old shame bubbling to the surface. When Serapio had saved him—and Serapio *had* saved him—Okoa had wanted to let his old life recede. And it had when he was with Enuka and her corps. It was hard to let that peace go and to wade back into the politics of the clans, but now it was time to face the consequences.

Esa first.

He waited for her at the door. When she joined him, they both slipped inside.

The hallway was cool and dark, flames glowing in sconces on the walls and bouncing off black walls and mosaic floors.

Okoa had turned, ready to explain, when he found himself suddenly embraced, Esa's arms around him and her head pressed against his chest.

"Brother!" she cried through her tears. "I thought you were dead. Oh, skies, I thought he had killed you."

Guilt rushed through him. "I'm alive, Sister. I'm alive."

"Oh!" She pulled back, her hands over her mouth. "The blood armor! Your throat. Did he cut your throat?"

"No, no," he soothed. "I am whole." He removed the helmet so that she could see.

"But . . . I don't understand."

"It is too much to explain, but I am whole and hale. I have aligned with the Odo Sedoh—"

"Aligned?" A hiccup.

He nodded. Here came the difficult part. "I came to kill him, as you are aware. But he already knew of our plans and was expecting me. We fought, and I had him at my mercy—"

"But you did not kill him?"

"We talked."

"Talked?" Her voice geysered in surprise.

"And he forgave me."

Esa stared, mouth open, and he knew he was losing her. He rushed on.

"He understood everything. Father, mother, Chaiya, even the matrons. He truly is our god."

Still she did not speak, only watched him. But he had run out of words.

"He is my brother," he said simply.

"Your brother," she echoed, voice barely a whisper. "And what am I?"

Oh, skies! He saw the mistake as soon as he made it.

"You are still my sister," he soothed.

He willed her to see, to understand how unburdened he was. How happy. But Esa had never been concerned with his happiness, so why did he believe she might be now?

"Benundah returned," he added. He wanted her to know.

She paced away. When she turned to face him, her eyes were fire, any tears of sympathy burned away by growing outrage.

"And so this past month and a half," she hissed, "while I have been mourning you and expecting the Tuyon to show up at my door at any moment to slaughter me for treason, you have been . . . what? Riding Benundah? Conversing with that *monster*?"

"I was helping the engineering corps."

"The . . . . what?" The last word came out as an incredulous shriek.

"Esa, please understand."

"Is this a game to you?" she demanded. "Skies, this has always been a game to you. From the moment you returned for Mother's funeral . . . you have never understood what is at stake!"

"I understand perfectly," he countered, his temper rising to meet hers. "I was sent to murder him, was I not?"

Her eyes narrowed. "Where is the knife? The sun dagger. Where is it?"

"I still have it. For safekeeping."

She jerked back, and then her expression closed. She had been all surface before, her emotions raw and her thoughts exposed. But he watched as she withdrew, and he knew whatever hope there had been for reconciliation had passed.

"Peyana made another," she said.

"Impossible. I was there."

"When you did not return, she had another forged."

"There is only one sun dagger." Even as he said it, he doubted his words. He tried to remember the conversation with the matrons in the cave, but it felt so long ago, and the details were lost to him. He did remember the Sun Priest's mask, the surprising weight of it, enough gold to make multiple weapons.

Esa smirked as she watched him think through the possibility.

He shook his head, unconvinced. "They would never trust you—"

She laughed, overloud and aggressive. "No, not me. They hate me."

"Then who?"

"Do you remember the last time we spoke, how you warned me that Peyana was plotting to betray us? Did you know then that you would hurt me more than she ever could?"

"I never meant . . ." He started but could not finish.

"Enjoy the wedding, Okoa. I know I will."

And then she shoved past him and out the door.

He let her go.

Not because he was heartsick over his sister, although he was. But because somewhere, possibly among the wedding guests, there was another sun dagger.

And he had to stop them.

Outside, a bell chimed. It was the signal that the ceremony was about to begin, which meant he must have been in the hallway with Esa longer than he realized. By now, all the clans would have arrived and taken their seats, and the amphitheater would be filled with Tovans, excited to witness the momentous day.

Okoa felt a rising panic.

He had no doubt that if someone was going to make an attempt on Serapio's life, they would do it while he was exposed during the wedding ceremony. He reached for the dagger he wore at his waist before remembering that by his own edict, no weapons were allowed on palace grounds today, even among the Tuyon. He had locked every spear, club, and dagger in the armory and given Maaka the key. It seemed prudent at the time, but the chime of the bell meant there was no time to find Maaka, no weapon he could quickly access.

No, there was one weapon he could reach.

Okoa bolted through the corridors of the Shadow Palace. The room he had claimed as his own for the duration of his stay wasn't far. He threw open the door, rushed to his bed, and tossed aside the mattress. He half expected the sun dagger to be gone, but there it was, wrapped in black cloth, still tucked in the sheath he had worn down his back.

He grabbed the weapon and ran.

He raced back the way he had come, out the same door through which he had led Esa, and within moments, he was sucked into the crowd. He couldn't see, bodies too close around him, so he employed muttered apologies and strategic shoves to work his way up the amphitheater steps to a better vantage point. When he had reached the first tier, he pushed sideways until he broke through to the center aisle.

He could see the rows below him now. Peyana was on his

right. She stood in the front with the rest of Winged Serpent. There were at least a hundred of her clan present, maybe more. And across from her, on the left and in lesser number, his sister and the scions of the Crow in their customary black. Any of them could have smuggled the dagger in somehow, and it would be his fault. Serapio had trusted him with his life. Okoa could not fail him now.

Voices drew his attention to the center, two dozen steps directly below him. There stood Serapio, his familiar baritone filling the space. And then Isel spoke, her voice as bright and crystalline as mountain air. They were reciting their vows, words of mutual commitment.

The couple themselves had their backs to him. They were shrouded in a cloud of incense, but Okoa could still make out Serapio on the left in his feathered cloak and Isel on the right in a bell-sleeved dress of bright jade.

Okoa gripped the still-sheathed sun dagger in his hand, undecided. Should he wait for the attack or warn Serapio now? If he warned him, would it be best to run down the steps and interrupt the ceremony? Or would that make the assassin act sooner? And from which party would it come? The vipers in green or his own people in black? Or from some unaccounted quarter?

Okoa began to work his way down the steps. He thought he saw Serapio lift his head, as if he heard his general's approach, but Okoa could not be sure through the fog of incense.

His gaze roamed the crowd, snagging on every movement, aware of even the smallest gesture, the first hint of intent. Blood pounded in his ears, and his nerves stretched thin. His palm against the knife hilt was slick with nervous sweat.

He would not fail. He would. Not. Fail.

Someone called his name, a distraction like the buzzing of a gnat. Maaka in the corner of his eye, and he was about to turn and gesture to the older man to join him when—

There, at Isel's wrist.

A glint of gold, barely visible at the edge of her sleeve.

Isel began to turn to face Serapio, and as she did, she raised her hand. Okoa could see Serapio's bare face, his exposed chest.

And it all came together. Serapio's concern about Isel's true nature, Peyana's quick agreement to the marriage when Okoa knew she would settle for nothing less than Serapio dead.

Okoa had failed Serapio before. He would not do it again.

He would not be indecisive, weighing options until he was crushed under the burden of choice. He would not be a disappointment like his father. His inaction would not be the cause of Serapio's death. Never again the lost boy, the faithless son, the inconstant friend.

Okoa drew the sun dagger from its sheath.

He intuitively registered its heft, the leather grip, the heat that seemed to emanate from the blade. He took the blade between his fingers and cocked his elbow back. His arm came down, wrist tight and controlled, and he released.

The knife flew, end over end.

It struck Isel in the back, below her left shoulder. The impact with flesh and bone made an audible noise, and Isel gasped, a sharp, shocked sound.

She stumbled, and Serapio caught her as she fell.

Blood spread across Isel's back, staining her jade dress to crimson.

Peyana shot to her feet, a look of incomprehensible horror distorting her face.

For a moment, time itself held its breath.

And then the world restarted as a rising murmur, confused and disbelieving, and quickly climbed to a howl.

Someone in green screamed, and the dam of disbelief burst wide.

Around Okoa, people were shouting. He turned his head. A woman was pointing at him, her mouth moving, but he could not hear her.

Someone tackled him from behind, and he crashed into the stone steps. His leg twisted beneath him, and he felt something in his knee pop. His head struck the ground with skull-jarring force. His helmet flew off and went tumbling down the stairs.

"Let me go," he growled.

Men dragged him to his feet. Tuyon, and one of them Maaka, his face contorted with rage, as if Okoa had personally injured him. The older man swung his arm, and his thick fist cut across Okoa's bare cheek. His head spun, and he tasted blood. Dazed, he did not resist as they dragged him down the steps.

He heard Peyana shriek a moment before something else smashed into his already smarting face. His neck snapped back from the impact, and he bit his tongue. The next strike broke his nose before the Tuyon intervened.

"She had a weapon!" Okoa's words came out in an unintelligible snarl, and he spit blood and bits of a tooth from his mouth. "Listen, you fools! She had a weapon!"

The Tuyon dumped him unceremoniously in front of the marriage altar. He felt the weight of Maaka's foot in his back, holding him down. Thick incense burned his eyes. He blinked the smoke away. His watery vision revealed Isel's body, close enough to touch. She was already dead; the knife that was more than a knife had cut clean through flesh and bone to penetrate her heart.

Her eyes were open, staring. Accusing.

"My brother." Serapio knelt before him on one knee. He

reached out a hand and pressed it to Okoa's cheek. He sounded infinitely sad.

"It was not meant for you," Okoa said, worried that Serapio had misunderstood, as certainly Maaka had. "Isel had a weapon, another sun dagger."

Some emotion—surprise? hope?—crossed Serapio's face. He turned back toward the dead woman, as if asking Okoa where.

"In her hand."

Serapio turned over her empty hand.

"The other one," Okoa said. "I saw it. Golden, like the Sun Priest's mask."

Serapio gently lifted Isel's other arm and drew back her sleeve. There, on her wrist, a golden bangle caught the light. Serapio tugged it free and held it in his open palm. He flexed his fingers, and the metal gave way, as soft as regular gold.

Okoa stared, confused.

"No!" Dread bloomed in his belly. "She had a blade! I saw a blade!"

"Okoa." The sorrow in Serapio's voice shattered him.

"It doesn't make sense," Okoa protested. "Esa said . . . !"

He turned his head to look back into the crowd that had gathered in a circle around him. Faces contorted in horror and disgust. All but one.

His sister.

Esa looked intrigued, almost eager, as if she had attempted a great feat and, to her surprise, succeeded.

Despair crushed him. He dropped his head.

"I thought she was going to kill you," he whispered. "That there was another sun dagger."

"I know," Serapio said.

Something struck him. A rock.

"Peyana!" Serapio stood. "Control yourself."

"Monster!" the matron screamed. "Murderer!"

Serapio left him and took Peyana in hand, arms around her shoulders. He lowered his head and spoke to her, but Okoa could not hear what was said. He only glimpsed Peyana's wild eyes, her grief-stricken face.

He could not blame her.

Okoa had only killed once before, the captain of the Golden Eagle Shield. It had been in self-defense, but that death still weighed on him.

For this death, there was no easy comfort. A misunderstanding was no excuse, intent no balm for the dead. He could have done a hundred other things. Told Maaka and had Isel arrested, interrupted the ceremony and restrained her himself.

But he had not trusted himself to wait, too afraid he would fail Serapio yet again.

Serapio was back, kneeling beside him.

"What now?" Okoa asked. He had begun to tremble.

"Peyana wants justice. The old ways."

Blood for blood. Okoa knew them well. He closed his eyes, defeated.

"Why did you take off your helmet?" Serapio whispered, his hand caressing Okoa's cheek. "Why did you show your face?"

Okoa looked up, sure he had misheard. Is that what troubled Serapio?

"You have put me in a difficult position," he continued. "The whole of Tova witnessed you kill their new queen."

"Can you not . . . ?" Was it too much to ask to be saved when he did not deserve it?

"It's not that easy." He sighed, as if he regretted what came next. "I must send you with Peyana now. She swears that when next I see you, you will still be alive and whole. She understands there will be dire consequences if you are not."

Okoa could already taste the pain Winged Serpent would exact upon him. He had known a Cuecolan at the war college who assured him that a good torturer could torment a man for hours and never leave a mark.

"Do not lose hope," Serapio whispered. "I am not done with you, General Okoa, and I will do my best to save you."

Four men moved in and hauled Okoa to his feet. Shield men in green. He recognized Ahuat, the Winged Serpent captain whom he had once considered a friend, but there was nothing kind in his face now.

Only loathing, and a promise of agony to come.

CHAPTER 33

The best way to win the war is to win the peace.

—Words inscribed over the war college at Hokaia

After the Winged Serpent had hauled Okoa away to face their tender mercies, Serapio retired to his rooms with strict orders to his Tuyon that he was not to be disturbed. He stripped off his wedding finery, the headdress Feyou had commissioned, and the uncomfortable sandals and flung them to the floor. He smashed his fist against the wall, frustration and guilt a volcano in his chest.

It had been so easy to ensnare Okoa in his plans. The man was so grateful, so eager to help. All Serapio had had to do was provide the opportunity, which he had done by suggesting that Isel was not trustworthy, placing Okoa in charge of his safety, and then gifting the girl with an early wedding present: a single golden bracelet.

It seemed Okoa's scheming sister had unwittingly aided in his plans by telling her brother that Peyana had crafted a second sun dagger. Fortuitous, and possibly the accelerant that helped speed Okoa's hand. He did not know, and now it did not matter.

Poor Okoa, to have such formidable enemies. And such black-hearted friends.

Serapio's scheming had not been entirely heartless. He had suggested the blood armor and given Okoa a chance to remain an anonymous killer. If only he hadn't removed his helmet, Serapio had hoped to substitute another of his Tuyon as the culprit. Someone who would have been a willing sacrifice if it meant serving the Odo Sedoh. But it had to be Okoa who did the deed. He was the most competent; none of the Tuyon had been trained as Shield or soldiers until their ascension. He had to make sure whoever he chose would not miss.

Serapio could not have done it himself. His delicate position would not allow it. The matrons would have turned against him in earnest, publicly denouncing him and making him into Tova's villain. As of now, all his actions, no matter how cruel, could be justified by his role as defender of clan and city. But to kill his bride, the daughter of a matron? He would have become anathema.

So, Okoa.

Another sacrifice.

Another way fate molded him into a monster.

A knock on the door pulled him from his rage.

"I am not to be disturbed," he growled.

"It is Maaka, and I bring news that cannot wait. News from Hokaia."

Hokaia. Serapio was so focused on winning the war by fulfilling the prophecy that sometimes he forgot that invasion was imminent. And in truth, for all he had done, all his dark deeds to meet the demands of the coyote god's song, he felt no closer to changing the tide.

"Enter."

The door opened, and two sets of footsteps followed. Maaka's he knew well, but the others were a stranger's.

"Who do you bring to my door?"

"A Crow scout, Odo Sedoh. Returned from Hokaia."

Serapio allowed himself a moment to resettle and then commanded, "Speak."

The young scout's voice was high and nervous. "The Treaty armies have set sail, Odo Sedoh. Me and Yendi saw them leave with our own eyes."

"Yendi?"

"My crow."

Serapio smiled at the scout's inclusion of their crow. "When?"

"There was a speech," the scout continued. "I was in the crowd, and I heard. They sail to Tova, meaning to kill you and liberate the city." They hesitated. "That was their word. *Liberate.*"

He waved away their concern. It was not news that his enemies cast him as an oppressor. "How many?"

"I counted two hundred ships. All kinds, but mostly Cuecolan canoes and those flat-bottomed Hokaia boats."

"Two hundred," Maaka said, sounding dismayed. "They must have commandeered every merchant ship in Cuecola and all the isles."

"Were there any Teek among them?" Serapio could not help but ask, his heart fluttering strangely. *She's safe now*, he thought. *You did what had to be done to make her safe.*

"None that I saw, but the fleet was vast."

He felt a mix of relief and disappointment.

"Two hundred ships possibly holding forty to fifty warriors each," Maaka lamented. "A force we cannot match."

"And we have not counted their sorcerers and eagle riders," Serapio reminded him.

"Their sorcerers will be no match for the Odo Sedoh," Maaka replied, confident, "and Carrion Crow will drive any eagle from the sky!"

It was all well and good that Maaka believed, but Serapio was not so sure.

The scout, who had been waiting patiently, began to breathe harder, clearly anxious.

"You did well," Serapio assured them. "Tova owes you a great debt. Yendi, too."

"Thank you, Odo Sedoh . . . and for Yendi." The scout sounded awed that the Odo Sedoh would remember their crow's name. Serapio guessed that would be something they could brag about for years to come.

If they had years.

War would come for the young scout, too, if Serapio could not stop it.

He dismissed the rider but motioned for Maaka to stay. "Bring me the captains of the clans and Enuka from the engineering corps. Let us see if they have a way to stop our enemies."

"Of course." Maaka hesitated.

"Speak, Maaka."

"Your bride, Odo Sedoh. I am sorry."

"My bride?" He had already forgotten Isel, his mind occupied by other things. He closed his eyes, feeling a spike of dismay at his own ruthlessness. Her blood still stained the steps outside the palace, and he had already moved on, another tick of the prophecy fulfilled.

"I . . . I don't know what happened," Maaka said. "What possessed Okoa? I can only believe he meant the blade for you."

Serapio considered. Would it be better for Maaka to think Serapio had been Okoa's target? Or to know that Okoa believed he was, in fact, protecting him?

Even he could not be so cruel as to do that to Okoa.

"I think he meant to protect me. After all, he had his chance to kill me and did not take it. Why would he try now before the clans and all of Tova?"

Maaka was quiet for a moment.

"If he is wrongly accused," Maaka said slowly, "if he truly believed the girl to be a threat and acted only to save you . . ." He took a deep breath before continuing. "Okoa is still Carrion Crow, still a prince of his people, still yours, Odo Sedoh. And no Crow son deserves the fate that awaits him in Winged Serpent's dungeons."

"If I had not let Peyana take him, I risked a riot. Everyone witnessed the murder, and Isel makes a sympathetic victim."

"In the moment, you had little choice if you wished to maintain your alliances," Maaka agreed. "But now."

Serapio leaned forward. "What do you suggest?"

"If the Odo Sedoh wishes to return Okoa to his ranks, no diplomacy, no consideration, and certainly no matron should stand in his way. Does not the Crow God Reborn take what is his?"

Death, the voice inside reminded him. *Your purpose is death. Anything else is not yours to claim. Any other path leads only to misery.* And yet Serapio felt a small stirring of hope. Perhaps this one time there was a path that was not death.

He would at least try.

"Thank you, Maaka. For the reminder."

"Of course, Odo Sedoh." He cleared his throat. "Shall I fetch the captains?"

Okoa would have to wait.

"Have them meet me in the war room."

· · · · ·

An hour later, the military leadership of Tova gathered in the war room. Once they were settled around the table, Serapio began.

"A scout has brought news that the Treaty cities have sailed for Tova. We can expect them to reach the mouth of the Tovasheh soon. They bring infantry and enough ships to block Tova's access to the Crescent Sea."

"How many soldiers?" Chela, the new captain of Carrion Crow, asked. He had stepped in to replace Okoa when he had vanished. Serapio had not met him until now, but Maaka had told him what he needed to know. The man had trained at the war college but never joined the Shield. Instead, he had been an agent of Carrion Crow in the greater Meridian, a speaker of dozens of languages: the rare southern dialects, the unwritten language of the Northern Wastes, even the tongue of the Empire of the Boundless Sea to the west. But most important of all, he was a crow rider, logging thousands of hours on his mount, a large male named Sagoby.

"Ten thousand on the ships," Maaka supplied.

"Ten thousand?" Suol, captain of Winged Strider, sputtered the number. "Even if a quarter of those are porters and sailors, it is too many."

"How many can Tova field?" Serapio asked.

"Fifteen hundred who are capable with a spear, another two hundred with bow, less than that with a hook spear." Suol had taken on the training and organizing of their ground forces in the Eastern districts. His forces would face the brunt of any land assault.

"And how many do we have in the air?" Serapio asked.

"Thirty-three crow riders, Odo Sedoh," Chela said. "Six are out on scout patrol but will be called back when the eagles attack."

"And what of the winged serpents? Does anyone know?"

Ahuat, the captain of Winged Serpent, was noticeably absent.

"Twenty-seven winged serpents," Chela supplied promptly.

"Combined, we should easily outnumber the eagles. Nuuma left with only thirteen, and an additional seven joined her when the families fled."

"Twenty? Are you sure that is all?"

"We believe thirty total, as there were some at the war college with the scions."

"Sixty Tovan riders against thirty eagles." Suol grinned. "I like those odds."

"The eagles are larger, more powerful creatures," Chela warned, "but a beast is only as good at its rider, and a third of their riders are mere students. What winged serpents lack in size against the eagles, they make up for in agility and speed. We will hold the advantage if we can keep the eagles corralled with no space to maneuver. The crows will work in groups to harry the eagles where we wish. With serpent and crow working together, it can be done."

"So we have the aerial advantage?"

"Aye, but barely."

"At least it is something. And what of water striders?" Serapio asked, turning to Suol. "How many of your beasts will be on the river?"

"Fourteen."

"Only fourteen? Against two hundred ships?"

"They are not cold-weather creatures," he said. "Many flounder under this long winter. But those we do have will serve as harriers, launching rapid attacks against their front line. We have mustered a fleet of water ships that will try to hold the channel open. Mostly barges and skimmers, but if the enemy is not content with their blockade and choose to move to attack Tova, they will not find the Tovasheh River an easy advance."

That was good news. "And how many are they, your ships?"

"Fewer than a hundred," he admitted. "Of varying size and speed, but all are ready to defend the river."

A hundred against two hundred? It was folly. "I do not doubt the bravery of your fleet, Suol, but the disparity is discouraging. Do we truly think we can keep them from reaching the city?"

Suol's sigh was heavy. "If they do gain Tova, runners will be stationed at all the bridges. If there is a breach, we burn the bridges."

"Leaving each clan to fend for itself?" Chela asked.

"It is the best we can do. It will make Shadow Rock inaccessible by foot, and that must be the priority. It will be impossible for the enemy to reach you, my king."

"You forget there are sorcerers among them," Serapio said. "Nothing is impossible."

An uneasy silence fell across the room. Terrible odds they could stomach, but magic made them unsure, afraid. These were people raised under the umbrella of the Watchers' reason and science. Countering any sorcery would be Serapio's burden alone. One he was not sure he could bear single-handedly if Cuecola brought its sorcerers, as he assumed it would.

Even the crow god had limits.

"What else?" he asked, trying not to let his concerns show.

"We stop them before they reach land." That was Enuka, and all attention turned to her.

"Explain," Serapio said.

The master engineer cleared her throat. "I have been working on a way to defend the Eastern districts, but I did not anticipate such numbers. I think I have been going about this poorly." She said it with some disappointment but no shame, as if now that she understood her fault, she would not dwell on the time lost but simply correct the mistake. "If their ground troops come on ship and once on our shores will outnumber us almost ten to one, the better thing would be to not allow them to reach our shores at all."

"We don't have the naval power to stop them," Suol warned. "We can station archers and spearmen in Tovasheh, but we face the same problem of numbers. They will quickly overwhelm us."

"I do not know how we stop them," Enuka confessed. "I am only suggesting that we do."

"It would end the war before it is even begun," Serapio murmured.

"Exactly, my king."

It was an intriguing idea, but that was all it was. An idea. And what use was an idea if it could not become action? He wanted to hope, but he found that hope alone was not enough.

"I will task you to think on it, then, Master Engineer. But do not take too long. The army will be at the mouth of the Tovasheh soon enough." Serapio stood. "Now, if there is nothing else, I have another matter to attend to."

The captains stood with him, each offering their condolences for his loss before leaving. Serapio accepted them graciously, even as he loathed himself for the hypocrisy, and was grateful when they were gone.

Despite their efforts, their willingness to sacrifice, and Enuka's brilliant mind, it was clear that they could not rely on conventional means to win this war. That was why he had done what he had done. That was why blood rose higher and higher around him.

That was why now he turned to the prophecy.

• • • • •

The crows showed him where to find Zataya. A windowless house in Coyote's Maw built into a cliff wall, whitewashed and marked with a climbing flower Serapio did not recognize. The crow that guided him and allowed him to borrow its sight named it a lupine. He entered through a door in the roof and descended a twist of stairs into an empty chamber. Square firepits sat long unused in the center, and the room was cold, neglected, and smelled of ghosts.

"I do not think anyone lives here," he told his crow, but the bird flew on, weaving down a hallway, sensing something that Serapio could not.

He followed as they descended farther and farther underground, his skin prickling at the close quarters and weight of rock around him. He did not like it here, below the earth. He was meant for the sky, being as much crow as man, and crows did not belong underground.

Finally, he heard singing, a half-mad warbling tune that seemed to cavort off the walls and echo around him. He followed it until he came to a door.

Heat greeted him as he entered the room. The scents of rosemary and lavender dominated the space, and his crow sight showed him that along the walls and all the surfaces lay bundles of dried herbs. He could not identify the varieties by sight, but he was sure that if he could hold each to his nose, he would recognize every one.

And there, in front of a blazing hearth, sat Zataya. She was the source of the off-key singing. A lone woman in a brown dress stirring something that boiled in a clay pot. She had yet to notice him, so he took his time observing her as she worked, wondering who she truly was and how she came to be alone in this place.

"I thought you were the captain of Coyote Clan Shield," he finally said.

She screamed, a short, sharp burst of surprise, and whirled to face him, eyes wide.

"It would seem to me," he continued, "that the Shield captain would not live alone in an abandoned house singing to herself as she brews . . . what are you brewing?"

She had not recovered from the fright of seeing him, and he smiled as he stalked around the room, inspecting the bundles of herbs. He leaned over and sniffed some of the more interesting-looking ones.

"Sage?" he asked, as he breathed in a pale green stem and ran a finger across the leaves. It was soft and slightly fuzzy.

"But this one . . . ?" He bent to smell the small yellow flower. It smelled like rain, earthy and pungent.

"Chaparral," she said, finally finding her words. "Good for stomach ailments or the rotting of the insides."

He made a noncommittal sound. "And are any of these herbs part of your divining?"

Her brow furrowed. "Prophesying's southern sorcery. Nothing to do with curing sickness."

"And yet." He spread his arms. "And yet you brought me a prophecy. And a cruel one at that, and you said all must be done or I would lose this war."

"Three wars, and yes, all must—"

He was across the room in four long strides, the flames in the hearth dancing in the sudden wake of his passing. His crow watched, indifferent, as he grabbed her by the throat, lifted her off her stool, and slammed her into the wall.

"I have fulfilled your prophecy, Witch." His words came sharp and biting, tiny flechettes of rage. "I have turned the rotten fruit of betrayal into loyalty, my unloved bride is dead, and the son has felled his sire. And yet the enemy comes, and my scout tells me they are an overwhelming force we cannot best. And now I wonder if you lied to me. If you thought to trick me."

"To what end?" she croaked, clawing at his hand that held her tight, dragging her nails across his skin.

"I do not know," he growled. "Is this a game? Something my enemies devised to break me?"

"I spoke the truth!" Her words came out in a throat-scraping gasp. "The Coyote song cannot lie!"

"Then you misunderstood."

"I . . . please . . ." She struggled to breathe, her hands beating weakly against his and her eyes rolling wildly.

Disgusted, he released her. She slid to the ground, wheezing and weeping.

But he had no pity for her. Not after what he had done at her urging.

Okoa, Marcal, Isel. They stained his soul, troubled him in a way nothing else had. The Watchers, Golden Eagle. They were the wages of war, the bloody hand of the Odo Sedoh or the Carrion King at work.

But Marcal and Isel were his. Their deaths lay at Serapio's feet, and Okoa's corpse would follow if he did not stop it.

She lay slumped against the wall. Serapio pulled her stool close and sat in front of her, elbows braced against his knees as he leaned forward. His crow fluttered down to rest on his shoulder. "Explain. And know that if I do not like what you have to say, I will not suffer you to live."

She coughed, and flecks of blood dotted her lips. "The Coyote does not lie," she repeated.

"No, but he is a trickster. I have done everything you said, and nothing has changed."

"Then you have not done everything. Something has failed. You have misread a sign, made a mistake in your reasoning."

"No." He recounted the rhyme as she had told it to him, counting off the elements with his fingers as he went. He did not dwell on the final line of the prophecy, that even in winning he would lose everything. He could already feel the cost of what he had done weighing upon him and had resigned himself to the sacrifice.

Zataya shook her head. "You've done something wrong."

"What, then? Tell me!"

"You cannot outsmart your destiny. Even the gods must bow to the fates."

His fingers flexed, the desire to kill the witch almost overwhelming. He found himself standing over her, the shadow rising unbidden, his veins blackening, inky tears gathering in his eyes.

Zataya cowered, arms over her head, her Coyote song bubbling from bloody lips.

She is not the problem. She is only the messenger. Killing her will solve nothing.

And in his heart, Serapio knew she was right.

He had tried to cheat the prophecy, hoping to avoid the price it demanded. But it was not to be.

And he knew why.

Xiala. It must want Xiala.

The only person he refused to give it, even if she had been standing before him.

With a scream, he turned and swept his arm across Zataya's carefully arranged herbs, sending them spinning to the floor. His crow rose toward the ceiling, screeching in sympathy.

Soon the Treaty cities would be at his doorstep, and he had no way to stop them.

CHAPTER 34

> Love is but a brief flash of lightning, quick to burn before it
> is gone. But oh, the power! The power! Never underestimate
> the lightning.
>
> —*The Obregi Book of Flowers*

Naranpa awoke to the sound of footsteps in the other room.
It took her a moment to remember where she was, but as light
streamed through the window, Kupshu's cottage came into
focus. The sun did not set for very long this close to the summer solstice, so, despite the light, she had no sense of the hour,
but the sounds coming from the other room suggested to her it
must be morning.

And Kupshu must be back.

Happy that she would get to see the old woman one more
time, she dressed quickly and slipped on her shoes. She was
careful not to wake Iktan, who still dozed naked on the other
side of the bed. It wasn't like the former assassin to sleep in,
or not to be woken by noises coming from somewhere in the
house, but Iktan was still recovering. Naranpa might have
healed xir physical wounds, but exhaustion and grief still lin-

gered around xir eyes and in the hunch of xir shoulders. It would take more than magic to heal that.

Naranpa slipped past the curtain that separated the sleeping room from the larger kitchen and living area to find Kupshu setting a fire in her hearth, a pot of water already hauled in and set to boil. She'd obviously been home for a while. What had appeared dusty with neglect yesterday was swept clean, and the windows had been flung open to air out the tiny house.

"Don't remember saying you could sleep in my bed," the woman complained, her eyes focused on the kindling as it popped and crackled, her voice as gruff as ever.

"I'm glad to see you, too," Naranpa said, taking no offense. It would have surprised her if Kupshu greeted her any other way.

"Oh, am I supposed to be pleased to see you? Sleeping in my bed." The fire had caught, and Kupshu waddled over to her cupboards. She opened a drawer, peered inside dramatically, and then slammed it closed. "Eating my food."

Naranpa winced as the bang echoed around the room. She hoped it didn't awaken—

Iktan rushed into the kitchen, eyes wild.

"Danger!" xe shouted, obsidian knife in hand, still stark naked.

Kupshu turned at the shout, took one look at Iktan, and grabbed a cooking pan. She assumed a competent-looking fighting stance and brandished it like a weapon. "Ho, villain! Get out!"

Naranpa had let out a small scream when Iktan had bounded into the kitchen, but Kupshu's challenge was like something out of a storybook, a very bad one, and she could not quite hold back the giggle that burst from her lips. She slapped her hand over her mouth, but it was no good. Laughter bubbled out. Shoulder-shaking, back-bending laughter.

Iktan eyed her, expression abashed. Xe lowered the knife.

"Are you unharmed?" xe asked.

Naranpa could only nod.

"Who are you?" Kupshu demanded. She had not dropped her makeshift weapon and was now quite brazenly staring at a very nude Iktan.

Naranpa pushed at Iktan's shoulder. "Go get dressed," she managed around a chuckle that split her mouth into a wide smile. "Please. I'll explain to . . ." She waved in Kupshu's direction.

Iktan slipped back behind the curtain without another word.

"Not only in my bed but with a naked stranger," the old woman muttered, sounding scandalized.

"Iktan is not a stranger," she explained. "Xe's the person I went to save."

"The one whose dreams you Walked?"

Naranpa nodded. "But I'm sorry if I overstepped by taking your bed. I truly thought you were gone."

"I was," she said, voice short. "I paid a boy in the village to tell me if someone showed up at my cottage. Ilo came last night to say he'd spotted two foreigners making themselves at home."

"Foreigner? Ilo knows me."

"Maybe, but you're still a foreigner, aren't you?"

Naranpa decided it was not worth arguing. She had a feeling that she could live fifty years in Charna and everyone in the village would still call her a foreigner.

The fire was burning steadily now, and although it was only days until the summer solstice, mornings along the lake always began chilly. The blaze warmed the room nicely in no time, and Naranpa could hear that the pot of water for morning tea had begun to boil. Out of habit, and respect for staying in Kupshu's home, she motioned for the old woman to sit and started making tea.

"Have you had breakfast, then?" she asked.

"Hours ago. While you were still snoozing away."

Naranpa pressed her lips together and counseled herself to patience. "Would you like something else? A boiled egg? A flat cake?" She set a steaming cup of tea down in front of the old woman and poured a bit of tuktuk milk in.

Kupshu grunted, but Naranpa could tell she was pleased. "I hope you don't expect me to train your friend, too. Xe's got an air of something, but it's not god-touched like you."

"No, Iktan's not here to train." Naranpa had her own cup of tea now and took a seat on the bench across from her. "And I'm not here to train, either."

"Then what?" Her eyes narrowed in suspicion.

"I need your help."

For the first time, she seemed to take Naranpa in, Kupshu's keen gaze reading her tired face, the hollowness of her cheeks, the resigned tilt of her shoulders.

"When you left, you said you were needed in your war."

"That hasn't changed."

"And yet you're here."

"Because I think from here is where I can strike the enemy the deepest blow."

"From Charna?" Kupshu's eyebrows rose in confusion and then fell as understanding dawned. "You mean the Graveyard."

Naranpa sipped her tea.

"And you want my help?"

She nodded.

"You foolish girl!" Kupshu hissed. "Did my story of Niviq's death teach you nothing?"

"It taught me that the Graveyard amplifies the dreamwalker's power and that a mind can be trapped in the dreamworld."

Kupshu spit on the ground. "You wish to lose your mind?"

"No. Not me."

"Then who?" Kupshu glanced over her shoulder toward the sleeping room. "Your friend?"

"My enemy. The jaguar lord who stalks my dreams. He threatens not only me but my city. I think I know a way to trap him in the dreamworld, but I will need your help to do it."

"At what cost, Naranpa?" Kupshu's voice rose. "Because there will be a cost."

"Whatever it takes." Her voice was flat and brooked no compromise.

She thought she caught movement behind Kupshu at the sleeping curtain, but Iktan did not appear, and Naranpa decided she had imagined it. She lowered her voice to a whisper.

"I don't want to die. But I know that I cannot hide from the jaguar man, and I would rather attack than wait for him to pick me off as he wishes. Every night I fear that I will dream of him; every morning I wake up wondering if my thoughts are my own or something he has planted in my sleeping mind. It is its own kind of madness, Kupshu, and I need it over with. The solstice approaches, the day when my god is the strongest. I will enter the dreamworld and open myself fully to my god. I will use that power to spring a trap and capture a cat. Now, you can help me do it, or I will do it myself. But I know without you, my chances of failure are greater. I am, as you said, a child still learning to swim. But I will do what I must, even if it means I drown."

The old woman stared at her, and Naranpa waited. She had not meant to confess everything quite so fully, but now that she had, she was glad for it. The truth was that she was terrified of what might happen to her when she confronted Balam, but it would not stop her. She had accepted that in order to trap him in the dreamworld, she might have to trap herself, too.

She would do it.

She only wished not to have to do it alone.

Finally, Kupshu made a noise, something between acceptance and disgust.

"Go feed the tuktuks," she grumbled. "Then we'll talk."

It was the closest thing to a "yes" that Naranpa would get.

She rose and walked to the other side of the table to kiss the woman's papery cheek.

"Thank you," she whispered, and then she slid into the sleeping room to change for the outside.

She found Iktan sitting on the bed, fully clothed. Head down. Waiting.

She swallowed. It was one thing to tell Kupshu of her plans, another to tell her lover and best friend.

"I had the strangest dream," xe said, voice soft. "I dreamed that I traveled across the entire continent to find the woman I loved. Only she conspired with an old village woman to come up with a plan. The very same plan, in fact, that killed the old woman's daughter."

"Iktan . . ."

"I might have some of the details wrong, but I assume 'my Niviq' means her daughter, and I very clearly heard the words 'death' and 'lose your mind.'" Xe scrubbed a hand through black hair and looked up, eyes wrinkled in concern. "But I feel like I'm the one losing my mind, Naranpa, because I just found you. And I'm not interested in living without you again."

She came to sit beside Iktan, the bed dipping under her weight.

"And I want to live with you. These days together have been the happiest of my life."

"Then why?"

"Because of power, Iktan. I have the power to help. And what kind of person would I be if I did not at least try?"

"An alive one."

"It is not enough."

"I know Balam. I have seen what he is capable of. Not as just a man of calculation but a man of magic. He is dangerous, Naranpa. And if this dreamwalking you speak of causes madness, he might already be insane."

"All the more reason I must try to stop him before he destroys Tova and unbalances the very heavens!"

Iktan shook xir head. "How am I supposed to protect you when you insist on throwing yourself into danger?"

"Perhaps you do not need to protect me." She said it gently, eyes searching, looking for the part of Iktan behind the biting wit and deadly sarcasm. "Perhaps you only need to love me, and that is enough."

Xe made a rude noise, tongue stuck between lips.

She laughed and leaned in to kiss away the vulgarity.

"I'm going to feed the tuktuks," she said, standing. "You're welcome to join me."

Iktan leaned back, hands behind head and eyelids heavy. "Absolutely not."

"Suit yourself." She changed into the day dress she had left folded on the shelf, the one she often wore to take care of the smelly animals. "There's hot water for tea, and despite saying otherwise, I think Kupshu would appreciate if you made her breakfast." She arched an eyebrow. "Or is that beneath you, too?"

Xe grinned, lazy and dangerous all at once. "The only thing I want beneath me is you."

She flushed at the innuendo, face hot, and fled before the ex-priest could say anything else to embarrass her. But even as she made her way to the animal pen, memories of what she and Iktan had done the night before in a borrowed bed flashed through her mind.

"Damn you," she muttered, realizing Iktan's flirtation had not only smoothly gotten xir out of doing any chores but had also been a change of tactic. A not-so-subtle reminder of what she would be giving up if she pursued her suicidal plans. And while her resolve did not waver, it did sway a bit.

• • • • •

She finished seeing to the tuktuks just as the heat of the day was beginning to set in. She stomped the loose loam off her boots and entered the cottage to find Iktan and Kupshu sitting at the table, empty plates between them and fresh mugs of tea in hand. And Kupshu, her grumpy old teacher, was laughing.

They were up to something, something of which she would likely not approve. Naranpa almost walked back out, but the scent of bread and hot lard kept her in place.

Iktan rolled xir head in her direction, the remnants of a smile still lingering on perfect lips. "Kupshu was just telling me about her poison collection. Did you know she had a poison collection?"

"Did Iktan tell you xe was an assassin?" Naranpa said, making her way to the stove. She helped herself to two boiled eggs, flatbread, and a few of the small salty fish she'd grown to appreciate during her time in the north, and then joined them at the table.

The old woman didn't even flinch at Naranpa's pronouncement. "Some people need to die."

Naranpa bit into an egg. It was soft and salty in her mouth. "Please don't encourage xir."

Kupshu cleared her throat, and Naranpa looked up, still chewing.

"We've been talking," the older woman said.

"I don't like the sound of that."

"You will," Iktan assured her. "We discussed the war and the dangers of it, even here, in little Charna, and we have devised a plan."

Naranpa licked salt from her fingers. "I already have a plan."

"Ours is better."

Skies. "Tell me."

"We set a trap, something to lure Balam in. He cannot be killed within the dreamworld, but his mind can be broken, and he can be trapped within."

Naranpa frowned. "That is my plan already."

"Ah, but you thought to use yourself as bait."

"He wants me. He will come if he thinks he can destroy me."

"Truly, he hates what you stand for, there is no doubt. And to bring down the sun god in the realm of the gods, it would be a victory. And it is too dangerous. If somehow you were to fail, you risk your god's survival. Your failure could cast the world into darkness forever. You worry about Balam unbalancing the world, but what of you?"

She hadn't thought of it quite like that, and uncertainty made her grimace. "But it is the only way."

"No, there is someone he hates not just symbolically but quite literally. And, bonus, is not the avatar of a god."

Her brow wrinkled, but Iktan's beaming grin gave it away. "You?"

"I did do my best to kill him. Let's hope he holds a grudge."

"Iktan, no." It was one thing to risk herself, but to send Iktan on a suicide mission for her cause? It was too much.

She said, "I'd like to speak to Iktan alone."

Kupshu looked as if she would protest, but something in Naranpa's expression must have swayed her. "Kicked out of my own house. Again!" But she left nonetheless.

Once she was gone, Iktan leaned back, arms folded across xir chest.

How to begin? Well, perhaps at the beginning. "Do you remember when we met?" she asked.

"You had a better lunch than me," xe said, blithe.

She smiled at the memory. "And you gave me that knife. To protect me."

"To impress you."

"Ah."

She envisioned a young Iktan, all arms and legs, scampering up the side of the tower like xe was as much squirrel as human. She took a long, slim-fingered hand between her own thicker, less dexterous ones. The next thing she wished to say was difficult, and she was not sure how Iktan would respond. She chose her words carefully.

"You have always tried to protect me from my enemies, and I understand the guilt you feel for failing."

Iktan's face tightened perceptively, but xe said nothing.

"But there is a difference between protecting me and smothering me. I tried to tell you that at the tower."

"Abah and Golden Eagle—"

She waved the words away. "It doesn't matter. It is my life. I choose what to do with it, mistakes and all. If I fail, then it is my failure. And if I succeed, then that is mine, too."

"So you want me to simply let you die?" Iktan's voice was icy with disdain.

"No. I have no intention of dying," she lied. "Once I have trapped Balam, I will find a way back to you. I swear it."

Iktan sat with her vow, face closed. Naranpa waited. The minutes ticked by. Naranpa became aware of a presence at the door. Kupshu, eavesdropping.

"Very well," xe finally conceded, expelling a burdened sigh. "What must I do to support you in this lunacy?"

Her heart sang, and she let her gratitude show on her face. "I will still need protection. The Graveyard is not without risks."

"You want me to fight demons?"

"Hopefully, there will not be a need, but when I am dream-walking, my body is vulnerable. I will need you to guard it."

Part of her had accepted that she might never return to her corporeal form if her plan was successful, but she had meant it when she said she would try, and it would give Iktan something to do while she Walked.

Iktan's eyes narrowed in thought. "How does one fight demons?"

"Kupshu?" she called, and there was an answering thud against the door, followed by cursing. She met Iktan's amused eyes, and they both laughed.

"Come tell me more about your poisons," Iktan called. "And let us devise a plan to keep my future wife safe and returned back to me after she saves the world."

Naranpa startled. "Future wife?"

"Yes. If I am going to stand aside and support this madness, I need something from you in return."

"Iktan, I—"

"Marry me, Nara." Xir voice was urgent, almost palpable with intensity. "Today. Before we go to the Graveyard. Kupshu can do it, or there must be some crusty local holy woman in the village who will be happy to hear our vows. I know it was forbidden for the priests of the tower to marry, but surely those rules no longer apply. And even if—"

"Yes," she said, cutting Iktan off.

"Yes?" Xe grinned. It really was a perfect face.

She nodded, and then Iktan was climbing over the table, knocking cups and bowls aside to pull Naranpa into xir arms and smother her with kisses. She laughed and held on, the whirlwind of xir affection making her giddy.

"What's going on?" Kupshu grumbled from the doorway. But Naranpa could hear a touch of sentiment in her tone.

"We're going on a suicide mission to trap a sorcerer in a magic realm and possibly fight the demon undead," Iktan said around an unending stream of kisses that kept Naranpa laughing. "But first, we're getting married."

• • • • •

The ceremony was small. There was indeed a wise woman in the village willing to hear their vows and bind them in matrimony for time eternal. And Kupshu bore witness, joined by Ilo, the village boy, who was happy to participate for a small fee. Naranpa borrowed a dress from Ilo's older sister, a yellow weave embroidered at the cuffs and hem, and another villager lent Iktan a robe of deep red.

"Anything but white," xe had said, and had genuinely smiled when red was an option.

Afterward, Kupshu made a fish dish that was divine, and someone else from the village, upon hearing that there was a wedding taking place, brought out a platter of sweets. After that, word spread, and within the hour, it seemed like the whole of Charna had poured into the streets to celebrate. A band was hastily assembled, flute and drum and bells. And everyone, even Iktan, danced.

It shouldn't have surprised her that xe was an exceptional

dancer. Xir physicality had always been a revelation, a gift from whatever dark god Iktan had pledged xir life to when xe became a Knife of the tower, but Naranpa delighted in the way Iktan smoothly turned and twirled her across the dusty village square.

Laughing and exhausted, she finally found a quiet bench and sat, happy to watch the festivities from a bit of a distance. Presently, her new spouse joined her, a clay cup of fermented milk in hand.

Xe sipped and made a face.

"You get used to it," Naranpa assured xir.

"I refuse," xe said, setting the cup aside.

They sat for a while, together but each in their own thoughts. Until Iktan said, "Did you know Kupshu was a spear-maiden?"

Naranpa gaped.

"I was suspicious as soon as I saw the way she wielded that cooking pan," xe said, "but then I told her I had recently come from Hokaia, and we got to talking."

Naranpa tried to contain her shock. "She never said."

"No one else knows. I might have flattered her a bit to get her to confess, but in truth, it did not take much."

"How did she end up here?" Naranpa gestured, taking in the little village. "I thought she was born and raised here. She made it sound like she was born and raised here."

"Born here, yes, but when her mother died and her aunt could not afford to care for both her and her sister, Kupshu, being the elder, went south to make her fortune. The spear-maidens will take any woman, of course, providing she swear an oath of celibacy."

"But she had a daughter."

"The oath didn't work out," Iktan observed succinctly,

"and neither did the father, so she returned to her childhood home to raise the baby."

"Niviq. Whom she lost." Something else occurred to her. "Is that how she knows so much about dreamwalking? Do the spearmaidens teach it still, even though it is forbidden?"

"Some, perhaps. I doubt the spearmaidens have forsaken the knowledge completely, Treaty terms or not. But most of her knowledge seems to come from local traditions. After all, this is where the first spearmaidens learned the arcane practice."

"On the shores of the lake."

"And in the Graveyard."

"And she told you all of this while you were dancing?"

"I am very charming when I wish to be."

That, she decided, did not warrant a comment.

Iktan slid across the bench to press against her, hip to hip, shoulder to shoulder. "Tell me, are you happy, Wife?"

She flushed and took xir hand. "Yes. Very."

And she meant it. It was perhaps the happiest she had ever been in her life. And she understood what Iktan had done for her, given her the best, last day xe could imagine, full of joy and life and food and so much love.

Because in a few short hours, they would make the trek up the hill to the Graveyard of the Gods. She sobered at the thought, some of her joy fading under the weight of reality. There were so many unknowns, so many gaps where things could go wrong. What if Balam never came? What if he did come, but Naranpa could not trap his mind? What if, while they slept, they were attacked, and Iktan, for all xir clever scheming, could not fight them off?

The more Naranpa thought about it, the more far-fetched the plan seemed. But what choice did she have? They had to try, didn't they? Naranpa could not simply leave the world to suffer when she might be able to help.

Night had fallen in earnest, and someone sent a lantern skyward on a puff of heated air. A wish for the newlyweds.

"We should join them," Iktan mused, voice thoughtful. "Make a wish."

"My wish has already come true," she said, leaning into xir side.

"Really?" Iktan cocked an eyebrow. "My wish involves a lot less clothing."

She laughed and allowed Iktan to pull her to her feet. And they went to join the celebration.

But the worry had already taken root, and she could not quite rekindle the free-spirited joy she had felt before. As she watched another lantern rise toward the sky buoyed by the good-natured shouts of the villagers, she only saw fire. And in that fire, just like in her dreams, Tova burned.

CHAPTER 35

> They say that when the Spearmaidens called down the Frenzy upon the City of Cuecola, Nightmares walked the Earth. Mothers fell upon their Children, Siblings upon Siblings, Husbands upon Wives, until the Pyramids and Temples ran with Blood. Few of the Ruling Class survived, and Those who did wished They had not.
>
> —From *A History of the Frenzy*, by Teox,
> a historian of the Royal Library

Okoa had not known the human body could endure so much pain and survive.

Once, during a lecture on the battle tactics used to defeat Cuecola during the War of the Spear, his instructor had assured Okoa's class that those who died in the Frenzy at the hands of the spearmaidens had likely felt no pain when the wild magic tore them limb from limb. The human mind, his instructor explained, shut off when pain became too great. Since the Frenzy, there had been experiments done, tests performed, and when the subjects had recovered from their tortures, they had claimed not to remember the worst of their suffering.

Okoa had believed it at the time, but now he knew his instructor had lied. Why, he could not say. Perhaps his teacher
had thought the deception a comfort for a reality too brutal to
face. Or perhaps the account had simply been an amusing tale
for a morbidly curious class of youths. Or maybe his teacher's
motivation had been something more sinister: disinformation
to reform the reputation of her ancestors and the horrors they
had visited upon the Jaguar Prince's men, a violence so devastat-
ing that it decimated the sorcerer class and convinced Cuecola
to willingly surrender its claim to magic for all the centuries to
follow. Or maybe it was simply ignorance, as Okoa's teacher
had certainly never experienced torture herself, had never had
her fingers broken or the arches of her feet whipped or the skin
peeled from her back.

Okoa suffered all this and worse. Or so he believed.

Because, despite the hours of pain, when he would inevitably return to his senses, sweat-soaked and confused, he would
find his body whole, his skin unblemished. But the snap of his
fingers breaking, the white-hot sting of the whip against his
bare soles, the screaming horror of the knife flaying him raw
remained.

He could not understand that it was his mind that the matron of Winged Serpent broke. There, in the deep caves below
the Kun Great House, snakes slithered from their pits and
crawled over Okoa's bound body. They sank venomous fangs
into his flesh, and the hallucinations of torture began.

But the worst was when Peyana came to sit beside him and
whisper a more potent poison in his ear.

Your clan has renounced you. You are a Crow no more,
Okoa No Name.

The Carrion King himself calls for your execution. He says that
you are mine now, to do with as I wish. And I wish you to suffer.

They were his worst imaginings made manifest, but even in his pain-addled haze, he thought of lies and the why of them. The matron Peyana, his sister Esa, his old instructor. All liars.

It was enough to keep his hope alive.

Until it wasn't.

The door to the room creaked open, and Peyana entered, bearing a torch in one hand and a basket cradled in the crook of her free arm. Her gaze cut across him, and she smiled, a cruel slash across her face.

"I've brought you a present," she crooned, and sat on a bench facing him. They had tied him naked to a stone chair, ropes constraining his arms painfully at the elbows and his legs wide and tied at the knees.

A serpent slid from around her neck, down her arm, and made its way to his exposed thigh. He could only watch, helpless and wrung out, as the creature sank its fangs into his leg. He imagined the toxin entering his blood, rushing to his brain, and resigned himself to another round of torture.

But Peyana only sat and watched, a starved smile twisting her mouth.

He thought to speak but couldn't remember how to form words.

The snake bit him again, this time the feeling of violation hot against his naked hip. Something like panic rippled through his body, and he thought to shake the reptile off, but Peyana reached out her arm and clicked her tongue, and the snake slithered up her arm and returned to its mistress. It curled around the matron's neck, docile, flat eyes watching him as if it knew what it had done and anticipated the result.

Peyana tapped a finger against the thing she held in her lap. Okoa forced himself to focus. It was a basket. It was woven from dried palm and had a handled lid. Peyana smoothed a hand across the lid before placing the basket on the ground before him. She did not open it but let whatever was inside remain hidden.

"I know your hours alone here are lonely hours, so I have brought you an old friend to keep you company." Peyana's mouth curved into venom and threat. "When I was a child, I used to admire the crow riders. Oh, you might not believe it, but it is true. Winged serpents are superior in many ways, but your corvids have their charms. So trusting. I think that is what I admired most. The relationships you build with your beasts. You raise them from hatchlings, do you not? Bond with them as they grow. It's quite beautiful."

Okoa's vision blurred and stretched, Peyana's face becoming grotesque, her eyes too bulbous, her mouth too cavernous. When she talked, he could almost see her words in the air as she spoke them. They were black and foul, like living rot.

"Benundah is your hen, is she not? A loyal creature. I heard that she screamed when we took you away. Became feral. Even the Odo Sedoh, the crow god himself, could not soothe her. She fled. Flew away. They feared she was lost."

Her tone grew sly, and her head seemed to flatten, her features widening at the cheeks and coming to a point at the crown, balanced on a narrowing neck.

"But she was not lost."

She tipped the basket with her foot. Not much, just enough to draw his attention to it. And to the bloodstains that soaked through the bottom.

"It is truly a tragedy that those we love most in the world must often bear the burden of our errors. My Isel. Your Benundah."

Cold horror made Okoa lightheaded, as if someone had opened his chest and exposed his heart, muscle raw and vulnerable.

"You know," she continued conversationally, "giant crows

are not so large up close. At least, their heads are not. In fact . . ."
She tilted the basket again, rolling the top with her toe. "I'd say
their heads are just about the size of this basket."

Okoa had that feeling, the one he had come to know well.
He was flying above the lake and had somehow lost his bearings, and then he was falling from a very great distance. Only
this time, there was no lake at the bottom to break his fall.

"Peyana," he managed in a hoarse whisper. "Please."

"Oh," she tsked, "it's too late to beg now." Hate flared across
her face under the torchlight, and a forked tongue flicked between her fangs. "You took everything from me, and now I will
take everything from you. And it begins here."

She kicked the basket over, and a mass of something bloody
and black rolled across the dirt floor.

Okoa's world tilted.

He squeezed his eyes shut. He would not look. He would not.
Remember the poison, the lies! It is not real, Okoa!
It. Is. Not. Real.

But his heart told him otherwise.

A moan emanated from somewhere within him, the sound
of his spirit breaking. It grew to a low, wailing keen, and then
he was screaming, screaming, until his lungs gave out, until his
throat bled.

And still it was not enough.

• • • • •

Okoa dreamed of crows. He was back in the rookery, tucked
under his mantle of feathers. A fire burned low, and there, beside him, the Odo Sedoh slept his restless, healing sleep. In the
morning, Okoa would wake and attend to him, and Benundah
would be there, and all would be well.

"Okoa, wake up!"

He turned in his sleep. There was a reason he did not wish to wake, a memory that dreams were the safer course.

Insistent hands shook him, and a familiar voice urged him to rouse from his slumber, but he knew something terrible waited for him there, something he did not wish to face, and so he resisted.

"Now, Crow son!" the voice commanded. "We must go!"

"Serapio?" Okoa opened bleary eyes, sure he was still dreaming of the rookery. But the face drawn in torchlight before him was sketched in grim lines, hints of outrage in the clench of his jaw, the furrow in his brow.

"What have they done to you, Okoa?"

Okoa tried to grip Serapio's shirt to pull him close, to whisper his terrible knowledge, but his arms were still tied to his sides. He flexed his fingers, broken, swollen, and clumsy.

"Skies," Serapio swore. He kicked at a snake that had ventured too close. "Have they poisoned you?"

Poison, yes, but it was his heart that was infected. "I have done terrible things," he murmured.

"You mean Isel. It was a mistake." Serapio felt his way along the ropes that bound Okoa. His deft fingers worked the knots.

Isel. Okoa could hardly remember her now. "No, not . . ." He heaved a great breath. "I have betrayed you."

Serapio paused. "What are you saying?"

Okoa's heart cracked, a fissure wide enough to break him. "The matrons. After Chaiya, I was so confused. My faith faltered. I took the mask to—"

"I know this, Okoa," Serapio said, voice gentle. "The poison has made you confused." He loosened the first knot. "And I have forgiven you."

"You should not." He searched for a way to tell Serapio about Benundah, mouth moving uselessly.

Serapio untied the last knot that held Okoa to the chair. Okoa tried to stand and collapsed back to sitting.

"You are in no condition to fight," Serapio murmured, "and it is best if they never know that I was here. We will move through the darkness together, but first . . ."

He lifted Okoa's legs, one by one, and forced the useless limbs into a pair of black pants. He held Okoa up to slide the fabric over his hips. It was strangely intimate, being dressed by the Odo Sedoh, his hands moving Okoa's body this way and that. *He cares for me*, Okoa thought, and then buried that sentiment. He did not deserve such care, and if the Odo Sedoh believed he did, it was because Okoa had deceived him. Shame shuddered through him, sending great heaving breaths from his bruised lungs.

Serapio threaded his arms through sleeves and slid a shirt over his head. Finally, a cloak was wrapped around his shoulders. Not feathered but black cotton. Good. He could not bear to wear Benundah's shed ever again.

"Hold on to me," Serapio commanded as he looped Okoa's arm around his neck and hauled him to standing. And quieter, to himself, "I should have never left you here this long."

"Nowhere to go . . . ," Okoa whispered, thinking that it didn't matter now whether he lived or died when there was nothing left for which to live.

"It is best that you do not return to the Shadow Palace," Serapio said, misunderstanding. "Benundah will take you to the rookery, where you will be safe." They shuffled forward. "I've brought you a bag packed with warm clothes and a few days' provisions. Anything else you will have to forage." He gently squeezed Okoa's shoulder. "You will survive this. And after the war, Benundah will bring you home."

"Benundah." The bloody basket, the black feathers. Okoa's voice broke around the words as they finally came to him. "Benundah is dead."

Serapio tilted his head, clearly confused. "No, Okoa. She came here with me."

"I saw her. She was dead."

"When?"

Okoa looked above and around, but he could not say. How long had he been here? Days? Months? A year? How long since the serpents' fangs had cut into his flesh, how long since Peyana had shown him her terrible treachery? He shook his head, hating that he could not answer.

"You are mistaken, Okoa."

He shivered, not with fear but with longing.

Serapio said, "I will show you that she lives."

"I want to believe . . ."

"Then believe! I tell you that she lives."

Please understand, Serapio, why I cannot. Okoa would have stopped, would have lain down on the cold dirt floor, there in the darkness, and wept for his failures, had not Serapio held him up. The hallway curved upward, out of the darkness, and they rose, step by excruciating step.

Okoa could feel the blood moving through his muscles, the creak as his bones returned to life after being tied to the stone chair for time eternal. The venom was fading, but he did not like the reality to which he was awakening. It stank of his perpetual lack of faith, his faltering doubts.

"You should leave me here," he murmured, mouth next to Serapio's ear.

Serapio said nothing, and Okoa continued. "I am a faithless creature," he confessed. "I deserve to live here in the darkness."

"What is darkness to a blind man?" A smile lifted the edge

of Serapio's mouth, the last thing Okoa saw before he guttered the torch.

They walked.

Okoa knew he sounded pathetic, but it was the truth, and he needed Serapio to understand. Okoa would never change. Never be the Carrion Crow son he was born to be, never the friend Serapio needed, never the general Tova required. There was something wrong with him. Some deep flaw that made him inconstant and unreliable. Even when he tried to be worthy, to become someone great, his flaw undermined his efforts. *Perhaps it is because my father was a traitor*, he thought. *The seed corrupts wholly. I am spoiled meat.*

"The venom still pollutes you," Serapio said, as if he could sense Okoa's grim thoughts as he led them through the darkness. "Your mind is not itself."

Serapio was wrong. His time in the snake pit had gifted him with a deep clarity. But Okoa said nothing. He knew Serapio would not understand. Would only try to save him when the time for saving had passed.

They moved through the night, slowly but surely, and eventually the world began to lighten. Not daylight but shadows in the place of emptiness, the outlines of walls, a floor, light somewhere above.

Okoa lifted his head.

"There are sky doors," Serapio explained. "I entered through one and followed this path down to you. Benundah waits just beyond."

Something like hope gripped him, made him shudder down a sob. He did not deserve, but he desired. "Promise me, Serapio. Promise me that she lives."

The shadow cut Serapio's fine features into something godlike in their beauty. "She lives, Okoa. Go and see for yourself."

They had reached the ledge, Tova spread before them. Faint lights shone from across the river in Titidi, a froth of yellow and orange was visible from the Maw, and somewhere below, the river rushed as loud as the flutter of a thousand wings.

A shout rose behind them. Okoa's absence had been discovered.

"Benundah?" Okoa asked, hesitant. Serapio had said she was here, but he could not see her.

Serapio's expression grew distant and then returned. "She is coming. Quickly!" He embraced Okoa, held him close for a moment, and Okoa felt his hope solidify. The voice of his failure nagged, persisted, but if Serapio could love him, perhaps he was worthy of love after all.

"I must go," Serapio said. "When Benundah comes, you must jump."

"Jump?" A gust of wind shoved him back.

"She will not let you fall. I will not let you fall."

Okoa was high above an icy blue lake. Always falling, always . . .

"Okoa? Can you hear me?"

The sound of running feet, of shouting guards, was drawing closer.

"Go," he said, shaking himself back to the present. "I . . . I will wait for Benundah."

"And you will go to the rookery? Or west? Somewhere until I call for you?" Serapio pressed a hand to his cheek. "There is destiny at work here, Okoa. Things beyond your control. Know that you did not fail me before, and you do not fail me now."

The feeling of falling threatened to overwhelm him again, but Okoa only nodded.

And then Serapio was gone, broken into a flock of crows,

black bodies and wings blending into the black sky. Okoa watched him dip low across the river and then circle up, up toward the Shadow Palace until he was gone entirely from view.

Alone, on the edge, Okoa thought, *My god has abandoned me. Peyana spoke true. I am unwanted, unnamed.* But why, then, would Serapio come for him? Lead him here, to the precipice of freedom? Taunt him with Benundah's survival?

Where is your faith, Okoa? What must you see to believe? He thought of Serapio, how he could not see but had the faith of a thousand men. *If only I could be like him. But I am not. I am . . .*

A familiar cry reached his ears, distant and faint.

Benundah!

Something in Okoa lifted. His spirit swelled, higher than the stars. Wider than the whole of the sky. Tears slipped from his eyes. The wind caught his long hair and flung it wildly around his face. Before he had always fallen. But now, the darkness around him, the unknown before him, he did not fall.

He leapt.

CHAPTER 36

Trust the heart to lead you home.

—*The Obregi Book of Flowers*

It had only been a few hours since Xiala had traveled through the shadowgate outside the war college in Hokaia to find herself on the banks of a river she strongly suspected was a branch of the Tovasheh. The forces of the Treaty cities had walked through darkness to arrive in darkness, out of the shadow and into the night. The moon above was only a sliver of a crescent above her head, but the stars were thick and numerous. Xiala almost wept to see it there. There had been nothing inside the shadowgate. No sky, but no earth, either. No up, no down, nothing but a vast hunger that licked the blood from the soles of her feet and sucked at her bones like a gluttonous child.

Even now, the memory of it sent a residual terror shivering through her. She had been certain that if she had lingered in that in between place, the shadow would have consumed her, flesh and soul.

But it had not, and one by one, each of them—lords, generals, soldiers, spearmaidens, eagles and their riders, and finally the cooks, sculleries, and porters—had stumbled out, shivering and drained. It might have only taken seconds to cross hundreds of miles, but in those seconds, her life had been leached from her in greedy handfuls.

She slumped on a nearby log, body heavy and aching, muscles depleted as if she had walked for weeks. She pulled the hood of her nondescript cloak tighter around her, making sure her hair was covered, and she was careful not to make eye contact with anyone. She thought the darkness hid her well, and she knew Teek mixed among the Hokaians in a way they did not in the other cities of the Meridian, but she was known to Terzha, Ziha, and Balam, and being found out would be disastrous. She wondered if they would kill her on sight, feed her to their shadowgate, or, most disturbing, use her as a weapon against Serapio.

None was an option that interested her.

Already the soldiers were erecting tents, the one in the center familiar to her from her travels across the plains with Golden Eagle. In fact, she saw the Golden Eagle sisters warming themselves at a hearty fire in what looked to be the command center of their encampment. Terzha was bundled in layers of white fur and, of all of them, looked the least affected by the bone-numbing cold of the shadow world.

Too bad, Xiala thought. *I would not mind if she suffered.*

A lean and long-legged spearmaiden approached Terzha at a run, and soon the Golden Eagle matron was joined by the Sovran of Hokaia and Lord Balam. They gathered around her, the spearmaiden speaking and gesturing expressively.

The woman was a scout, that much was clear. She must have been sent through the shadowgate earlier and was now returning to report.

Xiala closed her eyes and thought of vibrations and reverberations and the nature of sound, the way she might if she were in the sea. She focused on the crackle of the flames, the muttered curses of soldiers setting up camp, and, there, the rushed, breathless patter of the spearmaiden.

They were west of Tova, the woman reported, and only a few day's march from the city. The knowledge that Serapio was only a few miles east filled her with a cacophony of emotion. Relief, excitement, doubt, fear. They all warred within her. She thought of the taste of his lips, salty at sea and honey-tinged in Tova, the touch of his fingers, the soft rumble of his voice.

But she was also not a fool. It had been almost six months since their night together, and if she had changed, certainly he had, too. Carrion King. Of course, he had changed and was not the same man he had been when they had traveled the Crescent Sea together. But she was not the same, either. She had been a queen, had vanquished her people's enemies, had called upon the creatures of the deep sea to do her bidding. And she had killed. Not once or twice but many times and many men.

Would Serapio even recognize the woman she had become?

"You!" A voice broke her from her reverie, but the command was not for her. A man with a captain's stripe edging his cloak kicked at one of the scullery boys standing at the far end of the log, arms full of foraged wood. "No fires!"

"But they have a fire," the boy protested, motioning toward the command center with a belligerent thrust of his chin. "And I'm freezing my tits off."

The boy did look half-frozen, his small form shivering enough to rattle the kindling in his thin arms. In truth, the captain didn't look much better, glints of frost glittering on his braided hair.

"No fires!" The captain's hand moved with a quick and casual brutality and struck the boy. The boy cried out and stumbled, his carefully gathered wood spilling from his grasp.

Xiala found herself on her feet before she knew what she was doing.

The captain's eyes turned to her, as if daring her to do something.

"Now, now, Captain," a voice soothed. "There's no need for such savagery." Balam's hand came down on the captain's shoulder, fingers perceptively tightening, and the larger man winced.

Xiala remembered that first time on the docks in Cuecola when Balam had perceived her Song when no others could. She swallowed her magic before it could gather in her throat. She tucked down, pulled her hood tight, and made herself small. She prayed to the Mother that Balam would not see her, but she could feel his curious eyes travel over her. Could sense his pause, as if something nagged at his memory.

Seven hells! Hadn't she just concluded that Balam and the others would likely kill her if she was found out? She wondered if she could kill him before he did, or if he would call his blood sorcery as he had before and turn aside her deadly Song. Her heart thumped in her ears as she braced herself, expecting at any moment to feel the grip of his fingers on her shoulder.

"Water!" the cook shouted, clapping her hands as she made her way down the line, oblivious to the tension. "We didn't bring you all this way so you could lay about. Fetch a pail. River's that way. All of you. Now!"

The cook handed a lantern to the nearest woman, who called, "Follow me!"

A perfect excuse, and Xiala grabbed two wooden buckets and joined the other women, not daring to look back. Balam's gaze stayed on her, heat against her back, and she pushed deeper into the clump of women headed to the river. But the Mother must have heard her pleas, because her luck held, and Balam did not follow.

Xiala's hands shook as she exhaled a nervous breath. She had been spared for the moment, but she could not stay at the camp. It had been reckless to risk the shadowgate, but it had been the right thing. But now she had to find a way to Tova to warn Serapio that his enemies gathered at his back.

And perhaps, perhaps, she could see him again.

"The blood's all gone," hissed a voice to her left. Xiala peeked around the edge of her hood and recognized the woman who had walked through the shadow in front of her. The woman's braided hair framed a plain, narrow face as she spoke to her neighbor on the other side.

"Did you feel it when it happened?" the neighbor asked, another Hokaian woman, who could have passed as the first's older sister save for the lighter-colored hair under her undyed cloak.

The first woman shook her head, her expression dismayed. "But it ate the blood."

"So that it wouldn't eat us."

The woman made a sign to ward off evil. "They say the Carrion King trucks with the shadow world, and that is why we must fight him. But how are these Cuecolan lords who lead us any better? Where is our Sovran to protect us from the darkness of these foreign men who only wish to devour?"

"Hush," the other woman cautioned. "If they hear you, you'll be the next one they feed to the shadow." Her eyes darted around, seeking out any eavesdroppers. Xiala kept her head down and gazed steadily forward, but she listened.

"Your mother was right," the first woman muttered. "We should never have come, even if the pay was high."

"A generous merchant lord should have been our first warning," the other woman agreed. "But here we are, so let's make the best of it and get home."

"The best of war," her friend scoffed. "Listen to you. There's no such thing."

They had reached the river, and the women stooped to dip their buckets into the water. Xiala moved down a way and did the same. She needed to escape. These women didn't seem the type to raise the alarm if she disappeared. They clearly had their own misgivings and no outsized loyalty to the cause.

"Who knew Tova was so cold in the summer?" the light-haired woman muttered as she dipped her hands into the river. "Between this and the shadow world . . . no cacao is worth this."

Xiala could not hold back a snort. This wasn't cold. Yes, the night was cool compared with the heat of the central plains, but this was only a cool mountain evening. Nothing like the mind-numbing freeze of Tova in winter.

"Haven't seen you in the kitchens before," one of the women asked as she glanced at Xiala.

"I joined last minute," Xiala improvised. She smiled. Harmless. "Although I'm not sure this is what I signed up for."

The woman grunted. "None of us."

"Sorry to hear about your queen," the short-haired woman said, voice sympathetic. "Mahina, wasn't it? She gave a rousing speech at the spring festival. We were surprised to hear illness took her."

"I was at sea," Xiala lied, and then dared the question she had been too rattled to ask the shopkeeper back in Hokaia. "What happened?"

The women exchanged a look. The nearer one pursed her lips, as if suspicious, but the other looked more understanding. "A plague. She was quarantined for a few days, but they said it took her and her household staff quickly. They burned the bodies. That's all we know."

Skies, as many times as she had imagined murdering her mother, she had not deserved such betrayal. She did not think she would be able to hold back the wave of grief that suddenly loomed over her, so she gave the women a tight smile, picked up her remaining buckets, and walked downriver, quickly fading into the darkness. There was a bend near a copse of evergreens, and she headed there. She could hear the women talking behind her, but it sounded as if they had moved on to something else and forgotten about her. She walked until she could no longer hear their quiet murmurings.

Once she was certain she was alone, she removed her clothes, wrapped them all in her cloak, and knelt by the rushing water. Bundle in hand, Xiala slipped into the river. It shivered her bare skin, but it was the flow of a normal spring thaw, nothing compared with the leaching cold of the shadow world. And it was not the sea. It did not greet her as its own, and she worried that land sickness would again plague her as it had on her trek across the grasslands, or if her newfound powers would protect her. For now, there was nothing to be done about it. She would have to wait and see. Nevertheless, she was glad to be in the water. With the help of the current, she could be in Tova in a matter of a day, maybe less. Enough time to give Serapio a warning and allow him to ready a defense.

She dove below the surface and let the river carry her toward Tova.

• • • • •

Much later, Xiala surfaced as the silhouette of something huge crossed overhead. She stayed low, watching as it passed through the light of the rising sun. When she realized what it was, her breath caught in her throat.

"Crow," she whispered, watching the massive bird glide in to land not far from where she treaded water. It disappeared behind the trees, but the flap of its massive wings still filled her ears, and the crack of broken branches echoed through the surrounding forest.

Her first thought was of Serapio. She remembered that Uncle Kuy had spoken of Serapio and a young scion of Carrion Crow riding a crow when they returned to the city after Serapio had killed the Watchers. But this could not be him. He was a king now, readying his city for war. Most likely this was a Carrion Crow scout.

"Good enough," she said as she swam to the bank and hauled herself out.

She wrung the water from her long hair and dressed quickly, her clothes sticky and damp against her skin. Wrapping them had not kept them completely dry, but it had prevented her clothes from slowing her down as she swam. She vowed that once this was all over and her need for disguises had passed, she would find herself a pair of the Cuecolan pants she favored and never wear another skirt again.

She wrapped her cloak around her shoulders and headed toward the place where she'd seen the crow scout land. It wasn't far.

"Soon, Serapio," she murmured, cutting through the forest to face whatever destiny lay before her.

CHAPTER 37

Power is never willingly conceded; it must always be taken.

—From the *Oration of the Jaguar Prince on the Eve of the Frenzy*

After the spearmaiden scout's briefing, Balam walked through the camp outside Tova, true wonder spinning through his veins. He was not a man easily impressed, but the magic he and Powageh had worked, with the unwilling help of Lord Tuun, had left him open-mouthed and blinking back tears of awe. The shadowgate reeked of the powers of old, of things not seen in an age, of high magic like that called upon by the Jaguar Prince during the War of the Spear. If anything could make Balam weep, it was power.

"We did it, Saaya," he whispered to the dead woman who walked next to him.

She smiled, and he reached for her hand before he remembered she was not there. Which reminded him that he was very low on godflesh, thanks to that cursed woman who had refused to sell him what was his back in Hokaia. He could have destroyed her. Drawn the blood from her veins, spread it across the floor, and taken what was his by right.

He blinked.

Such violent thoughts.

That, too, seemed to be a side effect of dreamwalking, one that worried him even more than Saaya's near-constant presence now at his side. Or perhaps it was the pressure of leading the army when he had expected Naasut to take command.

Whatever it was, he would not let worries about his slipping sanity cloud his good mood. They had achieved something wondrous, something the scribes would write of for ages. And by the time he was done, Balam would be what he had always dreamed of.

The next Jaguar Prince.

And to think, if Tuun had not so completely failed at her conquest of Teek, he might have never dared such magic. It was desperation that had driven him to attempt to open the shadowgate. That and an admittedly large ego.

But, he thought, *I am not without fault. All this time I have been using a thief's blood to open passage through the shadow world, and I could have been using a sorcerer's and opened gates more potent by a magnitude.*

Well, it was live and learn, and now he knew, thanks to Tuun's sacrifice. Although, to be fair, sorcerers were uncommon. He would have to work his way through the merchant families of Cuecola where sorcery was a bloodright to find enough sacrifices. And if he started slaughtering the elites of the city, someone would certainly take notice.

Even he understood that was impossible.

If only there were more sorcerers to bleed.

The thought made him look to his cousin.

As if sensing his interest, Powageh glanced his way, eyes narrowing in suspicion. They had spoken little since arriving at the camp, Balam sure that Powageh was harboring resentments for having to participate in the killing of the prisoners.

"Cycles of life demand death," Balam had insisted when his cousin had balked at his plan to move a portion of the army through the shadowgate.

"Killing a hundred men for their blood is not part of the cycle of life!"

"According to whom? You?"

"Yes, me." Powageh had paced away, pulling at xir hair. "Seven hells, Balam. You are not making that argument with a straight face."

"The shadow must feed. It is only natural."

"The shadow does not belong to our world. It is entirely unnatural."

"There is where I must disagree. We may not understand it fully, so much was lost after the war, but it is a place of the gods." More and more, Balam was convinced of the similarities between the dream world and the shadow world and that they were both god realms. He longed for another lifetime to wring the secrets of magic from the world but feared most had been in the tomes destroyed after the War of the Spear, when magic had become anathema. Such a waste, such a terrible, shortsighted waste.

"Balam?"

"I was saying that just because it unsettles you—"

"Skies! My comfort is not the problem!"

"Don't curse at me." Balam's reprimand was mild but pointed. "Either you help me do this, or Tuun will."

In the end, they both had helped, albeit Tuun had done so unwillingly.

And it had been glorious.

Even Powageh had had to admit that. Once xe had stopped vomiting.

But xe looked fine now.

Balam gave a friendly wave, which did little to assuage his cousin's dark look.

Very well. He would let Powageh sulk. He was sure that his cousin would come around once they had Tova in their grip.

Raised voices drew his attention. He looked over just as one of the Cuecolan captains casually backhanded a scullery boy. The boy reeled, firewood spilling from his skinny arms.

Such unnecessary violence. Balam abhorred it.

He approached the scene and gripped the captain's shoulder. "Now, now, Captain. There's no need for such savagery." He squeezed the narrow dip between the bones of his shoulder to make his point, and the man crumbled in pain.

And then Balam sensed it.

Magic.

Ocean magic.

Impossible! They were a hundred miles or more from the Crescent Sea, and the nearby river was fed by mountain streams and snowmelt, not saltwater.

He scrutinized the crowd, looking for the only practitioner of ocean magic he knew, but he saw no one who looked like Xiala. There were spearmaidens, but even Xiala, clever as she was, could not hide among spearmaidens. And despite Tuun's wild assertions, he did not truly believe Xiala was a shape-shifter who had stalked her halfway across the continent and had come back to Hokaia.

Although *if* she had returned to Hokaia, and *if* she had somehow come through the shadowgate undetected, she might warn Serapio, and that would not do.

He spied Terzha near the command fire and headed over.

"I need you to put an eagle scout in the air. Can you do that?"

The matron was chewing on a twig, the sliver caught between her teeth. Her freckled face bunched in concern.

"We prefer not to fly at night, but . . ." She shrugged. "What worries you?"

"Do you remember Xiala?"

"The Teek woman?" Terzha's voice filled with some emotion Balam could not name. "I know her."

"I . . ." *Smelled her?* No, that would not do. "Someone reported there was a woman among the kitchen workers matching her description. It is probably a coinci—"

"I'll go." Terzha was already on her feet.

Balam's brow rose. "A scout would suffice."

"No." Terzha spit the twig from her mouth. "I know this land well. Flew it regularly before I went to the war college. If she is out there, I will find her."

"Very well. Then I . . ."

Terzha was already pulling her gloves from her belt and striding toward the pen where the eagles were kept.

". . . wish you luck."

Well, that was efficient.

Despite all the excitement, a yawn took Balam, cracking his jaw wide. He was tired, more than he cared to admit. He had not properly slept for weeks, relying on the dried yaupon to keep him awake, and when he did sleep, it was under the influence of god-flesh, and his dreams were bizarre and frightening but not restful.

What he wished for, and what he did not dare have, was a proper night's sleep.

"Where is she going?" Powageh asked. Xe had come up behind Balam, eyes watching Terzha saddle her eagle and take to the sky.

"An errand. For me."

Powageh's look was incredulous. "I swear you keep secrets from me by habit alone. It is a simple question, and I deserve an answer!" Xir complaint ended in a shout.

Balam looked around. A clutch of spearmaidens were staring, no doubt amused by Powageh's chastising.

"I give you the world, and you complain it is not enough," Balam muttered, and motioned toward the command tent. If they were going to have this conversation, and it seemed they must, they would not do it in public.

Powageh followed, and they ducked inside. Unfortunately, it was occupied. Naasut lounged on cushions around a plate of dried fruits and nuts, accompanied by yet more spearmaidens and a very pretty Cuecolan warrior Balam had never noticed before. Upon seeing Balam enter, the Cuecolan man blushed and made to stand.

"Don't do that," Naasut drawled, reaching for his hand. Balam didn't see a bottle of xtabentún anywhere, but the Sovran had obviously partaken. "Lord Balam doesn't care if you stay." Her eyes flashed, and she showed her teeth. "Do you?"

Balam gave the warrior a look of pity. "Better he than I. Now, if you'll excuse us."

He and Powageh dipped out of the tent.

"She really is useless," his cousin murmured.

At least on that they could agree.

Balam snatched a resin lantern from a table and took the time to strike flint and light it. He looked around, but the camp was sparse and held little luxury or privacy, stealth and speed being of utmost importance when planning the mission. After all, Balam hoped they would not be at camp very long. Golden Eagle had reported that Tova was only a few day's march from the city. Once there, Balam would sleep in whatever palace of the clans he wished. Perhaps a different one every day.

Or, more likely, he would claim the Shadow Palace for himself.

Thinking of the Shadow Palace made him think of the Carrion King. He still marveled at how they had come to this. So much work, so much painstaking work, to birth the boy at an auspicious time, to raise him in isolation, to cultivate the proper mix of naivete and resentment into a righteous, unyielding fanaticism.

How had it gone wrong?

But then again, how had it come so close to succeeding?

They had been teenagers when they conceived of the idea, and somehow among the five of them, they had nurtured the plan for two long decades. He had lost Eedi and Paadeh, and each death did wound him. But it was Saaya's absence that ached most of all, that left a gaping hole in his chest where his heart belonged.

For a moment, he saw her face again. Sharp chin, big eyes, a blazing intelligence that surpassed even his own. Of course, her son had become something incredible. Of course, their—

"Are you coming?"

Balam looked up. Powageh was already striding into the forest, xir own lantern in hand.

They didn't go far. Just out of the circle of light that marked the camp boundaries. He could hear the river rushing nearby, the soft rustle of small animals in the underbrush, the call of night insects welcoming summer. It was pleasant in the mountains, if a little cold for his blood. He missed the jungle heat, the towering palms and thick ferns, the profusion of colorful flowers.

Perhaps he would not claim any palace in Tova. Perhaps he would simply go home.

He shook off the indulgent nostalgia, wondering if his melancholy was another sign of the madness brought on by the godflesh, or if his unusual wistfulness was something else, an awareness that his greatest achievement was reaching its conclusion.

"Talk to me, Balam," Powageh said. Xe had found a felled trunk and taken a seat.

Balam preferred to stand, leaning against a mossy boulder and folding his arms across his chest. "What is it that you wish me to say?"

"Let us start with the hallucinations. I know you see things."

Balam had not expected that, but that was no secret between them. He had admitted as much before. "The godflesh takes its toll."

"It is Saaya? Still Saaya?"

"Among others."

"But it is her the most?"

Balam nodded.

"Do you ever wonder why it is she who haunts you?"

I am only grateful that she comes to me. "No."

"You can't even admit it." Powageh shook xir head. "Here, where we are alone with no one to hear us and no one to ever know."

"I don't know what it is you wish me to admit. Perhaps you could be a bit more specific—"

"Your son!" Powageh roared. "Admit Serapio is your son!"

Balam folded his arms tighter, holding himself in.

"Ah, skies," Powageh said, voice soft. "All the signs were there. How could I not see it? The timing was close enough that her Obregi husband was unlikely to suspect, the boy's intelligence, his propensity for sorcery which is a bloodright. Of course, he was Cuecolan. And Saaya would have never left his parentage to chance. It was your genetics she wanted for her godchild, not some unknown country lord."

"She doesn't haunt me," Balam said softly.

Powageh frowned. "What?"

He raised his voice. "I said she doesn't haunt me. She keeps me company."

Powageh threw up xir hands. "That is your answer? I tell you I know you are Serapio's father, and you prattle on about a ghost while there is a living, breathing boy who is your son out there."

Balam shook his head. "He is not mine."

"Don't deny what is right before my eyes!"

"He is my progeny. I admit that. But you are more his father than I am. What do I know of fathers and sons? Mine was a failure."

"Then be the father you never had for *your* son."

"Ah, Tiniz." Balam's smile was sad. "You always were too softhearted. It was too late the moment Saaya left Cuecola and I did not stop her."

They both sat with the reality of it, Balam knowing he was right and Powageh coming around to it.

"Perhaps," his cousin finally admitted. "But you don't have to kill him."

"Not just softhearted but foolish. The boy stands in my way."

"He is my kin, too."

"And what? You will stop me?" It was ridiculous. "You were sick in the bushes over the bodies of a few criminals you'd never met. Do you truly believe you could strike me down?"

"I don't want to."

"Your wants have never mattered to me." Balam felt reckless, almost drunk, words spilling from his mouth as if beyond his control. "It is your abilities that matter, and in this, you and I both know you are outmatched. If you refuse to help me, Cousin, then step aside and stay out of my way."

Powageh bowed xir head as if gathering courage. "Do you remember what you said to me?" xe asked. "That night on the balcony when I was late to the dinner party and Saaya shared her plans?"

Balam's eyes narrowed, wary.

Powageh said, "You told me that you loved her and that what you were doing, helping her down that path of self-destruction, was love." Xe shook his head. "But love does not help someone destroy themselves." Powageh looked up. "I will not help you destroy yourself."

The wind, barely a breeze, could have toppled Balam, his shock was so great.

"I used to think you were smarter than me," Powageh admitted. "Skies, you were more than smarter than me. You were richer, more athletic, better-looking." Xe laughed, a bitter sound. "Certainly more ruthless. And I thought that meant you were better than me. Could do things I couldn't do, and that's why Saaya loved you. Because she did love you. You know that, yes? But she was not the only one. I loved you, too, Cousin. Foolishly, I still do. And so I tell you this now. This path you pursue, it asks too much of you. It has taken your heart, it is slowly taking your mind, and after what I witnessed in the field outside the war college and what you have confessed to me now, I know it has taken your humanity. What is the point of winning the world if you lose yourself in the process?"

Powageh looked up, and perhaps for the first time in as long as Balam could remember, his cousin met his gaze completely.

"I am done, Balam. I want no part of this anymore."

Shock morphed to something else. Rage? Panic? An unfamiliar feeling of fear, and Balam's next words came out, dripping with disdain.

"You always were a coward."

Powageh shook xir head, as if unaffected, but xir voice trembled. "Call me names if it makes you feel better, but I am speaking my heart to you."

"Cowardice and envy. They are your defining features."

Powageh flinched. Even in the lamplight, Balam could tell he had drawn blood. *Just like your father*, a voice whispered in his head, and instead of feeling shame at the comparison to the man he loathed more than any other, he embraced it.

"You are right," Balam went on relentlessly. "I am better than you. That is why Saaya chose me. That is why even after, when you could have moved on and found a love of your own, you clung to us like a stray dog begging for crumbs. How many times did you watch us together and wish it was you?"

"Balam, stop," xe whispered.

"And now you say you love me?" Balam hissed. He had moved closer, crowding Powageh, towering above where xe sat on the log. "And you think what? That I will be moved because I love you, too?" He leaned in to whisper near xir ear. "Would it surprise you to know that after Tuun's spectacular showing, I was contemplating whether you were worth more to me alive or dead?"

Powageh turned xir head, as if to avoid hearing Balam's vitriol. And part of Balam did not know why he had said it at all, since he had not seriously contemplated hurting his cousin.

Because Powageh was not just his cousin.

Xe was his closest friend, the only person who had not left him, the one ally who had never betrayed or disappointed him.

Until now.

Now, when Balam was hours from achieving his dream, Powageh wanted to rip it from his hands.

Balam shook.

He had a vision of his father leaning over him when he was a child, no older than seven or eight. The elder Balam had seemed a giant then, a powerful and intimidating man. And once, when his son had received a failing report from his tutor, his mathematics not as advanced as it should be for a child his age, young Balam had been made to face his father and answer for it. The elder had come around his desk, the bulk of his body shading the small boy, and whispered, *You don't deserve my love.*

Balam had never forgotten it. In ways he would never admit, it had defined him. Pathetic that something that happened to him as a child would mold him still. But he could recall everything about the moment. The feel of those words as they sliced into him, the wound they tore in his heart, and the pain he had lived with ever since.

And so he used them now as the weapon they were, hoping to cause his own pain.

Hand cupping Powageh's cheek, mouth against xir ear, Balam whispered, "You don't deserve my love."

Powageh roared and shoved Balam away.

Balam stumbled. His heel caught on something—a rock, a branch, a rut in the ground—and he fought to keep his balance, arms wheeling inelegantly before he tumbled backward. Something struck his head, bending his neck awkwardly. He bit through his tongue, the pain sharp, blood instantly filling his mouth.

For a moment, he lay there dazed, the dropped lantern flickering wildly, the night loud and threatening around him.

A strangled shout came from far away, and then a muffled voice shouted, "Oh gods, oh gods, are you hurt?"

"Tiniz?" The name slurred thickly around his tongue. There was something wet dripping down his neck. Balam touched the back of his head. His hand came away sticky. It took him a moment to realize it was his own blood.

He did not even have time to panic before everything went dark.

CHAPTER 38

City of Cuecola

Year 302 of the Sun

> You were not only my sun and moon. You were the entirety
> of my heavens. What is there now for me but darkness?
> What is death but a desire long denied?
>
> —Inscription on the Jaguar Prince's tomb

Balam stood on the balcony of the house he had inherited from his father, and his father's father, and his father even before him, and looked out over the city of Cuecola. From his vantage point, he could see the glittering Crescent Sea on the edge of the horizon and watch the hustle and bustle of the docks as the great ships of the merchant city flowed in and out, ferrying the riches of the Meridian across the vast expanses beyond. Many of those riches belonged to him and traveled on his ships. Rare quetzal feathers, mounds of salt and turquoise, vats of thick brown honey brought in from farther south than even Cuecola and traded across the continent.

It should have been enough. Wealth, and the power that came with it. And yet he found himself restless, dissatisfied, unfulfilled. As if something was missing.

There was, of course, his old dream. The dream of becoming

a great sorcerer like the Jaguar Prince. But that dream had waned under the weight of maturity and responsibility. He still studied the bloodright arts, still spent time with Saaya among the scrolls and manuals that were his family's magical inheritance. Still listened to her talk of divine vengeance and ancient rituals. And yet, if he were honest, he found her single-mindedness was growing tedious.

Wanting to bring down the Watchers was understandable when you were a teenage refugee, fresh from witnessing the slaughter of your family. But the years had passed, and Saaya was the consort of a merchant lord now, the whole of Cuecola at her feet. What did revenge offer her that Balam could not, especially when he had given her a new home, a new life? His mother had once told him after a petty spat with another merchant family that the best revenge was a life well lived. Did not Saaya have that?

Movement in the street below caught his eye. Even weighed down by troubling thoughts, he felt a lightness as he watched Saaya scurry across an intersection busy with foot traffic and palanquins, until he realized she was unaccompanied. He had asked her a dozen times to travel with at least one bodyguard. He was an important man, an attractive target to his political rivals, and they could not reach him, but they might seek out the person he loved most and hurt her. Could not Saaya obey him in the smallest thing, especially when it was meant to keep her safe? Did he have no say in her life, even after all this time? After the loyalty he had shown her? The love?

Anger soured his mood, not that it had been bright to begin with.

He heard her enter the house and call a greeting to one of the servants, who directed her to the balcony and Balam. He waited, considering what he would say, how he might bring her to reason. Make her realize that he had her best interests at heart, be it when she walked through the city or planned for the future. That now was the time to put away childish fantasies and settle into a life here.

In fact, perhaps it was time for them to marry. He had only delayed it because she was not Cuecolan, not from a House of Seven, and it would cause complications. Saaya had never pressed the matter as other women might. But now his hesitancy shamed him. How could he expect her to commit to him and this life when he could not even make her his wife?

"There you are," Saaya said as she breezed onto the balcony. She rose on tiptoes to kiss his cheek, her eyes bright with excitement. "I have news."

"I have something to share, too," he said, voice more solemn.

"I'll go first," she said, grin stretched wide. She touched her hands to her belly and leaned forward to whisper in his ear. "I'm pregnant."

A frisson of terror, very small, that sounded like his father's voice, that felt like the chill of his disregard, shivered through him. But that quickly dissolved, replaced with wonder. A new purpose rose within him, a thing that filled in the places where something had been missing just moments ago.

"A child?"

She nodded, the happiest he had ever seen her.

"Then it was meant to be," Balam said, amazed that only moments ago he had decided they should marry, and now fate had brought them this.

"Yes," she agreed.

"How much time will you need to arrange the wedding? Not that I would expect you to do all the planning, but if you would like? And my mother will help. Not that you ever cared for each other, but . . ." Why was she looking at him so strangely? Had he done something wrong, presuming she wished to arrange the ceremony? Suggesting she talk to his mother? True, they had never agreed on Saaya. In fact, his mother's disapproval was one of the reasons he had delayed asking. But now, with a child on the way, surely his mother's disposition would change.

He had been holding her hands, but now she broke away. Took a step back, something like anger clouding her face.

"I'm not marrying you, Balam."

Joy and pain, how tangled they were that he could feel the heights of one and then the depths of the other so close together.

"But I thought . . ." His gaze traveled to her stomach. She did not look pregnant, but what did he know of children? How long did it take for the mother's body to reveal the child? Days? Months?

"The only time I need is time to plan the ritual. Our child's dedication to the crow god."

And her death. She did not say it, but Balam remembered what sacrifice it would take to bind the god to the child.

"No." As soon as the word crossed his lips, he wished to take it back. But then again, did he not mean it? It was ridiculous, this suicide mission whose very foundation was cracked through with what-ifs and never-befores.

Saaya stiffened. "We agreed, Balam. From the very beginning, you knew . . ."

"Yes," he admitted, "but that was in theory. *Before.*"

"Always."

Now she was being irrational, stubborn. And selfish. How could she only think of herself?

"And if I refuse?" he challenged, anger turning his voice dark.

Saaya frowned, confused, and he felt triumphant. He found himself falling into the same pose he used to speak to the council of merchant lords, the one he knew made them seethe with dislike, but which never failed to secure him the thing he wanted.

"Cuecolan law is clear, Saaya. The child is mine. You are the vessel, and you do have rights as the mother, but the male heir of a House of Seven—"

"You do not know if the child is a boy."

"Any heir," he corrected, although he remembered how she had been so sure it would be a boy before. To deny it now just to spite him was silly.

"And what would you do?" she asked. "Lock me away until the child is born? Force me to give birth whether I wished to or not?"

"Of course not, but . . ." But now that she had said it, he did consider the possibility.

Her tone matched his own in darkness. "I see."

Seven hells, this conversation had gone all wrong. They were supposed to be happy, to be celebrating. A marriage, a child. The life he wanted and had not realized it. He need only convince her that it was what she wanted, too.

He took her hands and led her inside. She resisted at first, but eventually they sat, the city still visible in the setting sun beyond the door. He would try again. Do better.

"What is it you want, Saaya?" he asked.

"The thing I have always wanted."

"What if we could destroy your enemies another way?"

She did not speak, but she pressed her lips together, listening.

"We could refuse to pay tithes," he said. "Not for long, but there are others on the council who would support me if I brought the motion to the floor. Or Cuecola could block the Tovasheh port, cut them off from trade. Or a public resolution condemning the Night of Knives. Cuecola might even issue a decree, claim they are in violation of the Treaty."

As he spoke, her face had only grown more distant, and he knew he was losing her. Why could she not be happy with what he offered her? Why did she not desire this life with him?

He felt himself shaking, his body filling with a wild kind of animal panic. He would not lock her up. That was . . . that was . . . what if that was the only way?

"I'm tired," she said, voice brittle. "I think I should go to bed early."

"What? The sun has not even set."

"It's the child." Her smile was wan as she touched her flat belly. "The midwife I consulted did say I would be unusually tired. Headaches, too. Swollen feet."

"Oh." Balam helped her to stand. "Should I send for something? Dinner? What can I do?"

"Nothing." She waved him away. "Just let me rest. And I'd like to be alone." She patted his arm reassuringly. "You have given me much to think about."

He felt a small glimmer of hope. "So you will consider it? The marriage? A family?"

She nodded, the same small smile still on her lips. "But don't press me. I need time."

Time. He could give her time. And in time, he knew that he could make her see reason.

"I will be in my office," he offered. "There are ledgers I must review anyway. I am meeting with the new heir of the House Tuun tomorrow about a possible venture to the east. It will give me the chance to gather the documents, and you"—he wrapped his arms around her and breathed in the scent of her hair, her skin, their growing child—"and you time to think."

She pressed her lips briefly to his cheek and then turned to disappear down the hallway. For a moment, Balam had that feeling he had had when he first met her. That he stood at a crossroads of fate and this woman would change his life forever if he allowed it.

"Good night, Saaya," he called after her, but she was already gone.

He stood for a moment, wondering if he should follow her. And decided against it. He would work. Prepare for the meeting, and then perhaps draft a resolution to bring to the other lords suggesting some censure of the Watchers. And once that was done, they could move on. Grow a family. Live a blessed and happy life.

$$\bullet \ \bullet \ \bullet \ \bullet \ \bullet$$

Balam awoke on the sleeping bench in his office, a ledger splayed open on his chest. One of the servants was throwing open the shutters to let the daylight in. He blinked against the light and looked around, his mind taking a moment to catch up with his location.

That's right. He had stayed up late working on the impending trade deal. And . . . He grinned. And he and Saaya were to marry and have a child. But he needed to give her time. Which was fair. He had pushed her too hard yesterday. Even knowing her temperament and how she did not like to be led but must always lead. He had not meant to cause her distress. It was just that the news of a child had elated him and, on the heels of that, her declaration that the child only meant that her sacrificial death drew closer had hurt him deeply. The extreme of emotions was untenable.

But he was not worried. There was nothing Balam could not acquire, no one he could not persuade. Saaya included.

"Nahil," he said to the servant who had gathered his discarded dishes and was halfway out the door.

The servant paused.

"I need you to go to the flower market. Buy the freshest, most beautiful blooms you can find." What was an auspicious number? "Fifty-two. No, why am I stingy? Four hundred. We will fill the room."

Nahil nodded in acknowledgment.

"And have the cook make a special breakfast and send it to Saaya." He grinned. "Have her cook double the amount she usually does. Saaya will need to keep her strength up."

After his servant left, Balam set about gathering the documents and figures he needed for the meeting, but his mind was elsewhere. It was difficult to concentrate as he waited for Saaya to rise. He thought to wake her himself, but he felt he should let her sleep. Although after another two hours had passed, he was entirely too restless to wait.

He left his office and hurried down the hall and then to the second floor and their bedroom. The door was closed, and a tray of corn cakes and congealed fruit jam sat untouched on the floor.

Balam frowned, his stomach fluttering with the first touch of worry.

"Saaya?" he called, and knocked. He did not wait for an answer but pushed the door open.

"Saaya?"

The room was empty. Not just of her but in a way that made Balam shiver.

"Saaya?" he called again, although he knew she would not answer, and for the first time in his life, Balam was afraid.

Calmly, calmly, he went to the trunk where she kept her clothing. He opened it. There were only a few dresses and shawls left abandoned inside, things that he had never seen her wear.

Breathe, he told himself. Breathe.

Next, he went to her jewelry case, the one he had filled with precious jade and turquoise for her to wear. The box was empty.

And now fear edged to terror. He stumbled back into the hall, shouting her name. A servant came. Not Nahil, another one. This one a woman whose name he could not remember even though he had seen her, spoken to her, a thousand times.

He couldn't think of her name. Why couldn't he think of her name?

Saaya wouldn't leave. Not when he had given her everything she ever wanted. Not when he had planned a life with her.

While part of him reeled in denial, another part of his mind was already dissecting the details of what it would take for her to run. The clothes, the jewels to trade for funds. A place to go.

She would need help, but who? He had tried to introduce her to the other heirs, but she had always complained that she didn't belong and begged off any friendships. The only contacts she had in the city were himself and their circle of conspirators.

Of course!

"Send for Ensha and Paluu!" he commanded the serving woman. And the one he suspected the most: "And find Tiniz. Find Tiniz first! I don't care if you have to drag my cousin here by the hair, xe will answer to me. Now!"

· · · · ·

Balam and the others sat around a room stuffed wall to wall with dahlias, the pretty rounded blooms turning his sitting room into a riot of color. And even though they attracted the eye and Ensha lifted a bloom to her nose, Balam saw only ash and smelled only the bitter stink of loss.

"Let us review it again," he said, rubbing a tired hand across his forehead.

Tiniz fell back against a nearby cushion. "We've already been over this a dozen times."

"Then we will go over it a dozen more."

His cousin groaned, and Enshu looked at him with a pity he could not stomach.

"One of you must have helped her leave," he accused.

"None of us knew she planned to run," Paluu said, voice weary with repetition. "You must have done something." He eyed the excessive number of flowers in the room. "Something that required an apology."

"We argued," he admitted. "But not seriously. Nothing to make her . . ." He waved a hand, unable to say the words aloud, to face the reality of his situation.

"Over what?" Enshu pried gently. "It might help to know."

Balam glared at the woman, resentful, even though rationally he knew that she was only trying to help. He would not tell them about the child. That was too private, too damning, especially as he remembered that he had threatened to lock Saaya away until after the birth.

"I asked her to marry me."

Silence, as the friends absorbed the news.

"Well, that's the problem," Paluu finally said.

Balam rose to his feet, fist clenched.

Paluu laughed, but it was high-pitched and nervous. "You have never asked for a thing in your life, Balam. Knowing you, you commanded her to marry you. Likely threatened her with a happy life or else. Which proves that you know nothing about her."

"Get out."

"Happily!" Paluu stood and made for the door but then stopped and turned. "Your problem, Balam, is that you are a tyrant. No wonder she ran away."

Balam raised a fist, ready to swing, but Tiniz stepped in to hold him back. "This isn't helping."

"Make him take it back."

It was a childish request, but there was too much truth in the accusation, and he felt exposed.

"He didn't mean it," Tiniz said. Xe turned to Paluu. "Did you?"

The woodworker only shrugged.

Tiniz sighed, always the only adult in the room. "It doesn't matter. Paluu is worried like the rest of us." Xe patted Balam's shoulder reassuringly. "We will find her."

"What if she doesn't want to be found?" That was Enshu, and they all turned.

The former spearmaiden shifted uncomfortably under their scrutiny.

"What do you know?" Balam asked, barely able to suppress the desire to throttle the answer out of her.

"Nothing. Just . . . you know Saaya. She has only ever been half in this world with us and half in a world of her own making. We all knew it was only a matter of time until we lost her."

"I didn't know!" Balam roared, tearing free of Tiniz's grip. He paced the room, helpless. "I didn't know," he repeated, and his voice cracked with emotion. Some terrible feeling that felt like the blackness of night closing in around him. And he knew when it did, he would never be able to find his way through it. It would only worm its way deeper into his being until it overtook him, blackening his heart, laying waste to his soul.

He felt an irrational hatred for the child Saaya carried. If only she had not become pregnant, she would still be with him, would still be alive in a year, ten years, fifty. And she would be his, and this foolhardy plan of revenge would be something they laughed about over a bottle of xtabentún in their old age.

"She still needs us," Tiniz said, and Balam saw that his cousin was speaking to Enshu and Paluu but not him. "No one else understands what will be required. It could be years, but . . ." Xe glanced at Balam and away. "She will return."

"And if she doesn't?" Balam asked, already feeling the blackness settle within him and start to make a home.

He waited for an answer from his cousin, from any of them, but no one spoke, because they did not know any more than he did.

CHAPTER 39

Even among your enemies there are allies, and among your allies, enemies.

—*On the Philosophy of War*, taught at the Hokaia War College

Okoa dipped his cupped palms into the river and let the clean, clear water fill them. He lifted shaking hands and drank. The water ran down his throat, cold and bright, washing away the last of the venom that had addled his mind.

What he could not wash away were his memories. The horrible pain of Peyana's torture still consumed him, remembered terrors that made him shudder, even though he knew they had all been illusion. What had not been illusion were his jumbled confessions, his faithlessness, his desire to give up and let the darkness take him. Remembering the words he had spoken made Okoa's face hot with shame. He forced a steadying breath through his lungs.

Although he was not entirely ungrateful. Those dark hours of despair had revealed a truth to Okoa. He understood now that he was flawed and would never be the perfect son or brother, would never become the faultless general, the best friend, the devoted follower.

But it didn't matter.

One great act. That was all he needed. A way to show once and for all that he was more loyal than his father the traitor, more honorable than his mother the betrayer and betrayed, more loving than his sister the faithless.

And he would find it. Somehow. And prove that he was worthy, not only to Serapio but to himself, once and for all.

He drank another handful of water.

And became aware of someone behind him. Not close. Hovering in the trees at the edge of the clearing.

His first thought was that Winged Serpent had found him, but he knew that no serpent riders could match Benundah's speed or distance, and he would have seen them in the air behind him. It was more likely someone from one of the nearby villages that were scattered along the river and through the valleys of the Western Wilds that stretched all the way to the Boundless Sea.

Still, he would not take chances. He sank his hands into the water again, careful to appear ignorant of the stranger's presence. He shifted slightly, using his body to mask his movement as he slipped a knife from his boot. He stayed hunched and low, the hilt of the knife gripped in his hand.

To his left, Benundah ruffled her feathers and emitted a soft questioning call. The stranger must have moved into the clearing, but Benundah's lack of alarm suggested that whoever was sneaking up behind him was more curiosity than combatant. Secure in his corvid's assessment, Okoa turned, knife in hand but not raised.

And gasped.

A woman stood before him, far enough away to run should he pose a threat, but not cowed as a villager might be when confronted by a crow rider with a blade in his hand. She was striking, thick coils of plum-colored hair escaping the hood of her green cloak, and even at a distance, the large eyes in her heart-shaped face seemed to reflect the rising sun in a kaleidoscope of colors. He had never seen a woman quite so arresting. His sister was beautiful in a cold way, and certainly there were alluring women among the scions of the Sky Made, but there was something about the woman before him that struck him momentarily breathless.

A siren. The realization came to him, and then *Teek.*

And he knew who she was.

"Xiala." He said her name as a declaration, an acknowledgment of a thing that was known.

The woman startled, blinking as if she did not recognize her own name. But it was her name. He was sure of it. He had never seen her, but Serapio had described her, and Okoa knew there could be no other woman worthy of the Crow God Reborn save for the goddess before him.

"Drop your knife," she said.

The knife fell from his hand.

Her voice was a melody that Sang not only in his ears but upon his will. He knew what it was immediately. Teek magic. He had heard of it, been warned against it, but never expected to experience it.

"Who are you," she asked, "that you know my name?"

"Your magic," Okoa choked out. His gaze darted between his knife on the ground and his empty hand.

Benundah let out a soft trill, as if she was speaking. But to whom?

Xiala glanced at the corvid but did not seem to have understood the great crow's language, and her eyes settled back on Okoa.

"You know my name, Crow son. It is only fair I know yours."

461

Her magic made him eager to comply. "Okoa. Okoa Carrion Crow."

"Stay where you are, Okoa Carrion Crow," she commanded, "and do not move." She stepped close enough to retrieve his knife, but only looked at it as if irritated. Of course. What use was a blade when she wielded such magic?

"You need not . . ." He blew out a breath and tried again. "I mean you no harm, Xiala. We have common cause."

Her eyes snapped back to him. "How? When I do not know you?"

"Serapio. I am his . . ." His general? His brother? His devotee? "I am his," he said simply, and then added, "I was once the Shield of Carrion Crow. I serve him now."

"Tell the truth," she demanded, and words bubbled to his lips.

Okoa found himself confessing, his history with Serapio pouring forth in a cascade of words he could not stop. He told her of finding Serapio after the slaughter on Sun Rock and taking him to the rookery to heal. He told her of his own doubts, of his sister's machinations, of the confrontation with Chaiya in the aviary that ended with his cousin dead and Serapio fled. He told her of his decision to betray Serapio to the matrons and of the forging of the sun dagger.

At that, she lifted a hand to stop him. "I thought you said you served him." Anger colored her voice.

"He . . . he saw my intent and showed me that we were not enemies but brothers." He shook his head. How could he explain? "He made me his general."

She pressed her lips together, her expression unreadable. "You came to kill him and left his general?"

"I never left, but yes. He has a way about him."

"That he does," she murmured, and a smile lifted her lips as if she was caught in a pleasant memory.

"There is something," he said, wondering if the carving was still tucked in the bottom of his bag where he had left it long ago. "I would show it to you."

Her eyes narrowed in suspicion. He gestured toward Benundah, where the bag hung from the saddle.

"I only want to retrieve it from my sack. Something of yours, I believe." He took a step and then another until he reached Benundah. The crow nudged him with her beak as he dug through his bag.

"Shhh," he murmured, and petted her head.

The crow cried out, clearly unsatisfied.

"But I don't have any grubs," he told her. "I'm looking for something else."

A noise drew his attention back to Xiala. She was laughing, quietly amused.

"She's used to her treats," he explained. "I usually have grubs for her."

She waved for him to continue.

Benundah made another sound of protest but seemed resigned to the lack. And at the bottom of the bag, Okoa found what he sought. He pulled it free and held it out to Xiala.

She was still wary, but she approached, and as she saw what he held in his hand, her expression softened. She reached forward and took the wooden carving from his outstretched palm.

"You were in the Great House at Carrion Crow when I was looking for him." She ran a finger over the mermaid in her hand. "What happened?"

There was no compulsion in her voice, just a need to know, and he explained it to her, how they had searched for her, but the crowd was too dense, too needy, and they had overwhelmed Serapio.

She bit her lip, distressed. "And then?"

How to explain, although this woman was clearly not a stranger to either Serapio or magic, so perhaps she would understand. Or perhaps she already knew.

"He transformed into a flock of crows." He knew no other way to explain it.

He had expected doubt, an expression of disbelief, but instead she threw her head back and laughed. It was a wonderful sound. Full-throated and free, as if a man becoming birds was not only to be expected but a particular delight.

"Of course he did!" she exclaimed, echoes of laughter lingering in her voice. "He was always as much bird as he was man, and what is this human form but a loosely held idea?" She swept a hand across her own body, and Okoa sensed there was a deeper meaning to her pronouncement that he didn't understand.

"So he looked for me," she said, voice soft with wonder now. And more than a touch of satisfaction.

"He has looked for you all this time," he told her. "His crows still look."

She nodded, as if absorbing his words. "I have been hard to find," she admitted. "But now I am here."

"And how are you here?" Okoa asked.

"It is a long story, and I would tell it, but it must wait. I need to see Serapio, and now."

"You have been long apart, and he will be glad to see you."

"No, you don't understand." Impatience twisted her mouth. "It isn't about me. It is about his enemies."

Okoa's awareness sharpened. "What do you know?"

"They are already here."

"Explain," he said, thinking of the matrons and their political maneuvering.

"The fleet that approaches Tovasheh is a decoy. The bulk

of the Treaty cities' army has come through a shadowgate west of here."

Okoa frowned, not understanding. "An army is here?"

"Nearby. I came with them. Disguised as a kitchen worker. I escaped as soon as I could and swam down the river all night. Depending on how far you tell me Tova is from where we stand, they can be upon the city in a matter of days. Maybe less with magic."

Okoa still didn't comprehend entirely, but her urgency was real. "Can you show me?"

She shook her head. "It will waste time, and there is no time to waste. We must get to Serapio now and warn—"

"I want to help," he said, gently cutting her off. "But I need more than news of an army. How many? Infantry only? Cavalry? Aerial forces? Are there sorcerers among them? How many? And their supply lines. You mentioned a gate. Is it still open? Can they bring more supplies and soldiers in and out? Can they retreat through it if we attack?"

She shook her head, obviously overwhelmed by his stream of questions. "I don't know," she admitted. "But it will take too much time to return."

He smiled. "Not on crowback."

They both looked to Benundah. The great crow had been digging for grubs in the ground to limited results. She lifted her head and cawed.

Xiala swallowed, clearly nervous.

"Have you been on crowback before?" Okoa asked.

"Eagleback."

His brow rose in surprise. "Golden Eagle?"

She nodded, looking miserable. "I told you it is a long story, but there is much I can tell Serapio about his enemies, once I see him again."

Okoa believed her. Not just that she had valuable information to share with Serapio about Golden Eagle and the traitorous Treaty cities but that she herself was to be believed. A more suspicious version of Okoa might have wondered if Xiala was a spy, someone who had gained Serapio's trust only to align with his enemies, but surely someone who meant Serapio harm would not confess such details to him, especially when she could have simply commanded him to walk into the river and drown himself and he would have happily done it.

"Will your crow bear two?" she asked.

CHAPTER 40

Safer to trust a lying Teek than a truthful man.

—Teek saying

Xiala was flying again. She distinctly remembered swearing to herself that she would never end up on the back of one of the great beasts of Tova again after her time with Golden Eagle, but here she was.

She had to admit she much preferred the crow over the eagle. Or maybe it was the company. When she had been with Golden Eagle crossing the plains of the Meridian grasslands, she was one step away from a prisoner, never knowing what came next and always wary of the others.

Okoa was much better company, and she felt more comfortable with the Crow man than she had among Eagles. She had not forgotten how the small crows had come to her defense on the ship as they crossed the Crescent Sea. An event that felt like a lifetime ago. But mostly, the crow reminded her of Serapio, and his presence had always been comforting.

As they rose higher, clearing the sloping valley, Xiala could see for miles. Below her, the river snaked through a narrow green belt of rolling hills and pristine forests. Along the river, visible only in bursts where the canopy of green cleared, a road followed the twisting waters, barely more than a trail. Balam's forces would have rough going on foot. Better if they took the river. She remembered the river looked serene from above but had been rocky and full of rapids on her trek down. Hopefully, that would slow the enemies' march to Tova.

But what did Balam need of overland travel when he had the shadowgate? Could he not just open another, this time perhaps within Tova itself, and push his army through? Or had he exhausted his supply of sacrificial prisoners and was now confined to more mundane means? She had no idea what traveling through the shadow world required.

Speaking of shadow, she looked eastward over her shoulder to see if she could catch a glimpse of Tova and how far, or near, it was, and gasped.

Behind her was a wall of shadow, not so different from the gate, but this was dome-shaped and didn't bubble and hiss like a living thing the way Balam's gate did. This wall of twilight looked almost solid, even though she knew it wasn't. She had traveled through it when she left Tova on a boat with Iktan, although she had done it at night, shadow and night blending seamlessly.

"The crow god's eclipse!" Okoa shouted in her ear.

"Seven hells, is that what it looks like from the outside? But how?"

"God magic." He said it with a finality that suggested he thought that was enough of an answer.

"Is the sun still eclipsed?"

"Still in the crow god's grip. Still winter. Still dark."

"It must be illusion," she said, thinking of how the sun could be one way inside the shadow and another outside. Or perhaps

Tova had fallen into another world the same way the two ends of the shadowgate framed a world of darkness in between, a shadow world triggered by the spilling of the Watchers' blood upon the Sun Rock.

She felt Okoa shrug, his heavy shoulders moving against her back.

"So much to understand," she murmured, thinking of how she could not even explain her own sea magic, so how was she supposed to comprehend that of the Crows?

"It is not unlike the shadowgate!" she shouted.

"That is how they brought the army through?"

"Yes."

"Did you see how it was done?"

Xiala thought of the prisoners' bodies, drained of blood and piled high, discarded like they were no more than dried husks of corn.

"Blood," she said, sounding grim. "They feed it blood."

"Skies. How much to do something like that?"

"Too much."

"Perhaps if we cut off the supply."

"They had pens of them."

"Pens of animals for slaughter?"

"Pens of men."

"Skies . . ."

They were quiet for a while after that. Until finally, Xiala spotted the more mundane smoke of campfires lifting in the breeze.

"There!" She pointed. "But if we can see them, can't they see us?"

"It can't be helped. I need to know what is there. How many warriors. Any possible siege weapons."

"Are you sure? There were eagles."

"You said they hadn't taken to the air yet."

"No, but that was last night. By now, they could be out on patrol." Hell, one could be above them right now. She craned her neck to look skyward but was happy to see nothing but sky and a distant bank of thin, wispy clouds.

"I'll stay high," he assured her. "By the time they see us and scramble their riders, we'll be out of reach. Benundah is faster than any eagle."

"I hope you're right." He sounded confident. If only Xiala felt as sure. But she was willing to trust. For now.

She held on tight as Okoa urged Benundah to climb. Unlike when she rode with Golden Eagle, Okoa had her sit in front close to the great crow's neck. The warrior sat behind her, enclosing her body in the cage of his thick arms. It was reassuring, albeit a bit tight, but she'd take the intimate quarters over a rope at her waist and a rider disinterested in whether she lived or died.

The wind was brutal up so high, snatching at her hair and biting at her skin. She shivered, but Okoa seemed unbothered or, rather, so happy to be flying that mundane annoyances like freezing to death were secondary concerns.

"When we fly over the camp, try to count. I need to know how many there are."

"Count what?"

"Soldiers. Spearmaidens."

Easier said than done. People were like ants from so far above. But she did her best, numbers moving across her lips as she squinted down below. She was so focused on counting that she did not see the arrow launched toward them until it was in the air. But it was a sorry effort. Xiala was closer to the clouds than the earth, and even the arrows of the southern warriors could not touch her up here.

But Okoa tensed at her back and muttered a curse beside her ear. "Time to go." He pulled on Benundah's reins.

Xiala was happy he had finally come to his senses. Flying was nerve-racking enough without the potential for attack eagles and warriors shooting arrows at you.

He had turned Benundah east, the dome of darkness over Tova faint in the distance, when Xiala spotted something moving on her right.

"Okoa. What's that?"

"Where?" His voice was sharp.

"Starboard." A crow wasn't a boat, but it was the first thing that came to mind. Okoa must have understood well enough, because he looked in the right direction.

"Seven hells." He snapped the reins, and Benundah flapped her wings, pushing forward even faster.

"An eagle?" But she need not ask. As if to answer her, the thing bounded forward, letting out a tremendous screech that could only be called a battle cry.

Mother waters. "What now?"

Okoa sounded grim. "Now we run."

He shouted a command in Tovan and gave the great crow her head.

Benundah had been accelerating, moving with speed toward the city, but now she climbed at an angle that had terror rising thick in Xiala's throat. Okoa stayed solid at her back, pushing her forward until they were both tight against the corvid's neck.

Xiala had thought that the wind was merciless before, but now it was as if the sky itself wished to see her dead. Her breath came shallow and labored, and with the little air she had, she whispered a prayer to her Mother, who, for all the gifts she had given Xiala, had not granted her the stomach for flying.

"Why . . . higher?" she asked through chattering teeth.

"We can't let the eagle get above us," he explained, his teeth chattering, too, their mutual suffering small comfort. "We're faster, but they're stronger, and the high ground is the advantage, especially for a bird of prey."

"Can we fight?" She remembered the ferocity of the small crows Serapio had called at sea.

"Crows fight in a pack, as a group. One on one, and we're dead."

Her stomach, already roiling, sank.

"But don't worry. I won't let that happen."

Trust, she thought again. *Because that's all there is.*

Despite their precipitous climb, the eagle and its rider were gaining on them, their advantage in the angle. Okoa cursed again, something more colorful this time, and with a sharp pull and a quick word, Benundah dived.

Xiala screamed. It was instinct more than fear, although there was fear, too, as her stomach plummeted.

The crow spiraled as she plunged downward, and Xiala squeezed her eyes shut, the forest rushing up to meet them.

And then they evened out, skimming over the trees, so close she felt like she could reach down and touch the leaves. Once she had recovered from the drop and could breathe again, although only in gasps, she peered back behind them. The eagle still followed, but it was not as agile as the smaller bird, and it had been forced to circle wide to change directions, giving them time to increase the distance between them.

Distance was good, but they were low now, and hadn't Okoa told her it was best to stay high? "I thought you said we had to stay above it!" she shouted, panic edging her voice.

"Evasive maneuvers," he said, voice clipped. "Eagles are awkward near the ground. And slow to change course."

She looked back again. "It's gaining!"

Their situation seemed impossible. Benundah might be able to evade the bigger bird for a while, but soon she would tire, and the eagle would look for an opportunity. It only needed one, and they would be crushed in its talons.

"We need a weapon!" she shouted.

"What?"

"A weapon!" Her Song did not work on birds, but there was a rider. If only she could get close enough, and if the damned wind would stop trying to rip her apart. But they were moving so fast, and she was barely able to hear Okoa, and he was pressed against her. Would the rider even hear her before the wind snatched her Song away? And if her Song accidentally killed Okoa, too, then who would fly the damned bird?

"I have an idea." Okoa said it in a way that suggested Xiala would not like whatever came next. "Can you take the reins when I tell you to?"

"Skies, why?"

"Do you trust me?"

"No!" The whole flight had been an exercise in trust, but she didn't want to encourage him.

He laughed, the sound snatched away as it reached her ears. "I need you to do it anyway. Benundah will know what to do. You only need to hold on. Loose! Don't pull. I'm going to let them get close."

"What? Why?" *Close* was a claw twice the size of her head. *Close* was talons sharper than an obsidian blade and a beak that could rip through her flesh like soft bread.

"You're right, Xiala. We need a weapon. And I know how to get one."

With encouragement, Benundah climbed again. Slower this time, as if she were tired, but Xiala understood it was to let the eagle rider draw near. She wondered briefly if crows could playact, and how they learned such skills.

Another quick glance, and now the eagle was so close that she could see the person tucked between the great expanse of its wings.

"Mother waters." She squinted. "I think I know who that is." Terzha. It was Terzha Golden Eagle. Tall and broad-shouldered even from afar, her distinctive seat recognizable to Xiala after following her across the Meridian for days, her brown hair trailing in the wind.

"The matron's daughter," Okoa noted.

So Okoa knew her by sight, too. Although he was wrong about one thing. "The matron now. Nuuma's dead."

"When? How?"

"Killed by the Priest of Knives is all I know."

Okoa made a sound of surprise, but there was no time to discuss it. Benundah had already come around and was rushing toward the eagle. The larger bird had matched their ascent, but Xiala could see that when they eventually came together like two lines meeting at the apex of the triangle, Benundah's speed would place her just a bit higher, rendering the eagle's fearsome talons useless. If the eagle wished to attack, it would have to do it on its back while flying.

Sure enough, the eagle came up too fast, and Terzha, intent purely on pursuit, had not anticipated their shift in tactics. Xiala could see her stumble to release a throwing spear from the buckles on the side of her saddle, but Benundah had sped past before the matron could succeed.

Xiala exhaled. That had been close. If Benundah had been a little slower, or Terzha a bit faster—

"Now!" At Okoa's command, Benundah pivoted, an elegant sweep that had her facing the eagle instead of fleeing.

"Take it!" He thrust the reins into Xiala's shocked hands. She felt him shift behind her, pulling his feet up to crouch on Benundah's back. He was going to jump. Stars and skies, he was going to jump.

"Okoa! No!"

"Tell Serapio what happened here!" he shouted as they rushed toward the eagle. "What we saw. And if I don't survive, tell him he was my brother in the end, and I hope I served him well."

Oh, skies, he was giving a death speech!

"And don't let Benundah come back for me. She will want to, but tell Serapio to make her stay. She's done enough."

Before them, Terzha rose in her seat, the spear ready in her hand.

"Okoa, look out!" Xiala shouted as the spear left Terzha's hand. She felt the weight lift behind her as man and spear launched skyward at the same time. Benundah dipped, and Xiala looked up, the world moving as if time had slowed.

Okoa flew through the air, graceful as if he had been born to it. He caught the spear as it sailed toward him. The force of the throw turned his body, and he let it swing him back toward Terzha, now with the spear in his hands. He plunged the weapon into the eagle's unprotected back.

The eagle screamed and careened wildly. Terzha, not recovered from overextending in the saddle, scrambled to hold on.

Xiala tried to watch as long as she could, but Benundah was moving away quickly, just as Okoa had commanded her to. She wanted to go back but doubted Benundah would do what Okoa had expressly forbidden.

And hesitating now would defeat the purpose of his sacrifice.

Her job now was to get to Serapio. To warn him of the

shadowgate and the army at his back. So she tucked in close to Benundah's neck, the reins loose in her hands, and let the great corvid take her to Tova.

She knew she had crossed into the crow god's domain when twilight fell like a veil around her. She saw the celestial tower, and beyond it the whole of Tova, bridges glittering with lantern light, bonfires dotting the districts like swarms of fireflies.

The city was familiar from the days she had spent there after the solstice looking for Serapio, but in some ways it had changed. Winter had taken its toll. No trade plied the river save floes of ice, and nothing grew on barren cliffs. She remembered that Aishe had told her of the beauty of the Water Striders' district in the summer and spring, but she could see nothing green grew there now. It had been late spring just beyond the city, edging into summer. But Tova was stuck in time, a winter unending.

She huddled closer to Benundah's neck as they soared across the city. And then they were approaching Sun Rock. Okoa had called it Shadow Rock, and she could see why. Before, when she had crossed the freestanding mesa that stood between the districts, it had been abandoned, Serapio's slaughter of the Watchers still fresh. Now a great structure dominated the land. Round like a Great House but turreted like some of the houses she'd seen along the southern coast. Several stories high and made of black stone. No, not stone. But not wood, either. *Bone*, her mind supplied, charred black and worked until it was as smooth and seamless as natural rock buffed by millennia of rushing water.

"Oh, Serapio, my love," she whispered. "What have you done?"

She had not let herself dwell on how he had earned the moniker of Carrion King, but this strange palace of black bone and shadow magic was foreboding, and she could not suppress the chills that shivered across her skin.

Ah, but maybe her transformation from the drunken sea captain she had been in Cuecola to who she was now would chill him, too. Her imprisonment with Golden Eagle, her murder of Lord Pech, and the unhappy reunion with her mother. The killing of her aunt and the wise women. Her time as a puppet queen. Alani. Teanni. Calling the kraken.

But what had transformed her most was bigger than her traumas. She had come into the power of which Serapio had only caught a glimpse during the storm on the Crescent Sea.

What would he think?

Ah, but perhaps he would understand completely. Was he not the crow god's avatar in the same way she was the Mother's? Did he not speak to the crows the same way she spoke to those who dwelled beneath the waves? Maybe they were more alike than different, a thought she clung to as they flew closer.

Benundah circled the rooftop of the bone and shadow palace once, twice, before landing. There was an aerie here, filled with crows of all sizes making their roost. There was even a giant white crow, the like of which she had never seen before, tucked into a nest.

Once Benundah had settled and Xiala was sure they were firmly on the ground, she slid from her mount. Someone had draped blankets across a nearby fence, probably to use as saddles. She took one and slung it around her shoulders. It smelled of crow, but it didn't matter. She'd grown to appreciate the musty scent, and she was grateful for the warmth.

She looked around, seeing only birds and bone walls. "Now what?" she murmured. Was she supposed to just go downstairs and announce her—?

"Xiala?"

She whirled. His voice. It had been months, but she would know that voice anywhere.

And there he was, materializing from the shadowy corner.

A breath shuddered from her throat, and she found that she was shaking.

He looked the same, but different. The days had worked their cruelty on him, too. Before, there had been something innocent about him, buoyant and easy despite the darkness he harbored within. But now he embodied the dark, and experience sat heavy across his lithe frame.

And then she noticed the little things.

His hair, first. It was longer, well past his shoulders, but it was still unruly, a curling mess around his face. She itched to smooth it down, to brush it back from where it fell across his eyes.

His eyes. Xiala could not hold back a small breath. Before, his eyes had been sewn shut. She remembered it had been something of which he had been self-conscious, but it had never bothered her. Now they were open, but that was not what made her gasp.

His eyes were solid pools of black, lacking the whites of normal eyes.

Eerie, yes, but strangely beautiful, and in some way, they looked entirely right, as if they had been that way all along under the crude stitching.

She saw that he had paused where he was, as if unsure.

She smiled. Perhaps some of the old Serapio remained after all.

"Hi," she said, and waved. And then remembered he could not see and said, "It's me." And then wanted to take it back because, *seven hells*, could she be more awkward?

"How?" he whispered, and she thought she saw him tremble.

"It's a long story," she began, and then laughed. "But you

like stories, don't you? If I recall, your favorite was the one about the naked sailor—"

And then he was there, pulling her into his arms, and she was doing the same, and skies, was she weeping? And Mother waters, was he weeping, too? Only his tears were black, and wasn't that something?

But her hesitation vanished as he murmured in her ear.

"I want to hear every story you wish to tell me."

She nodded, her cheek against his, and his tears against her lips, and wouldn't you know it, they tasted like salt.

"I promise," she whispered. "But first, Okoa needs you."

CHAPTER 41

I would know you in the dark, the reflection of my heart, the mirror to my soul.

—*The Obregi Book of Flowers*

Serapio had come to the aerie because Benundah had called him. The great crow was exhausted and hurting, and she was bringing someone back to the Shadow Palace: a woman Okoa had found in the forests west of Tova. And there had been an army of spearmaidens and men wearing animal skins and a giant eagle and Okoa, Okoa, Okoa.

Be calm, Benundah, he had soothed her. *I am coming.*

At first, he had not believed. Even when the scent of ocean magic filled his nose. Even when she had spoken, although her voice was the sound of waves and deep waters and life itself washing over him. But then she had laughed and promised him a story, and he knew she had returned.

How and why, he did not know. He did not care. Just that she was there and that he had to touch her, to hold her, to know for a fact that it was Xiala.

And then Xiala's body was against his, warm and alive,

and Xiala's arms were around him, and Xiala's cheek lay soft against his own.

He breathed her in. Some part of him that had been so desperately alone cracked wide, and he remembered who he had been before it all. Not just before the witch's prophecy had moved him to monstrous acts, and not just before the slaughter of Golden Eagle or the construction of the Shadow Palace.

But before the massacre of the Watchers.

Before he had gone to Sun Rock, when he had imagined a life where he was simply a man. A man who loved a woman, who gathered his friends around him and built a world for them both, one full of love and wonder and beauty.

Holding Xiala reminded him of that, and for a moment, he dared hope for it, again.

And then she said, "Okoa needs you," and reality rushed back.

"Where?"

"West of the city. The Treaty cities have an army—"

"West? We have reports that they will come up the Tovasheh."

"You are meant to look to the river. It's a distraction. They plan to crush your forces between two fronts or to sneak up and take this palace while you look toward the water."

Was this the knowledge that the prophecy had promised? Had he, despite his doubts, truly fulfilled it? Or was there something else, something elusive that he could not quite grasp yet?

He would have to untangle the ravel of the prophecy later. Right now, there were more pressing concerns. "Come with me. I need you to tell my captains what you have seen."

He turned to go, but she pulled at his hand. "What of Okoa? I left him there."

Serapio paused. He reached out to Benundah and asked her what he wished to know.

"Benundah fears he is dead."

He heard Xiala sigh. "I fear it, too, but we have to look."

He gathered Xiala's hands in his own. "And we will. I owe him much." *And yet you did not hesitate to manipulate him to your own ends, not once but twice. Do you truly care about his fate? What happens when you weigh it against that of the city? Against your own?*

Serapio shook the recriminations away. "I will not have Okoa's sacrifice be in vain," he said, as much for himself as for her. "Come. Report to my captains, and I will send crow riders to find him." *It is the least I can do, even if you are dead, Brother.* "The longer we delay, the worse the odds for us all."

He led her down the steps, calling for Maaka as they went. He felt her hand slip into his, and he could not help but smile.

"The steps can be treacherous," he acknowledged. He knew them well, every dip and rise, had walked them a thousand times, but they were new to her.

"Then don't let me fall. And perhaps you could add some lights for the rest of us." She said it, laughing, and tripped against him.

He was there to catch her. "I'll lead you through the darkness. I will not let you fall."

She laughed. "Ominous, crow man." And then, "Did you make this place?"

He was not sure how to explain this place made of blood and bone, a palace that likely smelled of death the way she did of life.

"It's certainly you." She sounded more amused than horrified.

He had not cared what anyone else thought of his home, but he found he cared very much what Xiala thought.

"Is it not the only part of me that—"

"Odo Sedoh?" Maaka greeted them at the bottom of the stairs. He could sense his Tuyon's curiosity, no doubt wondering who this woman was who held his god's hand.

"Rally my captains, Maaka. Xiala has brought news of the Treaty cities' armies. And tell the Crow captain to ready his riders."

"Xiala? The Teek sea captain?" Maaka must have remembered her name from the times Serapio had spoken of her.

"Ah, you've heard of me." She sounded proud. "Good to see my reputation has not dimmed in my absence."

He felt Maaka's hesitation, as if unsure how to respond to Xiala's audacity. It was a serious place, the Shadow Palace, but already Xiala brought something light and joyous to it.

"She will explain everything," Serapio assured his Tuyon, "but to everyone at once. Go! Time is passing."

"Odo Sedoh!" And Maaka moved, calling for runners to fetch the captains.

"He is your man?" Xiala asked, and he could tell there were many questions behind that one.

"My most loyal."

"There is something about him . . ."

Did he explain that he had made Maaka cut his throat and then rebuilt him with shadow magic into something different from what he had been before? That Maaka was man and not man, not dead but perhaps not entirely alive, either?

She had a right to know of that and everything else that he had done. It was not fair to have her hold his hand, kiss his cheek, and think him kind.

His voice came hoarse and low. "There are things you do not know that I have done, and if you did . . ." *You would not stay, Xiala. You would run far away, and I would not blame you.*

"Serapio." Her tone was gentle. "I am only curious about

who you are now, who the people around you are. I will not judge you." She squeezed his fingers. "Perhaps while we wait for your captains, you can show me this place you call home."

"You have already seen the place I love the most, the aerie. But if you would like, there is something else I'd like you to see instead."

It was the human part of him, the part that lingered when all else felt changed. And he wanted her to see it, to know that he was not simply destruction. That he could create, too. So he took her down the hall, past the Tuyon who stood guard at his door, and into the large private room beyond.

"Your bed?" Her voice had a teasing lilt. "So forward, Serapio. You are indeed changed."

He felt his face grow hot. "I . . ."

"Shhh . . . I'm teasing. Ahh . . ." Her quick footsteps crossed the room. "These are beautiful. Did you make these?"

"Yes." He joined her in front of the shelf where he displayed his wooden carvings. "They are sea creatures, mostly. I have never seen one, but I remember your stories, and our time at sea."

"Is this a crab?" She sounded delighted. "Their shells are more rounded, but you have the claw right. And oh, what is this?" She sounded confused.

He took it from her and felt the contours of the carving.

"A turtle."

She laughed, light and affectionate. "Not quite, but yes, I can see it now."

She took the turtle from him, and he heard her place it on the shelf. "Here." She put something new against his palm. He ran exploratory fingers over it and recognized it immediately. The female form on top, the tail below.

"Okoa gave it to me," she said, "to prove he was who he

said he was." Her voice shifted in amusement. "Although the giant crow was proof enough."

"I am glad it is yours again."

She sighed, and he sensed she had something to say, something that came reluctantly from her mouth.

"Tell me," he said. "I will not judge."

"Using my words against me."

He stiffened at that, thinking of the prophecy, of how he had used words to manipulate people. He did not wish to do that to Xiala.

"Oh, no! Your face. I didn't mean it." She took his hands. "Only that there are things you do not know about me, too. Things I have done. The world, my magic, has not been idle these past months." She took a deep breath. "You are not the only one who is an avatar of their god."

He was not surprised. He had known from the moment of her transformation on the ship that she was more than just a sea captain. "The ocean. I feel it. You are redolent with it, the power of your god simmering within you. You are life, Xiala. Full of it to bursting."

"I am death, too, Serapio. I have killed." She shuddered. "Too many, and without remorse. I have seen more dead than I ever wished to."

He dropped his head, took a step away from her before he realized he had. "Death has become my way, slaughter my name."

"The Carrion King."

He nodded. "And sometimes I worry that it is less about the demands of the crow god and more about my own desires. I've done things, Xiala. Unforgivable things. You say you do not judge, but if you knew the depth of my crimes, you would not want to be here with me. But now that you are here, I cannot imagine what I would do without you."

"Hey . . . hey." She touched his shoulder, ran a hand down his arm. She pressed her forehead to his, their breath mingling. He wanted to kiss her so badly that he ached with it. But there was something he must tell her first.

"There was a woman."

She stilled but did not pull away.

"I could not expect you to wait for me," she said. Her words were fair, but she sounded infinitely sad. "But since we are telling our stories, there was a woman for me, too. She offered me comfort and her bed when I thought I had lost you."

He had thought he might be jealous, but he was not. Only glad that Xiala had not been alone when she needed someone the most.

"You did not love her?" he asked.

"No, Serapio. I did not."

"I did not love my bride, either."

"Your bride?" She sounded startled.

"It is complicated." Reluctantly, he pulled away. "There is a prophecy."

"Ah, you and your prophecies. What did I tell you about those?"

"That they could not be trusted." He remembered well her words on the barge as they came upriver on the Tovasheh, the evening he had confessed his mission. "That they always had a way of going wrong."

"And this one demanded you marry?"

"This one said that my unloved bride must die for me to win this war." He did not tell her of the other parts, of how even if he won, he would lose everything. But he would, just . . . not yet.

"Oh." She was quiet for a moment, and then, after a deep breath, "Well, then, perhaps I am grateful that you chose another." He could almost see her following his words through to their conclusion. "Ah, the girl is dead. By your hand?"

He found the nearby bench and sat. "No, but by my design. I am not without guilt." He rubbed his hands across his face, as if he could scrub away the misdeed. "All I knew was that it could not be you. I could not let the prophecy claim you."

"You thought 'bride' meant me and thought to beat the prophecy." Her voice lightened, as if trying to pull him from his dark thoughts. "I'm flattered, but I'm not sure I'm the marrying type."

But the guilt of Isel's death, of maneuvering Okoa into bloodying his hands, was too great to be diminished, even with kind words. He held his face in his hands, overwhelmed.

And then she was beside him. "I'm sorry. I shouldn't tease."

She pulled his hands away, and then, to his surprise, she pressed her lips to his.

She had kissed him before. Once, on the ship. But she had been drunk, and he had been focused on getting to Tova. Not that he had not wanted it, wanted her, but it had not been the time.

And perhaps this was not the time, either. War at their door, the captains on their way, distance and dark deeds sitting between them.

But her lips tasted faintly of summer, and her scent filled his nose, and she was love, something he had never had. He wrapped his hands in the soft coils of her hair to pull her closer, and she made a small noise of surprise and pleasure.

Desire roared to life within him.

But so did shame.

"I do not deserve your love," he whispered, breath short, heart aching. He did not want to say it, but he would not mislead her.

"You do not have to earn my love, Serapio." Her breath was warm, her fingers gentle against his cheek. "Love is not a prize to be won or a sign of one's merit. It is a gift freely given."

"All I can give you in return is death."

"I do not believe that. You are here with me, are you not? Then you are capable of love."

"Sometimes . . . I do not know. I fear I am lost."

"Then let me help you find your way back."

And her mouth moved against his. Her touch that had been gentle tightened. She climbed into his lap, wrapped her legs around his torso, and pressed her body to his so that the only thing between them was a thin layer of fabric, and even that melted away as Serapio's hands slipped under the edge of her shirt. His palms moved across her back and then her stomach and up to her breasts.

"Wait," she whispered, and he thought he had done something wrong, until she moved away just enough to hoist her shirt over her head.

"Now, then," she said, pulling him back.

He kissed her bare skin, and she tasted like salt and the heat of the islands, her curves molding to his lips, his tongue.

He reached under the hem of her skirt, hands rubbing the insides of her thighs. The skin there was as smooth and pliant as new honey.

"Oh," she breathed, and moved against him. The friction as their hips came together left him stuttering and helpless.

Home, he thought. *This is my home. Not this palace made of dead things, not this city that I have forced to accept me at knifepoint, not even my god who takes and takes and will never stop taking.*

But this woman.

This . . . love.

He opened his mouth to tell her so—and was interrupted by a hammering knock on the door.

He froze.

"Mmmm . . . ignore them," Xiala whispered against his ear, her delicate teeth nipping at his lobe.

"I would very much like to," he admitted, voice hoarse with emotion, "but we asked the captains to come, remember? And they are waiting for us."

"Let them wait." She said it, but he could feel her ardor already cooling, the slight shift that put space between them.

He pressed his forehead against her chest and slid his hands down her sides, resting briefly at the dip in her waist, and then he was helping her stand, and she was pulling on her shirt, and he was straightening his clothes and wondering if his guards had heard them. And then he decided that he didn't care.

Another knock, louder this time, followed by Maaka bellowing, "The captains are here, Odo Sedoh."

Xiala sighed, notes of both regret and satisfaction in the sound. "All right, then, shall we go? Oh, wait. Your hair. Let me . . ."

She brushed his hair back and patted it down. A small thing but done with such care and concern that his breath caught in his throat.

Brazen, he pulled her close. Kissed her again. Desperate to have her taste linger on his lips. Afraid that once they left the room, he might never taste her again.

She kissed him back.

"It is not the end," she reassured him.

But he was not so convinced. He knew that despite Xiala's distaste for prophecy, he was bound up in it, and rarely did stories like his end with love.

• • • • •

His captains were all gathered in the war room. Chela introduced himself to Xiala as the Crow captain and beside him, his partner, also a skilled and respected crow rider. Then Suol and Enuka, both captain and master engineer from Water Strider. To Serapio's surprise, Ahuat of Winged Serpent attended this time, perhaps because the fate of the city impacted Winged Serpent as much as any other clan but also because Okoa's escape from their dungeons had no doubt roused Peyana's ire and her captain meant to interrogate Serapio about it.

And then there were Maaka, Feyou, Xiala, and himself.

Once the formalities were done, Serapio asked Xiala to tell her story. Of how she had traveled from Tova with the former Priest of Knives on an errand for Golden Eagle and of how they had ended up in Hokaia among the Cuecolans and the spearmaidens and planned their war. She explained that she had left briefly for Teek and then returned, skipping the details, although Serapio could tell there was much there that she did not share. He would ask her about it later, should they ever have the chance to be alone again.

She told them of a Cuecolan lord who opened a great shadowgate and brought an army through it only a few miles west of the city. At this, murmurs rippled around the gathered circle.

"Golden Eagle must have shown him the location to open his gate," Suol said. "They also know the city's weaknesses."

"There are Eagles among them," Xiala confirmed. "We fought one."

"We?" That was Maaka. He turned to Serapio. "You were there, Odo Sedoh?"

"No."

"Okoa Carrion Crow," Xiala clarified. "He fought the Eagle and ensured that I brought back news of the army, and I worry that his bravery cost him his life."

The room fell silent, the tension suddenly thick.

"And how did Okoa Carrion Crow end up in the western forests when last he was in our dungeons?" Ahuat asked, not bothering to soften his accusation.

Before Serapio could reply, Xiala said, "He came on his great crow, and he was alone. Perhaps your dungeon is not as secure as you think."

"He should have never been in your dungeon to begin with," Chela challenged. It was a surprising assertion. Chela had benefited from Okoa's fall, and Serapio had not expected he would now defend him. He wondered how Esa felt about her brother's imprisonment and her small but vital role in it. If she now had regrets and had communicated those to Chela, or if there was another motivation for the new captain's vigorous argument on Okoa's behalf.

"He was invaluable in planning the eastern defenses," Enuka added.

"Winged Serpent overstepped to arrest the brother of the matron," Maaka added.

"Who killed the daughter of a matron and the Carrion King's bride!" Ahuat reminded them, indignant.

Serapio closed his eyes as voices rose around him. He could feel Xiala's eyes on him, no doubt wondering what exactly had happened and how it had happened. He had told her that Isel had to die and that he had a hand in it even if it was not his hand that moved the blade, but he had not shared the details.

"Enough!" Serapio slammed a fist against the table to silence them. "Did you not hear? Tova is now caught between two armies. Our odds were dismal when there was only one. Now they are that much worse. If they are successful, Peyana will lose more than a daughter, as will we all. I need solutions, not recriminations. We win together, or we do not win at all."

That shamed them enough to end their bickering.

"We know what we face," Serapio said. "Give me options."

Chela spoke first. "I will take the crow riders west to engage the eagles and this secret army before they reach the city. And I will look for Okoa, whether he be dead or not."

Ahuat made a disapproving sound.

"Speak, Ahuat," Serapio commanded the Winged Serpent captain.

"Okoa is a problem."

"We don't even know if he lives," Maaka interjected.

"But if he does . . ."

Voices rose again. Serapio cut them off with a sharp chopping gesture. He said, "If Winged Serpent cannot put aside your grievances, tell me now so I do not waste my time!"

Ahuat's silence filled the room, and then, "We will do as we are commanded," he said, chastened. "The Crows will need us if they hope to defeat the Eagles."

"Good. Then the matter is settled."

"If I may, my king." Suol spoke.

Serapio gestured for the Water Strider captain to continue.

"We must confront the forces to our west. That is not a question. But if we lose our riders—"

"We will lose no crows," Chela objected.

"Or winged serpents," added Ahuat.

"You cannot know that," Serapio said, although the thought of even one great crow dying in this war chilled him. "Go on, Suol."

"We spoke of stopping the infantry before they reach the shore. How can we even think to do so without our full complement of aerial forces?"

"You don't need crows to stop them." This was Xiala. "You have me."

"With all respect, my lady—"

Serapio held up a hand to quiet Chela. "Go on, Xiala."

"You speak of stopping the fleet before they reach land? They are on the Crescent Sea now, no?"

"That is our understanding," said Suol.

"Then leave them to me."

A stunned silence settled across them until Enuka spoke. "I have heard of how the Teek control the seas, but to defeat a navy of two hundred ships? Forgive me if I have my doubts."

"I do not blame you for your doubts, Master Engineer. But know that the sea and all that live within her are mine as much as the crows are yours, Captain Chela, or your beasts, Captains Ahuat and Suol, or the ways of science yours. Two hundred or ten thousand. If I wish it, they will not come to these shores."

The captains murmured. It was a bold assertion, as bold as Xiala herself, and Serapio did not doubt her abilities. But he did worry. He knew that whatever magic it was, it would not come without a price.

"You don't have to risk yourself, Xiala," Serapio said quietly. "This is not Teek's war."

"But it is." She touched his shoulder. "I have not told you everything that happened when we were apart. Of the Cuecolan who killed our wise women, of the slavery she wished to impose upon us, and how my mother, our queen, was betrayed by those who were meant to be her allies. This is very much my war, and if I can help bring these monsters to ruin, then I will do it."

Now sounds of appreciation filled the room. And something else. Awe. Serapio's chest swelled with pride but also fear. Had he done enough to keep the treacherous threads of the prophecy away from Xiala? The lack of an answer worried him like gristle between his teeth. He could not guarantee that the prophecy was done with her, but he could at least stay by her side.

"Let us first defeat this threat to our west and recover Okoa. Afterward, Xiala and I will go to Tovasheh. Riders, how much time to prepare?"

Chela and Ahuat consulted. "Best if we can catch the eagles on the ground, where they are clumsy and slow. Perhaps we can end this quickly." Chela's voice shifted, as if he had turned his head. "How far to the camp, Queen Xiala?"

It took a moment for Serapio to understand, but Xiala's words finally sank in. *My mother, our queen.* Chela did not call her Queen because she stood by the Carrion King or even because she defended Tova. She was a queen in her own right.

"Two hours, maybe three."

"Then we will leave at the third hour after midnight to arrive at dawn and hope to catch them unprepared." Serapio heard the shift of a cloak and the jingle of a weapons belt as the captain bowed.

"By your leave, to prepare my riders," said Chela.

"Go. I will meet you on the aerie at the dedicated hour."

The Crow captain paused. "You are coming, Odo Sedoh?"

"The enemy is my responsibility, and Xiala says that they travel with at least one southern sorcerer. You will have no defense. I will come."

"Odo Sedoh." Chela sounded troubled, but Serapio did not have time to linger on his unease. With another murmured acknowledgment, Chela and the other crow rider left.

Ahuat said, "I will gather my riders and meet at the edge of the city above the celestial tower."

Serapio rose to grasp his forearm. They made their farewells, and then he was gone, too.

That left his Tuyon and the Water Striders. Suol and Enuka

were both already in discussion with Xiala about the abilities of the giant insects and how best to support her on the water. And then Maaka approached him to talk about how the Tuyon could aid in the impending battle.

"If I do not return tonight, you must ensure Xiala's safety," Serapio said.

"Nothing can hurt you, Odo Sedoh!" Maak protested.

"I do not know what awaits me among the southern sorcerers," he said quietly, so that the others would not hear. "But I must know that you, my friend, will watch over Xiala for me. It will soothe my heart to know it."

Maaka's voice vibrated with emotion. "It will be done, Odo Sedoh."

"Good." He gripped his Tuyon's arm. "Then may we see each other again, in victory."

"Odo Sedoh." And then he and Feyou departed, and the Water Striders soon after.

And then he and Xiala were alone.

"What did they suggest?" he asked Xiala, gesturing to where Enuka and Suol had been standing moments before.

"They wish to go to the celestial tower tomorrow to look at some of the old maps of the undercity and the Tovasheh coastline. Enuka thinks there is knowledge there that can help. I told her that I didn't need it, but she insisted. We have time, so I will humor her."

"I have only been to the tower once," he shared. "And not under the best of circumstances." He remembered his desperate flight there after the crowds had driven him to break into a flock of crows to escape their clutching hands, and how he had found the Sun Priest there and chased her through the tower's winding halls.

Xiala dropped onto the bench behind him. She turned him

so that his back was toward her. Her warm hands pressed against his shoulders, and she began to knead. He smiled, very much liking the way she touched him. Everyone else kept their distance, would never think to move him this way or that, but Xiala never even hesitated.

It made him feel human. It made him feel loved.

"They are men of power, and you handle them well," she commented as she worked his tired muscles.

He half laughed. "The men are not so difficult. They are used to taking orders. Their matrons, however . . ."

"Women." Xiala snorted.

He knew she jested to try to keep the atmosphere light, but, "They plotted to kill me."

"Only once? Women who lack commitment, then."

"They sent Okoa to do it."

Her hands stilled against his shoulders and then started again. "He seemed very loyal to you."

"Now, yes. But it was not always so."

"What changed?"

He turned to face her. Her breath brushed his face, and he cupped her cheek against his palm. And then, feeling bold and a bit desperate, he took the opportunity to kiss her again.

She allowed it, even let his lips linger on hers, but the moment he moved away, she said, "Tell me."

And so he did. Not only of Okoa. He began with the day of the Obregi eclipse when he was twelve and he drank the drugged milk, and continued with his mother Saaya's suicide that sealed his fate and set his destiny in motion so long ago. It all poured like brackish water across parched lips, both bitter and sweet. He skipped past the parts she knew of their time on the Crescent Sea but spoke of what happened after the massacre on Sun Rock. He talked until his mouth was dry and his tongue thick and clumsy, and when he got to Zataya's prophecy, he stumbled. He did not share the last lines which warned that even if he won, he would lose everything, but he did tell her of the tasks the Coyote song demanded had to be fulfilled for him to win.

He did not make excuses for the desperation that had propelled him to commit his dark deeds but confessed it all, and waited for her judgment. Waited for her to recoil in horror and cast him aside, to run from what he was and what he had become.

But there was only her hand against his knee, her breath caressing his cheek. Her acceptance in her silence. "Is that all?" she asked finally.

"Now that you are here, I worry that you are still in danger," he admitted. "That I have failed somehow."

"I am not your bride," she said gently, not to counter him but to assure him that she was beyond the prophecy.

But Xiala, who disdained prophecies, did not understand. They were rarely straightforward, and a song from the Coyote even more so.

"Bride could mean several things," he said. Had he not vowed his love to her? His very life? Were they not married in his mind, the bond between them more real than the duplicity between him and Isel?

King and queen.

Husband and wife in all but deed.

He told her this, the words clumsy with sincerity, his face hot and his voice shaking, until she grasped his face in her hands and said, "Then let us assume you have miscalculated, and I am your bride. There is one sure way to defeat the prophecy."

He stuttered to a halt, hope so hot within him that it burned. "How?"

"The prophecy called for a 'bride unloved.'"

He nodded, morose.

"Then love me."

"I do love you."

"No." She moved his hand to cup her breast, and her hand slid down to press against his groin. "*Love* me. And let fate do its damnedest to get around that."

CHAPTER 42

CITY OF TOVA
YEAR 1 OF THE CROW

May your love be steadfast as the sea,
Who kisses the shore eternal and never tires of the sand.

—Teek wedding blessing

A bed would have been nice, but Xiala had never been the type to worry about a bed. And the table in the war room was as big as a bed, even if it wasn't as comfy. But she had waited so long for this, and it had seemed so impossible as the months stretched, that she did not want to wait any longer.

Even for a bed.

But as she pulled Serapio close, he resisted.

"No?" she asked. She didn't mean to rush him. He had seemed eager, even hungry, before.

"Maaka's map," he said. "I wouldn't want to ruin it."

She laughed. "Then we will move it."

Together they rolled the map into a scroll and set it aside. But Serapio still looked troubled.

"Something else?"

He disappeared through the door, his footsteps echoing through the throne room. But he was not gone long, and he came back with a cushion, black and stuffed with down. He handed it to her awkwardly. She placed it on the nearby bench.

"We don't have to—"

"No." His head whipped up, eyes wide, a touch of panic in the furrow of his brow. "I want this. I want you." He swallowed, throat bobbing. "Perhaps more than I've ever wanted anything."

"Then what is it, Serapio?"

She took his hand and led him to the table, where they both sat side by side.

He was nervous. Skies. This man who commanded a city and believed himself a dark god incarnate was nervous. She had to remind herself that not everyone was as open about such things as the Teek.

"I . . ." He rubbed his hands against his thighs. "I was very sheltered growing up. I did not have friends, much less lovers. And my life has never been my own."

Ah, so it was not simply the difference between Obregi and Teek. It was the difference between Serapio and everyone else.

"You have never been with a lover?"

He shook his head. "And you have been with many."

"Ah, but none of them have been you," she said, and meant it. She took his hand in hers, raised his fingers to her mouth. "And never like this."

"You mean the war room?"

He was so earnest, so terribly sincere, her heart felt like it might overflow.

"I mean with you."

She took his face between her hands and kissed his forehead, his nose, his lips. Gentle touches. And then his throat, his collarbone. One side and then the other. And then she brushed his wild hair back and kissed the place behind each ear, using lips and tongue, trailing fingers in her wake.

"Xiala." His voice was a strangled rasp.

"Tell me what pleases you, and if you want to stop, we stop, prophecy be damned. Understand?"

He nodded, seemingly beyond words.

She removed his shirt, and he leaned back until he was flat on his back against the table. She straddled him, his hips caught between her knees.

She looked down at the haahan that crisscrossed his chest. She had not forgotten the brutal scars that marked his body, but she had not quite remembered. They were his history, the pain and essence of who he was, and she took care now to trace each line. First with a delicate finger and then with her mouth until he trembled.

"Good?" she asked.

He answered with a kiss. Not gentle, and certainly not hesitant. He took her mouth with his tongue and teeth, his fingernails scraping through her hair and across her scalp.

Skies, was this what hid behind that quiet, almost preternatural reserve?

He picked her up and flipped her onto her back so quickly she yipped a very unsexy squeak, but it didn't matter as her clothes came off and she found his head between her legs. She remembered how attentive he had been in the bath, the one night they had shared together. It was that, but more. An exquisite dance of pressure and penetration, his tongue against her, his fingers demanding and then soothingly light.

"Are you sure you've never done this?" She panted as she climbed toward climax. He didn't answer, thank the heavens, because that would have required him to remove his mouth, and she definitely did not want him to do that.

Her back arched, and a cry bubbled from her lips. His hand clamped across her mouth, and she bit into the flesh of his palm. He huffed, pain and pleasure on his breath, and she screamed her bliss into his hand.

A tangle of limbs, laughter, an awkward moment when her legs refused to work, and then they were reversed again. He on the table, she on top.

He was hard in her hand, his face slack with desire, his hands tight on the crest of her hips, but she wanted to be sure.

"Yes?"

He pressed his thumbs against her pelvis, a gentle weight to pull her down, and she took him inside her.

And slowly, slowly, she moved against him. Hand braced against his chest, toes curled across his thighs, as contentment rolled through her body.

They found each other in the rhythm of it. A sensual roll that left them both gasping and breathless. And through it all, she watched his face. How could she not when he was the most beautiful thing she had ever seen? A man of contradictions, dangerous but unbearably gentle, loving but cruel.

She did not lie to herself. He had done terrible things, and his path to redemption, if there was one at all, was narrow and precipitous. And it would not be her duty to lead him there. She would be his beacon on shore, but he must sail those waters himself.

That would come later. First, there was this moment.

First, there was this love.

She watched as his expression shifted from hunger to delight and wonder and, finally, satisfaction.

"Are you . . . ?" she began, before he pulled her tight and wrapped his hands in her hair and pressed his mouth against hers.

"Yes," he whispered against her lips after he had thoroughly kissed her.

"You don't know what I was going to ask," she teased, relishing his touch, his taste. The faintest hint of honey on his breath.

"The answer is yes, Xiala. Anything you wish. Anything at all. For you, the answer is always yes."

· · · · ·

They did eventually make it to a bed. His bed, where they spent the better part of an hour doing it all over again, and even exploring a few new things that Serapio explained he had heard about and wished to try. After, they both lay exhausted, bodies languorous and spent, and talked of everything and nothing all at once. He told her of his crow Achiq and how she had appeared one day, sick and hurt, and how he had nursed her to health. And Xiala told him of calling the kraken and sinking a ship and what it felt like to Sing with the sea.

He had smiled at this and told her he wished that he had been there to see it, although perhaps from a nearby shore, as he could not swim. And she had promised to teach him, because what self-respecting crow god couldn't swim, and he had very solemnly sworn to learn.

And so it went, as they traded adventures and heartbreaks and even a certain recipe for a kind of pie Serapio had recently discovered and vowed to make for her when this war was over, even though he had never baked a thing in his life.

They both knew the hour for parting was drawing near and this stolen moment between them was almost at its end, their promises of swimming lessons and pie baking likely empty. But they refused to rush to its inevitable conclusion, stretching their time together for as long as they could.

"Do you not wonder what game Balam plays at?" she asked idly, fingers tracing across his stomach.

"I know what game he plays. He was one of my mother's co-conspirators. And her lover before she met my father. Powageh told me they all studied the forbidden ways of magic to accomplish my making."

"Powageh?" She sat up. "An older bayeki, gray hair? Balam's constant companion?"

"His cousin, as I understand it, and a former Knife of the tower. Xe was my first teacher in the ways of shadow magic."

"Skies, Serapio. Are these not the same Cuecolans who wage war against you now?"

How to explain to her in the simplest way? "It is because I did not die."

"What?"

"I was meant to die that day upon Sun Rock. I was to allow the crow god to possess me so that when he . . . when *I* killed the Sun Priest, avatar of the sun god, both the Watchers and the sun god would fall in one fell swoop."

"To what end?" she asked, breathless.

"I did not make it my concern, Xiala," he admitted. "I was naive, content to be devoted only to my god, ignorant of human scheming. I let them use me and knew no better."

"Seven hells." She wanted to ask if anyone had ever simply loved him. Wanted what was best for him, and not to use him for their own benefit. But she already knew the answer, and she would not make him say it to her.

"Well, it's not all terrible," she joked. "That damned cat lord brought us together. I suppose we owe him for that."

Serapio seemed to think it over. "I would have found you anyway. Even if I had to cross the continent a dozen times. If my way is death and yours is life, then you are my other half."

She had never been one for romance and certainly did not believe in fated mates, but she liked his poetic talk and so did not counter him. And there was destiny at work in both their lives, whether she believed in such things or not.

· · · · ·

The hours passed too quickly, and soon it was time for Serapio to leave. A servant had brought them hot bathwater and a light meal. Thank the gods, because she was starving. No surprise, considering their earlier activities, a memory that made her smile wickedly as she chewed on a slice of cactus.

"Are you sure you don't want me to come with you?" Xiala asked.

"No. I would not put you in danger. You are safer here in the Shadow Palace surrounded by my Tuyon."

Xiala shifted into the warm place where his body had been and watched him bathe, enjoying the way the muscles in his back bunched and stretched as he slid the wet cloth across his bare skin.

When it was time for him to dress, she rolled out of bed and helped him pull on the shirt, leather cuirass, and long skirts.

"I hate a skirt," she observed, even as she admired how impressive he looked in his.

"They offer a freedom of movement when fighting preferable to pants," he explained as he smoothed his hair back to tie it at his neck.

"Perhaps," she conceded, "but they're shit at sea. They get soaked, and you're done for. All that fabric's like a fucking anchor."

He smiled. "I will remember that." He leaned over to kiss her. "And I am happy to see your language is still more drunken sailor than Teek queen."

She shrugged, unrepentant, and ate another slice of cactus.

He padded over to his shelf, the one with the animal carvings. There was a small wooden chest among them, obviously another treasure he had created. He turned over a crow carving beside it and shook loose a key from its hollow insides. He inserted the key into the box and withdrew a bundle of cloth. He brought it back to the bed and slowly unwrapped it.

Inside was a dagger in a leather sheath attached to a thong that was meant to hang from the neck. It had an elaborate hilt inlaid with jewels, but its blade was pure, blinding gold, and it glowed like a small sun.

"This is the sun dagger," he explained, "forged from the Sun Priest's mask."

"It's beautiful."

"It was meant to kill me."

"Ah, then not so beautiful."

"I think it will be an effective weapon against any shadow magic, including the kind conjured by Balam."

He motioned for her to lean forward and then draped the thong around her neck. The sheath nestled against her chest.

"Do you think I need this?" she asked.

"My motive is twofold," he admitted. "I trust you with the only weapon that, with a certainty, could take my life. And I'm giving you the power of a god to defend yourself, should anything threaten you while I am away."

"I have my own divine power." She cleared her throat meaningfully.

"Then simply keep the dagger safe for me. You hold my life in your hands, Xiala, in more ways than simply this."

She pressed a hand over the blade and felt it warm and alive.

And then there was nothing else to do but say goodbye, but how did you say goodbye when you had barely said hello?

Thankfully, Serapio knew.

"Once again, you have given me a gift, Xiala," he said, pulling her close. "I know you said I need not earn your love and that it is freely given. But if I survive this day, I will spend the rest of my life striving to be worthy of you."

"Let's both just focus on today," she said. "And tomorrow we will worry about tomorrow."

"Today," he agreed. He kissed her one last time, and then he was gone.

CHAPTER 43

Asnod is dead! Oh, my sister, my oldest friend! Odae curses me now, saying we never should have come to the Graveyard, never should have eaten the flesh of fallen gods. But I say she is wrong. Great power requires great sacrifice.

—From *The Manual of the Dreamwalkers*, by Seuq, a spearmaiden

Naranpa, Iktan, and Kupshu arrived at the entrance to the Graveyard of the Gods somewhere around the second hour after midnight. Naranpa had decided the time between midnight and dawn held the best opportunity to catch the jaguar lord asleep.

"So this is where the gods died." Iktan lifted a lantern to illuminate the great rocks that towered before them. Xe toed the line where, quite dramatically, the trail they had followed from Charna morphed from pale pebbly sand to a deep, unsettling red that susurrated underfoot.

Naranpa lifted her lantern, too, but the resin fires did little to penetrate the thick shadows. Shivers crept across her chilled skin. She had come here before, but the Graveyard was much more foreboding at night, and in the unsettling darkness, all the stories of demons seemed entirely plausible. She glanced over at Kupshu, who had been unusually quiet.

"Can you feel it?" Kupshu asked, catching Naranpa's look. "The walls between the worlds are thinner here."

"Kupshu says that there are many worlds besides our own," Naranpa explained to Iktan, who had not had the benefit of living under Kupshu's tutelage. "The dreamworld is but one. There is the shadow world, too. And many others."

"Mythic realms," Iktan said.

"More than myth," Naranpa corrected. "You and I have met within the dreamworld, have we not? Was it real or myth?"

"You touched the shadow world, too, Naranpa," Kupshu said. "Do not forget your own death."

Iktan's curious eyes settled on her. Naranpa flushed. Even after all she had been through, there was a soft embarrassment at explaining her transformation into an avatar.

"There was a witch in Tova who once bathed me in divine smoke and salt made from the bones and sweat of a god. Collected from the shores of the nearby lake, in fact. Or at least, that is what she told me."

"A witch?" Iktan's tone was dryer than the red sand. "How colorful."

"It brought me back from the dead." It was almost worth it to see Iktan's expression. "Although perhaps I wasn't entirely dead," she added. "I don't really remember it very well."

"You passed through the shadow world," Kupshu said confidently. "Else, how god-touched?"

"So this world-jumping opens you to the touch of the gods?"

"Death," Kupshu corrected. "Death opens you to the gods, the path smoothed by sacrifice. It is old magic."

"Fascinating," Iktan murmured.

"The worlds of the living and the dead, the waker and the dreamer, they are not so distant from each other," the old woman continued. "And the barrier can be crossed by those with knowledge."

Iktan's light bobbed in the darkness. "It's all very . . ."

"The opposite of what we were taught in the tower?" Naranpa understood. She had harbored the same doubts before she was dragged into belief. "So much was suppressed after the War of the Spear, out of fear. The knowledge was lost for generations, and only now do we find our way back."

"In the north, we don't keep our knowledge in books that can be burned," Kupshu said. "It is passed down, teacher to apprentice." She glanced at Naranpa, who returned the look with a smile. It made her realize what a sacred gift she had been given when Kupshu chose her.

"Thank you," she whispered, and reached to squeeze Kupshu's shoulder in gratitude.

"Walk faster," her teacher admonished, shaking off Naranpa's affection as she pushed ahead. "I have a location in mind."

Iktan chuckled at Naranpa's wry look. "Love shows itself in myriad ways," xe intoned.

The old woman led them deeper down through the winding caverns than Naranpa had ever ventured on her godflesh hunting, and the night grew thicker around them, the dark more insistent. They passed places the sun had never breached, even on the brightest days, and their lanterns did little to pierce the darkness now, casting only enough light to see a few footfalls in front of them. Still they moved on, Kupshu unerring, Iktan and Naranpa following.

Soon silence engulfed them as thoroughly as the darkness had, their banter anathema to a place so heavy with portent. The only noises were their own feet shuffling across the sand, the breaths that huffed from their lips, and the gutting flames of their lanterns. Even animal life was absent. Normally, the night would be full of the chatter of insects or the rustle of small beasts, the whisper of a gust of wind birthed from the swirling, restless heat. But here in the Graveyard, Naranpa felt they were the only living things for miles. That, even more than the darkness, made her stay close to the others.

And yet, after a while, the trickle of water reached her ears. Naranpa looked down to see they were almost on top of a small creek, not much more than a dribble of melt originating from some stubborn snowpack and cascading downhill through the high stone walls, most likely destined for the lake now miles behind them. Her light caught the darting shapes of small silvery minnows in the shallow water. She marveled at how wrong she had been. Even in this place of the dead, life persisted.

The sighting of the creek seemed to break the spell of silence, and shortly after, Iktan said, "Tell us of Seuq and her spearmaidens, Kupshu. I have always found her story intriguing. Oh, I know what the celestial tower teaches, but you were a spearmaiden once. Tell us what Seuq's own people say of her."

The old woman considered for a moment. "She was the greatest of her sisters. Brave, bold, but foolish." She nodded toward Naranpa. "Not unlike you."

Naranpa's brow rose. "Me?"

"Rushing off on an adventure, not thinking through the consequences."

"But she discovered great magic through her daring," Iktan pointed out.

"And started a war that broke the continent and killed thousands."

"Details." Iktan's smirk caught in the lantern light.

"It was not the magic that killed thousands," Naranpa said. "It was too much ambition. Her desire to conquer her neighbors, to use the power of the gods for her own gain."

Kupshu snorted. "As it always is with people and will always be. Power is impossible to untangle from our own desires. God magic belongs to the gods, and to them alone. It is too dangerous for humans to wield it."

"Well, it's a bit late for all that, no?" Iktan said breezily. Xir last word was punctuated by a bitter laugh.

"We're here," Kupshu announced.

Naranpa raised her lantern. They had come to a dead end, a semicircle of crimson-colored sand enclosed by white stone cliffs five times as tall as she was, all smooth and sheer, as if they had been burnished by a great hand or were not stone at all. *Bones*, her mind supplied. These rocks were said to be the bones of gods.

"What is this place?" she asked, awed.

"It's defensible," Iktan said approvingly. "Only one side open to attack, walls at your back."

Naranpa rubbed her hands up and down her cold arms.

Kupshu had continued forward to a small pile of rocks against the far wall. She had fallen to her knees, her head bowed, a prayer murmuring from her lips.

"This is where they found your daughter, isn't it?" Naranpa asked, understanding that what she had taken for a pile of rocks was a grave marking. "Are you sure we should be here?" She didn't mean to sound disrespectful, but what they had planned already felt dangerous without the complication of the body of a former avatar buried nearby.

"It is where her god spoke loudest to her. It will be the place where your power is amplified the most."

"Then let's get on with it," Iktan said crisply.

"Where shall I lie?" Naranpa asked, looking around.

"There." Iktan gestured to the farthest corner of the enclosure.

Naranpa went to the wall, as instructed, and unrolled her sleeping mat. Normally, she would only take the godflesh and meditate, but for this, she must sleep.

The sleep of the dead, her mind supplied. She swallowed down a sharp burst of fear.

Iktan chose a place a dozen paces away to unpack the myriad clay bottles and botanicals xe had assembled from Kupshu's cupboards. Xe had been vague when Naranpa had asked what exactly xe had brought to fight the undead spirits that might interrupt their work, only responding "fire" and "boom" and grinning like a maniac. So she had left xir to it, knowing that it only needed to be enough to keep Iktan occupied and, hopefully, safe until she could do what needed to be done.

"Here."

Naranpa looked up to find Kupshu proffering her a finger-sized clay vial that sloshed when the old woman shook it. Naranpa knew what the vial contained. They had discussed it earlier while Iktan compiled xir various combustibles.

"Death," Kupshu had told her, face grave. "You will not wake up again unless you find a way back."

Back from death. Well, Naranpa had done it once before, and that was without the full power of her god on the most dominant day of the year and in the most porous place between the worlds. And that had been with only her own life to live for. Now she had so much more to lose. She would not allow death to claim her willingly.

Her fingers tightened around the vial.

"You are very brave, Naranpa," Kupshu said, and Naranpa flushed under her teacher's praise. "Or very stupid."

She laughed, remembering that Denaochi, her brother, had once said much the same. "It seems to be my fate."

The old woman grunted and tottered away to see if Iktan needed help. Xe had poured liquid from one of xir many vials in a wide semicircle enclosing the three of them, Naranpa's sleeping mat at the center. In addition, xe had placed small crystals in a larger arc and at the entrance to their cove.

"An old assassin's trick," xe explained when Naranpa eyed the arrangement.

"How does it work?"

"I set the fire, and the crystals reflect the light, spreading it wider that it would shine otherwise. If these creatures fear light, as Kupshu said, then it should create an effective barrier to keep them out."

"Wouldn't it be easier to simply burn them?"

"We do not know if they burn," xe said, looking doleful. "We do not even know if they are embodied or simply spirits. Let us hope we do not find out."

And then there was nothing to do but begin.

First, the godflesh. Naranpa had brought a container of the sacred tea, and after positioning herself on the mat, she uncorked the canteen and drank it quickly. She knew it would not take long to work, and she still had Kupshu's deadly vial to consume, so she took that up next.

"Wait." It was Iktan. Xe came to crouch beside her. "Promise me you will come back, Wife."

An overwhelming feeling of loss threatened to smother her. She was not afraid for herself, but she did not want to lose the thing that was precious to her. She pulled Iktan into an embrace. "I promise."

Lips against her ear, xe whispered, "I would suffer it all again for you. Every hour buried in the cold ground, every minute on that ship with my rotting feet and poisoned blood. Know that it was worth it, Nara, for this time we've had together. You have been my redemption, my peace. Never doubt it."

She held on, memorizing the feel of xir flesh against hers and the scent of xir skin in her nose. Xe would be her beacon back from the dreamworld and death, her light through the darkness.

"I promise," she whispered again.

She lifted Kupshu's vial and drank. The potion was surprisingly sweet.

She lay back and folded her hands over her chest. The last thing she saw was Iktan's smiling face before she closed her eyes. She had always Walked in a meditative state before, and a small needle of fear at this new unknown element made it hard to focus. But she assured herself that this first step, at least, was all the same.

And then she realized it was not.

Her hands, folded across her chest, were empty. She was missing her amulet, the one with the firebird, which helped to ground her in the here and now. She had long ago traded it to the boy at the plank house where she had found Iktan.

"Wait!" she cried, panicked. How would she know what was real and what was not without her talisman?

She had begun to sit up when a deep moan wafted through the darkness, freezing her in place. She shivered in a sudden gust of cold, and the moan came again, as if the very stones around her had suddenly exhaled in pain.

The gust kicked into a punishing gale that sent her hair flying around her face and red sand scraping across her eyes. The smaller camp supplies tumbled away, and she threw her body over her sack to keep it from following.

Deadly cold prickled her skin a moment before the wind screamed and the lanterns went tumbling, light dancing across the ground before another unnatural gust blew them out entirely, plunging them into darkness.

Iktan cursed. "The lanterns, Kupshu. Don't lose the lanterns. I need light!"

The old woman shouted something and scampered across the sand, chasing the lost lanterns. Outside Iktan's precious circle.

"Iktan?" Naranpa called. "What is happening?"

Her words were lost in the wind, and another unearthly moan echoed around the ring of stones. What had once felt like a haven now felt closed and claustrophobic.

Naranpa was suddenly aware she was not alone. Something hovered beside her, a presence that raised the small hairs on her neck and arms, and where there had been silence a moment before was now filled with the whispers of a hundred lips, their words rising and falling like a living tide.

"Hungry . . . ," they murmured. "Cold . . ."

Someone screamed, a human voice, high and terrified.

Naranpa called fire to her hands.

A face appeared before her. Drawn and starved, mouth opened like a gaping wound. She reared back.

White hands reached for her.

A staff came down across the creature's skull. It shattered.

Iktan stood before her, panting and disheveled, Kupshu's walking stick in xir hand. "Not ghosts after all," xe said, satisfied. "Which means they can d—"

Skeletal fingers encircled xir ankles and pulled. Iktan flopped to the ground. The stick went flying. Iktan's eyes met hers, shocked, and then xe was gone, dragged into the darkness.

"No!" She threw fire into the sky, illuminating their camp.

Dread froze her heart, enough that her light sputtered. There were hundreds of them. Hollow-eyed, razor-teethed, human-shaped, but pale as curdled milk.

"Hungry . . ."

"Cold . . ."

"Lonely . . ."

To her right, Kupshu shrieked. Naranpa whirled to see one of the creatures had sunk its teeth into the old woman's arm.

Naranpa ran, feet clumsy and slow in the sand.

She grabbed the creature's head and shoved fire into it. The skull exploded, but Kupshu screamed as her arm blistered and burned, too close to the fire.

"No!" Naranpa cried, horrified at the damage she had done.

But she had no time to regret her actions as another creature attached itself to Kupshu's leg. And then another. She looked at Naranpa, terrified. And they both understood. Naranpa could not burn them away without killing her teacher in the process.

Kupshu closed her eyes, as if resigned to her fate.

Naranpa reached for her.

But it was too late.

The creatures dragged the old woman into the darkness.

Naranpa's body burst with power, clear, unadulterated light that flared as bright and deadly as the sun itself. Heat hurtled from her form in undulating waves, sending the red sand twisting into howling whirlwinds. White stone juddered down from the hoodoo walls in a deadly avalanche.

The power she harnessed was pure force, god magic, and it threatened to tear her apart. Her ears popped under the energy of the conflagration, her limbs shook, her breath singed her tongue before it left her parched throat, but she held it as long as she could. And then she could hold it no longer. She screamed as fire raced down the canyons, melting rock and setting the red sand ablaze. It spared no corner, no crevice. She felt the sparse grass in the hidden coves sizzle, the water in the creek turn to steam, the fish within wither to bone and then dust.

And somewhere within it all, Iktan and Kupshu.

Finally, starved of air, the fire ran its course and was extinguished.

Naranpa collapsed to her knees.

And all was silence again. No whispers of the undead, but no sounds of the living, either.

CHAPTER 44

> The best luck a man may hope for is to die neither too early
> nor too late but at exactly the right time.
>
> —*Exhortations for a Happy Life*

Okoa brought the eagle to ground somewhere north of the river. It had been a terrifying, stomach-twisting drop from the sky, the ground rushing up to claim them. He had only meant to cripple the great bird so that it could not pursue a fleeing Benundah, not bring the eagle down.

After all, keeping the beast airborne was keeping him alive.

Terzha had not been so lucky.

She had no doubt been shocked to find a madman flying toward her and had done nothing to counter Okoa's leap beyond gape, mouth wide. It had been easy to wrench her from her unsteady seat in the saddle and fling her into the sky.

He had watched her fall, arms flailing and legs kicking, but as she neared the ground and her end, he had turned away, his hands full with keeping her eagle in the sky.

In the end, he had only slowed the great bird's inevitable

descent, and as the earth came up to meet them, Okoa flung himself into the river.

The water closed over his head in a chilling wave. His feet hit the rocky bottom with a knee-jarring impact. He immediately launched himself upward and broke through the surface, gasping for air. He swam to the shore, pulled himself out, and collapsed.

Alive.

He was well aware that he had narrowly escaped death in a half dozen ways. First Peyana's dungeons and the leap from the Great House. Then the jump to the eagle's back, the sickening dive, and, finally, the river. He did not know how much more he could ask from his luck.

He allowed himself to lie there for a moment, working to catch his breath. The sun pressed against his eyes, and he wondered if Xiala had made it back to Tova. Likely not yet. The fall may have felt like an eternity, but it had only taken minutes. Xiala could not have flown all the way to the city so quickly, but she would be there soon.

He was not foolish enough to think there would not be more eagle patrols in the sky, especially when Terzha failed to return. He hoped Xiala did not linger and look for him. He had been clear that such chivalry was not only unwanted but foolish. He had not done what he had done simply for another eagle to chase her and Benundah down.

He pushed himself to sitting and assessed his surroundings. The trees were thick here, but a trail paralleled the river, and there were some animal tracks that wandered off into the forest. Good places to hide. He could conceal himself in the thick forest until nightfall and then make his way back to Tova under the cover of darkness.

Back to Tova.

The wild euphoria of the aerial chase dropped away.

He could not go back to Tova. He was an escaped criminal, still wanted for murder. The only thing that waited for him back in Tova was more time in a dungeon, a show trial, and likely the same fate as his father's: death at the hands of the matrons.

He could ask Serapio to protect him, but any aid Serapio offered would no doubt antagonize the matrons and compromise Serapio's leadership. Okoa refused to be the cause of Serapio's weakened political position.

He could go back to Esa, but she might simply turn him over to Peyana, and smile as she did it.

His heart sank under the weight of his fate, as heavy as his body plummeting through the icy waters.

No, there was no going back.

Only forward.

Run, a voice inside him whispered. *Do as Serapio suggested and go west to the Empire of the Boundless Sea. Or go north and join the wild men of the wastelands. Surely they will take in a warrior of your skills, and they are known not to ask questions of strangers.* He could even go south to Cuecola. He knew the language well enough, and he could fade into anonymity in a city that large.

But all those were the coward's path, and he dismissed them as quickly as they sprang to mind.

He looked west. Xiala had floated down the river from the enemy camp, which meant Okoa only needed to follow the rushing waters toward the setting sun to find it.

There is destiny at work here, Okoa. Those had been Serapio's last words to him, and Okoa had believed. Believed enough to find his faith again, and his faith had not failed him. It had led him here. He only needed it to lead him a little farther.

· · · · ·

The enemy camp squatted under the cover of darkness, light coming from a handful of pit fires marking the perimeter and, conveniently, the location of the guard posts. Okoa crouched in the deep shadows and watched the sentries until he had the rhythm of their patrol. One soldier always stayed stationary, tending the fire, while groups of two circumnavigated the encampment. Their routine left a consistent gap of almost half a minute between overlapping circuits where the sedentary sentry was left alone. Plenty of time for Okoa to slip through.

He still wore the black clothes Serapio had brought him, so he blended well into the night. And he had retrieved the knife that Xiala had so contemptuously tossed aside, but it would not be much of a weapon against a soldier with a club or a spear. He would have to remedy that.

He waited until the foot patrol had passed before sneaking past the sentry. No reason to kill him, as it would only raise the alarm that much sooner, and Okoa didn't relish killing a lowly guard, despite the blade gripped against his palm.

It was a good ten paces to the nearest cluster of tents. Once he was past the sentry fire, Okoa walked through the camp as if he was meant to be there. His skin prickled, sure that someone would call out for him at any moment, but the guard was focused outward, not inward, and took no notice.

He grinned. His luck still held.

On his way down the river to camp, he had thought of a plan. There was not much a single man could do against a camp this size, but he remembered some basic disruptive strategies he had learned at the war college.

The first idea was to poison their water supply, but since a river of fresh water ran the length of the way to Tova, it seemed a waste of time to attempt such a sabotage. A few people might fall ill, but not enough to slow their march. Spoiling the food supply might be a better gambit, but there was plentiful game here in the Western Wilds to replace bad meat, and their larder was well guarded. Most likely to keep out greedy hands more than malicious ones, but the effect was the same.

He had decided that he could do the most damage if he targeted the command tent. It was painfully obvious that that was where the leaders of the expedition were in residence. They had erected an oversized tent in the center of the camp and encircled it with spearmaidens. Xiala had said that both the Hokaia Sovran and the Cuecolan lords were housed within, with the Golden Eagle sisters in an adjacent tent beside the giant eagle pens a hundred paces away. Okoa planned to cause enough of a distraction to draw the leadership out and then kill as many as he could. It was a suicide plan, but it was the only plan he had.

Until he saw the giant hook spear.

Normally, the butt of a hook spear "hooked" into a handled thrower. By gripping the thrower and using momentum and speed, a man could launch a spear forward with more power and velocity than he could using only his arm strength. Hook spears were a formidable weapon that could cover great distances, but spears were heavy, and while they covered more forward distance, they could not rise much higher than the height at which they were launched.

The device before him looked like the hook spear he was familiar with, only it was twice its size, and the hooked end fit into what looked like a hand crank. The shaft of the spear slotted into a base that rotated in a half-circle, which meant at its apex it pointed directly up.

Okoa immediately understood what that meant. This hook spear could travel with a power and velocity unmatched by any other weapon, but more to the point, it could cause terror in the skies. This weapon was built to take down a crow in flight.

Okoa's head pounded with a blinding rage. The thing was obscene, and he swore he could almost smell the foulness of its purpose like a wafting rot on the wind. But he forced himself to study the weapon, looking for a weakness. Its only limitation, as far as he could tell, was that it would take two men to operate—one to crank the hook back and another to aim the shaft. Which meant its use had to be planned, unlike the quick draw of a bow. He guessed that fact was the only reason they had not attempted to bring Benundah down; he and Xiala had caught them unprepared.

Again, his luck.

But he could not allow them to take this abomination to Tova. The crow riders there would be caught unaware. He had to destroy it.

The march of feet and a murmur of voices pressed him back into the shadows. A pride of spearmaidens turned the corner, moving toward his hiding place. Nestled within their ranks was a woman in spearmaiden armor wearing an antler torque at her neck. He recognized the torque as a symbol of leadership from his studies at the war college and knew he was looking at Hokaia's new Sovran.

The spearmaidens continued on, and Okoa followed, staying small in the shadows as they made their way through the camp. Finally, they stopped before a tent marked with the healer's symbol. The Sovran called out. A moment later, a Cuecolan with a gray-streaked topknot and a blue-edged robe appeared in the doorway.

"What news?" the Sovran asked, voice thick with worry.

"He lives." The Cuecolan's face was haggard in the flickering torchlight. "His pulse is strong, but the healer is unable to wake him."

The Sovran growled. "This is a catastrophe!"

"Only a delay," the Cuecolan soothed. "I am sure Balam will awaken by tomorrow, and then we will—"

"Will he be in any shape to launch an offensive? He said we must attack on the solstice. You know it yourself, Powageh. 'When the crow god is at his weakest.' That's what he said!"

"To motivate you, Naasut. To motivate. Yes, the Day of Stillness will be to our advantage, but we have the better-trained fighting force, stronger eagles, and the element of surprise."

"They have a reborn god!" Naasut shouted. "And we don't even have our sorcerer anymore!"

"You still have me," Powageh corrected her calmly.

Naasut had been working herself into a frenzy, but the Cuecolan's unflappable manner seemed to slow her. In a more measured tone, she said, "Terzha said we should open a shadowgate into Tsay. That the former home of Golden Eagle is a superior vantage point."

"Balam thought it too risky to open a gate directly into Tova. The eclipse could change the magic, and if the gate closes too soon before the army is through, people could be lost in the shadow world."

Naasut glanced at the sky. "Where is Terzha, anyway?" She turned to a nearby spearmaiden, but before she could speak, the piercing cry of a crow broke across the night.

Okoa looked up.

A ghostly white apparition in the form of a great crow drifted across the night sky. There was no rider on her back, but Okoa recognized her anyway.

Achiq? And if Achiq was here? *Serapio!*

Okoa was not the only one who had spotted the giant

white crow. The Sovran and her spearmaidens stared into the sky, mouths wide. Shocked silence rippled through the enemy ranks, as if even they knew something divine moved among them.

A shout rose in the distance, followed by a bloodcurdling scream, and Okoa knew that a god now stalked the camp; the Odo Sedoh had come.

Naasut was the first to break. "Rally the warriors! Eagles in the air! Someone—"

She cut off abruptly. Her eyes bulged. She slapped a hand against her neck. Her mouth worked like a landed fish as she grasped the nearest spearmaiden, dragging her down as they both crashed to the ground.

A ripple of iridescent jade and turquoise scales caught Okoa's eye. There, crouched behind a barrel. Winged Serpent.

The armored figure lifted a delicate flutelike instrument to their lips and huffed. Okoa could not see the venom-coated dart that flew on that secret breath, but he saw it strike another spearmaiden in the throat. She made no sound as she fell.

Light flared nearby as a fire ignited, and Okoa flinched. When he looked back, there was a spear protruding from the Winged Serpent assassin's chest. They fell to their knees, just as another spearmaiden rushed forward to bash them into the dirt.

"Find the eagle riders!" the one who had killed the assassin yelled. "Get them in the air!" She pointed to a nearby Cuecolan soldier who looked shell-shocked from the sudden turn of events. "You! Take someone and arm the spear. Take down anything in the sky that isn't an eagle."

"I'll go," a nearby spearmaiden offered, and dragged the Cuecolan soldier with her.

Okoa waited for the rest of the warriors to clear the area,

the spearmaidens dragging their limp Sovran into the nearby healer's tent with the sorcerer on their heels, before sprinting after the two who had gone to arm the giant hook spear.

Even as he ran, the sky filled with the cries of crows and the answering shrieks of eagles. He looked up as two crows buzzed an eagle, sending the larger bird spinning. But it quickly recovered, its rider pulling it steady, and launched off in pursuit of the crows. He wondered if Benundah was somewhere in the sky at this very moment, possibly in danger. Panic pushed him to move faster, arms and legs churning.

He had only his small dagger, but he gripped it in his hand, ready. He rounded the corner of a supply tent just as the first giant spear launched into the air. It made a terrible sound, a hissing whoosh, as it barreled skyward. Okoa watched in horror as it clipped the wing of a crow. The corvid screamed and listed to the side, its rider scrambling to recover. An eagle descended on the injured crow, talons extended, ready to tear the smaller bird asunder. But before the bird of prey could reach its target, a flash of color whipped toward the eagle. He could not see the venom glistening on the winged serpent's fangs, but he heard the screech as the creature clamped its jaws around the eagle's neck.

Okoa turned his attention back to the giant hook spear. The Cuecolan soldier was working the hand crank as the spearmaiden rotated the base, looking for their next target. He had only seconds before they launched another spear, and this time they might not miss.

Okoa threw his dagger, aiming for the woman. The blade flew true, striking the woman just below the throat. She gurgled and staggered backward, tumbling off the platform.

The Cuecolan at the crank looked up, eyes wide. He bent, scrambling to retrieve his bow and draw an arrow from his quiver. Okoa raced forward, but the Cuecolan had an arrow notched and released in seconds. Okoa flung himself sideways. The arrow thudded into the dirt in the place he had been moments before. He scrambled forward and plucked the arrow free. He hurled it back at the bowman. Nothing more than a distraction, but it bought him a few precious seconds.

He searched desperately for a weapon. His gaze landed on a spear propped against a nearby barrel, no doubt the downed spearmaiden's weapon. He raced toward it, grabbing it just in time to turn and block the next arrow with a desperate downward swing.

He lunged toward the soldier, spear extended like a club. The bowman pushed his strike aside with the wooden back of his bow and tackled Okoa, taking them both to the ground and making it impossible for Okoa to use the long spear. They grappled, rolling back and forth, fingers looking for soft targets, knees and elbows flying, until Okoa drew an arrow from the man's hip quiver and plunged it into his leg.

The Cuecolan screamed. Okoa's hand closed around the discarded bow even as he rolled and twisted. He flipped the man onto his stomach, looped the bowstring around his head, and dug his knees into his back. And he pulled, bowstring slicing across the Cuecolan's throat until the dirt turned red and his gurgling breaths diminished and then ceased altogether.

Okoa fell back, out of breath and shocked at his own brutality. But he didn't have time to dwell on it. The crow killer was still usable. He climbed to his feet, mind already thinking of how to destroy the abomination, when a sound from behind sent him whirling, hands raised to fend off another attack.

At first, he didn't understand what he was seeing.

A human shape, with legs and torso, but with great black wings instead of arms and the familiar skull of a carrion crow. He had flung himself toward the ground, grasping blindly for the discarded spear, when the creature spoke.

"Okoa."

"Serapio?"

Okoa watched as the wings folded in and became human arms again, sheathed in black cloth, the shape of the head less black-beaked, and the more familiar delicate beauty of the Odo Sedoh restored. He was not sure what to make of it, whether it had been real or imagined, but when Serapio offered a hand, Okoa let him help him to his feet.

They embraced, brothers finding each other once again, and Okoa felt lightheaded with relief.

"I did not know if I would find you alive," Serapio whispered, mouth at his ear.

"I did not know if I would be alive," Okoa admitted, emotion tightening his chest.

"You sent Xiala to me," Serapio said. "I can never thank you enough."

"And Benundah?" He had to ask.

"She is well." He tilted his head toward the sky. "Somewhere nearby, waiting for you."

The knot in Okoa's chest loosened, but the talk of Benundah reminded him of why he was there. "There is something you need to see."

He led Serapio over to the crow killer and explained how the weapon worked and its purpose. Serapio ran his hands across the hook spear, exploring. Okoa had never seen such a dark look on his face, not even when discussing the Watchers' wicked deeds or the matrons' betrayals.

"I thought to break it," Okoa said. "But perhaps fire is best. Or . . . what are you doing?"

Serapio had wrapped his hands around the base and closed his eyes. "Not fire," he said. "Shadow."

Okoa watched in fascination as shadow flowed from Serapio's hands. The shadow moved like it was alive, and it devoured

529

the wood, burning through the base and the giant spear alike as if they were nothing, leaving behind only shifting ash.

"How?" he asked, awed.

"Wood is a living thing, and every living thing can be killed."

Once again, Okoa was confronted by Serapio's strangeness, but this time he did not falter. He kicked through the ash, sending it away in small puffs.

Serapio was resting, back bent and hands braced against his knees. "Calling the shadow is not without a cost," he explained. "It feeds from me if I cannot give it what it desires."

Okoa did not need to ask what the shadow desired. If he had not already known from the massacre at Sun Rock, Xiala had reminded him with the opening of the shadowgate.

"It's eating you from the inside out."

Serapio's smile was tight. "That is an interesting way to phrase it, Okoa Carrion Crow."

"Odo Sedoh!"

The two men turned as a crow rider approached at a jog. "We've done what we can, but many of the soldiers have fled into the forest. Chasing them in the dark will cost us too many casualties, but we can return in the daylight and hunt them down. They can't go far."

"You cannot wait," Okoa said. "They mean to open another shadowgate and come through to Tova. By tomorrow, they will be in the city."

The rider stared, horrified, but Serapio only looked thoughtful.

Okoa said, "I heard them talking. One of the Cuecolan sorcerers is injured, but there is another, and they claim to be able to open the gate alone. The Hokaian Sovran seemed doubtful, but . . ." He paused. He had almost forgotten. "But a Winged Serpent assassin struck her with a poison dart. If she's not dead yet, she will be soon."

Serapio's brow rose. "The Sovran is dead? You forget the little details, Okoa."

"Terzha Golden Eagle is dead, too," Okoa added. "Another small detail."

The rider grinned. "So we hunt these sorcerers down, and the will of the army will be broken."

"There are still the naval forces coming up the Tovasheh," Okoa reminded him, "with the bulk of the land army."

"Xiala will handle the sea." Serapio sounded confident. "And what is any army without its leadership?" He spoke to the crow rider. "Return to Tova. Tell them what has happened here. I will hunt down the sorcerer, kill him, and ensure that this war ends before it touches Tova."

He turned to Okoa. "I am placing you in command here. Finish what needs to be done, and return to the Shadow Palace."

Okoa flushed hot. "You honor me, Serapio, but perhaps you should pick another."

"And why is that?"

"You forget that Winged Serpent—"

"Peyana will do as she is told. I am her king, and I need my general." He gripped Okoa's arm. "It has been difficult, but it is done now. The Shadow Palace and the Crows will make amends to Peyana for her loss, and we will move forward. All will be well. You will see."

Hope sparked. Okoa grinned. "Let it be as the Odo Sedoh commands."

"Good. Now, let me find this Cuecolan sorcerer and end this."

Okoa thought to offer his aid, but he remembered the winged man and the shadow that bled from Serapio's hands and understood that he would be no help in such a confrontation.

He wished Serapio well, and Serapio left to hunt his sorcerers.

Which left only Okoa and the rider. Okoa had recognized the red feather insignia on his chest and knew this to be the new captain of Carrion Crow. He could not deny the disappointment he felt that Esa had replaced him, but it was to be expected. Besides, he was Serapio's general now. Esa's approval was moot.

"I am Okoa Carrion Crow," he said, the introduction awkward, but he was not sure what else to do.

The new captain bowed. "Chela Carrion Crow." He paused, a spark of something in his dark eyes. "Captain to the matron Esa."

Okoa swallowed the bitterness flooding his mouth.

"Casualties?" he asked, gesturing for Chela to follow him as they headed back toward the heart of the camp.

"Only one," Chela said from behind him.

Okoa paused. That was wrong. He had heard the fighting, could hear it still, and he had seen the Winged Serpent assassin go down with the spear through their belly.

But before he could turn and ask Chela to explain, something struck him in the shoulder. The pain was sharp and sudden and stole his breath away. He gasped, thinking the enemy must have hit him, but that didn't make sense. The only person here was Chela.

Another strike, and another, as Chela stabbed him in the back.

Okoa swung wildly, knocking the captain away. He could feel the blade still in his flesh, a weight too close to his spine. He reached over his shoulder, searching. His hand finally closed on the hilt, and with gritted teeth, he wrenched it free. Blood, hot and sticky, flowed from multiple wounds. He coughed, bright red blood bubbling on his lips.

Lungs, he thought, even as he wheezed, struggling for breath.

Chela had recovered from the glancing blow and stood just out of arm's reach. He watched Okoa, eyes hooded, torchlight dancing across an emotionless face. "Your sister sends her greetings."

Esa, he thought. *How could you?* But ruthlessness had always been her strength and trust his weakness. He should have known she would never let him go, and if he was not hers, he would belong to no one, especially not the Odo Sedoh.

He shook his head, trying to clear his growing dizziness. His grip tightened on the bloody dagger. Esa might try to kill him, but he would not go down without a fight.

He made to attack Chela but found himself on his knees, the blade tumbling from his fingers.

"It was poisoned," the young captain said, the sound echoing strangely in Okoa's ears. "A gift from Peyana Winged Serpent."

He looked up, blinking, as Chela's form faded in and out in the dark. He opened his mouth to speak, but only blood answered. He tried to move again and found himself facedown on the ground, dirt scraping his cheeks, body failing as the poison reached his heart, and it stuttered . . . and then stopped.

And Okoa knew his luck had finally run out.

CHAPTER 45

> It is said that He had made his peace with Death, but
> Those who knew Him best whispered that Betrayal broke
> his Heart.
>
> —From *A History of the Frenzy*, by Teox,
> a historian of the Royal Library

Balam ate as a dead woman whispered in his ear. It was not Saaya but the unknown spearmaiden who had haunted him since his arrival in Hokaia. She sat on the bench next to him, her now-familiar desiccated face close enough that should he tilt his head toward her, their brows would surely touch.

"Persimmon?" he asked, and offered her a bite.

Around them, war raged.

It was the screams of the dying that had woken him, and now they popped and shimmered outside like a hellish chorus, rising in terror one moment and dropping to an eerie silence the next, the singing throat no doubt cut. There were also the clang of clashing spears and screeching birds and, more recently, the distinct crackle of fire.

He glanced at the corner of the tent again. The hide fabric

had been stripped and coated with some mixture that repelled both rain and flame, a remarkable innovation. But it didn't stop the edge of the tent from smoldering and emitted an increasingly dense, greasy smoke.

He coughed at the thought, even though he knew the fire was not real.

Just like the dead woman, the chaos of battle was only a dream. One he could no longer distinguish from reality, but logic told him that if he were sharing a piece of fruit with a corpse, then surely the rest must be an illusion, too.

He touched a hand to the compress that was wound around his head. Another strange element of the dream, and something entirely new. He had tried his best to ignore it, but he hated the way it squeezed his skull and made his head throb. Exasperated, he clawed at the cotton until his fingernail caught. Unfortunately, his compromised nail went with it, and he hissed in pain. He examined the jagged nail, the exposed fleshy bed, and thought again how strange this dream was and wondered what it meant.

There was a knife on the table, the one he had used to cut the persimmon, and he took it now and sliced through the thick cotton. The bandage fell away, and he sighed in relief.

"Balam!" a hoarse voice cried as a figure barreled into the tent.

Balam calmly looked up. It was Powageh. How strange. His cousin had never been in his war dreams before.

"Persimmon?" he asked the apparition and extended his hand.

"You're awake!" Powageh shouted, voice somewhere between shock and fear.

"An interesting choice of words," Balam observed. Did dreamers have awareness that they were dreaming? Even when they weren't the subject of the dream? Or was it his mind that supplied Powageh with words now, and he himself was being the clever one? It was all very philosophical, contemplating the nature of dreams and reality.

"You're awake and . . . eating? What are you . . . ?" Powageh waved the questions away. "Never mind. We must go!"

Something outside crashed to the ground with a loud boom. Powageh flinched.

Balam took another bite of fruit. He looked around. Surely there was a bottle of xtabentún in this . . . . Where was he, exactly? With these raised mats and an open trunk full of medicinals. How funny for his dream to place him in a healer's tent. Ah, well, that did explain the bandage.

The dead woman next to him whispered her garbled warning again, and he favored her with a smile.

"I'm afraid I don't understand," he informed her, and not for the first time.

Powageh was kneeling in front of him now, that bloody discarded bandage in hand. Xe tried to wrap it around his head, but Balam pushed his cousin away.

"I don't want to wear it." He turned to the spearmaiden. "Tell my cousin that I'm fine, and I don't need that damned bandage."

Powageh stilled. "Who are you speaking to?"

Really? Did the various entities in his dreams not communicate with one another? So inconvenient. But he would play along.

"I'm talking to . . . what is your name?" He had never thought to ask.

The woman's jaw clicked, bone against bone, and emitted a hiss of breath. "Sssss . . ."

"Again, please," Balam said, once he had gotten over the moment of surprise that she answered him at all.

"Ssssseeeeeuuuuuuq."

Ah. He turned to Powageh. "Her name is Seuq."

Balam's pulse stuttered.

Revelation broke open his mind.

"Seuq?" he asked the woman, voice sharp.

She did not repeat her name, but he was sure he had heard correctly. Seuq. The spearmaiden who had waged war upon the Meridian, whose manual he had been studiously devouring these past months. She had been with him all along, and he had failed to realize it. Seven hells, was she trying to help him? Is that what all the whispering was about? *Beware . . . beware . . .* Beware what, though?

"Balam, are you listening to me?" Powageh shouted.

Balam reluctantly wrenched his attention back to Powageh. "What?"

"Did you say you are talking to Seuq? A woman who has been dead for three hundred years? Is that what you said?"

Balam stood abruptly, forcing Powageh to stumble and drop onto xir backside. "Where is Naasut?" he asked, an idea already forming. "She is always bragging about her classical education, and we all know she had an annoyingly comprehensive knowledge of the War of the Spear. Surely she speaks ancient Hoka."

It was brilliant, wasn't it? Why hadn't he thought to ask Naasut before? He mouthed Seuq's unknown word, marveling at how it pressed against his tongue.

"She's dead! That's what I'm trying to tell you. Naasut is dead, and Terzha is missing, and the camp is under attack."

The world shuddered and shifted.

The smell of burning hide, the taste of offal threatening the back of his mouth, the screams of the dying in his ears.

"I'm not dreaming?"

Powageh, eyes wide with fear, shook xir head.

"What *happened*?" He looked around, finally grasping his surroundings. "I'm in a healer's tent," he murmured. His gaze fixed on Powageh. "Why am I in a healer's tent? The last thing I remember, you and I were talking."

Powageh flushed, eyes down. "You fell."

A lie. Or, at least, not the whole truth. His cousin had always been a terrible liar. So many tells.

"You hit your head," Powageh rushed on. Xe still held the bandage and lifted it now, as if to provide evidence. "It must have truly addled your mind."

"Seuq has been with me since Hokaia," he said dismissively. Trust Powageh to misunderstand such a wonder. Of course, xe would think Balam compromised when the very opposite was true. He had finally been enlightened.

"It doesn't matter," Powageh quickly amended. "What matters is we have to go!"

"Go where?"

"Abandon camp. We'll regroup with the naval forces. Or return to Cuecola, rally the other houses, and once you get some rest, try—"

And it all blazed back. Their conversation in the forest, Powageh's maudlin confession, the way xe wished to abandon Balam, rip his dreams from his hands because xe was jealous.

Balam trembled, the acute terror of loss twisting his gut.

"I need to find someone who speaks ancient Hoka."

"There's no one, Balam! They're all dead . . . or dying. And we will be dead, too, if we don't—"

"The tower. There will be texts in the celestial tower. Vocabularies. We will go there."

As soon as he said it, he knew it was the right decision. All his dreams of standing atop a tower in Tova. They made perfect sense. Seuq had been trying to tell him that this military venture with his flawed allies and perfidious cousin was a mistake. All he needed to do was go to the celestial tower, decipher Seuq's words, and claim his victory.

Powageh stared. Xe was still half sprawled on the floor, and Balam held out a hand. After a moment, Powageh took it, and Balam lifted his cousin to xir feet.

"Open a shadowgate," Balam commanded.

"What?"

"We go to the celestial tower by shadowgate. It is the only way."

"And bleed whom? Have you forgotten you need a human's worth of blood to open even the smallest gate?"

Balam smiled. It was his old smile. His predator's smile.

"I have not."

He still held the knife, the one he had used to cut the persimmon. He buried it in Powageh's stomach. His cousin gasped, jaw falling open.

"Thank you for volunteering," Balam murmured, mouth against Powageh's ear.

Powageh gripped him by the shirt, his eyes ablaze, and Balam was sure his cousin would fight back. Would draw on xir long-neglected lessons in violence learned in the celestial tower or call shadow magic to xir defense.

But Powageh did not strike. Balam saw the moment when xir eyes went flat, xir muscles lax, and xe bowed xir head.

"Coward to the end." Balam sneered. But he knew it was not true. It was not that Powageh was craven. It was that Balam had finally broken xir heart.

And as Balam knew well, what good was living when your heart was in pieces?

He quickly banished the thought and the horrible guilt, the

first murmur of regret that accompanied it. But he could not stop the tear that rolled down his cheek.

"Would that you never loved me, Cousin," he whispered, as he let Powageh tumble to the ground, blood pouring from his midsection. Balam slipped off his sandals and stepped into the growing pool. He coated his feet and then bent to cover his hands. With a bloody finger, he painted stripes across his face.

Powageh lay silent and did not try to stop him.

Balam spoke the words to conjure a doorway. He stepped over his dying cousin and into the shadowgate, his mind already on Seuq.

CHAPTER 46

> And I cried, Is this my destiny? To be bound by blood
> To those who would deny me? That my own kin
> Would seek to lay me low
> And forge a weapon of my grief?

—From *Collected Lamentations from the Night of Knives*

Serapio stalked through the enemy camp, searching for the Cuecolans that Okoa had told him were still there. But it was difficult to discern anything through the chaos. Sound and smell and feel collided in a frustrating and tumultuous cacophony that assaulted his senses. He had not called a small crow to help him see, although he knew some nested nearby. He had not wanted to subject the creature to the chaos of battle, and besides, he preferred to fight without sight. Others might think it foolish, but he had learned how to fight blind, making the appropriate adaptations. Under pressure, he preferred it, as with it came the muscle memory and reaction time he relied on. But there were drawbacks, as now, when he might do better if he could simply see where the Cuecolan lord had gone.

Something burned nearby. He could feel the heat against his skin, and on the billowing tide of smoke, he caught the medicinal smell of wild ginger and thistle. He paused, remembering what Okoa had said about one of the sorcerers being injured. He moved toward the fire.

He found what he thought must have been the healer's tent. It had collapsed, flames busily consuming one side. But the smoke rose at an angle, which suggested part of it still stood, so Serapio circled until he found a place to duck in on the far side away from the fire.

He took a moment to search the interior but found only discarded sickbeds and supplies. No people. Frustrated, he turned to go.

Someone called his name.

He stopped, unsure he had truly heard it. But there it was again, the voice a rasping echo plucked from his memories.

"Powageh?" He turned in place, listening.

Above the crackling flames and distant sounds of war: "Serapio."

He went to the sound and bent to the floor. Hands grasped his legs and then moved up, pulling at his clothes, as if to draw him closer. He registered their sticky touch, the slickness under his bare feet, and knew he was standing in Powageh's blood.

"How are you here?" Serapio asked in wonderment. The last time he had been with his old tutor was in Obregi before he left for Cuecola. Powageh had confessed that xe had conspired with Serapio's mother and the Cuecolan lord Balam to rebirth a god who would not only destroy the Watchers but topple the very order of the heavens.

Ah, you came with Balam. Of course. Xiala said as much. But why turn against me? I spared your life once, for my mother's sake. I did everything you asked of me. I wade through blood because of you, even now.

"I'm dying," Powageh whispered, as if Serapio could not discern that for himself. "There's no time."

Threads of nostalgia threatened to ensnare him in some moment of mercy, but even if he wished to help, he was no healer. There was nothing he could do here.

Serapio gently disentangled himself.

"Wait!" Powageh cried. "There are things you must know."

Despite his unwillingness, mercy came anyway. He crouched and ran a hand across Powageh's head, pushing back wet hair from a hollowed face.

"I know already," he said. "You and Balam have turned against me."

"Balam . . . He has gone to Tova."

Serapio froze. "Where?"

"The tower. He has lost his mind. Cannot tell reality from dream. He . . . he seeks knowledge there that will help him win this war."

Something in Serapio's chest tightened. He thought immediately of the Coyote song. Was that knowledge not meant for him alone? Or, like the trickster that he was, would the coyote god give Balam the knowledge he needed to win the war, too, pitting them against each other?

"What is it, this knowledge he seeks?" he asked urgently.

"I . . . I don't know. Something about Seuq. A spearmaiden. Dead. Long dead." Powageh coughed, a terrible racking sound.

Serapio cupped his old tutor's face. "My crow is here, and she is swift. I will follow, and I will stop him."

"He travels through a shadowgate. It's too late. He's already there."

A shadowgate? His heart fluttered in alarm. Xiala had told him of the strange door made of shadow that allowed movement across great distances.

But his next thought calmed him. Did he not know shadow as intimately as a lover? Was he not made of shadow himself?

"I will walk through this gate, too. Tell me how."

543

Powageh did not tell him in words but took his hands and pressed his palms in blood and drew a wet finger across Serapio's cheeks. And again, as he drew a series of lines across his lower face. "So that it will not steal your breath," xe explained. "Speak where you wish to go, envision it. And then call the shadow. Beware. The shadow must—"

"The shadow must feed." Serapio's smile was grim. "I know. You taught me well, Powageh. Is there any other thing I must know?"

"For you? No. You are shadow's master. It will do as you wish. It always has."

Serapio bent and pressed a kiss against Powageh's forehead. The gesture surprised him. He should feel anger, resentment for his old tutor's betrayal. There was a time when Powageh was both friend and parent figure, the only person Serapio trusted. Even now, Powageh was trying to help him. No, he would not let Powageh die thinking Serapio had only hate in his heart.

"Rest well, old friend," he murmured, and then stepped away.

As he had a hundred times, Serapio called shadow. He could feel it bubbling into this world, birthed into existence as if all this time it had only been waiting for him to beckon it forward. This time, he asked it to shape itself into a doorway and let him pass.

He made to step forward.

A hand clawed at the hem of his skirt. He paused.

"Do not kill him. Please." Powageh's voice was a terrible scraping, a person breathing their last. "Love has broken us both, and his mind . . . he is lost. If I could save him, bring him back . . . for your sake . . ."

Serapio frowned. "Who?"

Powageh's cough was wet with his heart's blood.

"Your father. Balam."

CHAPTER 47

Life is but a tiny island in death's vast sea.

—Teek saying

Xiala was dressed and waiting when the master engineer arrived at the Shadow Palace. The hour told her it was dawn, but the sky was the same twilight of the eclipse that it had been for months. She had forgotten how strange it was for time to not exist, for an entire people to be stuck in this in-between, neither day nor night. She wondered how long the city could continue like this. She had not asked Serapio if he knew how to end it, or if he even wished to, but surely even he, creature of shadow that he was, could not survive without balance.

"A better choice." Enuka greeted her, critically taking in Xiala's new clothes.

"Feyou," she said by way of explanation, and the master engineer nodded.

The first thing Feyou had given her was a pair of fur-lined boots, and then, with a sly smile, pants. Xiala had gasped and held the thick dyed cotton up for inspection. They were the right size. Black, but then, she was among the crows now and

545

should expect no less. Socks, a shirt, and a thick fur-lined cloak were next. She had greedily layered on her new warm clothes and gave Feyou a hug out of sheer gratitude.

"He's different when he is with you," Feyou had said.

"Hmm?" Xiala had run a hand down the fabric of her cloak. It was decorated with intricate whirls and small black beads, not plain at all.

"The Odo Sedoh."

"We are friends."

Feyou's gaze had flicked toward the bed and the crumpled blankets.

"Ah, more than friends," Xiala had amended, and could not suppress the edge of a smile. A little wicked, a little possessive, and why not? She had thought she had lost him, had worried her love was unrequited, and to find it was neither? That he desperately wanted her, that he loved her? It felt like fate, and she was not a woman who trucked with fate. *No fate but that you make yourself.* Wasn't that the Teek way? Well, somehow she had made this fate for herself, and she would hold on to it as long as she could.

"It is good to see him happy," Feyou had said. "You bring a life that is needed here."

"Balance," she'd said, thinking of the eclipsed sun. "His god has made him unbalanced." And then, remembering to whom she was speaking, added, "No offense meant."

"Life is necessary, too," Feyou had agreed thoughtfully, "and you are brimming with it." She had said the last with an approving smile. "I do not think the crow god would disapprove."

The woman had meant it as a compliment, that much was clear, but Xiala frankly did not care whether the crow god approved or not. Besides, she knew that death was her business, too. The sea gave, and the sea took away, and so it was with her.

She had thanked Feyou for her help and then went to wait for Enuka.

Now the master engineer led them away from the Shadow Palace and across one of the great woven bridges that branched out from the mesa and connected the various districts of the city. It was not the same bridge where Xiala had witnessed so many people meet their deaths on the day of the Convergence, and for that she was grateful. Those terrible memories stayed with her, and even though she had made peace with them, crossing the bridge made her uneasy.

This bridge deposited them on a beautiful esplanade paved with white stone and ornamented by majestic stone carvings. She spied at least four different eagle motifs and knew where she was.

"It's empty," she said. "Did all the Golden Eagles join with the Treaty cities?"

"The scions were traitors," Enuka replied, "and the Odo Sedoh treated them as such. The rest were sent to live with the other clans. The clan called Golden Eagle is no more."

Their fate was not spoken, but it was implied, and Xiala's heart broke a little. Despite his ruthless reputation, she could not believe that such slaughter didn't bother Serapio. She wondered why he had felt he must do something so dark, but then she remembered her own desire to destroy Tuun and her invading army, and how betrayal made one irrational with fear. So she did not press Enuka for details.

"There's something I wanted to ask you," Enuka said, obviously eager to change the subject. "Something about your Song. That is what you call it?"

Xiala nodded, wary, but the woman continued, oblivious and obviously excited.

"I'm developing a new weapon," Enuka said. "Well, several. One that uses sound to attack."

"You are a sorcerer? Or . . . god-touched?"

"Neither," Enuka rushed to clarify. "My method has to do with turning sound into sight. Well, perhaps that's not the best way to explain." She paused. "There is a man in my camp, a clanless. He spoke to me of seeing sounds. That they did not simply exist in his ears but had shape and form. Sometimes color."

"Go on."

"It is not so strange. Sound can be felt, after all. I can shout at you"—Enuka demonstrated, and Xiala winced as the woman's breath hit her face—"or even clap"—another demonstration with the same result—"and you feel it. My theory is that it may be possible to render sound perceivable to the eye."

It did not seem so strange to Xiala. The voices of the sea creatures came to her not only in sound but in sight and feel. Perhaps Enuka's theory was not so different.

"Shall we try it?"

Xiala startled. "Now?"

"Something small. Just a note."

She shook her head. She had killed with a single note, after all.

"Perhaps you can just visualize it. Theoretically, of course. Say you were to describe your Song. What would it look like?"

"The blue-green roar of the sea." That seemed obvious. But then, "The lightless depths, silent and black. The splash of red blood pooling in the water, an invitation to feast. The white of a screaming man's eyes before he drowns."

Enuka stared. "A little scary," she murmured. "But I like it. Is there perhaps a description that is a bit less . . . murder-y?"

Xiala laughed. "The lapping sea. Sand underfoot."

"Those are calming sounds?" Enuka asked. "Then perhaps we can try something like that. Not now, but on our journey to Tovasheh. It may prove useful to our defenses there."

Xiala agreed, and they continued on, the next bridge already rising before them. Soon they were on the tower grounds.

"Have you come here before?" Xiala asked, curious. She had only seen the famed home of the Watchers from a very far distance, and it was much larger than she had anticipated, an imposing spire that challenged the sky for supremacy. Hubris was the word that came to mind once the awe at its very existence wore off. Who would build such a thing except as a challenge to the gods themselves?

"I used to come quite often," Enuka said as they walked the grounds, drawing ever closer. "The Watchers presided over the greatest collection of knowledge in the Meridian, perhaps beyond."

"A library."

"Not simply a library. *The* library." She cocked her head toward Xiala. "Do you read?"

"Enough to sail a ship," she said. "And maps."

"Maps are what we seek." Enuka warmed to the subject. "My people, Water Strider, have stories of secret caves through . . . well, thundering piss!"

Xiala startled. It was a curse she had never heard, but she liked it. Maybe she would add it to her repertoire. She made a note to ask Enuka where exactly she was from. The accent that colored her voice was certainly not all Tovan, and she'd never heard a Tovan use the colorful expression.

They had stopped in front of the entrance. Enuka beat a fist against the wooden doors. They did not budge, and there was no handle on the exterior. They were clearly bolted closed from within. She cursed again and walked the length of the portal, pressing here and there to test its sturdiness.

Xiala tilted her head back. "There's a window." She pointed upward.

Enuka joined her. "Are you offering to climb up? If you fall, the Carrion King will have my head."

"Then we won't tell him."

Xiala approached the wall. The stone was rough and uneven and offered plenty of hand- and footholds. It had been a while since she'd climbed anything, but she had always been nimble, and the window really wasn't that high.

She handed Enuka her cloak, whispered a quick thanks to Feyou for the pants, and climbed. The stone was jagged and frozen, and it bit into her hands. Even a few lengths from the ground, the wind picked up, dragging at her hair and clothes. But it was not so difficult, and after a few moments, she was hauling herself through the window and into the celestial tower.

She dropped to the floor and listened. It seemed abandoned enough, but looks could be deceiving. She called her Song to her throat, ready to fend off any crazed Watchers or nesting thieves who might have claimed the tower. But she was very much alone.

"Everything well?" Enuka shouted from below.

Xiala leaned out the window. "I'll come down and open the door."

Enuka waved in acknowledgment.

She eased out into the hallway, still alert. The hallway led to a circular central stairway that hugged the stone walls as it wove its way skyward to an open hole in the ceiling. The front door and Enuka were two stories below, the barred door visible from where she stood. She was about to take the first step down when she heard a noise.

She made to retreat, and realized with alarm that it was too late. She froze, breath tight in her throat. She dared not Sing with Enuka so close.

The golden dagger! It still hung around her neck, and she

had begun to reach for it when the approaching figure came into view.

Her first thought was of a ghost, but ghosts didn't clomp down the stairs muttering to themselves, did they? Especially in Cuecolan.

He walked right past her, eyes barely skimming over her, as if *she* were the ghost. For a moment, she had the wild impulse to call out to him but quelled it.

And then he was gone, disappearing out of sight.

She stood there, unsure what had just happened. Perhaps she had lost her mind, because surely Lord Balam had not just come down from the roof of the tower and looked at her with less interest than he might show a potted plant.

She shook her head in wonder. How was he here? Well, the "how" she could guess easily enough. But why?

Distantly, she heard Enuka call from outside. She retreated to lean out the window and hold up a finger for patience, and then she slipped out the door to follow Balam.

She caught the flutter of his cloak as he disappeared through a door. She looked up at the inscription over the great doors. She could not read it, but the curling scrolls suggested that the famed library of the Watchers resided within. What was he looking for?

She slipped through the doors and followed. He was louder now, muttering about language and difficult women and his own shortsightedness, but she could make no sense of his babbling. She followed at a distance as he prowled past rows and rows of scrolls, manuals, and books. Occasionally, he would pause and pull one from a shelf, but inevitably, he would cast it aside unsatisfied and move on to the next.

Eventually, he worked his way to a rounded room that was set apart from the others. He went through the entrance and moved out of sight.

Xiala hesitated. If she followed, they would be face-to-face, and there would be no way to avoid a confrontation. Was that wise? Perhaps she was wrong, and he hadn't seen her before? No, he had seen her, even acknowledged her. He knew she was there but didn't care.

It was too much, too strange, and concern even more than curiosity compelled her forward.

With a steadying inhale, Xiala pushed through the door.

Balam was hunched over a lectern, an open manuscript before him. *I could kill him now*, she thought. *One long note that would burst his heart or shatter his skull.* But then she would never know what information he was so desperate to find and how he meant to use it against Serapio. And if Balam sought it, would others come after him who would, too?

She crept forward, intent on getting a better look at the scroll.

"Xiala." Balam's voice was a shredded rasp that froze her where she stood. He lifted his head but faced forward, away from her. "Since you are sneaking up on me and not simply making yourself known, I can only ascertain that you are not a figment of my imagination and are indeed real."

Now he turned to face her, and the lamplight hit his face. She gasped. He had always been so well groomed, a man of control and polish. Now he was not. Blood matted his unbrushed hair, and his eyes were black hollows in a face etched with misery. He looked like a man who had not slept for weeks, and when he did sleep, his dreams were nightmares. But his mouth was set in a determined line, and as he stared her down, he did not waver.

"So that *was* you in the camp," he said. "Stinking of the sea."

Hold still, she told herself. *Wait to see what he does.*

She had her Song ready, confident that she could overcome any sorcery he might call to try to counter her. She was no longer the untested drunk she had been in Hokaia, lashing out haphazardly. She was an avatar of the Mother and did not fear him.

"Well, don't hover," he said testily. "If you're going to interrupt me, you may as well be useful."

She stared.

He huffed, exasperated. "You speak a number of languages, do you not?" His eyes were sharp. "Cuecolan, Tovan, Teek, Trade."

She nodded. Wary. Song ready.

"Ah, but do you speak Hoka? Not this corrupted hodgepodge the city speaks now, but classical Hoka. From the time of the War of the Spear."

He looked at her expectantly.

She shook her head.

"No? Then you are no use to me."

Something seized her heart and squeezed. She gagged on her own blood, her pulse suddenly pounding in her ears. She tried to Sing, but her breath huffed out uselessly, and she realized, belatedly, that Balam was not the same sorcerer he had been in Hokaia, either. And now there was an awful throbbing in her head, as if a million hammers were suddenly battering her skull, and she could not think around it.

Balam had his arm extended, hand open and fingers splayed. Blood dripped from a fresh cut across his palm, and he muttered Cuecolan words she did not understand.

"It seems unfair, doesn't it?" he asked conversationally as he drew closer. "I have mastered every contemporary language from Cuecola to the Northern Wastes to the Boundless Sea, but one word in *fucking* Hoka eludes me. One word!"

He was close enough to touch her now, his eyes wild.

"*Liyemi.*"

Her eyes widened in recognition.

He saw it, and his power stuttered in surprise. For a moment, the hammers stopped.

She struck.

She spit a single note, bright and razored, and it sent him stumbling back, his hands clamped across bleeding ears. She hurled another burst of sound toward him. Only this time, she felt her lungs seize with the effort, as if her magic had carved some small piece from her, too, as payment.

So far from the sea, she thought. *Here my magic struggles.* She could wound him, a hundred cuts with a sharp knife, and it might eventually wear him down. But Balam could control the flow of blood, his own and hers, and he realized his advantage at the same time that Xiala realized her limitations.

He threw his hand out.

Her blood caught fire in her veins. She screamed, her back arching, her whole being pulled upward, as if some massive hook was dragging the life from her body. She choked, unable to call air to her throat. Unable to make a sound.

She hung suspended as if by invisible strings as blood oozed from her skin and dripped to the floor. And slowly, she began to die.

"Teek!" she finally croaked, no more than a whisper.

Balam stared. He flicked his wrist, and air came rushing back.

She heaved in a breath. "Word. Same . . . Teek."

"Of course," he murmured. "An isolated island where nothing has changed in three hundred years." He focused back on her. "What does it mean?"

Her mouth worked. Blood ran from her scalp, covered her eyes, trickled salty and awful into her mouth.

"What. Does. It. *Mean?*"

Thunder rumbled nearby, and a strange popping sound ripped through her ears. It hit Balam, too, and he staggered, a pained cry on his lips. She felt his power release her, and she dropped to the ground, landing hard, knees and palms stinging, slipping in a pool of her own blood.

A black roiling mass of shadow slashed a doorway into the room.

"Impossible," Balam whispered as he stumbled back from the churning darkness.

But it wasn't impossible. It was very real. And they both watched as Serapio stepped through the shadowgate.

CHAPTER 48

Gods are greedy things.

—Kupshu, former spearmaiden and wise woman
of the Northern Wastes

Naranpa snuggled between her two brothers and watched the first rays of the sun break through their window. Not every house in the Maw had a window where the sun came through, and although theirs was small, no more than a sliver near the roof to let light and air in, there was always a sunrise.

Today's sunrise was special. Today was the day Naranpa would go to the celestial tower. Her mother's employer, the matron of Water Strider, had been true to her word and arranged for Naranpa to work in the tower as a serving girl. She would cook and clean and wash, and maybe, maybe, she might learn to read.

She had not even confessed her secret desire to her mother but harbored it close to her heart. The very idea made her shiver with excitement. She had never touched a book, but once a merchant had come to the Maw and set up a stall selling small palm-sized scrolls of folk stories. No one bought one, so he didn't linger, but Naranpa had watched him all day and wondered what it might be like to unroll the bark paper and decipher the glyphs, to read for herself the wonders they held locked inside.

Murmuring voices drew her attention to the mat where her mother and father slept. She watched sleepily as her father, already dressed and ready for the day, kissed her mother before creeping silently out of the room. A small part of her felt sad that her father hadn't woken her to say goodbye. Mama said it was difficult for him, having Naranpa leave. But Naranpa also knew she was another mouth to feed. It would be hard to be gone, but it was best for her family. Best for her brothers, especially. They were growing quickly, and Mama always complained about how much they ate.

The door opened and closed, and her father departed for his backbreaking work in the fields.

Naranpa rose and tiptoed across her sleeping brothers. There was a small chest where she kept her things, and draped across it was a new dress. It had been a gift from one of the Water Strider matron's nieces, a castoff she no longer wanted. But it was the finest thing Naranpa had ever owned, and she slipped it on now with pride.

She found her mother crouched over the communal cooking coals outside the front door, already beating out the day's bread with her hands. Normally, that was Naranpa's duty, because her mother left for work with the sunrise, but the matron had granted her mother the day off to escort Naranpa to the tower.

She glanced over. "Good, you're up. Careful, Nara, don't get that dress dirty before it's time to go."

The hem was well above her sandaled feet, but she lifted it anyway. "I won't," she promised.

Her mother straightened and dusted the cornmeal from her hands. "I'm glad you're here. There's something I want to show you. Come with me."

"What about the bread?" she asked, following her mother, casting the half-finished flat cakes a lingering glance.

"They will keep, or Akel can do it once he's awake. Come!"

Naranpa hurried to catch up, and together they walked through the barely stirring streets of the Maw. Her mother led them upward through the warrens, climbing until they were on the top level.

Naranpa hesitated. This was where she came sometimes to gaze out of the city. She did not know her mother knew of the place, but it seemed clear that Naranpa's secret overlook was their destination.

"Come on," her mother said, smiling.

Once they were there, the city glittered before them. It was the most commanding view in Tova, Naranpa was sure of it. From here, she could see Sun Rock, the great mesa rising in the center, the shimmering woven bridges connecting it to the four Sky Made districts. As dawn broke in earnest, the bridges gleamed like spidersilk in the morning light, and the districts—Kun and Odo, Tsay and Titidi—glowed as they came to life. And there, on a far mesa on the very western edge of the city, was Otsa and the celestial tower.

It captured her heart like nothing else. More than Titidi with its greenery or Kun with its terraced hills. More than Odo with its black stone fortress or Tsay gleaming white and pure.

"What do you see?" her mother asked, eyes sparkling with curiosity.

Naranpa thought carefully. It would be easy to give her mother a simple answer, but the moment and the question felt important. She did not want to answer without thinking.

"I see my destiny," she said finally.

Her mother crouched down so that their heads touched. "I

see it, too, Naranpa. I knew it from the very beginning. You are special. Should you wish it, this city will be yours."

Her mother was wrong, of course. The city was never hers. Certainly not as a child. And not as a dedicant in the tower, or even as the Sun Priest. It was not even hers when she stood on Sun Rock as the avatar of the sun god and battled the Odo Sedoh for Tova's soul.

Because she was a Maw brat. Because no matter how hard she worked and how much she raised herself up, she would never be Sky Made, never a scion, never blessed.

She thought she had come to terms with that. The reunion with her brother, the alliance with the Maw bosses, and, finally, her choice to walk away from the city that was as fickle, demanding, and inconstant as an unrequited love.

And so why now did she return to this place in the dreamworld, to stand on that same precipice where her mother had taken her that morning? Why did she return at all when she could have stayed with Iktan in the Northern Wastes or studied with Kupshu or done anything else? She could have lived. They all could have lived.

She had only to let Tova go.

The city of her birth, the city that had killed one brother young and the other eventually. The city that ground her parents down in poverty, the city of class and privilege disguised as enlightenment.

As she stood looking over the city that was still encased in the crow god's eclipse, the sun god whispered of destruction in a voice so deafening that she could not remember why she wished to save Tova at all.

Has the city not prostrated itself to the crow god and betrayed the sun? Is this once holy city not rotten? Unsalvageable? What does Tova matter to you now that Iktan is gone, and your brother, and anyone you cared about?

She bowed her head as the truth of the sun god's words wormed into her soul. And it was the truth. The city had taken and taken and taken, until she was left with nothing.

There is only one path, one destiny, one satisfaction, the sun god breathed. *Let Tova be nothing, too.*

Some part of her resisted, fought against the coming horror, but she could not stop herself. She lifted her arms and the sun god rushed in. It was not simply fire to her hands as she had done before, but an act of supplication, a concession of self that allowed her god to fill the empty places within her and take command.

She gasped as her body caught fire, flames haloing around her torso and streaking down her outstretched arms. The city had lived under the threat of shadow for a season and learned to fear the crow god and his shadow. Now they would fear the light.

It's not real. It's only a dream, Naranpa told herself.

But even as she thought it, she knew it was not true. The walls between the worlds were thin, and gods did not respect the boundaries of life and death, waking and dreaming.

And what was she but a thing caught in between?

"Burn!" she cried in a ringing voice not wholly her own.

All at once, sunlight burst across the city. The sun had been a sliver of orange behind a black sun on the horizon. Now it returned to its proper place in the sky. Only brighter, only more, as the world shifted and the summer solstice reigned . . . and the eclipse of the crow god shattered.

Heat broke across the city like a tidal wave, dense and suffocating. She imagined people suddenly blinded by the light, scorched by the heat, struggling to breathe. She would have cared about their suffering before, but her compassion had been seared away under the force of her god's will.

She turned her attention to the glittering bridges, the marvel of Tova. Except there had never been a bridge to the Maw. The Sky Made had saved such wonders for themselves alone and left the people of the Maw to scrounge for what they could find.

With a thought, she set the bridges afire.

All at once, the rope walkways sparked into infernos, long, snaking whirls of blue flame strangely elegant in death. She watched until the bridges disintegrated and collapsed into the river below.

She turned to her next target, the Great Houses themselves.

The Great Houses were populated by the matrons who had never accepted her, by the privileged families who sneered down their noses at her low birth. *And servants like my mother.* The thought flickered, but her god refused to let it take hold.

She willed the palaces of the matrons to conflagrate.

And the districts burned.

She turned to the Shadow Palace. A thought, and the black building made of bone and blood and shadow began to smolder. *It resists*, the sun god told her, *but it will eventually succumb. On this day, nothing can withstand the light, not even the crow god.*

She saved the celestial tower for last.

But when she flung out her hands, her god ready to rain fire down upon the place that deserved it most, she balked.

Why do you stop? her god cried. *Where is your hate?*

"No!" she screamed. Because there was hate, yes, but love, too. The celestial tower was the place of her worst humiliations but also her greatest triumphs. The place where she had met Iktan, the place where she had become a leader, the place where she had found her calling and embraced knowledge over superstition.

She had a memory of the first time she had seen the great

library. She had been assigned to clean the floors, a task reserved for only the most trustworthy of the servants. Learning to read would come later, but that first day, she had only walked among the shelves, reverence slowing her steps as she swept the aisles, the task as holy as anything she had experienced in her small life.

Still holy. Even more so than the divine voice that drove her now.

She lowered her hands and turned away from the tower, and the thwarted sun god howled with rage even as the rest of the city burned.

Tears of fire seared her cheeks as she looked out over the city.

Tova looked like all her dreams.

With a sudden start, Naranpa realized that it *was* the Tova of her dreams. In all the nightmares she had had of Balam and the city burning, she had thought the carnage the work of the jaguar lord. The carnage she was meant to stop.

But it was not Balam who destroyed Tova.

It was her.

Naranpa crumpled to the ground, her hair singed, the skin on her hands peeled away, charred bones showing through.

"Iktan," she whispered, tongue blackened to a rotten thing. "Show me a way back."

But xe could not. Xe had died.

It is only a dream.

Kupshu was right. Gods were greedy things, and now Naranpa's god claimed her and everything that had been hers.

It is only a dream.

But Naranpa did not believe in dreams, not anymore.

CHAPTER 49

CITY OF TOVA
YEAR I OF THE CROW

There is always a choice.

—The Crow God Reborn to his tutor upon leaving Obregi

Serapio stumbled through the shadowgate and into sunlight. He felt it immediately, the presence of the Sun Priest. The way his god turned his attention to her and little else. His old enemy close, and Serapio compelled to kill her.

"No!" Serapio roared with a defiance of which he had not known himself capable. With tremendous effort, he wrenched his attention back to the scene before him. The sunlight cast shadows in the room that helped him see, and sound and movement and scent told him the rest.

A man, shouting. Balam, although his voice was changed. But he was still the man he had met in Cuecola who had secured him passage on a ship, smelling of copal and jungle and magic.

Xiala, on the floor to his left, the scent of ocean and life and everything precious.

And blood. So much blood. The room reeked of it.

But Serapio did not have time to determine its source before he was under attack. He sensed the displaced air, the movement toward him. He called his feathered form and ducked low behind his wing. The projectiles struck, penetrating the outer layer of his living armor. The pain was sharp, a dozen thick needles peppering his arm. His jaw clenched against it as his mind reeled. Always before, his crow armor had repelled arrow and spear alike, but whatever Balam had hurled at him was neither.

It was sorcery. Blood formed into a weapon sharper and more deadly than even obsidian. The knowledge came to Serapio just as another volley of blood daggers sought him out.

He rolled to the side, avoiding all but one that sliced across his shoulder. He swallowed the fiery agony and launched a counterattack. With a thought, his armor transformed. The feathers of his arm became small, quilled projectiles of their own. He sent the sharp quills flying. Balam shouted as he moved to avoid the blows.

For a moment, the only sound was breathing. His own, Balam's, and Xiala's.

Xiala. He called her name.

"I'm here," she answered, and, staying low behind the shelves, he began to make his way to her.

"We can continue this exchange all day!" Balam shouted, voice rough with exhaustion. "But you will eventually succumb. Look out the window. The eclipse is no more. Your god is losing and your city burns!"

With the mention of the crow god, the compulsion to seek out the Sun Priest thundered back. Serapio stumbled under the weight of the call, knees hitting the floor.

"Serapio!" Xiala sounded panicked.

He did his best to wave her concern away, but inside he felt like he was being torn asunder. He had never defied his god. From the time he was a child, he had embraced his fate as a way forward after his mutilation. The crow god had been his guide and comfort, the thing that filled him and gave him purpose. Even when the crow god had abandoned him after Sun Rock, Serapio had stayed faithful, longing only to know his god's presence again. And now the crow god had returned, determined to impose his will upon Serapio's own new and fragile one, and Serapio seethed.

One thing. He asked for only one thing in exchange for all he had done, all he had sacrificed.

And his god would not allow it.

"No!" he roared, and forced himself to move toward Xiala.

He thought he heard Balam laugh over the roaring in his head.

Hands touched Serapio, pulling him close. He let Xiala hold him and drew strength from their contact, her scent, her weight against his body. And then he realized she was sticky with blood.

"Are you hurt?" He gasped, his own hands gently searching her for injuries.

"It looks worse than it is," she said, her voice strained. And then, "Or feels. He has a sorcery that draws blood from the body."

"Blood magic," Serapio confirmed. "His magic must feed, and so it will take his own blood or another's if he so wills it." It was the same principle as shadow magic, and what he used to create his Tuyon's armor. But it also meant there was a limit to Balam's power, and as with any magic, if there was not another source, the magic would draw from the sorcerer. Balam had to be struggling to remain on his feet already.

"My veins may run dry," the sorcerer shouted, "but not before your god has taken everything from you! The shadow feeds, and your god will need more of you if he wishes to battle the sun."

"Is that true?" Xiala asked. "Is the crow god hurting you?"

"A war within," he acknowledged through clenched teeth.

"What can I do?" she asked.

"Can you run?"

"I . . . yes."

"Then run, Xiala. You must run."

"I will not leave you."

"This battle is mine. I must kill Balam if I wish to cut the path." Serapio hesitated. "He is my father."

"Your . . . Ah." He could feel her concern, a sudden whisper of doubt as to where his allegiances might lie. An acknowledgment of what he had told her before of the prophecy's demands. "It is too much to ask you to kill your father, Serapio. Even of you."

He took her hands in his, pulling her close until their foreheads touched.

"You are my home, Xiala. My present and my future, and in the face of that, what is the past but the dust of memories best forgotten? He is a stranger to me, and one who once abandoned me, and abandons me still in pursuit of his own glory. You came back when you did not have to, risked your own life, sacrificed so much. You are my heart, my home. I want for nothing else."

And as he said it, he understood it to be true.

He wanted nothing else. Not power, not Tova, not the acceptance of this stranger who was his father. He knew that. But what was new, what shook the very foundation of who he was, who he had been for so long, was that *he did not even want his god.*

When Powageh had confessed that Balam was Serapio's father, he had only felt a rising horror. Not because this man who had been his mother's lover and co-conspirator was his sire, not even because he had mistakenly killed Marcal, a man who, if not his father, was a victim to Serapio's desperation. But because as long as Balam lived, the prophecy stayed unfulfilled.

And so now it came to this. If Serapio managed to kill Balam, he could still win all three wars—the one against the Treaty cities, the one the crow god waged against the sun, and the one within himself.

But if he won the wars, he would lose everything. Was that not what the prophecy promised?

When Zataya had first brought him the coyote's song, it had seemed a worthy sacrifice. After all, what were his *things*? A palace? Power? His life?

But he had not understood the price the trickster god demanded. Then he had thought Xiala beyond his reach and that the best way to protect her was to slay the unloved bride in her stead. But now his mistake was clear.

Xiala was his everything, and if he won, he would lose her.

He would rather lose the wars.

The war against the Treaty cities was in the hand of his commanders now, and while Balam claimed the sun was winning the war against the crow god, the final result was still undetermined. That left only one war fully within his power to decide: the war within himself.

And he decided.

Another wave of compulsion gripped him, this one worse than before, as if his god knew his heart and meant to break it.

He screamed as he collapsed, the voice of his god a deafening howl in his head. And then he was crawling, not by his own choice but as if he were a puppet being commanded by invisible strings, his fingers clawing into the stone to pull him across the floor toward the door.

To find the Sun Priest. To kill his true enemy.

Serapio was dimly aware of Xiala moving, of Balam's shout, and then his world went dark.

CHAPTER 50

> Victory then to the Carrion King
> who in winning loses everything.

> —Coyote song

Xiala watched in horror as Serapio set his will set against that of his god, and paid the price of his defiance with his pain. She yearned to help him, but instinctively knew that he must fight the battle against the crow god without her.

Balam was another matter.

She pushed to her feet, spread her arms, and stepped into view.

"I will tell you your word!" she shouted before Balam had even registered that she was vulnerable before him. He turned his focus to her, eyes wary, as if suddenly she was the predator and he the prey. There was fear there, but was it fear that she would deny him his answer or that the answer would destroy him?

She knew which one it would be.

"I will tell you the word if you spare Serapio. You promised me, back in Hokaia."

Balam's expression shifted, amused. "What a terrible thing

love is. I loved once, and it brought only misery." He glanced toward Serapio. "Even if I wanted to help, he struggles with a greater force than my own at the moment. And I cannot imagine that this time he will survive."

"Help him!"

Balam's face shut down as he withdrew into himself, the desperate animal retreating. "I cannot."

"Even though he is your son?"

Balam jerked his head back, as if Xiala had hit him. He hesitated, if only for a moment, and then shook his head. "Look at him. He is barely human now. And only a god can hope to defeat another god. And godhead was denied me!" His expression darkened. "Unless . . ." He grew sly again. "Unless Seuq knew. She spoke of it, attaining godhood. Is that the word that you keep to yourself? The secret to the power of a god?"

He had stepped forward, eager.

"I learned something today," Xiala said, circling wide, keeping out of his reach and moving him away from Serapio, who still writhed on the floor. "I learned that sound can be seen. Waves in the air instead of on the sea. Colors."

"The word," Balam growled.

"Of course, visual sound would be useless to a blind man."

"Enough games. The word!"

"But to you, Balam, it would be death."

He seemed to process her threat a moment later, but by then it was too late.

It was dangerous, what she was doing. After all, Enuka had explained it to her only once, and even then, it was only a theory. But she could think of no other way to defeat Balam and spare Serapio.

This time, when she called her Song, she did not think of sound, of the feel of notes gathering in her throat and moving across her tongue, although she knew that they did. She did not contemplate the press of air passing between her lips, although it did.

She thought of waves. Of an ocean's powerful surge, the force of a great tsunami, inevitable in its rise. It climbed from the depths of her being and exploded from her mouth as the terrible whiteness of oblivion.

Her Song made manifest as color and sight . . . but not sound.

She watched as it struck Balam, his eyes widening in shock and then a brief moment of terror as he saw his own death on the crest of a wave breaking over him. Drowning him in a sound he could not hear but could only see.

And like the soldiers on the beach in Teek, Lord Balam of the House of Seven, merchant lord of Cuecola, patron of the Crescent Sea, White Jaguar by birthright, and sire of the Crow God Reborn, shattered.

It was a horror, and Xiala shut her eyes as blood and flesh and bits of what had once been a man burst across the room, spattered the room and herself with gore.

The room had smelled of blood before, her own and Balam's, but now it smelled worse, the hint of innards lingering in her nose and the back of her mouth. She shuddered at the feel of wetness against her own skin, but it was done.

Balam was dead.

"Ambition," she whispered. "The word was ambition."

Seuq had tried to warn him, but he had failed to understand.

She turned to Serapio, praying that she had been right, and sound made into color and sight would not harm him, and was both relieved and distressed to find him alive and still fighting his god.

She rushed to his side, horrified to find his fingernails torn from their beds, his hands trailing bloody tracks as he struggled to drag himself across the floor. His face was caught in a rictus, his mouth open in a silent scream, his black eyes swirling with something foreign and hostile.

She grabbed his arm, hoping to pull him back, but his flesh was ice, the burn searing her own skin. She jerked her hand away, and it trailed shadow.

"What do I do?" she cried, not sure if he could hear her.

Serapio's mouth worked, struggling to speak. Xiala leaned close to listen, aware that to touch him would burn, but willing to risk it.

"Dagger," he whispered. His body shook with a sudden spasm, as if his god had heard and disapproved.

But she understood.

She still wore the sun dagger on a cord around her throat, and she pulled it free now, dragging it from its sheath.

The thing, the god, that battled to possess Serapio turned its attention toward her. She hesitated at the malevolence that swirled in his black eyes, the strange grin that curled his lips. This was not Serapio. She knew that, and she also knew that he was losing this war.

And so Xiala did not apologize, did not weep and profess her undying love, did not look for another way.

With a single powerful blow, she buried the dagger in his chest, aiming for his heart. He rose to meet the blade, back arching as it penetrated his flesh. He screamed, the most horrible sound Xiala had ever heard. Perhaps not a killing Song, but her heart shattered all the same.

He fell back, the golden knife embedded between his ribs, light leaking from the wound, and reddish ichor already spreading across his torso. She wanted to look away, but she did not.

She took his hand, no longer burning cold, and watched his eyes clear as the sun dagger drove the crow god from his body.

"Free," he whispered, his smile genuine and real. He lifted a hand, cupping her cheek, but she could see what the effort cost him. The way his arm shook and his brow buckled under the strain.

She leaned into his touch, not sure what else to do, tears gathering in her eyes as her own chest tightened with loss. He was dying, she could see it. Free of his god, his own man at the end, but the price was his life.

"Balam?" Serapio's voice was less than a whisper.

"Dead. I told you," she said, her laugh bitter through tears that now freely flowed. "Prophecies are shit. You're free." Her breath caught in her throat. "So don't leave me now."

He grimaced, and some emotion—regret, sorrow, hope— flickered across his delicate face.

"Promise me," she said, her fingers tightening in his. "Please, Serapio. Promise me you won't leave me."

He closed his eyes. He coughed, blood coating his lips, and whispered something too low for her to hear. She leaned closer, and he said it again, words on his final breath, and then he was gone.

She took him in her arms and held him close, his face against hers, his wild hair soft against her cheek.

I promise. Those were his last words. He had promised not to leave her, but here she was, alone.

And she wept, the salty tears of the sea, her grief as wide and vast as the Mother could bear. *He's free*, she told herself, *and he promised*. And it helped, but not enough. Not enough.

It took her a moment to notice the change, lost as she was to sorrow.

It began as the brush of a feather against her face.

And then the soft cry of a crow.

She lifted her head from where she had rested it against his chest and watched as what had been his body moments before shifted into something else. At first, she thought it was only his feathered cloak caught in a trick of the light, but when the small black bodies began to move, she realized Serapio himself had . . . changed. Shifted, as Okoa had once told her he could.

No longer did his body lie before her. Now there were crows. Dozens of crows that ruffled feathers and shook themselves free of his clothing.

Xiala scooted back to give them room and then watched as they rose in silence, a black flock that circled above, her at the center. She had a vivid memory of the crows on the ship that had killed her crew in her defense, but these crows did not peck or claw. They wheeled through the library in silence, the echo of their beating wings loud in her ears, the brush of the wind they made tousling her hair. She closed her eyes and breathed in their scent.

It was familiar. It was his.

The flock whirled, building momentum before they fled through the open door, rising through the center of the great central staircase to exit through the open roof. Xiala pushed herself to her feet and followed, reaching the top of the tower in time to see the corvids traveling west, away from the city, away from the Meridian, across the Wilds and toward the Boundless Sea.

"You promised!" she shouted, but the crows did not acknowledge her cry, and then they were gone, disappearing from view.

And the jagged pieces of her heart, and her fragile belief that somehow Serapio might keep his word, went with them.

CHAPTER 51

And in the God Wars, the gods of shadow and light, of
fire and stone and sea and wind, all fell one by one. Only
Coyote, who was a god of the thin places in between,
thought to bide his time.

—From *Songs of the Coyote*

Zataya stood on the grounds of the district of Otsa, shaded by
the shadow of the celestial tower, and watched the delegation
from the Northern Wastes bring the body across the newly replaced bridge. Summer had already begun to wane, and the
days were growing shorter, but there *were* days, and there were
nights, each lasting as long as they should, the heavens having
returned to their normal course once the gods and their avatars
had been driven from the earth.

Stories of what had happened on the Day of Stillness had
run rampant through the city. Some said the Sun Priest had
returned and defeated the Odo Sedoh but, in her anger at the
city's capitulation to the shadow, razed Tova with fire. Others
said the jaguar lord had killed the Carrion King and burned
Tova to cleanse the city, but they had no answer for where the
jaguar lord was now. And yet others said the Carrion King had

574

taken pity on the city and brought the sun back or, alternately, had abandoned the city on the summer solstice as the crow god decreed, his reign only meant to last a season.

Zataya expected the truth was somewhere in between.

"There she is." Sedaysa stood beside her, her breath shortened by grief. "It is better Denaochi did not live to see this," the Coyote matron continued. "It would have broken his heart to see his sister so."

"They say she is not dead but only sleeps," Zataya observed as a palanquin carried by four men in fur mantles passed them by.

On the palanquin was an almost transparent obsidian box the size of a human. Through the thin black glass, Zataya could just make out a figure dressed in gold that appeared to be sleeping.

It was Naranpa.

Beside the palanquin walked a lean figure in red. Sedaysa dipped her chin as the red-cloaked figure passed, and Zataya followed suit, but her surreptitious gaze was irresistibly drawn upward in curiosity. The stranger had an attractive and somewhat androgynous face marked by large, intelligent eyes and a long nose. Hair, midnight black, hung in soft waves to their shoulders, and, for no reason that she could discern, a shudder of alarm juddered through her body as those dark eyes focused on her.

She quickly looked away, dropping her gaze to her feet, willing the stranger to look somewhere else.

"The Priest of Knives," Sedaysa murmured. "Iktan Winged Serpent. I have never had the pleasure, but xe was with Naranpa when the sun god claimed her. They say xe has not left her side."

Zataya remembered the rumors now, of how the former priest had stood watch over the comatose Naranpa just as xe had once done as her guard at the tower. And how xe had stayed for days in the Graveyard of the Gods waiting for

Naranpa to return from the dreamworld. But she had not. So xe had convinced the local villagers to build this coffin and palanquin and bring her south to Tova so that she might rest in her beloved tower among her books.

It seemed a folly when it was clear to all who saw her that the sun god had claimed Naranpa's mind and left her body an empty shell. But it was a shell whose heart still beat and that did not rot, and who was to say she might not one day return? Moreover, who dared cross the former Priest of Knives?

Both Sedaysa and Zataya raised their heads once the procession had passed. With a shared glance, they fell in behind as representatives of Coyote clan. The other districts had sent delegates as well, but Zataya did not know all of them, or at least could not remember everyone's name.

The three matrons of the Sky Made were dead. Peyana Winged Serpent and Ieyoue Water Strider perished in the Stillness fires, and Esa Carrion Crow was deposed in a coup that rocked her clan in the following days. The deaths in the fires were indeed a tragedy, but the coup was something else, something that portended a change to the fabric of the city.

Chela Carrion Crow, a man, was matron now. He had returned from the Crow's mission west with news of Okoa's death and the decimation of the secret forces that had tried to attack Tova from the rear. Chela's bravery had won him many followers, and when he had revealed that Esa had tricked her brother into killing Isel Winged Serpent on the day of her marriage to the Carrion King, the Crows had risen up and overthrown the sister, replacing her with the hero captain.

None outside of Carrion Crow knew the details of exactly what had been said and done within the walls of the Great House, since it was Crow business, but rumors claimed that Chela locked Esa in a sky prison to await banishment, and the former matron had decided to take her fate into her own hands. Her body was found downriver in the same place they had found her mother's body. Her corpse had been quietly burned, a star map in her hands, sent to join the ancestors.

Okoa Carrion Crow's body had also been burned after being recovered, along with the handful of Tova's soldiers who had died there in the Western Wilds. He had been hailed as a hero and forgiven for his role in Isel's death, the city aghast at the treachery of his sister.

Okoa's crow, a great hen named Benundah, had circled the city for weeks, joined by the white crow named Achiq that had been the Carrion King's. Until one day, both crows were simply gone. Zataya liked to think they had found comfort in each other and gone somewhere beyond the reach of humans, but she did not truly know, and it was only her own wish to think it so.

The procession had come to a stop at the doors of the celestial tower. Zataya craned her neck to see. There, in a flowing gown of sea blue—no, she wore wide, draping pants—stood the queen of the Teek. Zataya had spent the past year among the matrons of the most holy city on the continent, but Xiala's shine was enough to steal her breath. There was something regal about her, befitting her royal title. But she also possessed a quality that was wild and untamed like the sea. It manifested in the way her gaze always seemed to drift east toward the Crescent Sea, in the play of the wind through her plum-colored hair, and in the sadness that swirled in her rainbow eyes.

She, too, had become a hero of the city. After the Day of Stillness and accompanied by the remaining captains, she had gone to the port city of Tovasheh and awaited the approaching naval forces of the Treaty cities. Those who witnessed it said she simply called the sea to swallow the ships. But others who had been there said the ships had been overrun by sea creatures both large and small, all called to do her bidding. Either way, their end was the same. Xiala destroyed the navy and the army they carried before they even came within striking distance of the shore. She had ended the war on Tova before it had even begun.

With the Sky Made clans in disarray, the Carrion King dead, and Xiala's power manifest, the city welcomed her leadership. But Xiala did not want it, she had made clear, and had called Sedaysa and the new matrons to the tower that first week and assured them that once things were settled, she would be returning to Teek.

When news of Iktan's planned return had come on the lips of swift messengers, Xiala had decided to stay until xir arrival, and now that day was upon them. Zataya watched as the two embraced, the Priest of Knives and the queen of the Teek. She wondered what they said to each other as they stood close together like old friends. But she was too far away to hear.

"Now what?" she asked Sedaysa.

Zataya suspected that Sedaysa would lead the council now, as she was the only original matron left. She chuckled to think that a pleasure-house boss from Coyote's Maw had risen to such heights. That she herself, a Dry Earth witch, would stand beside her.

"Now we entomb the body in the library," Sedaysa said.

"And then what?"

"And then Tova rebuilds."

There was so much work to do, and it was unclear what purpose Tova would embrace now that the Watchers were gone, the Treaty was ended, and the leadership was new. It was a city that had lost its identity and now, for better or worse, must find a new one.

As they moved to follow the crowd into the celestial tower, Zataya thought she heard something. She paused to listen. At first, she thought it was the sound of a woman crying. But then she recognized the cry for what it was.

The high-pitched yip of a coyote.

CHAPTER 52

I end my report with a note on Teek: It is my deepest regret
that I was unable to include a visit to the mysterious island
in my report, for I suspect that should they ever again open
their borders to the outside world, their ideal location, rich
island resources, and mastery of shipbuilding would make
them a powerful force with which to be reckoned.

—*A Commissioned Report of My Travels to the Seven Merchant
Lords of Cuecola*, by Jutik, a traveler from Barach

Iktan stood on the bow of the Tovan ship as it entered the
newly dredged harbor of the Teek capital. All around, vessels
of various shapes and sizes crowded the busy port. Some xe
recognized. A Cuecolan long canoe here, and there a Hokaian
barge modified to sail the open seas. But there were many ships
hoisting flags that xe did not recognize. Banners from cities far
from the Meridian, particularly from places to the east where
trade had recently exploded. Some of the finest fabrics xe had
ever seen came from a place called Awon, and xe had heard of
many wonders from other cities. Perhaps xe would visit someday once xir other business was settled. The world was very

wide, much wider than xe had ever thought, and xe had an enviable skill set that was still very much in demand, should xe wish to place xirself on the market. But that option was far in the future. For now, Iktan was . . .

"Ambassador?"

Iktan turned.

"We're approaching port," the steward said. "Shall I send a message to the queen?"

Iktan smiled. "I am sure Queen Xiala has already taken notice of our approach." Ships flying the Tovan flag were still rare in Teek, and this particular one had once been a gift from the Teek queen herself.

The steward sketched a bow and hurried away to prepare for docking.

Iktan eventually followed and was ready to disembark when the plank touched land. Even after a half dozen years as the Tovan ambassador, Iktan was not quite used to being the focal point of a parade. Xe much preferred stealth, alleyways and rooftops being more to xir liking, but now xe led an entourage of gift-bearing stewards and porters down the main street of the newly minted capital. The town bustled with trade, the faces and fashions as diverse and colorful as in any city in the Meridian. In six short years under the visionary leadership of their new queen, Teek had truly become the power of the Crescent Sea.

The new palace was a graceful, sprawling white stone house that sat atop a rising hill overlooking the bay. Female guards greeted the Tovan entourage at the outer gate and diverted the porters with their gifts fit for royalty down a hallway. They escorted the steward and Iktan's personal guards to a garden of thick island foliage, where xe knew they would be offered refreshments and prodded to share any gossip. Xe understood.

It had been almost a year since xe last visited, and there was much to be shared about the state of Tova and its clans.

The entourage sorted, Iktan walked alone down a white stone hallway. Presently, xe passed through a colonnade that overlooked a sheer drop to the rocky sea below. A sea breeze sighed through the open-sided room, as soft as a woman's touch against xir cheek.

There is only one woman's touch I crave, xe thought, *and the breeze is a poor substitute*. For a moment, Iktan's mind traveled down a dark corridor, this one made of white hoodoos and the whispers of dead gods. An immense sorrow welled in xir chest, but it was a familiar one, the same one xe had carried for six years, and now xe welcomed it as an old friend, a reminder of why xe traveled the known world and how xir mission was not done, would not be done, until xe had found the knowledge xe sought.

Xe tucked that thought away as another set of guards parted wooden doors and let Iktan enter the queen's receiving room.

Xiala stood on a balcony that ran the far length of the space. She was beautiful, as always. Her thick, coiling hair was piled into an intricate braid at the base of her neck, and she wore pants and a sleeveless tunic in a flowing aqua color that reminded Iktan of sea foam. Her sun-kissed brown skin glowed in the afternoon sun, her gaze on something beyond the balcony.

Xe knew there was a small hidden cove just visible over the railing where the waters were calm and warm. And that the cove was protected by a creature aquatic and inhuman. Xe had never seen the mysterious guardian, but xe knew it to be there, had heard stories of the thing sailors called a kraken. It conjured such fear that no one dared to attack the Teek queen from sea unless they wished to die a terrible death.

"Iktan." Xiala looked up, smiling.

Iktan found xirself bowing, not simply because that is what ambassadors did but because Xiala's presence commanded it. And xe did not mind. She had long ago earned such respect.

"Please," she said, laughing, and drew Iktan into an embrace. "Are you thirsty? Hungry? I can send for something."

"Last time I visited, you had a wonderful elixir. Something with melons . . ."

"Of course. Come. Sit."

Xiala exchanged a few words with one of the women at the door, and within a few minutes they were seated at a table on the balcony, a spectacular view of the harbor below and a chilled melon drink in their hands.

Iktan leaned forward to peer down at the cove. On the small, secluded beach were two figures: a woman and a child. Iktan knew for a fact that the child was a few months shy of his sixth birthday. And the woman was not the child's mother but his caretaker. His mother, after all, was a very busy woman.

"How is he?" Iktan asked when Xiala's gaze followed xir own down to the beach.

"Wonderful," she said, face softening. "Growing. Skies, I've never known a child to eat so much."

Iktan smiled. "Still cursing like a Tovan, I see."

Xiala flushed. "I'm trying to curb the cursing, for the boy's sake."

"Once a pirate, always a pirate."

Xiala's eyes widened. "I was never a pirate. I was a legitimate merchant captain."

"And now you are a queen." Xe sipped from the fruit elixir. "And how goes your queendom?"

"Teek is changing very quickly, and not everyone comes along willingly." Her eyes cut to the child. "Sometimes it is the small things that threaten people. What harm is there in a child?"

"Not just any child."

"A boy child, I know. Despite all we have lost, some Teek still wish we . . . returned our boy children." She rubbed her hands across her arms, as if suddenly chilled. "It was a barbaric practice born of fear. And with our population decimated, it was even worse."

"He is not just a boy," xe corrected gently, "although I do not doubt what you say. But for him . . ." They both watched as the boy carefully walked along the edge of the water looking for whatever children sought on sandy shores. "You cannot deny his parentage is somewhat . . . unique."

Xiala's small smile was an acknowledgment of the truth.

"Do they know?" Iktan asked. "Does he know?"

"Paternity has never been something that concerned Teek. That buys us some time." She smoothed her hands across her lap. "When I am ready."

"He looks more like his father every time I see him. Someone will realize it soon enough."

"And I will deal with it then." Her voice had risen slightly, her temper pricked.

"I may have some news that will ease your burden. Only a rumor. On the lips of one of my agents in the far western mountains."

"They say you are a spymaster."

"Please. An ambassador." Xir mouth quirked. "Do you wish to hear the news?"

She nodded, although her gaze fell to the floor, and her shoulders curled inward.

"My agent was caught in a snowstorm in a small village, forced to stay until the passes cleared. Over a shared barrel of balché, she met a local guide who told her of a hermit who lived in an abandoned monastery not far from the village. It seems the hermit comes down the mountain occasionally for supplies and such but never stays the night and rarely talks to the villagers."

Xiala breathed. "It could be anyone."

"He's blind. The hermit. Not the guide. The guide was astounded that a blind man could navigate the mountain pass and thought it worthy of a story about the local's heartiness."

Xiala held the idea, and Iktan could see the moment she let it go. "I couldn't possibly. It's a wild rumor, that's all. And I am a queen now. I have too much responsibility."

Iktan took a folded paper from xir coat pocket and set it on the table.

"What is that?"

"A map."

"I . . . I can't."

"You can," xe said gently. "Go. If not for yourself, for him." Xe nodded toward the boy on the beach.

"It's not safe."

"I will stay with him." Iktan brushed a hand across xir hair. Xe had let it grow back these last few years, and now kept it long and tied in a topknot. "My motive is not entirely selfless. Naranpa still sleeps." Xe said it quickly, as if it might hurt less if the words did not linger on xir tongue.

"I'm sorry."

"I am not. As long as she sleeps, she is not dead. If that day comes, then I will . . ." Xe never allowed xir thoughts to go past that day and did not allow it now. Naranpa would wake. Xe had to believe that.

"I have traveled the entirety of the Meridian," xe continued, "spent months reading every text known to the world, consulted witches and sorcerers both, and found nothing."

"I know."

"So you see, I am hoping that the one living shadow sorcerer might know something more, and, well . . ." Xe sighed. "I find I cannot give up hope, no matter how foolish it is."

"Hope is never foolish."

"Neither is love."

They exchanged a look, old friends with more in common than they wished.

Xiala sat back with a wry laugh that they both understood too well. "Then I guess I am going on a trip."

"My ship is at your disposal," xe said, "should you wish for something a bit more discreet. Traveling as a queen might draw eyes."

She stood and walked to the edge of the balcony.

"Akona!" she called down to the boy. "Come here. I want you to meet someone."

The boy shouted some complaint in Teek before his mother insisted, and, trailed by the bitter laments that only a five-year-old could muster when forced to do something against his will, Xiala's son trundled barefoot up the sandy path. He paused on the balcony, eyeing Iktan, his black hair tousled and his bare brown legs coated in a fine layer of salt and sand.

Iktan smiled, and the boy shyly smiled back, and then, having decided that Iktan was an acceptable presence, he rushed toward his mother.

"Look!" Akona carefully opened his small hand. Lying in his palm was a bird's egg.

"A gull?" Xiala asked. "You should put it back in its nest. You don't want the mother to reject it."

"He insists it is a crow's egg," the caretaker said, "but I told him we don't have crows on the island."

Iktan stilled and saw the same wariness in Xiala.

"A crow?" the Teek queen whispered. "How does he even know of crows?"

"He told me," Akona said, small voice solemn.

"Who told you?" Xiala's voice was soft with wonder.

"My friend." Akona lifted the egg to his face and kissed the shell. He crooned a sweet song to the egg.

Iktan wondered if those notes had more sea or sky in their making, and what it meant for it to be both.

Iktan stood and went to the boy. Xe knelt so they were face-to-face. Iktan had not lied. The boy looked very much like his father.

"It seems you have a new friend." Xe gestured to the egg. "You will have to care for it. Can you do that?"

Akona nodded with the weight of his new responsibility.

"Very good. I will be your new friend, too. Is that all right with you?"

Another solemn nod.

"Then I will keep you both safe while your mother is away." Iktan smiled. "Or better yet, I will teach you how to keep yourself safe. Did you know that I am very hard to kill? Would you like to be very hard to kill, too, Akona? Yes? Good. We will start your lessons tomorrow."

CHAPTER 53

OBREGI MOUNTAINS
SIX YEARS AFTER THE FALL OF THE CARRION KING

I have saved a place for you, my love,
In the quiet spaces between the stars.

—*The Obregi Book of Flowers*

Xiala climbed the last few steps to the village with Iktan's map clutched in her hand. The journey had taken longer than she expected. The sea travel was easy enough, but once she had reached the mountains, she was forced to join a traveling caravan, and their trek was slow and ponderous. Unlike her, they were in no hurry.

But she was here now at the map's terminus and, according to the caravan master, just in time. It was the autumnal equinox, and the first storm of winter was expected to strike in the next few days. Once it did, the mountain passes would close to travel until the spring thaw.

She walked toward the travelers' inn. The only one in the village, she suspected, and she had reached for the door handle when something in a shop window the next building over caught her eye. She paused, mouth open.

She stepped toward the shop window, barely conscious

of a couple exiting the inn who pushed past her, jostling her shoulder.

It can't be, she thought. But it was. She was certain of it.

She walked inside the shop and was greeted by the rich smell of freshly carved wood. A variety that scented the air with sharp, rich pine and thick sap.

"Looking for something special?" the shop owner asked. He was an old man, surely someone's grandfather, as wiry and wrinkled as a walnut, his white hair no more than a collection of wisps upon his head.

"The carving in the window," she said, slightly breathless. "It's beautiful. Is it . . . yours?"

"Ah, no." The old man chuckled. He lifted a gnarled hand for her inspection. "Can't carve much anymore at my age, but I recognize true craftsmanship, as do you." He hobbled forward and carefully lifted the carving from the window display. "This is the work of a master."

"It's incredible," she agreed.

"I call it 'The Lovebirds.'"

The carving was large, larger than she could remember Serapio ever making before. Every other carving he had made had always been small enough to fit in his palm. This work required two hands simply to pick it up.

On a branch sat two birds, so close that the curves of their shoulders touched. One tilted its head upward, as if reading something in the sky. The other nestled near the first bird's neck, gaze turned inward.

"How do you know?" she asked abruptly. "That they're lovebirds?" *What if one bird stabbed the other? Would they still be lovers?* She thought of her son's small egg, so easily crushed by careless hands, and how he had held it so gently as if it were the most precious thing on earth.

"I guess I don't," the old man confessed. "But I like to think that they are."

"I do, too."

"Would you guess that the artist is blind?"

Xiala's heart thumped a little more loudly in her chest.

"Difficult to believe," he continued, oblivious to Xiala's quickened breath, "if I hadn't met him myself."

"Do you know where I can find him?" she asked carefully.

"He comes into town to sell these carvings. They're popular with the caravans. It's good money. Enough that he could afford a place here in the village. But he lives up the mountain. There's an old monastery there. I used to make the trek on occasion, to take him his earnings from the sales when he hadn't come down for them. I'm an honest man, but nobody should hold another's man's money for too long."

"Can you take me there?"

"To the birdman?"

The birdman. The shopkeeper surely meant the man who carved the birds, but the moniker stirred something in her heart.

"I'm sorry," the shopkeeper continued, "but I don't think he'd take too kindly to visitors. He's not the type, if you know what I mean."

"I . . ." She thought quickly. "I'd like to commission a piece. A very expensive piece."

The old man hesitated.

"I would be happy to pay you a percentage, of course," she added. "For the introduction."

His reticence melted away. "I can't make the hike anymore," he said, sounding apologetic. "But my grandson can take you. Although he would be missing a day of work . . ."

"I'll be happy to pay him, too. Lost wages."

The shopkeeper grinned. "I'll send for him now." He paused, eyeing her fine cloak, the jewels in her ears and around her neck. "'The Lovebirds.' Would you like to take that, too?"

"I dare not yet," she said, "but perhaps you can hold them for me."

• • • • •

The shopkeeper's grandson was a lanky teenager who scrambled up the mountain as easily as Xiala might swim through calm waters. But she was not swimming, and moreover, she was used to flat land, where the air was plentiful and breathing was easy, as the Mother intended. This was something else.

"Almost there," the teenager assured her with a smile she found mildly patronizing. But she didn't complain. He was carrying her bag, after all, and, unlike her, had thought to bring extra water. Which she was very grateful for. She had entirely underestimated how far and how steep the climb would be. But eventually, they crested a rocky outcropping, and a red stone structure shuffled into view.

"There it is," her young guide said, pointing to the building.

Xiala studied Serapio's home. It was rounded and at least two stories tall from the placement of the narrow windows, perhaps three. Someone had repaired sections of the curving wall, the new parts notable for the mismatched stone, and thatched the roof. It looked sturdy and well cared for but a very far cry from the Shadow Palace.

Her guide stepped over to a post Xiala had not noticed. He pulled sharply on a rope that was attached to a bell mounted to the top. It clanged out a greeting that echoed across the high peaks.

"Best to let him know we're coming," he said, as he led her up the trail. "Last time I brought something up from my grandfather, I found a knife at my neck." He shook his head, rueful. "He may be blind, but he's very fast."

She touched his arm, and the boy looked back, questioning.

"Would you mind if I went the rest of the way on my own?" She pressed a small purse of cacao into his hands. "And you don't have to wait." She glanced at the setting sun. "I'll find my own way back."

Her guide hesitated.

"I'll be fine," she assured him. "We're . . . well, we used to be friends."

He shrugged, as if to say it was her life to do with as she wished, and then turned to work his way back down the path to the village.

Which left Xiala to finish the journey alone.

The remainder of the walk was surprisingly pleasant. After she crossed the last rocky outcropping, she found herself in a meadow thick with late-summer flowers. They perfumed the air, dancing in the afternoon breeze. From there, she followed a meticulously manicured path that cut through a copse of trees heavy with fruit. The path ended at the entrance to a small vegetable garden.

And there he was, kneeling in the soil and picking thick bunches of some kind of leafy vegetable with a red dangling root. She watched him as he worked. She had always enjoyed the way his hands moved, his long, graceful fingers and assured motions.

He lifted his head and turned his face toward hers. He had aged, as no doubt she had, too. He had always been thin and birdlike, but now he was more solid, a man more than a boy, with not simply the lithe muscles of a trained fighter but those of a man who built houses and worked the land. His delicate face had settled into something that was more enduring than ethereal, but his hair was still wild. Long now, longer than her own, which meant almost to his waist, and held back with a tie.

Still beautiful, she thought, and that old familiar longing tugged at her heart. *Now or never, Xiala. Still time to run before he knows it's you.*

"I hope you plan to stay for dinner," he said, voice slightly raised to carry on the breeze.

Too late, although she knew full well that she had never had any intention of running.

"I would very much like to stay for dinner," she said.

He gestured to the basket at his feet. "Grab these." And then he turned to walk the short path to his door.

She scooped up the basket of vegetables and followed. The inside was even cozier than she would have guessed. A kitchen area, a workbench, a simple bed, and the most beautiful table and benches she had ever seen, constructed in vertical stripes from three interspersed shades of wood. Intricate animal carvings adorned the edges and sides.

"It's beautiful," she whispered, as he took the basket from her and went to the small cooking area. He set a fire in a beehive-shaped clay oven whose flue ran along the side of the building to release the smoke outside. She'd seen similar ovens in Tova but never indoors. He must have designed it himself.

"The table?" he asked, bringing her thoughts back. "It took me two years to make. The benches almost as long."

"And you cook?" She could not hide her delight.

"I had to learn," he said. A smile curved the edge of his mouth. "I did promise you dessert once."

She laughed, pleased he remembered, happy to catch a glimpse of the Serapio she had known. And who had known her.

"Perhaps we can start with washing vegetables," she said, joining him at the cooking station. She filled the clay pot with water from a nearby bucket, and together they worked in silence, washing and gently separating the leaves, stems, and roots.

After everything was cleaned, Serapio took out a knife and began to chop, first a small pile of stubby purple tubers and next a mound of dark green chiles.

"Stew, then?" Xiala asked, her stomach already rumbling. "I'll put the water on to boil."

"There's cornmeal in the barrel." He pointed with his knife. "I don't grow corn, I trade for it. But there's plenty if you want to make bread."

"Serapio . . ."

"You smell like the ocean," he said, voice soft, almost wistful. "Even here, so far away. I missed it." And the part he did not say, but she heard in his voice. *I missed you.*

Something within her shuddered and broke, a wave of hurt and heartache she had held on to for six long years.

"Where did you go?" She had not meant to ask, but to see him here, to understand that for all this time, they could have been together and were not. It was a terrible, shattering realization. Her son had helped ease her pain, but she had been so lonely, so terribly lonely.

"Here. Well, not at first. I don't know where I went at first." His hand stilled, and he lowered his head. "It took a very long time for me to become a human again."

"Oh." She had not expected that.

"And longer still to remember who I was . . . and what I had done."

"And the crow god?"

He looked up, dark eyes unerringly drawn to hers. "Gone. You severed our connection, Xiala. Permanently."

"I'm sorry."

"It is what I asked you to do." He resumed his chopping, the rhythmic slap of knife against wood filling the room.

She rubbed her hands across her suddenly shivering

shoulders. "It was the hardest thing I have ever done," she admitted.

"And yet you did not hesitate."

"I made a promise."

"So did I, and one I meant to keep. Someday. Only I did not know how. I am sorry I left you alone. It was the last thing I wished to do."

"I was not alone."

He paused, and she could see his own heartache in the fall of his shoulders, the unsteady hand that stuttered over the knife. "Of course."

"It is not what you think. I was not alone because I had a son."

He nodded, but she could tell he didn't understand.

"Our son," she said gently.

And now he stilled.

"He looks just like you, or so Iktan insists. Xe is the only one who knows Akona's true parentage, but others are likely to figure it out soon enough. Teek are loose about such things, but . . ." There was no way to say it but as the truth. "He seems to have an affinity for crows."

"His name is Akona?"

"A Teek name. It means black-winged."

He smiled. "You named our son black-winged, and you don't think anyone will notice?"

"He was born with a thatch of the blackest hair. Your hair. I could always say it was the hair." She shook her head, smile rueful. "Would you like to meet him? I mean, not now, but . . ."

"Someday."

She nodded. "Yes. Someday."

"I would like that."

He scraped all the vegetables into the pot of boiling water. And stood there looking lost.

"What's wrong?" she asked, alarmed.

"I would very much like to touch you."

"Oh." She came to stand before him. He was shaking, she realized, as he lifted a hand and moved it toward her face. She took his hand and pressed his palm against her cheek. Only when his fingers cupped the curve of her jaw did she realize she was crying.

"The stew will take a while to cook," he said softly.

"Oh," she said, smiling despite the tears. "Perhaps, while we wait, I can tell you a story. I know a great one, about a crow and a mermaid."

"How does it end?"

"However we want," she said, voice careful.

"Pirates?" he asked, hopeful.

Xiala laughed. "You want there to be pirates?"

"I have always wanted to capture a ship."

"Then there will be pirates. Anything else?"

"Stars?"

"So many stars, Serapio. A night's sky full of stars, and the darkness between them, too."

He took her in his arms and pressed his lips against her hair. "I very much like the way you tell a story, Xiala of the Teek."

"Then listen well, Serapio. This is only the beginning."

Acknowledgments

Mirrored Heavens is the culmination of a dream. For as long as I can remember I have wanted to read (and then write) an epic fantasy inspired by the cultures of the Pre-Columbian Americas. A story with both grandeur and grit, love and loss, that celebrated the unique beauty of these cultures and decolonized gender and love in a way that felt true to me. I hope I have done that, both for myself and for you, the reader. I did my best. Along the way I fell in love with my sometimes broken but always fighting characters, many who embody elements of my own struggles writ large but who became their own people with their own particular journeys. It has been challenging, but it is everything I ever wanted as an artist and as a brown kid reading science fiction and fantasy.

I did not get here alone. Thanks first and foremost to my readers. Each and every one of you who picked up *Black Sun* and gave it a chance, who continued on to *Fevered Star*, who found yourself holding that gorgeous cover for *Mirrored Heavens* in your hands and reading the pages within. Your support has made this trilogy a reality, and I will be forever grateful.

Thank you to Turquoise Apocalypse who read the earliest drafts of this behemoth: Brian Hinson, Rae Oestreich, Lauren Teffeau, Ian Tregillis, and Sarena Ulibarri. Thanks also to AnnaLiza Bella. Thanks to all the Bookstagrammers and Booktokers who hosted readalongs and made videos and celebrated the first two books with me. Thanks to my Serapio baes and

Xiala girlies, my Iktan ride or dies, my Naranpa stans. Thanks to the reviewers, even the bad ones, because at least you're reading.

Thanks to the team at Saga Press: Amanda Mulholland, Lauren Gomez, Zoe Kaplan, Chloe Gray, Erika Genova, Jéla Lewter, Caroline Tew, Savannah Breckenridge, and Christine Calella. Special thanks to the copyeditors and cold readers and anyone who ever caught a typo. It was a Herculean undertaking, and I appreciate you!

Thanks to the incredible cover artist for all three books, John Picacio. Stunning "soul portrait" art every time, but on this one you outdid yourself. Thanks to my fantasy map maker Robert Lazzaretti. Still the coolest job ever.

Thank you to my agent Sara Megibow. I wouldn't be here having this much fun without you.

And thank you to my friend and editor extraordinaire, Joe Monti, who knows all too well that no good deed goes unpunished, but a great deed is punished twice. I hope we did something great. Whatever may come, it was worth it.

And lastly, thanks to my husband, Michael, and my daughter, Maya. You inspire me and keep me going through all the lows and celebrate the highs. You are my reason. Period. I couldn't do this without you and wouldn't want to.

City of Tova

Tsay :
Golden Eagle Clan

Otsa

Tovasheh River

Sun
Rock

Odo : Carrion Crow Clan